Destiny
Mine

JANELLE TAYLOR

>>>>>>>>>> <<<<<<<<<<

Destiny Mine

>>>>>>>>>> <<<<<<<<<<

KENSINGTON BOOKS

KENSINGTON BOOKS are published by

Kensington Publishing Corp.
850 Third Avenue
New York, NY 10022

Library of Congress Card Catalog Number: 94-078680
ISBN 0-8217-4824-6

First Printing: February, 1995

Printed in the United States of America

To my daughters,
Angela Reffett and Melanie Taylor
And my grandson,
Alex Reffett

To my Cheyenne friend,
Christy Johnson,
And,
The Cheyenne People

To my agents,
Jay Acton and Adele Leone

ACKNOWLEDGMENTS

My husband, my hero, and research assistant,
Michael Taylor

My friend,
Joe Marshall,
who provided facts on weapons and customs of the Plains
Indians and who is a talented writer, teacher, craftsman, and
special person.

R. W. Adamson,
who wrote "Kionee's Destiny" poem and made the "Kionee,
The Huntress" ceremonial mask from my novel. Thanks for
your talent and for your generosity.

KIONEE'S DESTINY

Touch me where the golden dawn,
Meets the morning dew,
And I will give my life, My Love,
To view our dreams come true.
Join me as the moonless night,
Conceives a bright new sun;
Then unity, birth's destiny,
To merge us ever one.

—R. W. Adamson ©

Destiny Mine

PROLOGUE

September 1797
Big Horn Mountains

"IT MUST BE DONE on the next moon, my love." Strong Rock told his grieving wife. "Kionee has seen the passings of five hot seasons, and *Atah* has given us no son. She is the oldest of our daughters; it is her duty, her sacred honor as a chosen one. It is the law of the Hanueva for her to take my place after my seasons are too many to provide for my family and to defend them and our people. If I lay ill or injured on my mat or if *Atah* calls me to Him while my hair is still dark as the night, she must step from behind Strong Rock and become as he was. We must do the marking ceremony for her to begin a walk on the *tiva* path as our Hunter-Guardian."

Martay's heart thudded in dread, though she had expected the bad news. "Forgive me, Strong Rock, for pushing no son from my body since our joining day. Four times I prayed to *Atah* for a boy to—" Her remaining words were choked off by sorrow and tears.

"Do not weep, Martay. If it is not the will of our Creator and Protector, He will give us a son before Kionee is sixteen summers and speaks her vows. The law of our people must be obeyed, and we cannot survive without a son to bring us food and guard us from harm when our seasons are many on Mother Earth. I will tell the shaman to prepare for the ritual here at our sacred mountain before we travel to our camp for the cold season. After the changing ceremony, Kionee will wear the marks of a *tiva* on her hand and face and will no longer live as a female. She must learn to think, speak, and be as a man in all ways but mating. On her sixteenth summer, Kionee will make a shield from hides of buffalo I slay and a bow from wood gathered in the sacred medicine forest. When her weapons are ready, she will place a tipi-of-power next to mine. She will receive a ceremonial mask and sing the *tiva* prayer. After that moon passes she will ride, hunt, and meet in council with the men until we live only in her memory."

"Unless she is taken from Mother Earth," Martay added. "If we are attacked by enemies, she must ride and fight as a warrior and defender. I fear for her safety and survival if that dark sun rises."

Strong Rock caressed his love's damp cheek. "She will be trained well by Regim and the other *tivas* to face and win any challenge. They will teach Kionee all she must know to accept her rank and to become one of them. Do not forget the Crow shaman believes *Atah*'s eyes shined on Hanueva by placing the holy Medicine Wheel and Great Arrow in our land. He told his tribe to leave us in peace or they would anger the Creator and His spirit helpers who guard us. He fears our *tivas* have great power and magic and it is bad medicine to slay one. Kionee will be protected by that fear. No *tiva* has been captured or slain and unmasked by a Bird warrior or their allies, so the truth remains hidden from them. It is a good trick and must continue for our safety. Crow chiefs believe the shaman's vision; they warn their bands to fight only Blackfoot, Lakotas, and Cheyenne, which are many and strong—fierce and skilled enemies. To keep their pride uninjured, Bird warriors say to others they do not attack us because we are too weak and worthless for earning coups; they say it would be as if riding against women, children, and old ones. We cannot allow such insults to provoke us to prove they lie, for they are many and are experienced in countless battles."

"What will happen when the shaman dies and his vision words are forgotten? What will happen if Crow cease to believe and fear them? Do you forget a few Bird warriors sneak raids on us in the hot season when we hunt buffalo on the grasslands in the great Basin of Thunder?"

"The foolish number small, Martay, and our protectors defeat them without provoking war or revenge. So it will be when Kionee is a *tiva.*"

"We have traded many times with those called Cheyenne; to this season, they are no threat to us. But what of other Crow enemies or their friends who are not bound by the Bird shaman's words?"

"They treat Hanueva as wind, as if they cannot see us. All know we do not ride against other tribes for coups or seek to steal their hunting grounds and possessions. All know we are too few and peaceful to be of help as an ally to any large band. Yet, all know we will defend our camp and families if attacked. Those who would be enemies do not want to lose warriors' lives and weapons fighting those they see as weaklings. As with the Crow, others believe *Atah* gave us the sacred Medicine Wheel and Great Arrow and He dwells near them. Kionee will be safe in my shadow and at my side."

"Will peace always blanket us, my cherished mate?"

"Only *Atah* sees into new suns. Do not blame yourself for bearing no son; that is for *Atah* to choose. You are a good wife, Martay. Your face is easy to look upon and you give me great pleasure on our sleeping mat. You are skilled in all woman's work. Our tipi is strong and warm. You have borne me four children and you teach them the best path to follow. It is a good deed for Kionee to become a *tiva*, so we must not fear or resist it. This has been our way since before we can remember, passed from father to son to son since Creator gave us life. He holds Kionee's destiny in His hands. Until He calls her to Him, she will be our Hunter-Guardian. If it is to change, only *Atah*, the High Guardian, can do so."

Martay grieved over the mother-daughter bond to be severed; it would be as if her little girl died. Kionee was her secret favorite—the child had been her shadow for five circles of the seasons. Her eldest child learned fast and helped with most chores, always willing and eager to do her best at any task. Kionee warmed her heart and made her smile or laugh many times each sun. When Martay tanned hides, cooked, or gathered food, water, and wood, Kionee handed her needed tools, fetched things to save her time, tended the three younger girls, and did other tasks. Kionee was learning to cook, learning which plants and berries to gather, and practicing with beadwork and sewing on small hides Strong Rock and Regim brought to her for that purpose.

Martay knew they would no longer share such times and joys after the marking ceremony. Kionee would be compelled to play boys' games, learn boys' tasks, do no girls' work, and spend her suns and moons until sixteen with *tivas* in training for her new role in life. Instead of awls, fleshers, beads, and babies, Kionee's hands would hold a bow, arrows, knife, lance, shield, and game. Instead of showing her beauty and gentleness, Kionee would conceal them and behave with the dignity and reserve of a man.

Martay wondered if her own mother had felt these same conflicting emotions when Regim became a *tiva* for their family. It was odd, Martay admitted, but she thought of her older sister as a man, as she could not recall Regim's feminine side. Would it come to be the same with Kionee? At that agonizing moment, she did not believe it would. Yet, on the next moon, the little girl sleeping nearby would be lost to her; and unbidden resentment nibbled at the distressed mother's heart and mind.

Martay scolded herself for wishing it was one of her other three girls who would travel the *tiva* path. Perhaps, she fretted, she was being punished for feeling more love and pride for one child than the others. It tormented her to think of perils Kionee would face on the hunt and in possible battles, as a female's strength and stamina—no matter how well honed—were never equal to a man's. Yet, no female had refused to accept her *tiva* role. She could not think of a single one who did not seem proud of and happy in that new destiny. All she could do was hope and pray it would be the same for Kionee, as she could not bear to see her beloved child unhappy.

As if his thoughts journeyed in a similar direction, Strong Rock said, "Soon Kionee must move her sleeping mat to the *tiva* tipi. She has many things and ways to toss aside, and many to gather and learn. The daughter of Strong Rock will become a great hunter, and a great warrior if that dark season comes. Strong Rock's seed must never dishonor our family or defy our customs. It will be done as *Atah* and our law command."

Martay sighed deeply, then gave her husband a sad smile. "Yes, Strong Rock; it will be done as *Atah* and our law command. I will do my best to make the change easy and fast for her." *And for me.*

A quarter moon rode the eastern sky like a silent spirit who was coming to observe this awesome occasion. An autumn wind cooled the evening air and whispered winter was trailing close behind it. Scents of pine, spruce, and lingering wildflowers mingled with the strong breezes that often blew over Medicine Mountain. A temporary camp was situated within riding distance, where mothers nursing babies and older children tending siblings awaited the tribes' return. Only Hanuevas of a certain age gathered at the holy site where numerous stones formed the sacred Wheel which was over seventy feet in diameter. Twenty-eight spokes radiated from the altar hub to its enormous rim. Seven stone cairns were spaced around the circle, all facing the direction of the rising sun. Weather-bleached buffalo skulls stuffed with and resting upon beds of sweet sage and herbs were positioned atop the hub, cairns, and where the spokes met the rim. Torches of pine stood in the ground at those same spots; their dancing flames brightened the setting and sent pungent smoke drifting upward in lazy patterns until breezes captured them and swirled them away. *Tivas* in ceremonial masks and their finest garments sat on rush mats inside the stone ring, while the tribe did the same beyond it. The shaman in full regalia waited near the altar with those requesting this rite—fathers and mothers and the two participants—ready for it to begin.

Drumbeats summoned the tribe and then prepared them to witness a sacred ritual, said to be handed down from ancient ones called the Nahane. Their tribe had lived in this territory longer than any could remember, and had watched other bands enter it and call it theirs. All knew of the Great Arrow of stones which *Atah* had placed on a mountain westward to point the way for His spirit helpers to this holy place where they gathered after the buffalo hunt to give thanks to the Creator and to evoke His future guidance. Time was short, for they must be gone before others arrived to do the same, especially the fierce Bird People.

After everyone was in place, the drumming halted and Spotted Owl shook his rattle to take charge of the event. The shaman's action evoked a venerable hush; even birds, animals, and insects appeared to obey his unspoken command for silence, reverence, and attention.

Spotted Owl lifted the buffalo skull from the altar and held it toward the darkening heaven while he entreated in a melodic tone, "*Atah*, Creator and High Guardian, see and hear your children this moon. Hanueva come to ask You to make *tivas* of these girls. We ask You to guide and protect them as they train to ful-fill new destinies, those chosen by You. *Atah*, Creator and High Guardian, we ask You to give them long life to serve their fami-lies and people, strong bodies to do their tasks and fearless spir-its to challenge all perils. We ask You to give them joy and pride in their new ranks, success on their hunts, and skills to defeat enemies if they come. We ask You to keep them true to their call-ings by You and our law. We ask You to remove their past lives as daughters and to give them new ones as sons. We ask You to give them strength, courage, and many good deeds. We ask You to let no man or thing blind them to their duty or pull them from their new path. *Atah*, Creator and High Guardian, we ask You to hear our pleas and to answer our prayers."

Spotted Owl replaced the skull on its bed of sweet sage and herbs. "Mothers, come forward and change their garments and hair," he said. As the shaman sent forth prayers of dedication, the women obeyed.

Martay wove two braids from Kionee's long black hair, for never again would she be permitted to wear only one or to let her shiny mane flow free. She removed Kionee's dress and put on the boy's garments she had made for this occasion: breech-clout, leggings, beaded belt, and vest. After she finished her part, she returned to her assigned position with a heavy heart.

The shaman instructed in a resonant voice, "Fathers, hold up their *kims* so *Atah* can capture their female spirits; He will place them inside and guard them in these sacred vessels in the *tiva* meeting lodge."

Two clay pots which were much smaller than the girls' heads were held aloft by their fathers. Spotted Owl lit his sacred pipe and wafted its smoke over the children, then motioned for the vessels to be lowered. He blew smoke into the containers, from which dangled downy feathers and were adorned with the col-ors of nature. Inside were miniature toys and dresses to repre-sent the putting away of feminine things, along with their female essences. Following more instructions, beaded pouches holding the dried ovaries of she-bears were attached to the girls' belts. The bags would be worn in that fashion until the girls reached sixteen. At their final ritual, the ovaries would be placed in a beaded medicine pouch with other chosen objects and worn around their necks even beyond death.

"Fathers, paint on the mask you have chosen," Spotted Owl said.

Kionee sat still, quiet, and respectful as Strong Rock applied the black covering from ear-to-ear and hairline-to-jawline. Her large brown eyes gazed at his serene face as he added blue, green, yellow, and red markings which he had selected as her pattern. The five-year-old did not understand the awesome and life-altering meaning of the ritual, but she knew this moment was special and that she was an important part of it. Pride and joy filled her because only she and her best friend Sumba had been chosen for this great honor. She watched her father smear liquid from the coneflower root on the back of her right hand, and felt it go numb with speed. She observed as he tattooed a beautiful mask into her flesh. She was surprised she did not feel pain as the porcupine quill pierced her skin countless times. She liked the colorful design he created for her to wear. She was eager to show it to the other girls tomorrow when they played with their small tipis and dolls, as no other children were allowed to attend the ceremony, and she did not know why. Kionee was sure they would beg to have their fathers give them one like hers and Sumba's.

Martay watched the lovely face of her precious child vanish beneath the paints Kionee must wear at all times, except during certain rituals which would be performed after her sixteenth summer when she would use a buckskin mask with a full border of flowing black and white feathers, special markings, and breast-length tassels with beads and tiny plumes. She stared at the clay jar which held captive her daughter's female spirit, one which would be placed in the *tiva* lodge with her own sister's and the other *tivas'*. Martay's eyes returned to the vivid mask on her beloved child's face; then her gaze roved those of the other *tivas*, including Regim's. She knew the reasons for the masking custom: to prevent men from thinking of a *tiva* as a woman during the hunts or battles or council meetings and from gazing upon one with desire. It caused other women to forget or ignore a *tiva* was a female, and give them proper respect. It also prevented men of other tribes from guessing the truth and attempting to steal and enslave *tivas*. Until a girl was old enough to reapply her face paint after bathing, other *tivas* were required to do so, using her hand tattoo for pattern guidance. Martay wanted to snatch the talking-feather from her belt and shake it for permission to speak to men in public. She wanted to tell them this practice of making girls into half-boys was wrong and cruel. Yet, she knew she felt this contradictory way only because Kionee was now included.

How can a female forget she is a woman when she has breasts and a lovely face to hide and is confined in the Haukau between the full moons when blood flows from her lower region? Martay fretted. She knew the alleged reasons why *tivas* could not have mates and children. *But if a girl must be a Hunter-Guardian, she should be equal with Hunter-Protectors in all ways!*

Martay rebuked herself for being selfish and angry, but she could not halt those emotions at this difficult time. If she had not been spared that rank by being born the second child in a family of only daughters, she would be a "man" this moon; she would not share a tipi and mat with Strong Rock. To never experience love, kisses, embraces, and children seemed a great sacrifice for only *tivas* to make. But the child of Strong Rock must not be the first chosen one to dishonor her family and people by refusing her rank or by fulfilling it badly. Martay realized she must pray and make offerings to *Atah* to give herself the strength and courage to do what she must, and to forgive her for wicked feelings and thoughts.

Spotted Owl motioned for the group of over forty *tivas* to come forward. He waited and listened as they promised to do their best to train the girls for their future duties and to teach them to be obedient to their fates. Afterward, the group returned to its assigned place.

Concealed behind rocks, the chief's eight-year-old son and the boy's best friend spied on the ritual with keen interest and amazement. They knew *tivas* of all ages but had not known they were girls and women until this moment. As they whispered back and forth, they guessed the secret was kept from children to prevent exposing it to outsiders who came into contact with the Hanueva. They talked of how other tribes would laugh at them for having female hunters and warriors, so they would never reveal the offensive truth. The secret explained to them why *tivas* did not swim and bathe with boys or men, and always kept their real images hidden. Wide-eyed and alert, they watched Kionee's pretty face disappear behind one of those painted designs. They heard her declared to be a boy now! She would play, hunt, and train with them when the new sun rose! At times, they had been jealous of the "boys" and "men" with colorful faces who were said to be sacred "chosen ones." Both boys sneered they no longer wanted to be *tivas*, and swore never to allow a girl to become a better hunter or fiercer warrior! When the climactic dancing, singing, and drumming began, the youths sneaked back to camp.

After the dreaded ritual ended and her child approached, Martay gazed into the upturned and colorful visage of her "son." A bitter fate had been forced upon them: from this moon until Kionee's death, she would wear the Mask-of-the-Hunter and live only for the survival of others. To hide her inner turmoil, Martay forced out a smile, which the "boy" returned with love and respect.

In a gentle but firm tone, Martay said, "You must go with Regim, Kionee; you will stay in the *tivi* tipi with the elders for a learning season. After you are trained and skilled, you will return home to us. This is a big task, little one, and you must do your best in it. Obey the *tivas'* words as you obey mine and your father's. Sumba will be with you in training."

Kionee smiled innocently and nodded before hugging Martay. She accepted her aunt's large hand and departed.

Martay's burdened heart cried out, *Good-bye, my little daughter; may you never experience the kind of searing pain which burns in me this moon.*

1

March 1813
Wind River Canyon

T HE SCENE BEFORE HER of three sisters working on a cradleboard for the first child of one of them became too much for
Kionee to endure. As the women stitched and beaded, they
made guesses about the baby's sex and destiny. Becoming a
mother was one of life's glorious moments for a female, a great
happiness and victory Kionee was denied in her *tiva* rank.

Young men were playing their flutes, giving doubleback
rides, and taking long walks with girls. Soon snow would be
gone; grasslands and trees would be green; flowers would
bloom. Mother Earth and Nature would renew themselves and
reproduce. Perhaps, Kionee reasoned, that was the cause of her
discontent, envy, and tension during this changing season: female urges and instincts buried deep within her were straining
to burst forth when she must hold them captive. It also was near
the time for her blood flow, another reminder she was female, a
reminder she was different and set apart from her true sex. She

hated those few suns she was confined to the *Haukau* and often prayed they would cease since they had no purpose. The cold season had been too long and harsh and given her too much thinking time. Suns spent at weapon-making and repairs while trapped inside by snow and strong winds had kept her hands busy but left her mind free to escape and roam forbidden territory.

Though her feelings were in a turmoil, Kionee was too well trained in deceit and self-control to let it show. Yet Kionee felt as if the emotions might boil over at any moment, burning her and those around her. She realized she could no longer witness the tormenting scene and stay reserved, and she must not risk losing her pride and honor.

Kionee drew a quiet breath in resignation of her fate as the hunter and guardian of her family, as the son her parents could not have. "I wait no longer for Sumba. I will speak with your brother on the new sun."

Before the *tiva*'s sisters could use their talking-feathers for permission to speak to a "man," Kionee ducked and departed. In an agitated state, she decided not to search for Sumba, who had taken the *tiva* vows with her at sixteen. Though Sumba remained her best friend behind Regim and Maja and had shared her existence in the elders' tipi for eleven circles of the seasons, Kionee had not exposed her inner conflict to her "brother" who was happy in "his" rank. Their winter camp was spread along the river for a great distance in the sheltering canyon, and Sumba could be inside any of the 258 tipis where over a thousand Hanueva lived. Kionee also needed to be alone to regain her poise and to clear her head.

"We go, Maja," she told the silver wolf who joined her the instant she was in sight. Ever since she'd rescued him from certain death ten years before, the powerful and loving animal had been her constant companion and loyal friend, the only one at this point in time to whom she could spill her heart. On the way to her family's tipi, Maja's head grazed Kionee's fingertips in affection and in comfort, as if he perceived her distress. In response, she glanced down, smiled, spoke to him, and ruffled the thick fur on his neck. "We are a pair for life, Maja, for we do not belong to our packs or have mates."

In the distance, Kionee saw her father entering a friend's tipi for a visit. He struggled with the crutches that enabled him to get around on one leg, as the other had dangled useless from his body after an enraged buffalo bull rammed his horse and trampled it two summers past. That was when she assumed the rank of sole provider and protector of her family. She was the youngest *tiva* with that responsibility, as most took control when their parents were older. She was aware of how much her family needed and depended upon her for survival. She could guess her family's fate if anything terrible happened to her. For certain, she could never break her vow and leave them helpless, shame them and herself.

Kionee entered Strong Rock's dwelling and told her mother she was going to hunt fresh game and to scout the departure of winter.

"That is good, my son. Watch the sky for danger," Martay cautioned, her eyes aglow and her heart warmed by her child's accomplishments.

"I need another deerskin, Brother, if you find one."

"The hide I bring home will be yours, Sister," Kionee replied to her oldest sibling, Blue Bird. "I will return before the moon comes."

Kionee retrieved the bow and quiver of arrows from a wooden tripod which held her many weapons, her tipi-of-power. She took a large bundle outside to untie and unwrap it in fresh air, as a clever hunter never allowed cooking or heating odors, smells which would warn animals or enemies of his approach and presence, to penetrate his robe. Nor did she use grease on her hair and skin to help retain body heat. At the trees where she kept her horses secured and tended, she tossed a white throw over the pinto to hide his brown markings and put a braided bridle around his jaw. She settled the albino fur cloak over her dark hair and buckskin-clad body to keep her warm and to conceal her from prey and predators' view. With Maja loping beside her, Kionee left the tranquil encampment.

Most of the ground was covered by a blanket of snow, but eager green shoots made their presence known here and there. Kionee passed the hot springs area where water refused to freeze even in the harshest weather. Nestled close to it, she saw plants with furry white heads which scattered like tiny feathers in a stiff breeze or if one blew rapidly on them. Pasqueflowers had pushed their stems through the frigid barrier and put forth blooms. Yellowbell had done the same, and it offered roots to be eaten raw or cooked. The white garments that trees and bushes had worn for so long were being discarded a layer at a time. The strong, bone-chilling winds had calmed for a while, and ice was deserting the ponds, rivers' edges, and streams' banks. Game was moving easily and more frequently through the forests, hills, and grasslands. In almost two full-moon cycles, Kionee re-called, her people would break winter camp to travel to the plains to hunt buffalo. Surely that would distract her from current worries. It must, as she would need all of her wits about her when racing with a huge and powerful herd of great beasts.

The *tiva* inhaled crisp, clean, cold air and enjoyed the gentle breeze wafting over her. She looked at the clouds in the pale-blue sky. More snow was coming soon. Perhaps it was Nature's final attempt to hold off the warm season.

The huntress approached a peaceful forest where green pines and fir mingled with naked branched aspen, ash, and cottonwood. Kionee knew from experience that game might be located feeding on tender new grass along riverbanks or nibbling tasty bark in aspen thickets. She glanced at the rocky cliffs of red, reddish brown, and gray which rose above the timber. Snowdrifts bordered the meadows and heaps of white filled crevices in the broken range on either side of her. She silently guided her mount into the densest section of the forest, as most animals preferred cover to open terrain. She liked the wild and often fierce beauty of this setting; and she liked being alone with her wolf and horse for companions.

As the sun glittered off snow and ice, Kionee squinted her large brown eyes to thoroughly scan her surroundings. She knew animals often became almost invisible in tangly underbrush. She saw a mule deer bolt and flee, and knew it was useless to pursue it. A coyote darted into hiding not too far ahead of her. His pelt was as bold and noticeable against a stark white backdrop as were those of dark opossums who traveled snow-topped limbs above her in sluggish caution.

Then Kionee found the tracks she wanted: elk, a big one, moving at an unhurried pace. She must trail him deeper into the forest. The skilled huntress focused on each tree before her, the limbs in particular, as antlers and horns were often mistaken for them and ignored.

Kionee dismounted to check a spot where snow was melted; it told her the animal had urinated recently and was not far ahead. The wind was in her favor, but it did not bring her the scent of her prey. She listened for hooves crunching in the snow or for antlers scraping against a tree, but there were none. She proceeded with caution until it was time to dismount and continue on foot. She ordered Maja to remain with and guard Tuka so the elk would not catch their smell, panic, and escape. Accustomed to living and working together for years, the wolf and horse obeyed without hesitation, unafraid of each other.

Kionee closed the distance between her and her quarry. Trees and a snowbank concealed her advance. She heard the animal snorting. She slipped behind bushes, still laden with snow in the shade, and hid her painted face behind a white deerskin mask. Kionee peeked from the hiding place and saw the creature pause to check its security. She eased two arrows from a quiver; one she stuck in the snow for swift and easy retrieval, and the other she nocked on her string. She made certain any movements were silent and slow.

Kionee counted the points on his rack: eleven, reaching high over his head. His large neck was covered in thick fur. His long legs were poised in readiness. She took a steadying breath, aimed, and fired. Her weapon swooshed through the still air and the tip thudded as it struck its target. Her arrow seemed to cast a mysterious shadow as she heard the shot echo through the forest. There was no need to fire again because, as the elk bellowed and twisted, she heard its legbone snap. While the animal snorted and thrashed in death's throes, she saw the reason for the echo: a second feather-tipped shaft protruded from the beast's chest on the opposite side. She seized and nocked the second arrow, then took a stance of self-defense and balance as she inspected the dense timberline across from her position.

Kionee saw a man watching her, surprise revealed for a moment in his expression. She heard the elk buckle to the ground, but kept her gaze locked on the intruder who had quickly mimicked her same precautions.

For several minutes, the two hunters stared at each other and waited to see what the stranger's next move would be. Neither had expected to encounter someone else, and both were amazed by their rival's prowess. Neither could determine if the other was a threat who would battle for possession of the mutual kill.

Kionee studied the man whose tall body was cloaked in a calf-length buffalo robe. Golden-brown hair—lighter than she had seen on any Indian—flowed over his broad shoulders; two thin braids framed an unscarred face that caused the breath to catch in her throat and her heart to beat oddly. Though his more than appealing face was unmarked with painted symbols and no coup feathers were in his hair, she surmised by his hunting skill that he was a well-trained and successful warrior. His expression was one of confidence; no fear was visible in his tawny gaze. She was—and yet was not—astonished when he lowered his bow until its arrow pointed to the ground.

Instead of putting aside his weapon to make intertribal hand signs, he asked, *"Ne-tsehese-nestse-he?"*

Kionee slightly lowered her bow but stayed alert as she said, *"Na-tseskee-tsehese-nestse,"*—"Cheyenne a little." *"Na Hanueva,"* she revealed her tribe. With her gaze locked on him and using one hand, she untied and removed the white deerskin mask and dropped it to the snow. His people were friendly to hers, if he was in truth Cheyenne as his use of their language implied. She watched his gaze study her facial mask, then saw him nod acceptance of her identity. She eyed him as he replaced the arrow in its quiver and headed for the slain elk.

Kionee did the same. When they met at the fallen beast, he looked at her again with great interest. The color of his eyes matched that of Maja's. He was a head taller than her, and his body much larger. He appeared to be a few winters past her twenty.

Using his language along with intertribal signs and words, they communicated with each other.

"Na-tsesevehe E-neha Ho-nehe. Ne-toneseva-he?"

She listened as he told her his name and asked hers. Lowering her voice as trained to disguise her sex, she replied, "Kionee."

"Tiva-he?"

She nodded she was a *tiva*, as her mask implied. "Son of Strong Rock and Martay of the Hanueva. I am the Hunter-Guardian for my family. Why does Stalking Wolf of the Cheyenne come so far to our forest to hunt?"

"We go to the sacred Medicine Wheel to seek a vision and to offer gifts to the Great Spirit. While Mother Earth still wears her white blanket, this path is best to ride. We need fresh meat. I will take a small share and you will take the large one for your family. Is that good?"

Kionee was impressed by his generosity and kindness. "It is good, since both arrows were true and matched in flight. Who travels with you? Where is your tipi?"

"Two friends. They wait in camp that way."

Kionee's gaze followed the line of his pointing finger. "Bird

People camp in the land where the earth bubbles as kettles and spews water into the air. They ride to the sacred wheel many times; they do not remain in camp when the ground is good. Crow and Cheyenne are enemies. They are many and you are three. If their eyes find you, they will attack."

"The son of Big Hump fears no Crow, but we do not seek a fight this moon. We use the land and our skills to hide our coming and going."

"You are the son of the Strong Heart chief?"

Stalking Wolf parted his robe and buckskin shirt to display the symbolic red hand over his heart. "I am the son of Big Hump and brother to Five Stars. My people camp fifteen suns from this place."

"Hanueva know the names and coups of Big Hump, Five Stars, Stalking Wolf, and the Strong Hearts. My people camp in the canyon of the river wind, near the boiling earth pot. You and your friends are welcome to rest and eat with us."

"*Ne-aese,*" he thanked her, but explained they were in a hurry to reach the sacred site, carry out their task, and return home before the move to the grasslands to hunt buffalo. As he spoke, Stalking Wolf studied Kionee. He recalled the man's prowess in tracking and slaying the elk and wondered how such a small, soft-spoken man could be so skilled and brave. His head was filled with many questions about the mysterious *tivas* but knew it was impolite to ask them of a stranger.

Kionee was disappointed by his refusal, as she yearned to study him longer. To guard their secret, *tivas* were not allowed to visit trading camps, and they remained at a safe distance when others came to theirs; yet she had heard many glorious tales about such famous Cheyenne warriors. She felt honored by *Atah* to be in his presence and to speak with him. The way he carried himself shouted that stories about his prowess and courage were true. Hanueva protectors, she mused, could learn much from a warrior like him.

Despite his distraction, Stalking Wolf perceived warnings of danger: with the wind in his favor, he caught scents of tipi smoke, cooking odors, and bear grease on skin and hair. "If you hunt alone, enemy eyes watch us," he whispered. "Prepare to fight. It is not the smell of my companions."

Kionee was not so lost in her observation and admiration of him that she failed to notice the same clues. She also glimpsed and heard movement behind the Cheyenne warrior. "They are not my people. Three enemies try to circle us; their faces see your back. Their garments say they are Crow."

Though the Hanuevan appeared to be looking at him, Stalking Wolf realized the clever son of Strong Rock was peering beyond him. He was impressed by the hunter's calm. "They have trees to protect them from our arrows. We will use the elk as our shield. When I signal with—"

Kionee's action cut off his remaining words as she lifted her bow, with its arrow still nocked, leapt to his left side, and fired. A loud yelp of pain and surprise said she hit her target as it moved from tree to tree.

With haste, the huntress and the Cheyenne dropped to the snowy ground and used the slain animal for cover. Two arrows slammed into the beast's body near their heads.

"I take him as mine," she said, selecting the enemy on the right with a nod of her head. "They are still three; the first is only wounded."

As Kionee wiggled on her belly and forearms toward the elk's rear end, Stalking Wolf did the same in the opposite direction. With the way the animal's neck was bent, the large rack was not an obstacle for him. Both spotted their goals from arrowtips left carelessly in view. Neither wasted weapons on unstrikable targets; they waited for the right opening to fire.

Without warning, fierce and loud growls filled the quiet air as a large silver wolf raced with lightning speed and darting agility toward the two concealed Crow. It was enough of a threat and surprise to flush them from hiding as they whirled to defend themselves against a ferocious enemy.

The Crows' panic placed them in sight and jeopardy. Stalking Wolf and Kionee jumped to their feet, aimed, and fired. Their shafts whizzed through the small clearing and struck home. After the dead men fell to the ground, the silver predator halted his advance and looked at the victors. It was the strange man who captured Maja's attention.

When the Cheyenne nocked another arrow, Kionee grabbed his arm and shouted in her language, "*Gat!*", as she shook her head to halt him.

The warrior glanced into doe eyes that were flooded with panic. "He is a crazed wolf to behave as he did. He might attack us next."

Fearful for her pet's survival, Kionee forgot to fully disguise her voice. "He is mine. He will not harm you unless I order it. He is Maja, my friend of ten winters. He helps me and protects me. You must not slay your spirit sign, Stalking Wolf. Come, Maja," she summoned him.

The Cheyenne watched the wild creature join his owner, and saw the slender hunter stand between them as if protecting the animal from him. Its muscled body moved with power and ease. He admired the wolf's courage, intelligence, and stealth: traits that obviously matched its owner's. He watched Kionee run his fingers over its thick shiny fur; The wolf nuzzle Kionee's small hands with affection and gentleness. It was clear these two were close friends, and he was not in danger since he presented no threat to the *tiva*. He recalled the prayer in his vision quest: "Make me as the wolf, Great Spirit," and wondered if Maja was meant to help him fulfill his destiny.

Noise from the brush reminded Stalking Wolf of the third enemy. "I must go after the one you wounded. He saw your face mask; he will think we are Hanueva. If he escapes, he will tell others Hanueva attacked them. His band will come for revenge. Remain here and I will return soon."

"I will go; it was my arrow that failed."

"Let me do this deed for you; I am a trained warrior, as is he.

You must live to hunt, to protect your family. I have no mate and children who depend on me. Come if you must, but let me defeat our enemy for you."

Kionee was warmed by his offer and—strangely—by the news about himself. "You are good and kind, but it is the duty of the one who wounded a beast to track and slay it. I am skilled with weapons and hands."

Stalking Wolf decided Kionee stated a fact, not a boast. Yet, he did not believe one so small and gentle could defeat a large, experienced, and brutal warrior in close battle, as the Hanueva were known to be a peaceful band of hunters. He gave a nonchalant nod, but assumed he would be the one to fight when the time came.

Kionee ordered Maja to guard their meat from scavengers. The wolf sat down and obeyed. She followed the warrior to the spot where their enemy had sneaked from his hiding place. Together they trailed the Bird man from crimson drops and moccasin tracks in the snow.

They reached the place where their attackers had left their horses. They saw the injured man attempting to mount to flee. Hearing them, the foe turned, drew his knife, and took a stance of self-defense.

That was not the main thing Stalking Wolf noticed: it was the horses and possessions of his two companions. He yanked a knife from his sheath. "You die this sun, Crow dog!"

"He is my duty," she reminded as she reached for her weapon.

"He is mine," the Cheyenne refuted between clenched teeth. "I must take revenge for my friends. The Crow have their horses and belongings; they are dead. He is mine, Kionee," the man stressed in determination as he shook off his buffalo robe to ready himself for battle.

She knew it was futile to argue when a blood lust filled a man's eyes. She nodded and said, "It will be as you say. May *Atah* protect you and guide your hand. If He does not, I will avenge you to the death. I will place your body and weapons upon a scaffold as is your custom, Stalking Wolf, and send word to your people."

"Stalking Wolf," the Crow warrior echoed in a surly tone as he recognized that legendary name. "If you fight no better than your friends, your scalp will be on my lance this moon and your weapons in my tipi. After you are dead, I will slay the coward with you. Hanueva are weak as women; they hide from real men." To Kionee, he sneered, "I will cut the mark from your hand and sew it on my shield; others will see *tivas* are not sacred and have no big medicine. And if you do have magic, I will steal it with my knife. Coyote Man will make me strong and swift; victory is mine."

The warriors hunched forward into stooped positions, feet apart, arms and hands hanging loose, and knees bent. Their expressions revealed their hatred and contempt for each other. Light glittered off their sharp and menacing blades. They circled as they watched and waited for the perfect opening to attack, cautious on the snowy terrain. The Crow lashed out at the Cheyenne but missed his nimble enemy, who easily dodged the premature thrust.

Stalking Wolf laughed and made no attempt to return the careless action. He saw fury—and unbidden respect—fill the Crow's eyes.

Half crouching, the Crow began another try for success. He knew, as did the Cheyenne, that the man who drew first blood had an advantage. He half turned partially to throw his rival off guard, then whirled and kicked at Stalking Wolf's groin as he lashed out with his knife. His enemy laughed again and parried the blows, and sliced through his shirt into his arm. The Crow gaped at the blood that oozed from a large gash and soaked his sleeve. "You will die!" he raged.

"Foolish words cannot harm me, Crow dog. Fight if you know how."

The Bird warrior desperately flirted with death to draw his

competitor into a reckless move, as he was weakening fast from his two wounds. He was angered and provoked by the way the Cheyenne danced in and out as the man and his knife chewed at his body with little nicks. The cold weather did not prevent sweat from beading on his face and torso. He hated the slashes in his clothes and flesh; he hated the warrior who might beat him, slay him. It would be a great coup to take the life and possessions of Stalking Wolf. It would be a larger coup to take those of a Mask Wearer afterward.

Evading and injuring his opponent, the Cheyenne stayed alert. A wounded man or animal was dangerous and unpredictable. He saw the signs of fatigue and worry on his enemy. It was difficult not to flaunt his superiority and imminent victory.

The Crow sank to his knees, taking deep breaths and lowering his head as if in shame and in resignation. Yet, his gaze locked on the Cheyenne's feet as he readied himself to act when his rival came forward for the kill.

Stalking Wolf guessed the ruse and pretended to fall into the trap. He came forward, even as Kionee yelled a warning to him.

"He cannot fight more," Stalking Wolf shouted. "I will finish this deed, then tend my fallen friends."

As the Cheyenne came within striking range with his knife hand lowered and in sight, the Crow used the last of his energy to lunge upward to his feet, lifting his blade high to stab forcefully. The Bird warrior's gaze widened in astonishment and fear as he saw the Cheyenne's other hand plunge downward and bury a second knife in his chest. He dropped his weapon as his hands clutched the death tool but could not remove it. He looked at his killer before sinking to the ground and closing his eyes forever.

The Cheyenne lifted his arms skyward and howled like a wolf before thanking the Great Spirit for giving him victory and revenge. He looked at Kionee who was observing him in awe.

"You are a great warrior, Stalking Wolf; your skills cannot be matched. I am honored to witness such a glorious battle."

The Cheyenne was pleased with the *tiva's* praise. He was touched by the hunter's earlier offer to avenge him if necessary. He spoke words of gratitude before he said, "I must tend the bodies of my companions before I continue my journey. It is too far and long to carry them home. I will take the Crow horses and you will take those of my friends; it is a good trade, and theirs must not be found in your camp. After I build their scaffolds and sing the death chant for them, I will come for my meat. If you must ride home, leave it where it lays."

"I will help you; it will be a long and hard task, for winter lives in the hearts of trees and they will not yield with ease. What will we do with the Bird warriors? If others come and find their bodies, they will attack us."

"I will place them on their horses and carry them far from your land. Fresh snow this moon will cover our tracks."

As he loaded the body and gathered the horses, she said, "That is good, Stalking Wolf; you are wise and skilled in head, heart, and body. My people will thank you when you come to visit us. To this sun, few Crow attack us, for they think we are weak and worthless, and their shaman told them it is bad medicine to slay those whose people were given the sacred Medicine Wheel. We offer no challenge to Bird warriors; they attack the Cheyenne and their friends, the Oglalas."

"Your people must stay alert and trained, for those few will raid again and will tempt others to join them. Many see *tivas* as holders of great magic and wish to steal it. Hunger and evil can dull even the sharpest wits."

"We train to fight, for we know peace will not always live with us. We do nothing to make the Crow forget their fear of us; it serves us well. *Tivas* are Hunter-Guardians; that is our purpose in life. We do not fear death, for *Atah* is with us and His will must be accepted."

"That is true," Stalking Wolf concurred. He led the horses to the attack site and loaded the other two bodies. He secured the bridle ropes to nearby trees until his departure.

While he did so, Kionee sent Maja to fetch her horse. The wolf returned soon with the pinto, and she stroked both animals with affection. Again she ordered Maja to remain with the elk to guard it, and he obeyed. She mounted her horse and followed Stalking Wolf.

Both read the signs that said the two Cheyenne had been attacked from hiding, refused a chance at honorable death in battle.

"They struck as thieves in the night and stole their lives."

"They have been avenged; they will sleep well and safely until *Atah* claims them. Let us do what we must before snow comes."

They constructed two wooden beds from limbs Stalking Wolf gathered and she tied together with his friends's ropes. He bound his friends in their robes, along with their weapons. He secured the bodies in place and used his horse to lift the burdens into the trees to rest on large branches where they would be safe from animals. When the task was finished, he sang the death chant to alert the Great Spirit to their fate and location.

"Does your brother go to meet the Great One?" she asked as she took a last look at the wooden mats above them.

"Five Stars remained in camp to hunt for our family and to protect them. The shaman picked the men to ride with me to Medicine Mountain. If I had come alone, they would still live."

"Only the Creator can choose the sun we die and knows the reason for that time; He guided the shaman's words. You are not to blame."

They returned to the elk to complete their work there. He packed the Crow weapons and possessions to carry with him to give to the families of those slain. He would keep their sacred tobacco pouches for himself as coups of this deed. He squatted to watch the *tiva* skin the elk, and noticed how slender and delicate the hunter's hands and wrists were. Without his white robe, Kionee appeared even smaller in size than he had imagined. His gaze traveled the Hanueva's profile and found the hunter's features were not large and they reminded him—even with a colorful shield—of a female's. Perhaps if all *tivas* were similar in shape and looks, that explained why the Crow called them women and weaklings. Yet, he had witnessed nothing to hint at the latter being true about Kionee.

The Cheyenne saw how the silver wolf lay close to his owner, many times touching the Hanueva, and many times staring at him. He perceived a superior intelligence in the animal and a keen sense of loyalty. He had no doubt the creature would defend Kionee to the death. It amazed him how well the animal understood and obeyed commands. As he watched the hunter wield his knife, he realized the drawing on Kionee's hand matched that of the facial design. He wondered if *tivas* ever washed off their paints and revealed their faces. He assumed the custom had a special meaning and he wished he knew what it was. His gaze drifted over Kionee's weapons and admired their craftsmanship. The Hanueva's hunting skills were obvious from the quality of his hides and garments. Yet, something about the younger man troubled him.

Stalking Wolf stood and walked to cast off a sudden feeling of tension and confusion. He wondered if Kionee had anything to do with the shaman's words to him about finding his destiny and himself on this trip. Had their paths crossed by accident or by the Great Spirit's intention? If the latter, what part would they play in each other's lives? Perhaps he would get answers to his questions during his vision quest at Medicine Mountain.

The Cheyenne went to join Kionee when the skinning and carving were done. "Put this in your medicine pouch as a token of our deed and meeting." He held out a ring he had taken from a Crow, as the Bird Warriors liked to highly decorate themselves, their horses, and tipis.

In the flicker of an eye, the silver wolf rushed forward and leapt against the Cheyenne warrior's chest. The beast's size, strength, and agility knocked the unsuspecting man to the ground. With its forelegs braced on Stalking Wolf's heart and with teeth bared, Maja stared into the man's eyes, ready to tear out the warrior's throat if he made even the slightest move.

2

"*G*AT, *MAJA!* *Jante. Ombeg.*" She told him to stop, that the man was a friend, and to come to her. Without delay, the animal responded and took a protective stance near Kionee's knees. "I am sorry. He thought you were a threat to me. He smells the dead wolf on you," she added, nodding toward the gray tails dangling from his quiver and robe.

"They were killed when I defended myself in a cold season long ago and they were crazed by hunger. I do not slay my medicine sign and animal protector unless it must be so to survive." He spanked snow from his leggings, brushed it from his long hair, and shook it from his robe.

"Maja must sniff your hand to know you are a friend. Offer it to him."

The Cheyenne extended his hand, palm side up. The wolf came forward and smelled it, placing the scent and action in his memory.

"It is good; you are friends now. I must return to camp. Do you want to eat and sleep with us? Dark and snow will come soon."

"I must ride far with the Crow bodies before others search for them. Mother Earth's blanket is needed to conceal my trail to this place and yours to your camp. We part as friends, Kionee. Perhaps we will hunt together another sun." He extended his hand and they clasped wrists in a parting gesture. "I thank you for the game and for your help this sad sun."

"I give *you* thanks for the game and help this sun. May *Atah* ride with you and protect you on your quest. Do not fall prey to Crow arrows."

Stalking Wolf released his grip on the Hanueva. Something about the way Kionee gazed at him made him edgy. He used a skin to wrap the hunk of meat Kionee had carved off for him. He helped load the hide and larger pieces onto his friends' horses. He stared into Kionee's face for a moment to dispel his uneasiness, then smiled and mounted. He gathered the ropes to the other horses and departed as large flakes began to fall.

Kionee locked her gaze to his back and tried to ignore the unfamiliar sensations that flooded her mind and body. He was a man above others, the kind of man she would want as a mate if that were allowed. She scolded her fingers for itching to touch him again. She scolded her lips for craving to meet his. She scolded herself for the curious heat and weakness racing through her. She scolded herself for praying and yearning to see him again when that would only distress her further. She saw him halt, twist on his horse, prop a hand on its haunch, and gaze at her. Her heart fluttered and the breath caught in her throat. It was if their gazes spoke words neither could understand. She lifted her hand and waved farewell to him.

The Cheyenne returned the gesture. He saw the silver wolf snuggle closer to Kionee's legs as if to say, this is mine. Against a white backdrop and with snow drifting down on them, the two made a colorful and dramatic sight. For a crazy moment, he imagined Kionee as a woman, a beautiful and mysterious and magical and irresistible female. He was almost reluctant to leave. He shoved that foolish thought and feeling aside, nodded, turned, and did not look back again as he rode northward.

Kionee squatted and ruffled the fur on her pet's neck. "He is gone, Maja. I do not understand and it is bad, but he touches me in a strange and powerful way. I trained, live, and look as a man; but I am not a man; I can never become a man. My life is as the canyon where we camp: it is as if *tivas* are on one side of the river which parts it and our tribe is on the other; we are always set apart from them. We share air, rain, food, and laws with men, but we are as different from them as the coyote to the deer."

Maja licked Kionee's hand to give the comfort he sensed she needed. He rubbed his head against her side to share closeness with her, and was glad when Kionee stroked his ears, then hugged him.

"We must go." She mounted Tuka and led the gift horses away.

As she journeyed homeward, that now familiar feeling of unfulfillment troubled her. Stalking Wolf had only increased her sense of loneliness. When she bathed in the river and her face was clean of paint, she saw her true appearance and shape: undeniable proof she was a female, a pretty one. Yet, she was called "son," "brother," and lived as a male, a man as barren as a stone.

At sixteen summers, she had made her shield and weapons, received her ceremonial mask and dewclaw rattle, and sang the *tiva* song of loyalty and obedience. She had filled her medicine pouch with sacred tokens. Charms from her first kills on land, in air, and in water and those she gathered to empower her with nature's forces rested in the beaded bag around her neck, along with the dried ovaries of a she-bear, the sign of a *tiva*. She had constructed and placed her tipi-of-power beside her father's. Afterward, she had sat with the council, spoken openly and freely, voted on all matters, participated in rituals, hunted, and even fought against a few enemies. It was no secret she could ride, fight, track, hunt, and shoot better than most of the real men in her tribe.

Her cousin, Little Weasel, was annoyed by her skill. It was his fault—not hers—that he did not have as many beaded symbols of courage, daring, cunning, and successes on his ceremonial sash. It was not her fault her father's accident had placed her as head of her family two summers past and she had done all she could to be the best hunter and guardian possible. Little Weasel should not envy her when he was free to live as he was born but she was captive to a sacrificial fate. The only man whose skills and deeds matched hers was the chief's son, Night Walker, her cousin's best friend; but she did not want to think about either man today. She wanted to think only of—

"*Gat*, Kionee! It is wrong and will make you suffer," she scolded herself.

Despite that warning, images of Stalking Wolf filled her head. They warmed her body so much that the lowering temperature and increasing wind and snow went unnoticed. She visualized his tawny gaze and virile body. She remembered the strange way he looked at her in parting and wondered at its meaning. She knew she had not given away her secret. She was certain he accepted her as a friend, as the son of Strong Rock and Martay.

Kionee knew she could have no mate to love her, to share her life, to hold her and comfort her in dark times. She could bear no daughter to give birth to future Hanuevas. She could bear no son to take care of her when her seasons were many, her parents rested in death mounds, and her strength was gone. She would be forced to live with the *tivas* elders in a separate tipi and she— like them—would depend upon the younger *tivas* and male hunters to be generous with game and hides to fill their needs. She would never experience the passion she had witnessed between her parents and other happy couples. She would never feel the pleasure and joy of bonding with a special man on the sleeping mat. Her only memories and deeds would be of giving to, protecting, and caring for others.

Kionee looked at her pet whose gaze seemed empathetic, as if he saw into her head. "What of my needs and wants, Maja? What of my happiness? Is a *tiva*'s life all I am to have while I live? Do I not deserve more, to have the same things other women possess, when I am in truth a woman? Must I sacrifice all I am and can be for my family and tribe? Must I be denied *Atah's* gifts. Are such things not for each of His children? Did He make such harsh laws, or were they made in olden times by men when girls were many and boys were few? Why can I not be a huntress and protector without painting my face or using a mask? Why must I hide my sex when being a female does not take away my skills? Will this law be here forever to ruin the lives of firstborn daughters in families without sons?"

Kionee went silent when she saw curling smoke from many Hanueva campfires. She had left this morning a *tiva* and returned near dusk a *tiva*; meeting Stalking Wolf had changed nothing for her. *That is not true; he has changed many things in your heart and mind. He—*

"Kionee!" Sumba called out and hurried forward to join her friend. "Your hunt was good. I am sorry you could not find me to go with you."

"*Atah* guided me to a big elk. I will give the *tivas* elders a share."

"Where did you get the horses? They bear Cheyenne markings."

"I will tell you as we go to the *tiva* lodge to give them meat and these horses to ride to the grasslands. I must summon the council to hear this bad news, for powerful evil winds will blow on us this season."

Sumba halted and stared at Kionee. "We are in danger?"

"Yes, my friend and brother, from evil Crow warriors. Already they sneak into our land and attack. Come, we will speak as we walk."

Kionee finished revealing the grim news and took a seat on a mat in the meeting lodge. She had been careful to control her expressions, movements, and voice to conceal Stalking Wolf's potent effect on her.

Chief Bear's Head was the next to speak in council. "It is good you gave meat and horses to our past *tivas;* your heart is kind and your victory with the Cheyenne warrior is large. Your mother must bead this deed upon your sash. Do you see trouble in your dreams, Spotted Owl?"

"I have seen many strange things," the shaman replied. "They have been clouded by shadows. When they are clear to me, I will reveal them."

"Are the cloud blankets light or dark, Spotted Owl?"

"They are dark, my chief, a bad sign, one I do not understand. When He is ready, *Atah* will uncover them and show us which path to ride. *Atah* never fails to protect and provide for His children; He will do so as long as we follow His commands."

"If Bird Warriors come to attack, we must fight and defeat them," Night Walker said. "We must show them our strength and courage to strike fear into their hearts. If we look afraid and weak, they will laugh and raid us. Have we forgotten *Atah* put us in this land first? He placed the Crow and others in lands far away. The Crow grew too large in number and parted into bands. Their longtime enemies forced many of those bands from their old hunting grounds and they rode into ours. All know that *Atah's* land cannot be owned. Even so, we did not strike at them when they and others came and called parts of it theirs. The old ones accepted them in friendship and peace. They do not desire such good things from us or from others. If we do nothing to halt their greed and challenge, soon Hanuevas will have no land and life. I say we must train hard to be ready to battle them."

"Once the war arrow leaves the bow, my second son, it cannot be returned to the quiver of peace. No trail must be ridden too fast and reckless. *Atah* must be the One to halt and punish them into retreat."

"Are we not skilled weapons for *Atah* to use against them? Where is our pride, my father and chief, if we allow Crow to trample it to dust?"

"Words cannot harm a strong and wise man, my son, but enemy arrows send our hunters and protectors to live in the stars."

"Some words are as strong as arrows and clubs, Father, for they have the power to make peace or war, to make friend or enemy."

"That is why we must speak and live for peace. Enemies cannot battle men who refuse to fight. What honor and coups can Crow find in attacking those who have no desire to war with them, who offer the peace pipe?"

"If we live as frightened deer, we will be hunted and slain as such, for the chase and victory are as breath of life to Crow. The season has come when hiding and retreat must be put aside. Soon the Bird People will hunger for all land and game. What of the Hanueva then?"

"My friend and brother speaks wise and true," Little Weasel concurred. "I say we make known the Hanueva prowess and frighten them."

"Our chief is wise; once a blow is struck, it cannot be recalled," Strong Rock argued. "We are a people of peace. War and coups are not our way, and all know this to be true. The Sun Dance is not our way. We do not change the names our fathers give us when we are born. We do not have warrior societies who seek to best each other. We do not steal from enemies or fight them for glory. To do so calls death to our lodges."

The chief's son asked Kionee's father, "Is not honorable death better than cowardly existence?"

"Hanuevas are not cowards," he announced firmly. "We battle when attacked."

"Defense is not the same as preventing attacks, Strong Rock. It is better to reveal strength and courage to stop them from coming than to tend our wounds and bury our dead while we wait for others to raid again. If we sneak to their growing ground and destroy their tobacco plants—their sacred medicine—and steal their Sun Dance Dolls, they will lose spirit and weaken. They believe they will live and prosper only as long as they perform their tobacco ceremonies when the seed is planted and when it is harvested and have seeds for the next season— and as long as they have the power of their dolls and the power of those before them who had them."

Kionee recalled that Stalking Wolf kept tobacco-seed pouches of the men who attacked them in the forest. She knew that to take one of the Crow's holiest objects was a great coup; even as children the Crow wore a tiny bag of it around their necks for protection and to show unity to that cult and its beliefs.

"Night Walker's words are strong with hate and with hunger for bad food," another hunter said. "Do you forget that bad food kills and hate dulls wits?"

"Does Runs Fast forget we did not begin this conflict?" Night Walker scoffed. "Does Runs Fast not know it will grow worse if we do nothing? They care not for our words and ways of peace. Does Runs Fast desire even a life of fear more than holding on to our land and honor for our people?"

"We do not hide, Night Walker, but we must not gallop into the arms of death to seek glory as our enemies do. If they come in war, I will fight them at your side, but I will not chase or challenge them first. They are strong and many, and such action is foolish."

"They *have* come to raid and to seek war, Runs Fast. Did

Kionee not find them on our land, near our camp, weapons ready and eager to kill?"

"The Crow attacked a Cheyenne band they found in their scouting path; they are fierce enemies," Strong Rock pointed out. "We do not know if they came to raid our camp and slay our people."

"Did they not attack Kionee to slay a *tiva?*" Night Walker refuted.

"Kionee was with a Cheyenne when they saw my son."

"Kionee's mask told them he is Hanueva. Still, they attacked. I say, if Kionee had been alone, Kionee would be dead by a Crow arrow. I say, Crow no longer fear or flee from what they believe is *tiva* magic, for their hunger to capture such powerful medicine makes them daring."

Spotted Owl reasoned in a soft tone, "We cannot know if your words are true, Night Walker, so to act on them is unwise."

"We will place guards each sun and moon to watch for Crow raids," Chief Bear's Head ordered. "We must wait to see if trouble strikes before we move to the grasslands. Do not go looking for sly death, my son; wait until it stalks you to lay a trap for it."

"Why do we not send peacemakers to Red Plume, Long Hair, and Swift Crane to see why they allow their warriors to attack us?"

"Your thought is good, Strong Rock; we will think on it until the council meets in ten suns and votes. Search your hearts, my people, for the path we choose to take will paint our destinies on our family hides."

Night Walker's heart pounded in excitement as he realized he had ten days to convince others to join his side against the weakling peacemakers. Somehow, he plotted, he and Little Weasel would provoke a conflict in which they could use their prowess to obtain glory. Never, he resolved, would he allow the Crow—or any others—to push him off this land or to make him cower in fear and ultimate defeat, no matter what he must do to prevent it.

"Where is my mate?" Martay asked Kionee upon her return.

"Father stayed behind to speak with friends. I grow weary, for there were many tasks to do this sun. I must sleep soon."

"Will the Crow come to attack us, Brother?" Blue Bird asked.

"I do not know, Sister, but I worry over them sneaking near our camp. The one who died last did not fear us or *tiva* magic."

"Will Runs Fast be called into battle?"

Kionee considered her sister's expression and tone. "You fear for his safety and survival?"

"Yes, my brother, though I should not when he is skilled in fighting."

"He has captured your eye and heart?"

"Yes."

"If war comes, Blue Bird, I will try to guard his back for you."

"That is kind, Brother, for your skills are as large as the mountain."

"What of the Cheyenne warrior?" Martay asked. "Did he offer help?"

"The Cheyenne will be busy with the buffalo hunt and defeating Crow who challenge them. His skills are great, for he has fought many battles."

"Would it not be wise, my son, to camp near them on the grasslands?"

"That is for our chief and council to say. None spoke for it, Mother. Little Weasel and Night Walker spoke for war."

"War? We cannot challenge the Crow, my son. They are too many."

"Do not fear, Mother; none took their bold words to heart."

Martay fretted over her "son" going into fierce battle with such hostile and experienced warriors. She had lost one daughter to sickness in the chest many winters past. Blue Bird hoped to be joined to Runs Fast before the cold season, and Moon Child would follow that path in one or two more summers. It had taken her many seasons to accept Kionee's change of fate, but her "son" had proven himself before and after Strong Rock's accident. She was proud of Kionee and at peace with their life. Perhaps becoming close with Blue Bird during Kionee's long absence from their tipi had mellowed her heart and taken away her anger.

Strong Rock entered the tipi, struggled to his mat, and lowered himself to sit on it. He put aside the wood supports and took several deep breaths. He was glad no one offended his pride by offering to assist him. He was grateful to Kionee who had found the sturdy and straight staffs with forked branches to fit under his arms. His clever son had wrapped their tops in rabbit fur to prevent chafing and soreness in his armpits, had rubbed the limbs free of splinters, and had secured leather strips halfway for his hands to grip. Strong Rock tried not to resent his ill fate, but at perilous times like this, unwanted bitterness and a sense of failure crept into his mind and heart.

Strong Rock knew he and his family were fortunate and blessed to have a son like Kionee to take his place. The worried father did not want to imagine life without him as their Hunter-Guardian. "It is a bad sign the Crow resist their shaman's words and steal near our camp for evil deeds. I do not want our protectors to ride the reckless trail Night Walker desires, but we must prepare for defense, for more are sure to come before we leave."

"Friends of those we slew will seek a path to revenge, Father, for that is their way. It is good the Cheyenne warrior took their bodies far from our land and *Atah* sent snow to hide our tracks and deeds. When Mother Earth warms her face, the Crow will be busy with tobacco planting for a time."

"You must picket your horses near our tipi, Kionee; Crow hunger for good buffalo and war horses. You have trained Recu to ride as one with you in the great hunt. You have trained Tuka for skilled riding and fighting. They would be great losses to you and our family. A strong and smart animal brings many hides and weapons in the trading camp. Few can be found and captured and trained well after they escape and run wild."

"Maja guards them for me; he will alert me to an enemy's approach. He knows all scents of our camp and will smell any strange ones."

"It troubles me, my son, that Crow no longer fear *tivas* and now crave our mask-wearers' big medicine. Bird warriors become leaders and chiefs by gathering many coups: by touching an enemy while fighting or in stealth, by stealing one's weapons in battle or in secret, by stealing an enemy's horse after a defeat or when it is picketed at his tipi, and by planning successful raids. Those with the largest number and highest ranking coups win those places. They are a people who love war, who seek it. We must pray for peace and survival."

Kionee realized her father was saddened by his helplessness when war might loom on their horizon and that he yearned to defend his family and people. Whatever came, she was ready to confront it, and she would do her best to obtain victory. Perhaps Stalking Wolf and the Cheyenne Strong Hearts would come to help them if— *Forget him.*

On the fifth day after meeting Stalking Wolf, Kionee and Regim went hunting. After spending the last few days in the menses hut, Kionee was charged with tension and needed the exercise and diversion. Regim sensed something was disturbing her niece and hoped to learn its source.

Kionee felt as if her emotions would get out of control if not discussed with someone who was loved and trusted. She needed advice, understanding, and comfort. What better source was there than the person who had trained and almost reared her, who was her mother's "brother," who was the *Tiva-Chu—*

leader of the Hunter-Guardian rank—and who would never betray her confession no matter what it was.

"I have worn my mask for fifteen summers, Regim . . ." she began, "but it has not become like part of my skin and life as I was told it would." Kionee paced and frowned as she disclosed, "When the sun blazes down like a fire in the hot season, water runs from under my breast band and slips down my body like tiny rivers. The deerskin tightens as it dries and I can hardly breathe, but I dare not loosen or remove it. With each circle of seasons, my mounds grow larger and it becomes harder to flatten them into hiding. When I am captive in the *Haukau* during my blood flow season, I grow restless and angry, for it serves no good purpose. Why does *Atah* not halt it and dry up our breasts? He has the power and magic to remove such reminders we are female. Why are they not captured and placed in our *kims* with our female spirits?"

Kionee halted her movements and looked at the older woman, but the *Tiva-Chu's* expression was unreadable. "No matter how long and how good we live as men, Regim, we remain females in body. *Atah* did not change us into the men we live as; we have not grown shafts and bags between our legs. We train, hunt, and council with men, but they do not seek us out at other times as friends; they still view us as females in their hearts and heads. We do not smoke the sacred pipe or share the sweat lodge or bathe with them; we are treated as females in those ways. Women pretend we are men—sons and brothers—but they know we are not; they are happy they are not *tivas* and must live as we do. When Mother Earth renews her face after each season of snow, strange and powerful urges call to me and attack me without warning and mercy. Their voices shout to me of mating and bearing children. When my hand lies across my chest at night, I think of children who will never feed there. Why must only *tivas* be denied such joys and victories? Why can we not be mates and mothers and still be Hunter-Guardians?"

Regim was astonished by this unexpected revelation. She

had guessed something was troubling Kionee but not a matter this serious. "If such unions were allowed, who would do the woman's work and tend the children while a *tiva* hunts or fights for her own family?" she replied. "A man cannot do so and it is not the duty of other women to do so, for they have their own tipis and families to tend. It would be dangerous and impossible for a *tiva* who is belly-carrying or breast-feeding a baby—or has other little ones and chores—to ride on the great summer hunt for the buffalo. If bound to a family, she would be unable to leave her children to battle enemies if we are attacked; that would deny her family and our tribe of a skilled fighter. Her presence would be required in camp to give her baby milk, so she could not go when long hunts are needed at times when game roams far from us in the cold season. And how could a joining between two 'men' be explained to visitors and children?"

Regim grasped Kionee's hands and gave them a gentle squeeze. "If a *tiva* cannot be a full-time mother and mate, she must not leave her rank and join to a man. She can join to one only if our *tiva* laws are met. Few men have the skills and strength to provide game and skins and defense for two families, three if he is responsible for his parents. It would risk the *tiva*'s family going in want, perhaps both of their families going in want. It is our duty as Chosen Ones to make these sacrifices. *Tivas* which number less than the fingers of a hand have joined with mates since before my mother's birth. By the time we are released from our duties at our parents' deaths, we are too old to bear children and most men have wives. Those who lose mates do not want one who cannot accept their seeds of life in old bodies. Only three times have girls in training had their *kims* broken to release their female spirits when their mothers gave birth to sons, all before they were ten seasons old and long ago. *Tivas* cannot allow themselves to have such selfish thoughts and feelings. You must do the same, Kionee, or you will suffer great sadness. To desire what cannot be causes a hardness to enter you."

As a vivid image of the Cheyenne warrior galloped into her head, Kionee asked, "What if a *tiva* cannot control such forbidden thoughts and feelings?"

"Do you wish to yield to Night Walker's desire for you? Is he the one who stirs such conflicts within you?"

"No, never him. He is not my destiny. There are many things about Night Walker and Little Weasel which trouble me. They whisper of rising hungers to battle the Bird Warriors for coups and excitement. Already they speak such words aloud in council. Each time they leave camp to hunt, I fear they will seek a path to provoke the Crow against us so we will be forced to fight them. I do not like or trust the burnings in their eyes or the strange eagerness in their bodies for war. I do not like the fire in Night Walker's loins for me. He has never accepted me as a man. He is careful with his words and actions, but I see what lies beneath their sly coverings."

"Your eyes and wits are sharp, Kionee, for you grasp how he looks at you and hear the softness in his voice when he speaks to you. As snow blanketed Mother Earth, I watched the hunger in his eyes grow larger and its fire burn brighter when he thought no one saw them. It will be hard to deny him when he pursues you after the buffalo hunt, for I am sure he will. He waits only for you to pass twenty-one circles of seasons, as is our *tiva* law, before he speaks openly to you and to others of his desire to join with you."

"I pray that is not true, but I fear your words are wise and knowing. I fear the trouble his chase will bring. Before his mouth opens to speak such unwanted words, I will do all I can to prevent them from spilling forth. I must halt him from trying to clear a path I do not wish to travel."

"Do not forget: he is our chief's son; he is a man of high rank. If his brother is slain, he will become our next chief. Most will think it is a great honor to become his mate; most will be angry with you for refusing him. He has the skills to provide for and protect his mate and children, and your family. He has the prowess to best you in the hunt, and in hand battle. He meets all of the commands in our law."

"No, Regim, he does not, for I will not accept him. I do not love him or wish to share a tipi and mat with him."

Regim studied the expression in the troubled gaze of her sister's child. "Is there another you would accept? Wish to accept? Has your heart been seized by a skilled hunter who does not meet our laws for freedom?"

Kionee tensed and wondered if she should expose the astonishing truth.

K IONEE'S GAZE LOCKED with her aunt's, whom she trusted, respected, and loved. Her decision came swiftly. "Yes, but he is not of our tribe. He does not know I am a woman."

The astute Regim added up the recent clues to Kionee's increased restlessness and withdrawal into herself. "The Cheyenne warrior from the hunt six suns past. Tell me about him and this power he has over you."

Kionee wondered how—with only simple words as a tool—she could describe such a potent force like Stalking Wolf. How could she explain this irresistible attraction to him? Yet, she must try. "Since we met, he steals into my thoughts when I am awake and he enters my dreams when I sleep. I am drawn to him as a bear to honey or as our people to the sacred mountain. I feel a strong and strange bond to him."

"You must forget him, Kionee, or you will be tormented by reckless longings for what can never be. Our people do not join outside our tribe; it numbers only thirty-two stones over a thousand, but we keep the Hanueva alive and pure with laws to ban joining with outsiders and *no* joining between close kin. If we mix our seeds with others, one sun there will be no Hanueva bloodline. If one is allowed to break that law, others will be tempted to do so. If outsiders are allowed to join us, they will bring trouble and changes, and expose our *tiva* secret. You must make this new sacrifice for the good of Kionee, your family, and our people. Drive him from your head and heart."

"That is like telling a river to stop flowing, or snow to cease falling in the cold season, or the sun to never rise again, or the wind to stop blowing. I yearn to see him, to touch him, to feel his embrace and kiss. But you must not worry or fear, Regim, for our paths will never cross again. We do not camp or hunt in the same areas. *Tivas* do not visit trading camps, for we must always stay apart from others to guard the truth, as you well know."

"Pray your feet and his never walk the same trail and your eyes never meet again," Regim still warned. "He is forbidden to you, and punishment for breaking our law is harsh. Even with your great skills and courage, you would not survive it."

Regim clasped Kionee's cold hands in hers. "I love you as my own child and I have helped train you since you were five summers. I beg you: let me help protect you and guide you away from this evil magic. Do not break your vows. Do not dishonor yourself and your family. Do not bring down *Atah*'s anger upon you and us. See this as a test, a challenge; and win it with wits and courage and strength. When we go to the sacred wheel after the buffalo hunt, make offerings to *Atah* for forgiveness and seek His help in walking the path He cleared for you. If you must step from it, do so either with Night Walker or another Hanueva of high rank and skills."

How so, Kionee wondered, when no Hanueva stirred her blood, enflamed her body, and enticed her to think of defying her vow as Stalking Wolf did? "Who made such laws, Regim? Why must we pretend to be what we are not? Why does the Creator allow us to have such feelings and thoughts if they are wrong? Does that not seem cruel?"

"It has been the way of our people since before we can remember," Regim reminded her. "There are many things we do not know or understand, but still must obey. We must not question or doubt the will of the Creator and High Guardian."

"With every *tiva* family circle that closes because she leaves no children behind to continue it, our tribe grows smaller and becomes more vulnerable to enemies," Kionee argued. "It would help our tribe be larger and stronger if *tivas* were allowed to join and bear those needed children, who will bear other children, so our people will not cease to exist one season under the evil hands of attackers." She raised pleading eyes to search Regim's face. "Have you never experienced love and desire for a male? Do you not understand how these emotions make me feel?"

"Yes," she answered quickly, "but I cut them from my heart and mind, for it could not be. You must do the same. In time, such forbidden and dangerous feelings will vanish and the joy in your rank will return."

"Do they ever leave, Regim? Will it return, my *Tiva-Chu* and friend?"

"Yes, Kionee, my loved one, if you do not resist the truth."

Kionee nodded as if in acceptance of that advice, but suspected the woman had lied to her for the first time. She forgave Regim because she saw the affection behind that tiny deceit.

Many days' ride beyond the Hanueva winter camp, Stalking Wolf came upon a sight that partly explained why Crow warriors were raiding in areas where they should not be. He considered visiting the Hanueva to give them a warning but decided against any delay in returning home. Bad weather had held him captive at the sacred mountain wheel two days longer than he wanted and needed to stay after receiving his strange vision. In twenty suns, he would ride into his camp and report the bad news and his suspicions.

Images of the white-clad Kionee with a colorful facial mask and a silver wolf at the hunter's side flickered through his mind, and he asked the Great Spirit to protect his new friend. *I do not know how or when, Kionee, but our paths will cross again, for I have seen it in my sacred vision. We have faced battle and death together and now we are bonded in a mystical way. When I reach camp, I must ask the shaman to tell me the meaning of my vision. If this is the season for me to take a mate, why does no woman of our tribe touch my heart and flame my body? What is the "powerful destiny" Medicine Eyes sent me to seek? Have I displeased the Great Spirit and He did not reveal it to me? I must have answers soon.*

"You make a new bow, Kionee. Is it for the hunt or a coming battle?"

"I will use it as Atah guides me, Little Weasel."

The man eyed the symbols on the discarded piece of choke-cherry, their colors indicating the deeds for which they were earned. Again, she had chosen chokecherry for her new weapon, the best wood to use but the hardest to find in the right length. He had watched her figure the needed size by measuring the distance between the tips of her fingers on an outstretched hand across her body to the opposite hipbone. He noticed the skill she evinced in attaching the leather grip that was edged with snowy fur. He observed as she stood and braced one end with her calf and ankle and pulled the other toward her chest to slip the boiled and dried sinew into a notch and lock it in place to test the sinew's tension. Nearby lay a wrist band for protecting her arm against string slap, a beaded carrying bag with a quiver attached, and two extra sinews for replacing a broken or weakened one. "You have many marks, old and new, to paint on it. Will the sun rise when your deeds are more than it can hold?" he questioned.

Kionee glanced up at her cousin and noticed his frown, one

that matched his bitter tone. As usual, she ignored them both with hopes they would cease one day. "Only *Atah* sees into suns not lived. He has given me many good deeds, and I am thankful. It has been fourteen moons since our men left to visit the Crow. Do you think they will return soon with good news?"

"*If* they return," Little Weasel responded to her obvious change of subject, "I believe they will be slain or held captive. Night Walker agrees."

"You are angry Chief Bear's Head and the council did not send you and Night Walker," she said.

"Crow hearts are as black as this night will be without a moon. We should scout and trap them, not cower in fear and beg for peace. The arrows you make would serve us better if shot into Bird hearts, for a dead man cannot raid and kill and cannot plant seeds in his mate for new enemies. We would have more people if *tivas* are allowed to have mates. Kionee could become a mother. Night Walker would take you as his woman."

"That is not our way, Little Weasel, and it is wrong to speak of it."

"Perhaps it is time for changes in our customs if we are to survive."

Kionee watched her cousin stalk away from her position at the edge of the forest. Her horses, Recu and Tuka, shook their heads, silent signs, it seemed, that they understood his words and fiercely disagreed. Maja nuzzled her arm as if to say, *I am here and I will protect you from harm.* She whispered to the large silver wolf, "They are bad, my friend, and I fear the threat they will bring to our people. We must pray and hope for peace. If the council had sent *tivas* to speak with the three Crow bands, they would listen. But it is good they did not send Little Weasel and Night Walker, who seek only adventure and glory. They crave to show their cunning and courage, Maja, but in the wrong way. If war is to come, my friend, *Atah* will guide us through those dark suns. We will fight together as one."

Kionee lifted her club. A skilled weapons-maker, she had

fashioned it from a willow rod while still green and wet enough to be bent and stretched over the head of a stone and attached with wet rawhide, which shrank and tightened as it dried. She wondered if she would use it as a weapon one day soon.

She fingered a hunting lance, which was longer and thinner than a war lance for battle. Hers was a head taller than her height, whereas a war lance was its owner's height plus the tip. She had no doubt she could pierce a foe with the blade, but would she be compelled to take lives with it?

Kionee's gaze drifted over a pile of arrows she had made, some this very day and some during the long winter, as each required long labor on shafts, tips, and fletchings. She had gathered the lengths of willow before winter while the sap was down, peeled and dried them, and secured them in bundles until she made them into weapons. Most were sized to the span she required for accurate firing, and painted with her ownership markings for joint hunts. Others were longer and unmarked for trading, as twenty good arrows were worth a horse or twenty superior hides. A good bow brought two horses or forty superior hides or other trade goods.

Of course, she mused, Little Weasel would never trade with her for weapons, though he was not as talented as she was. She wished her cousin could make weapons, hunt, and fight as she did so he would not be jealous of her superiority. *I know that is why you wish me to throw away my* tiva *vow and join to Night Walker after the buffalo hunt. I see, his hunger growing larger. I have felt his presence in hiding when I bathe; he has seen my face and body and knows I am a woman. But I will not be a woman for Night Walker. If a man is my destiny, it is Stalk— No, Kionee, do not let him fill your thoughts.*

Nine days passed as the Hanueva men and *tivas* readied weapons and practiced fighting skills afoot and on horseback to prepare themselves for a conflict that most prayed would never come. The weather went back and forth between warm spring days and cool nights to chilly days and nights with light to heavy snow as Mother Nature resisted a seasonal change. Everyone noticed that the six men sent to the three Crow camps did not return or send messages of success or failure, so worry increased and training intensified.

Kionee spent another two days in the *Haukau* during her menses, a visit which made her more restless and dissatisfied with her sacrificial rank. She tried in vain to keep thoughts of Stalking Wolf from her mind, and finally accepted the reality that was not possible, but she pined in silence even with Regim. She hunted with others as usual, but now all remained on alert. She knew Night Walker did everything he could to prevent her from being one of those chosen for scouting parties; twice he reasoned with her about her family's need for a hunter more than a protector. Yet, Kionee decided he was only safeguarding her for himself.

She watched the romance between Runs Fast and her sister grow warmer and bolder, and it brought envy to Kionee's mind and sadness to her heart. He would accompany Blue Bird when the girl went to fetch water and wood and to gather spring plants for cooking, but always with people around to avoid shame. The couple would stay in sight each time they talked at the edge of the forest or rode doubleback. He played his flute for her enjoyment and to show his selection of her to others. Kionee concluded they would join after the buffalo hunt and ceremonial visit to Medicine Mountain. She told herself she must hunt extra hard and long this season to help Runs Fast obtain enough buffalo hides for their tipi. After Moon Child came of age next summer and joined, that would leave only herself and her parents to provide for and defend. After they were gone, she would be alone, alone with the elders in the *tiva* tipi, unless . . .

No, Kionee, you cannot join to Night Walker. You cannot lie upon his mat, in his arms, your bodies united into one. His lips—his children—are not those you desire.

"Come, Kionee, we go to hunt. Red Bull and Tall Eagle say a herd of antelope and deer feed near the river where it bends toward the rising sun."

"I will get my weapons and horse, Sumba. Maja, stay and guard." She ordered the wolf to watch over her family during her absence. Others did not care for hunting with a predator whose scent might spook their prey. Maja lay down quietly near the tipi entrance; though eager to accompany her, he was obedient.

Taysinga, a *tiva* two years older than Kionee and Sumba, and Goes Ahead joined the group as they rode from camp. The six traveled northward along the Big Horn River for two hours to the location where scouts had reported sighting the herd. The animals had not left the area. Even if the hunters had not descented their bodies, there was no wind for a time to carry their smell to the grazing creatures. The three men and three women planned their approach from several angles. After leaving their extra horses secured by reins in a copse of trees until needed to carry home the meat and hides, they carried it out with skill and speed.

As the hunters neared their targets, the herd realized their peril and bolted in many directions. The band separated and pursued their goals. Arrows were fired and hit their marks, but the game raced valiantly onward. Finally, strength depleted, each deer and antelope struck stumbled and collapsed to the ground.

Kionee dismounted and retrieved a knife to give a merciful and swift end to one animal's futile struggle for life. She lifted her brown eyes skyward and said, "Thank you, *Atah*, for this gift of meat and skin for my family." She stroked Tuka's neck and forehead, pleased with the pinto's performance. Kneeling beside the deer with her marked arrow embedded in its chest, she eyed the quality of its hide as she skinned the creature without damaging it. She removed and placed antlers, choice teeth, and furry tail in a large parfleche for various uses later. After gutting the animal, Sumba joined her and helped load it onto an extra horse. Kionee secured it there with its legs roped beneath the horse's belly. Kionee did the same task to assist her friend, then both went to aid Taysinga who was slower at the deed and—as always—crinkling her nose in displeasure at the smell and feel of death.

Afterward, Sumba and Kionee tracked and prepared the antelope they had slain for older *tivas*. Almost at the moment the two females finished that task and stood washing their hands, Red Bull shouted that Crow warriors were galloping toward them with weapons brandished. The warning was unnecessary for Kionee, who had already heard them. She squinted at the three Hanueva men separated from them by the river and hurrying to come to their defense.

"Taysinga, get the horses and game into the trees for protection while Sumba and I guard our backs!" Kionee ordered the frozen eldest *tiva*, who stared in fear at the peril riding toward them: eight armed Bird warriors. Kionee seized the immobile girl's arm, shook her, and commanded, "Sharpen your wits and move fast or we die!"

Taysinga glared at Kionee for a moment, but obeyed. She scurried into the trees, secured reins to the horses and quickly grabbed her weapons, all as she observed the unfolding scene in near panic.

Kionee watched three warriors break off from the band to challenge the Hanueva men who were crossing the river. They knew they were at a disadvantage while in the water, and rushed to get on land. The other five warriors charged toward the *tivas* with obvious intent to attack and kill. "Sumba, they hold strong shields to defeat our arrows," Kionee noted with displeasure. "We must trick them. Fire at the first one's head; when he lifts his shield, I will fire into his belly. Fire next at the second one's leg; when he lowers his shield, I will fire into his chest or neck. Two will be gone before they learn our trick and guard against it. Fire twice on my signal, then get behind the trees."

"*Dwil*," Kionee told Sumba to loosen the first arrow. The instant the Crow jerked up his shield to ward off the shaft, Kionee fired into his stomach and saw him double over in pain and surprise. "*Dwil*." She coaxed the second shot and struck another enemy in the chest as he protected his leg. "*E'fa! Ombeg!*" She complimented Sumba and ordered a retreat as the astonished men halted in caution and to check their friends' conditions.

The odds were now three to three, with the *tivas* having protective cover. The Bird warriors grouped close and whispered as the women awaited a new assault. With loud yells, the enemies whirled their highly decorated mounts and headed to fight with their companions.

"Six skilled warriors are too many for our three hunters to battle."

"You are right, Sumba. We must help them. Come, Taysinga."

"I will wait here and guard our horses and game. I am a bad fighter."

"If you come, our numbers are the same," Kionee pointed out. "We must ride fast before our friends die."

Kionee and Sumba mounted and galloped after their attackers before the aggressors could join their friends who were nearing the hunters' position. The frightened Taysinga did not join them.

Within moments, the three Crow whirled again and galloped toward the two *tivas*, fanning out to engulf them. It was clear the warriors had not intended to aid their friends, only entice the *tivas* into the open and into a trap. Kionee and Sumba reined in and began to fire arrow after arrow at their assailants because it was too late for a safe withdrawal; it was face and fight or take a shaft in the back while trying to escape. Sumba called for Taysinga to help them, but the terrified girl remained in hiding. It was fortunate for the two brave women that one Crow headed for the trees and the concealed target cowering there, evening their odds.

Kionee wounded her attacker in the arm and caused him to drop his shield. He yanked a knife from a sheath and charged her in fury. Quickly she dismounted, knowing she had more chance of success on the ground and could prevent her horse from taking a deflected blow. The warrior leapt from his horse and ran to meet her challenge. In his anger, he slashed wildly and missed striking her each time. Kionee cut his wrist and then his calf as she ducked and darted past him. Before he could react, she buried her knife in his back.

Kionee finished in time to see the other Bird warrior lift his blade to plunge it into Sumba's heart. She heard him taunt Sumba with vows to take her horse and possessions, and to skin the painted masks from her face and hand to adorn his shield with them. Kionee could not come to Sumba's defense because the third warrior had halted his charge at Taysinga and focused on the "brave *tiva*" whose "magic and power" he craved to steal with her death. He shouted to Taysinga that a coward had no value to him.

Kionee prepared herself to battle him. She was tired and tense, and he was fresh and calm, yet, Taysinga still did not come to her aid. The Bird warrior aimed his war lance and flung it at her, an action she sidestepped by inches. The moment it struck the earth, she seized it and drove a lethal blow to the warrior's belly as he reached her. Without delay, Kionee ran to Sumba's opponent and jumped on his back to prevent him from mutilating her dead friend's body. She clawed, scratched, and pummeled him as he tried to rise and shake her loose. Kionee took an elbow to the mouth which split her lip and sent blood flowing down her blackened chin, and sent her falling backward. She wished Maja was there to aid her or Tuka could respond to a summons or Stalking Wolf would appear and— *Do not dull your wits!*

"You and your magic are mine now, *tiva*, and those of your friend." Her attacker grinned malevolently. "I will have great power when your masks are on my shield and your scalplocks are on my coup stick. As One-Eye says, we will show others it is not bad medicine to slay those with painted faces. Come, *tiva*, and kiss my blade with your skin and blood. You die this su—"

As the cocky man reached the position Kionee wanted and he took a spread-legged stance to tower over her to gloat, she kicked upward with haste and drove her foot into his groin. When he doubled over, she bolted to her feet and slammed her knee into his chin. The jarring blow knocked him to his back. She leapt on him, grabbed his armed hand, and shoved his knife into his chest before he could recover in time to react. She hurried to stand and check her surroundings for another challenge. She saw the one remaining Crow riding northwestward and two of the Hanueva men riding toward her. She noticed in dismay that they led the horse of Tall Eagle with his body lying across it.

The Hanuevas had witnessed Kionee's prowess, courage, and loyalty to Sumba. All knew the peril of a *tiva* body falling into the hands of an enemy and their secret being unmasked. They knew Kionee had prevented Sumba's exposure at great risk to herself. They had many questions to ask of her.

"Where is Taysinga?"

"He waits in the trees, Red Bull."

"Why did he not fight with you and Sumba? Five were many for two."

"I do not know, Goes Ahead; you must ask him." *Perhaps she acts more like the female she is than the male hunter she pretends to be. She hides in fear and will know great shame from this dark deed.*

"We must take our friends and game home before our enemy brings others to fight with him," Red Bull said.

"He will not return, for he will not reveal their defeat and shame at the hands of five Hanuevas."

"Perhaps that is true, but we will hurry."

"How did you and Goes Ahead defeat your attackers?"

"While you battled many, we killed two and the other ran away. But one took the life of Tall Eagle before we defeated them," he explained sadly, then said they must go.

As they retrieved their horses, loaded their last burden, and mounted to depart, Kionee noticed the bitterness in Taysinga's expression. For some reason, the girl blamed her for what she would face for being a weakling and coward! Taysinga's sorry attitude worsened during the men's praise of Kionee's skills. Kionee did not attempt to lighten her mood, as she held the girl partly responsible for Sumba's death.

The hunting party entered the winter village and were met by people shocked to see Tall Eagle and Sumba dead. News of trouble swept through the camp.

Kionee let Red Bull and Goes Ahead reveal their successful hunt, fierce attack, defense and victory of sorts, and their two losses. It did not escape anyone's attention that Taysinga's name was darkened or that the *tiva* rushed to her family's tipi to avoid humiliating questions.

Everyone praised the exploits of five of the six Hanuevas who had left camp only to hunt. A council meeting was called for later that evening to make defense plans and to mourn the deaths of their two friends. During that meeting, it would be decided how Taysinga must repay the families of Tall Eagle and Sumba for their losses, which might have been prevented if she had not failed in her duty. It was revealed they recovered all telltale arrows and signs, and they took no possessions from the fallen Crow to be found in their camp. Most agreed with Kionee that the survivor would hold silent to "save face."

Before Kionee reached her tipi, Night Walker halted her and said, "You must not endanger yourself; your family has great need for you alive. *I* have great need for you alive; I will make those words clear before snow blankets our land once more. You are brave and skilled, Kionee, but do not become bold and foolish. If there is fighting to be done, I will do your part."

"I did not seek a battle this sun or on any sun, Night Walker. My friend has joined *Atah* and my heart is sad, so speak no more words." She moved past him and entered her tipi to grieve for Sumba. Maja snuggled close to her on the sitting mat and offered his friend comfort. "She is gone, Maja," Kionee whispered into the wolf's ear. "I could not save her. She will never know the joys of love and mating, or bear children; that should not be so. I will miss her, for she was my best friend behind you and Regim. Protect her and guide her feet to you, *Atah*."

The peace-talkers sent to Red Plume and Long Hair returned with words which relieved and elated the Hanuevas, but the two men sent to Swift Crane's camp never returned, if they reached it alive . . .

The weather became unusually warm in the day and almost balmy at night. The remaining snow melted and trees and grasses flourished in green splendor. Scrubs and plants sprouted in abundance; yellow bell, fireweed, spring beauty, snow lily, arrowleaf, and others were gathered for food. Birds and animals returned and sought mates. Insects did the same.

But the glorious weather coaxed more and more Crow to hunt and scout too close to the mouth of the Wind River Canyon. Guards were a routine sight around the Hanueva camp, and a warning system was ready for speedy use. Kionee and her people also hunted and scouted, but in larger groups than usual and with great caution. Whenever Crow tribesmen were sighted, they were avoided; whenever they were encountered,

Hanueva made signs of peace and left that location. So far, no more attacks or raids had come. Still, the Hanueva could not relax or trust their enemies, though two bands had sworn peace and appeared to be honoring their word during chance meetings. It was concluded the band they should fear was Swift Crane's, the one Night Walker and Little Weasel yearned to challenge.

Several days and nights had passed in rigid alert and increasing edginess when Kionee was heading to take over Goes Ahead's guard position. Along the way, she met the sister of Blowing Rain, who was mate to Red Bull. The young female was frantic as she halted Kionee to relate that she and Blowing Rain had been gathering wood and plants when her sister's baby decided it was time to be born, fast and on that spot.

"Go for help. I will guard Blowing Rain. You are too far from camp," Kionee scolded. She did not have to ask the pregnant woman's location, as shrieks of pain and fear were loud in that direction. "Go! Hurry! If enemies are close, they will hear her cries and follow them."

As Kionee neared the scene, she heard sounds which halted her for a few moments as they warned her of grave peril. She whispered cautions to Maja, who already had detected the problem and come to full alert.

Kionee listened: a grizzly was making its way toward the helpless woman. She saw bushes shake as the great beast passed them and left the trees upriver. The huge creature had a dark and sleek skin, and appeared deceptively slow and lazy. Its nose was dirty from work in the earth. Its mouth was open, pink gums and long white teeth in view. She knew from experience that the enormous and deadly bear could charge across that shallow water and attack either her or Red Bull's wife with ease. Kionee watched the back muscles ripple and hunch beneath the

protrusion between its powerful shoulders. She saw the animal
stand to sniff the air, to listen, and to get a view of his intended
meal. She noticed the claw scrapings on nearby trees at heights
of seven feet, a bad sign. Rotting logs revealed teeth and claw
marks where the bear had foraged for insects and chipmunks
earlier in the day. She knew the bear could not be outrun; and
running usually provoked an attack. Fortunately, Kionee did
not see any cubs, as a sow would be more threatening than a
foraging male.

Kionee and Maja worked their way between the grizzly and
Blowing Rain. She motioned to the suffering woman to remain
silent and still to avoid luring the awesome predator to her vulnerable position. Obviously the baby's birth could not be slowed
or stopped, and soon its wail of life would entice the threat
closer. Kionee had her weapons ready, as she must defend
Blowing Rain with her own life if necessary. She sighted several
squirrels across the river and wounded two with hopes those
noises would cause the bear to reverse his movements to inspect
them.

The grizzly paused for a few moments, glanced toward the
fussing squirrels, then continued onward toward the Hanue-
vans' location. The bear halted five tree heights away and
looked at Kionee, Maja, and the woman on the ground. He made
a bluff run at them using a short burst of speed at a loping gait.
When they remained still and quiet, he seemed to debate
whether to leave them alone or attack. Kionee knew he was test-
ing them as a threat and assessing their strengths. He would not
charge unless he was certain he could defeat them or they
threatened him. Kionee guessed he was about to ignore them
and depart, but Blowing Rain could not suppress a scream of
anguish as the infant's head surged from her body and its shoulders tried to free themselves.

Kionee saw the grizzly stretch his thick neck, flatten his ears,
assume a stiff-legged challenging stance, and glare at them: all
ominous signs. He shook his massive body and growled his

change of mind about leaving. Kionee watched in alarm as the fierce predator lowered his head and ran toward them at full speed, a target too huge to take down with one or several arrows.

Atah, help us, for my skills are not as large and strong as this peril.

4

KIONEE LIFTED HER BOW and fired an arrow into the grizzly's chest beneath its mouth. While his massive head was raised to sight her, she had aimed for the vulnerable soft spot where he breathed with hopes of cutting off his air. If she succeeded, it did not slow or halt him. She shot an arrow into his right foreleg, one into his left leg, then another into his upper chest. Still, he continued his determined charge as if unwounded. Maja rushed around the creature and began to snap and bite at his hind legs. Kionee fired an arrow into the center of his furry chest when he lifted himself to a towering height and pawed the air as he bellowed in rage and pain and snapped off several shafts. Doing so caused his fury and agony to mount. Too close to shoot again, Kionee drew her knife and tried to lure the bear away from Blowing Rain by yelling, stomping her feet, and flailing her arms.

The bear lowered his forelegs and took her bait. With him racing after her at an amazing speed, she darted around trees and logs to elude his claws and teeth. She hoped to slow and deter him with obstacles, and to get him as far away from the woman and child as possible. Kionee surmised he must be losing blood and strength at a good pace, so she must continue her actions to weaken and exhaust him until she could slay him with Maja's help; or until he decided to give up his chase and leave. If not, she reasoned, her distraction might give Blowing Rain time to birth the child and to recover enough to flee.

The huntress prayed for *Atah*'s assistance and guidance. If only, she worried, the creature was not so powerful and angry, he would yield defeat and escape to lick his many wounds. It soon was apparent to Kionee that he would not give up; that she was entangled in a battle to the death.

Calling upon all of her skills, courage, and stamina and those of Maja, the two friends fought with the enormous threat until they also weakened and tired. For a frantic moment, Kionee feared there was nothing she or *Atah* could do to save their lives. Just as she was about to give up hope, the bear turned and ambled away. In renewed alarm, Kionee realized it was heading back toward Blowing Rain. Nothing she did called the grizzly's attention back to her, so she and Maja pursued in haste to turn him. Panic gave Kionee a jolt when the challenger whirled on the snapping wolf and made slaps at her friend with quill-sharp claws which could open up a man or animal with a single slash.

The agile wolf evaded the lethal blows and circled the dark beast with nimble speed as he nipped several spots, causing the bear to go round and round in pursuit. At last, Kionee saw the huge predator slow and stagger, then sink to the earth. She grabbed a heavy limb and used it as a club to render the animal almost senseless. Without hesitation, she leapt on its hump and seized its lower jaw to yank back its head. Without delay, she drew a sharp knife across its throat and ended their peril. The grizzly collapsed in death, and Kionee went limp on its body for a short while to recover from the exhausting ordeal. She thanked *Atah* for survival and victory and for allowing her to take His creation's life to save theirs.

The calling of her name rent the now quiet air. Kionee rushed to Blowing Rain's side.

The fatigued woman smiled gratitude through misty eyes. "My heart beats with joy to see you live. You risked much to save our lives. Red Bull will reward your courage and kindness."

Kionee watched Blowing Rain nestle her first child in her arms; that tender sight warmed and saddened the *tiva* who would never experience such a special moment. When Blowing Rain closed her eyes to rest for a while, Kionee glanced at the blood of new motherhood on the woman and the blood of a hunter on her own hands; their colors, smells, and meanings were so different: life and death, a female free to be a woman and a female forced to live as a man.

How, Kionee wondered, did *Atah* choose which path each would follow, and why? If not for Sumba being the eldest, Blowing Rain would not be enjoying this glorious experience. And if not for Kionee being the eldest, her sister would not be joining to Runs Fast soon. And if Blowing Rain's two sisters were not at joining ages, the next in line would be trained as a *tiva* to take Sumba's place. It was rare for a *tiva* to be killed or to die young, as her friend had. Now, when Sumba's father was too old to hunt and protect, the other *tivas* must help her parents. *How lucky Pine Tree and Blue Bird are to escape this grim destiny! As for you, Taysinga, you were not punished enough for your part in Sumba's death. Hate me if you must for speaking the truth, for I do not care.*

Within a few minutes, several people—including Red Bull—ran to join them. After hearing the frightening tale from his weary wife, Red Bull embraced and thanked Kionee for rescuing his family at such a great risk.

"The bear skin belongs to your child, Red Bull, to make its first mat. The meat is for your family to help them regain strength."

"Your heart is good and large, Kionee; your skills and courage are as big as *Atah*'s land above us. My life is yours if danger seeks you one sun. Our child will carry your name while it walks on Mother Earth. I will place the claws on a thong for you to wear to reveal your deed for all to see and know."

"You are kind and good, Red Bull, my friend. I must go watch for our enemies after I wash in the river. Blowing Rain is brave; she held quiet and still while suffering; show her great honor and love for her deed."

As the other hunters gathered around the bear to admire it, Red Bull nodded and went to kneel by his wife where two women were tending her. He kissed the woman's forehead and stroked her cheek and hair. "You are brave and strong, Blowing Rain, and my pride in you is great."

"Our child is a daughter; she is uninjured and unafraid. We would not live if Kionee had not come to save us. His deed is large and generous."

As the couple admired their newborn and talked, Kionee noticed the love and closeness they shared. Envy wafted over her as did a gentle breeze. As when she had watched Blowing Rain and her sisters preparing the cradleboard for this child, the touching sight was too much to endure. She glanced at the other hunters who were skinning the bear for Red Bull. She heard them speaking their amazement of her victory and praising her skills. Yet, her anguish overshadowed the glory of the event. She headed to the river to wash her hands and arms of blood and to escape the wrenching scene.

Afterward, as they walked through the trees toward their guard site, Kionee stroked the wolf's head and ears. "If you had not been with me and helped, Maja, I would not live, and Blowing Rain and her child would not live. You are my best friend and I love you. Since your pack is gone and no other will accept you as is the wolf's way, we will remain like mates for life."

The silver creature licked her hand and nuzzled its head against her leg.

That evening, Red Bull came to the tipi of Strong Rock to return Kionee's undamaged arrows and to give her a necklace of bearclaws and beads, a gift quickly made with help from his friends and their mates. Red Bull suspended the token around Kionee's neck and thanked her again.

"Our child was given the name of Ae-Culta-Kionee," he announced.

Kionee smiled as she heard the girl would be called She-who was saved by-Wind of Destiny. "You show me great honor, Red Bull; my heart sings with joy and pride. If a dark moon rises, I will be ready to hunt for and protect she who carries my name. If the need comes, she will join the family of Strong Rock and live as my . . . sister."

Martay felt twinges of anguish and guilt as she empathized with her daughter who would never have her own baby. It had taken eleven spans of seasons to make Kionee a son in her mind and heart. But hearing the strained tone in Kionee's voice and seeing a certain gleam in Kionee's eyes as the word "child" almost escaped her lips, Martay wondered if Kionee yearned for the life of a woman.

Before Red Bull could leave, Night Walker entered the tipi without asking for or awaiting permission to do so. "I was hunting and returned to hear of your great peril and deed, Kionee. Are you injured?"

"No. With the help of Maja and *Atah*, we defeated the bear. All are safe."

"Danger seems to stalk you this season. I will remain nearby when you are not in our camp. My heart would be cold and dark without your warmth and light."

"You are a good friend, Night Walker, as a brother to me, and I thank you," Kionee felt compelled to reply before witnesses to the man's first romantic overture. She was angry with him for being so bold, and revealing his desire. But from the looks and reactions of the others, no one of them seemed to have noticed his true meaning . . .

With the exception of Martay. She was surprised by it, caught the undercurrent of displeasure in her child, and tried to help extricate Kionee. "My son must eat and rest; this deed took much of his energy and strength. The family of Strong Rock thanks you, Red Bull, for honoring our son with such gifts and praise. I will make a garment for your baby with the first skin he finds."

After the guests' departure, Strong Rock embraced Kionee and said, "My love and pride are large this moon, my son, for you bring great respect to my tipi and family with your prowess, courage, and giving spirit. *Atah* chose my son well, for I could have no better one. I have no fear with you as our Hunter-Guardian. May *Atah* guard your life and skills and keep you with us until death, for my tipi-of-power is weak and we would be lost without yours."

"Do not worry, my father; nothing and no one will steal me from your family circle or from the rank *Atah* gave me many seasons past." *For the only temptation I face and gift I crave are beyond my reach and power.*

>>>> <<<<

The following evening as Kionee tended her horses, Night Walker joined her, his action bringing her to alert and causing dismay.

"I find my thoughts on you each sun and moon, Kionee. You are a good hunter and fighter. Our people give you praise and are happy you are one of us. Our tribe would not wish to face you in battle as an enemy."

Kionee forced a smile. "You are kind. It is good we are hunters and brothers together. With your great skills, you would be a bad enemy to fight."

Night Walker leaned against a tree. "We are well matched in that area. I try to teach my brother all I know, for Gray Fox will be chief and hunter for my father and mother when that moon rises. Soon I must seek a mate, leave my family's tipi, and bring more Hanueva to life. It is a great honor to make our tribe larger and stronger. It is the duty of a Hanueva to do so."

"Your deed will bring joy and respect to your family and people. You have lived twenty-three circles of seasons and proven yourself more than worthy to take a mate. Your friend Little Weasel already races ahead of you with children; he has a fine son and daughter. If you hurry, in a few buffalo seasons, you will be training your son with his to follow you, and they will become good friends as their fathers are."

"It is a hard choice, for only a *tiva* warms my heart and body."

"I have seen Taysinga's eyes when they are upon you. Perhaps he will break his *kim* and free his spirit to become a woman to join with you."

"My eyes and heart do not look in her direction."

Kionee continued her chore, ignoring his clue and the use of "her." "That is bad, for no other *tiva* has the desire to leave our rank."

"Do you never feel and think as a woman? As a mate? As a mother?"

She focused a look of mingled disbelief and near insult on him. "That is not our way, Night Walker. I am a son. I am a *tiva* in all ways. I have lived, trained, and sworn to honor my vow and duty."

"Have you never wished to become a woman again?"

"This has been my life since I was five summers on Mother Earth. To Kionee, my family, and our people, I am a son, a hunter and protector. That is the will of *Atah*, for He chose me to walk this path. No man should ever look upon a *tiva* as a female, or tempt one to leave our rank out of season."

"Heads do not choose the ones we love; our hearts do that task."

Kionee's tension mounted as the man's gaze roved her face and body. "But a strong man of honor does not place his moccasins on a path he should not and cannot travel; that is our way."

Night Walker moved closer and murmured in a voice made husky from her nearness, "It is also our way to use that path if *Atah* changes our destiny. Creator has done so in past seasons. There is a slit in the *tiva* lodge through which one can leave that rank if tests are met. I will face them."

"Do not bring suffering to yourself and to this *tiva* you desire if your choice is not Taysinga, the only *tiva* who would leave our rank. To speak to one who is unwilling will cause trouble and bring pain to both hearts. It will cause trouble among our people to seek what cannot be won."

"I will think on your words, but they do not change my feelings for her. I have loved and desired and waited for her for many seasons. I will find a way to win her heart and acceptance and will challenge for her release. I am sure we will be joined before the next snow falls. Our people will accept the choice of their chief's son, for both are worthy of becoming mates. She has earned the right to freedom and joining; she will bear strong and brave children, for she has strength and courage. Perhaps one will be chief if my brother Gray Fox falls prey to Crow and I take his place to lead our tribe."

Kionee realized in dread that if Gray Fox *was* slain and Night Walker followed his father, it would be almost impossible to reject him without causing great shame and trouble, and difficult to elude the war he craved. "Do not speak of such things to her until she is willing to hear them."

"I will wait and look for the sign to approach her. It will come."

Kionee watched the grinning man depart. Night Walker was strong, handsome, brave, and smart. He could provide for and protect his family along with that of a *tiva*'s. Most females would be eager to join with him, but she was not. She hoped her words would dissuade him from further pursuit. At least he could not speak his desire clearly and loudly until after the buffalo hunt. Between now and then, she plotted in panic, she must change his mind, his target.

Taysinga . . . She was the only other *tiva* who resented her change in life and who loved a man. If she could get them together, it would solve many problems. If not, Taysinga would dislike her even more. Perhaps the woman was not to blame for hating to hunt and for being afraid of powerful warriors, as Taysinga did do her first task with acceptable skill. Perhaps she should not fault Taysinga for acting like a female on occasion.

Kionee went to her tipi and sought sleep to ease her mind. Kind slumber came to free her and give her strength for the hunt in the morning and for watch duty the next evening.

An early awakening full moon appeared low in the sky, faint against a pale-blue background. As Kionee watched it from her guard position, she counted the days until their move to the grasslands: twenty-one or less. The journey would be lengthy and slow. Once they reached Thunder Basin, the hunt would be rewarding. Perhaps with all tribes doing the same task, the Crow and Night Walker would be too busy to—

Kionee's gaze widened in astonishment as she watched Stalking Wolf ride toward her hiding place, heading in a direct line to the Hanueva camp. He sat straight and alert on his mount, as if he sensed eyes on him. Even so, he continued along his chosen path. Yet she knew he was not careless, only confident.

An open-throat shirt exposed the sun-bronzed skin of his muscular chest. His long hair was golden brown with two thin sections braided near his handsome face and secured behind his head. Two eagle feathers dangled downward from where the braids joined, and they fluttered in the wind. A medicine pouch was suspended around his neck and peeked from beneath his buckskin shirt which was adorned with tiny locks of enemy hair that signified he had performed a great deed for his tribe or shown enormous courage and victory in battle. The red stripes on his leggings revealed he was a member of the Dog-Men Society, the largest and most powerful group of his people. Tiny hairlocks also decorated them, declaring he had been a "dog-rope" wearer in the past; not only a sash wearer, she realized, but one of the two of four bravest men selected for that position for the span of a circle of seasons. While holding that high rank, one had to be last to leave the battlefield. To be a sash wearer was an honor and a terrible danger. It would be a big coup for an enemy to slay one and to steal his treasures. Was there no end, she mused, to Stalking Wolf's valor and deeds? Was there a man anywhere to compare with him?

She continued to observe him. A bow and quiver case rested upon his broad back. He rode a tall and sleek snow-colored stallion whose name she recalled as White Cloud; he led another horse whose markings and burdens revealed its purpose was for carrying his possessions. She studied his face with strong and perfect features. He was a virile and magnificent creature, a man of elite prowess. Her heart lurched in excitement as he came closer.

Then something startling caught her eye as he shifted its position: he was carrying his war shield uncovered, and its design almost matched that of her ceremonial one! A large black wolf's head was painted in the center with white elk horns painted across its forehead and its nose. Several arrowheads, a weasel skin, eagle feathers, and grizzly claws were attached near the edges in various locations. She noted there were only a few differences between their shields: her skin was ermine; her feathers, hawk; and her claws were dew from the deer. How strange, she thought, that their patterns would be so similar . . .

After composing herself and ordering Maja to remain hidden, Kionee stepped into view, and he halted. She watched his tawny gaze sweep over her and the lowered weapon, an arrow-nocked bow. He urged his horse to within two arms' lengths of her. His smile and nearness caused her heart to beat faster and her wits to scatter. Why, she worried, did he or any man have such an effect on her, a *tiva*? How could she halt these wild and forbidden emotions? Why did he evoke such conflicting reactions: happiness and anguish, anticipation and reluctance, fear and courage?

"*Haahe. Na-hoe-hoohtse,*" Stalking Wolf said.

She listened to him greet her and say he had come to visit, but she was so filled by disbelief and questions that her tongue did not move.

When the Hanueva remained silent and watchful, Stalking Wolf said, "Kionee, son of Strong Rock, it is good to see you, my friend and ally." When the hunter still did not speak, he asked, "Do you not remember me, our elk hunt, and battle with three Crow?"

She had to compose herself again, but was pleased he recalled her and her mask pattern. She hoped her voice and expression did not expose her emotions as she questioned, "Why have you come to visit, Stalking Wolf, when it nears the sun to ride to the grasslands to hunt buffalo?"

"I must speak with your chief and council. Our shaman's visions say trouble is in the wind. My father and our council sent me to smoke the peace pipe with Hanuevas and to help your people escape the Crow."

Kionee glanced behind him and queried, "You come alone?"

He nodded and replied, "*Heehee.*"

"You are a great warrior and son of a great leader, and Cheyenne are known for their large skills in fighting and raiding, but how can one man hold back a flock of Bird Warriors if they fly to our land to attack?"

"I have battled as one man in past suns as a sash wearer and not been defeated. I do not fear them, or death with honor. I walk the sacred path. I seek *Maheoo*'s guidance, approval, and protection in all things. As long as Our People follow *Maheoo* and Sweet Medicine's prophecy and keep our Four Sacred Arrows, we will survive and gather victory over enemies. Our shaman's vision from *Maheoo* told him how to save your people, and we have been commanded to do so. I was chosen as *Maheoo*'s shield and weapon."

"It is true you are brave and strong and skilled, for you bear those marks and symbols, and they are many. But your presence may endanger us if Crow learn you are here. What greater coup can a Crow earn than to defeat Stalking Wolf? We are a people of harmony; we are hunters, not warriors or raiders. We fight only to defend our camp and tribe: all know this and most leave us in peace."

"The season of peace is gone forever, Kionee. You know this, for you stand guard against raids. I will speak my words to your chief and council; you can resist them there. I ride to your camp. Do you come with me?"

"I will go with you." She summoned Maja from the bushes.

The Cheyenne watched the silver animal join Kionee, its golden eyes never leaving his face. The wolf's ears were erect, but the ruff on its neck was calm. There was a controlled power and fearlessness about the creature. His strong shoulder grazed Kionee's legging when he halted, as if he needed the contact. The Hanueva's gaze was filled with respect and love as his fingers stroked the wolf's head. It was as if the two shared an emotional and spiritual bond. "It is good to see you, Maja, my friend and symbol of my animal helper," Stalking Wolf said. "Come, we go."

With Kionee and Maja walking beside the white stallion, Stalking Wolf rode to the Hanueva camp along the river in a lovely and sheltered canyon. Excitement and suspense engulfed him as he headed to fulfill the sacred visions and to find his true destiny.

5

S O THAT EVERYONE COULD hear and see to the best advantage, the voting members of the Hanueva tribe met in a large clearing away from the women and children and their noisy activities. Several hundred hunters and a group of over forty *tivas* sat in a circle around their chief, shaman, eight council members, and their unexpected guest. It was their way for the ten leaders to govern the tribe, but all hunters possessed a vote, with the majority controlling the decision. Usually, most of the band followed the leaders' advice.

"It is a great honor to welcome the son of Big Hump to our camp."

Stalking Wolf thanked the chief and said, "I have brought good words and hard words for the ears and hearts of the Hanueva."

"Speak them, our friend and ally," Bear's Head gave him permission to address his people without interruption.

"Soon all tribes go to seek the buffalo, Giver of Life. Before that sun rises, enemies grow restless and eager to raid for horses and captives, to renew their fighting skills as Mother Earth renews her face, and to strike the first coups of a new season. All know how the Crow values his tribal rank: a position in his chosen society and leadership among his people depend upon his prowess on the battlefield and success in gathering coups and many possessions. In suns past, Crow did not attack Hanueva in large parties, only in small numbers and in secret. That will not be true this season, for they no longer view the Hanueva as weak and unworthy and having great magic which cannot be defeated or stolen."

"Is that not what I told you, my father and people?" Night Walker heatedly reminded him.

"Silence, my son! Do not ride into another's words."

"I am sorry, Father, but my anger against them and a fear for my people's survival and safety stole my tongue."

"Speak, Stalking Wolf, and all must be silent until he is quiet."

The Cheyenne nodded gratitude to Bear's Head, and made a mental note to keep a watchful eye and ear on the chief's disquieting son. "The shaman of my tribe, Medicine Eyes, saw things—good and bad—in two sacred visions. Many moons past, he sent me to the holy Wheel to make offerings to the Great Spirit and to fulfill part of his first vision. *Maheoo* placed my feet on a path to seek my true destiny. He says the slayer of my parents still lives and it is my duty to find and punish him; his face has not been revealed to us to this sun, but it belongs to a Crow."

When the Hanueva looked confused, he explained, "Big Hump was my grandfather until he took me as his son after my parents were killed. I am to remain with your tribe and to help you reach the buffalo grounds alive and unharmed. He says one among you is destined for a great deed among Our People and that Hanueva must be protected." Stalking Wolf did not think it necessary to mention he was also to find his mate before the next snows came, according to the vision. "There are those among the Crow who no longer honor and obey the words of their past shaman's vision about the Hanueva; Calls-On-Spirits is dead, and his power over them is vanishing as mist beneath a hot sun. Medicine Eyes saw many Bird Warriors flying to attack Hanueva if we cannot trick them into retreating or shoot them from their land skies." When Stalking Wolf paused to see if the chief or shaman wanted to ask any questions, he noticed Kionee's keen attention on him, and an odd sensation danced over his body and teased through his mind.

"How do you know Calls-On-Spirits is dead?" Spotted Owl asked.

Stalking Wolf focused on the shaman. "As I rode from the great Wheel, I found his resting place. His tipi sat alone on the land between the mountains. It was painted with many colors. He was wrapped in a yellow robe, bound with sinew, and placed where he took his last breath of air, as is their way. The tipi entrance was sewn, but I cut the strips and looked inside. He waits for the forces of Nature and the spirits to claim his body."

"We sent men to speak of peace to the three Crow bands, but only those from Long Hair and Red Plume returned. The others must have been slain,"

"Chief Long Hair honors his word not to attack Hanueva, only to fight Lakotas and Blackfoot. Red Plume honors his truce with Hanueva. It is not so for the band of Swift Crane; he does not wish to fight with Hanueva, but many of his warriors do, and it is their right by leadership of high rank. If his life is taken, those who desire war will control the tribe; that is bad. To survive, Hanueva must ally, travel, and camp with Cheyenne."

Kionee's cousin responded to their guest, "Eight Crow warriors attacked one of our hunting parties eight suns past, and five Hanueva defeated them, killed all except the coward who fled in fear of their skills."

"But two of our hunters were slain in that attack, Little Weasel," Strong Rock pointed out. "Tall Eagle and Sumba. If Kionee had not struck death blows to five, others would be walking in the stars. I do not wish my son to face more Crow with blood lust in their eyes, for they number many."

"We have almost three hundred trained fighters; we can defeat them."

"That number is less than those in one Crow society, Night Walker, and the Crow have many among them," Stalking Wolf reasoned. "It is unwise to challenge them to war. So it is true with Our People; we have many societies whose members number more than all the hunters of your tribe."

"Why did your father and council not send us many warriors to help?" Spotted Owl queried.

"That was not in Medicine Eyes's vision, and it would be viewed by Crow as a war challenge. The last vision says Stalking Wolf and the chosen Hanueva will trick the Crow and defeat their hunger for horses and captives. We will clear a path for your people to reach mine in safety."

"How will we trick the Bird Warriors?"

Stalking Wolf noticed the excitement in Night Walker's voice as those words were spoken. It was obvious to him that the loosely bridled spirit of a warrior lived in the chief's son, but it was a dark and dangerous one. The same appeared true for the man sitting beside him, Little Weasel, a man also eager to fight for the wrong reasons. Yet, news of Kionee's glorious deeds amazed and impressed him; that was the hunter who should ride with him soon.

"That will be revealed to us when the time is right," Stalking Wolf answered. "I am to live and travel with the Hanueva, to conceal myself among you, until camp is broken. On that day, two groups will leave this place for the buffalo grounds. Most will travel away from the cold wind land, round the mountains, and go toward the Medicine Bow Forest. Near it, they will travel along the banks of the river until it bends toward Cheyenne land. They will journey then into the grasslands and camp near Our People in the Basin of Thunder. Stalking Wolf and three Hanuevas will ride northward along the Big Horn River to where it is Ten Sleeps to the shooting water and bubbling earth kettles land. There, we part and take separate trails. One party of two will journey over the mountain and canyon passes to the summer camping location. The other party will journey over the mountains and along the three forks of the big rivers and meet your people as they near the Medicine Bow Forest. The scouts will watch for Crow and halt any raids. We will find their tracks and see where they go to camp to hunt buffalo, for it is best to know where the enemy lives."

The worried chief said, "We have been a people of peace since being placed on this land by the Creator. We respect *Atah*'s land and do not waste His creatures. That is our way. Once we challenge Swift Crane's band and make an enemy of it, the conflicts between us will not end until we are destroyed or captured. We must wait and pray for peace to continue. The Bird Warriors will weary of coupless rides and cast their hungry gazes on those who can feed them."

"That will not come to pass, Bear's Head. The one who escaped the battle with Kionee and the other hunters will tell his friends of their skills; they will return for revenge and to regain the fallen ones' honor. Your people have proven they are worthy opponents with great medicine to steal."

"He is right, Father," Night Walker urged. "You must hear his words and follow them."

"To the death and suffering of many, my son?"

"If it must be. Only *Atah* can choose the sun we join Him. I am ready to battle for my people. I will ride behind my brother, Gray Fox, or I will lead our warriors if he is needed in camp to protect our chief and people."

"Your heart burns with wild fires I do not understand, my son. I fear they will consume you and those who follow you."

The shaman said in a reverent tone, "An owl whispered to me in a dream last night, my chief and people; *Atah*'s messenger told me a cunning and powerful wolf would come to lead us to safety. I believe that sign and leader are here. This Cheyenne comes on a full moon to enlighten us. I say we listen and obey his words."

"You speak for war, Spotted Owl?" the chief asked in disbelief.

"No, I speak for trickery and survival, as does Stalking Wolf. We must not ride into the large nest of Bird Warriors, but we must not allow them to take our land or steal our women and children for slaves and mates. It is against our law to join with those outside our tribe, even by force."

Stalking Wolf was pleased with the shaman's first words, but troubled by his last ones. If a female was taken captive, she had no power to resist her owner's desires and would suffer great harm or die for doing so. Was it not better, he mused, for her to obey to be able to escape and return home? Afterward, revenge could be taken for her abuse.

"We must continue our guards and watch our camp and horses with eyes like the eagle's and hawk's. We must practice to be ready to fight. We will prove to the Crow and others we are not afraid or weak. We will not allow them to steal our land and possessions or capture our people. We must not beg for what is ours to use from *Atah;* we must prove we are worthy to keep it within our grasp. We must resist and fight as brave and honorable men, or run and hide and die as the weaklings Crow say we are."

"Night Walker speaks wise and true," Little Weasel concurred. "We must use our courage, cunning, and skills to battle them; that is why the High-Guardian gave them to us. Where is our pride if we do nothing to defend our families and ways?"

As the men talked for and against resistance and challenge, Kionee studied their guest. His life was so unlike hers. His people were warriors and often raiders. They joined societies, with each having its own rituals and rules. They had a tribal council of forty-four minor chiefs and one head chief. They possessed four Sacred Arrows with special ceremonies to ensure the Cheyenne's survival. Though the Cheyenne worshipped at Medicine Wheel, their most sacred location was in the Black Hills, claimed to be the home of the Holy Ones, their spirits. They honored the

sun and faced their tipis to its rising face as a reminder that their
god sent its heat and light to make things grow and to symbolize
their own enlightenment. They endured agonizing rites where
they offered bits of their flesh to the sun during a great dance
after the buffalo season. Without viewing his chest, Kionee
knew Stalking Wolf had done the Sun Dance because of the
bloodred plume attached to the feathers on his thin braids.
Whether one agreed or not with that harsh custom, it proved he
possessed enormous stamina and courage.

All males over fifteen winters were members of their warrior
rank, but each had to seek a vision to receive his name and signs,
and must prove himself in battle and be chosen to join a society.
When the Cheyenne rode into a great battle, their chief always
led them, and no man dared to place his horse beyond Big
Hump's unless given permission for an important reason. As
chief, Big Hump was the one to perform the Great Medicine Ceremony and was Keeper-of-the-Sacred Arrows, which made his
life and those objects the targets of enemies. But few bands were
rash enough to attack a large and strong Cheyenne camp, even
to recover captives.

Kionee believed it was wrong to steal people—especially
women and children—from their families and way of life. The
Hanueva did not need slaves to do their work for them, and did
not cause the sufferings of others.

Yet, there were many similarities between the two peoples.
Both worshipped the Creator of all things, even if they used different names for Him. Both tribes were hunters, their main prey
the buffalo which provided meat, hides, and various other
needs. They respected Mother Earth, their families, their tribe,
and their laws; and defended those things to the death if necessary.

The way they governed themselves was also similar. All
warriors had a vote in the tribe's affairs. Both councils made
suggestions, but the members decided which path to ride. With
the Cheyenne, the chiefs of the societies spoke with its members

to gather their feelings and thoughts on a matter, then those chiefs told the council their desires, which were always accepted. Even so, most honored the head chief's, shaman's, and council's wisdom and words.

Careful to conceal her interest Kionee continued to appraise Stalking Wolf. His eyes were a mixture of brown and yellow, not as dark as most Indians'. His skin was also different. Even his features were not as sharp and large as those of other Cheyenne she had observed. It was as if he were not all Indian, as if one parent were not Indian; yet how could that be true of the son or daughter of a chief? Perhaps she would learn the truth later. It did not matter to her, for she admired this unusual male.

Kionee was forced to halt her perusal when she was asked about the name she had heard during the fight with the eight Crow. "The enemy who buried his knife in my friend's heart spoke of a warrior called One-Eye," she revealed. "He said they will prove to others 'it is not bad medicine to slay those with painted faces.' They have feared our masks and magic in past suns; that time lives no longer. I took revenge for Sumba, as you did for your friends."

"What of their horses and possessions, Kionee?"

"We left the warriors where they fell. We gathered our arrows, removed our tracks, and left no clues to their slayers."

"What of the one who escaped and will reveal your deed?"

"Will a warrior tell others of the weakness of himself and seven friends at the hands of only five hunters? To do so would evoke great shame. They say we are weak, unworthy, but we defeated them with fewer fighters."

"To save his face, Kionee, he will say there were many."

"I say he will blame Cheyenne or Oglalas, fierce enemies and skilled warriors. He will not tell it was peaceful Hanueva. But if he does so, they will fear the magic, medicine, and power of our protectors and guardians."

"Fear them, yes, but a craving to steal those powers will make them bold, even reckless, in their quests," Stalking Wolf refuted in a gentle tone. "Tell me; how did a small party of Hanueva defeat a larger one of Crow?"

Red Bull answered for her when she waited too long to respond. "Kionee does not boast of his great deeds. I will speak them for my brother and friend, for he saved my family from the claws and teeth of the grizzly."

As Stalking Wolf listened, Red Bull related those two events in detail. "We will call our daughter Ae-Culta-Kionee. She-Who was saved by-Wind of Destiny," he translated for their guest. "The naming ceremony and our new season dance is on the next moon; you are welcome to join us."

"That is kind, Red Bull, and I will do so. I have spoken my words and we will make plans on another sun," he announced to let them know he was finished. As Stalking Wolf reflected on the man's revelations, he was astonished to learn that a male of Kionee's diminutive size and almost feminine appearance could defeat such awesome forces. Though he had seen Kionee in action long ago, he knew he had misjudged the extent of the mask-wearer's skills. Surely, he reasoned, his new friend was the person who would help fulfill the sacred visions.

To end the meeting, as darkness was near and a meal waited to be eaten, the chief said, "We will smoke the pipe of peace with the Cheyenne and offer thanks to *Atah*, Creator and High Guardian, who sent him to us."

Spotted Owl prepared the redstone bowl with tobacco and lit it. He drew two puffs, one of truce which he blew straight from his mouth and one of thanks which he sent spiriling upward toward *Atah*'s domain. He passed the pipe to his right, to the chief who did the same.

Following the eight council members, Stalking Wolf took his turn. As the *heohko* made its rounds of the hunters, occasionally being refilled with more *peeonoe*, the Cheyenne warrior noticed the *tivas* did not share the pipe or even touch its stem to pass it beyond their position. Yet, they made the signs for *peace* and *thanks* in unison as one man rose and carried the pipe to the man on the other side of the group. He could not determine the meaning behind such an omission. Perhaps it was a sacred vow or sacrifice, as they were not a warrior or social society. Another point troubled him: in their visions, both he and Medicine Eyes had heard the spirit wolf speak the words, "The wind of destiny will blow over you this season." That had to mean there was a mystical bond between him and Kionee, and a great quest stood before them. *Soon I will understand.*

As the men and *tivas* were leaving the area, Strong Rock approached Stalking Wolf and offered, "You are welcome to eat and sleep with my family. My tipi is large and good, for Kionee is a skilled hunter and provider."

The Cheyenne warrior pretended not to notice the man's crippled leg as he smiled and accepted, "That is kind, Strong Rock."

"Come, we eat, talk, and rest. Kionee, we go. Stalking Wolf stays with us, my son."

"I will join you after I check my horses and Maja," she responded. She needed time and privacy to master her rampant emotions at that news. Her father did not even suspect how dangerous it was to place that great temptation within her reach! She must remain on guard at all times to prevent weakening toward him and exposing herself. *You should not have done this deed, Father, for it is hard to be near him and control myself. Please help me to resist him and his magic, Atah, or I am lost.*

6

IONEE WAS NOT GIVEN time or privacy. Stalking Wolf accompanied her to the secure area where their horses were tethered near the woods so he could check on his stallion and gather his belongings.

During their walk, she coaxed, "We must hurry, for Mother has the food prepared and it grows late. Our talk was long and grave."

Stalking Wolf stole a glance at the hunter. How, he wondered, could one so small and almost feminine be such a great fighter? To beat one Crow warrior was a large coup, but to have victory over five in the same battle was an awesome deed. If news of it reached enemy ears, Kionee's big medicine would be sought by many. "Do not worry, my friend; Our People will protect your tribe during the buffalo hunt. Before we join them, I will see no harm comes to the Hanueva. You will be my companion, for your skills are many and few warriors possess those to match yours. You are well trained and blessed. On this moon, I do not grasp the vision given to me at the sacred Wheel, or those given to our shaman, or *Maheoo*'s joint plan for our tribes, but they will all be revealed to us when the best sun rises."

She dared not look at him as her gaze might be filled with desire. She struggled to master the tone of her voice to keep her feelings hidden. "Your words please me, Stalking Wolf, and I will help you and my people. No greater warrior could be chosen to be our shield and weapon."

He detected a strange tension in his companion and realized the hunter was refusing to look at him. "Your words please and honor me, Kionee. I do not know why I was chosen by *Maheoo*, but I will not fail Him or my duty. I vow to protect your people with my skills and life."

"No harm must come to you!" she blurted out. "It is not our way to bring suffering to others," she added to cover her odd outburst.

"It will not, for you will ride with me as my shield and friend. It is an honor to have a child named for you and your brave deed. I have fought the great bear and only defeated him with *Maheoo*'s protection." He paused and pushed up his right sleeve to show a scar. "I carry the marks of his claws and anger. We battled a long time. I jumped on his back and rode him as a wild horse. My blade crossed his throat before he shook me off." He noticed the hunter's touch was soft and light as Kionee halted to finger the healed slashes and stare at them. Again, that odd sensation chewed at him, but he brushed it away in annoyance. "It is good Red Bull's child is female and will carry her name until she lives with the Great Spirit."

Kionee walked faster to escape the delight she'd felt in touching him. "Hanueva do not seek visions and change the names our fathers give us. We are called by what is seen or felt or where we are when we enter life. When my time came, a great wind blew over our camp and took down many tipis. We moved to another place which was safe and calm. The one we left was covered by rushing water; many lives would have been lost if we had not changed camps. Father called it a wind of destiny, for it saved us from death. I was born that moon. Why are you called Stalking Wolf?"

"When I received my vision, I saw a man dressed in wolf skins," he began his explanation. "He was a hunter of skill and silence. I was told to learn the way of the wolf and to take it as my sign. Many times I ride at night with the moon to guide me as I stalk my enemies. I must be swift, bold, and cunning. I must have courage, strength, and be wise. As with my spirit sign, when I join, it will be with one woman and it will be for as long as we live. Do you have a mate and children?"

Pain stabbed Kionee's heart. "No, it is not the *tiva* way. We allow no person or thing to distract us from our duties to our family, tribe, and *Atah*. As with all creatures, *Atah* gave each a different role; for me, it is that of a *tiva*. You protect well, Maja," she spoke to her pet to change the disturbing subject. She ruffled the hair on his neck and smiled when he licked her hand.

Stalking Wolf was sure he perceived bitterness in his friend's voice. Perhaps, he reasoned, Kionee had been chosen to become a *tiva* and it was not the destiny he wanted. During his stay with them, he would observe the *tivas* and see what he could learn about them, as he could not ask questions; that would be rude and unacceptable.

His tawny gaze followed the gentle curve of Kionee's jaw-line. He studied the hunter's features: small nose, soft lips, thin brows, and delicate bones. When Kionee leaned forward to stroke Maja, Stalking Wolf saw something else unusual: Kionee's neck was slender for a man's. Perhaps the *tivas* concealed their appearance because they were too feminine and pretty and might encite teasing from men of other tribes. And perhaps those feminine traits were what made him uneasy at times.

Kionee sensed the Cheyenne was making a furtive study of her, and it warmed her body and thrilled her entire being. For a wild and crazy moment, she did not care if he guessed her secret and almost wished he would. If he did, she mused, what would he do? If he saw her unmasked and unclothed, would she be appealing to him, as he was to her? In haste, she scolded herself and regained her control.

Stalking Wolf finished collecting his possessions. "I am ready."

Kionee nodded, not trusting her voice, and led the way.

The family of Strong Rock and their guest sat in a circle around the cookfire. As was the Hanueva custom, women and children did not have to wait until the men finished before they enjoyed their meal. They devoured the venison stew Martay had prepared. It was flavored with wild onions, dried thistle, sage, milkweed buds, dried fruits and berries, and newborn roots of yellow bell. Corms of spring beauty, slowly roasted in dying coals, were served. Drinking water was poured in buffalo horns which were balanced in holes in sturdy wood blocks. The men sat on rush mats, while the women relaxed on squares of thick hide padded with soft fur. A refreshing breeze wafted through the circular entrance and left with smoke via the pinnacle opening where many poles were lashed together. Burning pine and spruce needles gave the tranquil area a fragrant smell.

Stalking Wolf noted the tipi was large, comfortable, and clean, attesting to both Kionee's hunting skills and Martay's feminine ones. The exterior was unadorned, and the flap opening bore only the symbol of Strong Rock on both sides, announcing its owner whether tied open or closed. Some possessions were stored in various sizes of parfleches; others were suspended from pegs and thongs at the top of a dewcloth, a decorative section which ran from shoulder height to the dwelling's base. Its main purposes were to divert rain which ran down the poles and to keep out winter drafts. Sleeping mats, rolled and secured by thongs, awaited their nightly use. Two tripods holding weapons and sacred items stood like guards on either side of the entry, and it was evident from markings which one belonged to Kionee. Perhaps, he thought, he would be given a chance to examine the young hunter's, as they appeared well made.

Stalking Wolf smiled, nodded, and held out his wooden bowl for another serving of stew to let Martay know how much he enjoyed her cooking and appreciated the Hanueva's hospitality. The females remained silent and respectful as Strong Rock told the story of how a wounded buffalo had half crippled him and how Kionee had come to be the family's sole provider and protector at such a young age. The proud father could not help but repeat the telling of his son's recent victories, while Kionee ate with his head lowered humbly.

"It is good the Great Spirit gave you a son with such great skills. I saw them with my own eyes when we battled three Crow together. But it is bad in another way: enemies will seek his big magic and medicine. He must be alert each sun and moon to guard against them. While I am among you, I will protect his back, as he would defend mine."

Strong Rock and Martay thanked him, and Kionee nodded gratitude.

Blue Bird retrieved her talking feather and shook it for permission to speak to a stranger. When her father granted it, she asked, "Will you teach my brother and his friends how to defeat our enemies? Will your people help us if we are attacked in large numbers?"

Strong Rock grinned and explained, "Blue Bird fears for the life of one called Runs Fast; he plays the flute for her and chooses her this season."

"If trouble strikes, I will keep my eye on the love of my friend's sister," Stalking Wolf answered solemnly. "Do not fear, Blue Bird, for I have seen no Hanueva who is not trained and prepared to fight well. My head tells me it is the same with Runs Fast."

"Thank you," Blue Bird said, and returned to her meal.

As Moon Child poured Stalking Wolf more water, he saw how she lowered her gaze in shyness. Perhaps she found him appealing. Even if she were allowed to join outside her tribe, the girl was too young to interest him. From her looks and manner, she had not reached the tipi to womanhood. Still, it was unwise to encourage such feelings in her.

When the meal ended and things were stored, Martay fetched and unrolled the sleeping mats, placing hers with Strong Rock's, the two girls' on their right, and Kionee's on their left.

Stalking Wolf placed his mat beyond his new friend's and sat down on it to remove his moccasins, leggings, and shirt. He folded them and put them with his belongings. With a guest present, the women removed only their moccasins, but Strong Rock did the same as he had, exposing the extent of his injury and evoking Stalking Wolf's empathy. The Cheyenne was aware Kionee did not wash off his mask or remove any garment except his footwear.

The huntress struggled to keep her gaze off the magnificent male nearby. She had glimpsed the Sun Dance scars and red handprint—symbol of the Strong Hearts—on his muscled chest. The warrior's body was sleek, hard, and strong; Kionee struggled to douse the flames of desire which Stalking Wolf kindled within her. She was glad she was tired. Sleep would help her escape his captivating pull, at least for a while.

After the fire died, darkness engulfed the tipi and slumber captured the six people inside it. But the dreams of two females—Kionee and Moon Child—were filled with images of the handsome and virile Cheyenne nearby.

As for Stalking Wolf, his sleep was disturbed by strange visions of a beautiful woman. Shiny black hair streamed down her back and strands blew in the wind. Her shapely body was cloaked in a white buffalo hide. Her arms were outstretched in beckoning for him to seek his destiny within them. Her expressive brown eyes glowed with love and desire and then a mysterious anguish. A silver wolf spirit paced back and forth behind her, then lifted its head to send forth eerie and soulful howls to a full moon. Each time he tried to approach her, a cloudlike barrier rose between them and he could not penetrate it and seize her for his own.

The next day, Stalking Wolf recalled the troubling dream and the words of his shaman which said he would find a mate this season, and also find his parents' killer. Perhaps, he reasoned, that was why his path had crossed with Kionee's; he was convinced the Hanueva hunter would be the one to help him locate and win the vision female and help him defeat his parents' slayer. That would explain why the shaman's vision said it was necessary to protect the Hanueva and have them camp nearby during the buffalo hunt. His true destiny, he felt, was at hand, and he would find it with Kionee's help.

The time arrived for the Naming Ceremony, spring dance, and feast. The men had hunted that morning and the women had cooked all afternoon. The men had bathed in one area of the river, the women in another, and the *tivas* in a third. Everyone had donned their finest garments or regalia, ready to share in the pride and joy and reverence of this occasion.

Parents with children born since the last naming ceremony were called forward to participate in the first ritual. Mothers held freshly washed and herb-rubbed infants who wore breechclouts and were wrapped in animal skins. Blowing Rain's child wore the hide of the grizzly killed by Kionee. Fluffy white breathfeathers were secured in the children's dark hair. Unlike most tribes, the names these babies received today would be carried for life, never to be changed through a vision-quest or by choice.

The shaman lit a cured braid of grass taken from the plains during the last great buffalo hunt. Entwined with it were sweet sage, blue flax, pine needles, and wildflowers. As smoke drifted upward, Spotted Owl used his medicine fan of eagle feathers to waft it over each child in turn as he prayed and dedicated them to *Atah*'s and their people's service. "Be true and generous to Creator, your people, and your family. Have courage, honor, and strength in all things. Do only good and kind deeds. Do not forget you are Hanueva. Never shame yourself, your family, people, or laws."

"Fathers, lift your children so *Atah* and His spirit helpers can view them as you speak their names," Spotted Owl instructed.

One by one, fathers held the infants high and spoke their names. Afterward, babies were returned to mothers' arms and warming skins.

Spotted Owl looked from couple to couple as he reminded them of their duty to rear their child by Hanuevan laws and customs.

All the infants were males except for the child of Red Bull. Kionee prayed a son would be given to the couple so her namesake would not be forced into a *tiva*'s sacrificial existence. She watched the parents' gazes glow with love, pride, and joy. She envied them. Then she realized the naming ceremonial prayer almost matched the *tiva* dedication and vow. Three of the words—"in all things"—echoed through her mind many times. Soon, parts of two other commands did the same: "Do not forget . . ." and "Never shame . . ." She told herself she had been weak and wrong even to consider doing so in a forbidden desire for their guest. The Cheyenne warrior had been sent to them to ensure their survival, not to sway her into disobedience and dishonor. She vowed she could and would resist temptation, as *Atah* willed.

The dancing and singing began. First came the celebration of new life and the continuation of the Hanueva bloodlines through these infants. Gifts for the children were placed on large hides near their parents' sitting mats. Kionee, a skilled weapons maker, presented the boys with small bows. To her namesake, she gave a small medallion with a bear beaded in its center.

That dance and song were followed by ones to entreat a good hunt, peace, and survival from their Creator and protector and to thank Him for past blessings. Only men and *tivas* performed and sang as drums sent forth a melodic beat and a huge campfire lit up the clearing beneath a waning full moon. Next, hopeful couples danced within shared blankets to ensure a fertile season on their mating mats. Single males made their future choices known by asking their loves to join them in the outer circle where they danced in place while facing each other. It was no surprise to anyone when Runs Fast invited a blushing Blue Bird to be his partner.

Stalking Wolf observed the ceremonies, the *tivas* in particular. He realized no coups were chanted, though—in his opinion, his new friend's recent feats deserved such recognition. He noticed no *tiva* participated in the last dance, and recalled they had not bathed with the other hunters. Tonight, the group of over forty sat together, and a little apart from others, but near his position. They were clad in highly decorated and colorful regalia: shirts, leggings, moccasins, and breechclouts were adorned with painted and beaded designs from nature, some with feathers and claws attached. Their black hair was worn in the same manner: two braids down their backs. It was their disguises that captured his attention: deerhide masks molded to their features with cut-outs for seeing and breathing. One had to look close at several to notice it was not real flesh. He assumed the deerskin had been treated in a special way and worn until it hardened into the shape of its owner's face. Feathers of various colors, kinds, and lengths banded those skin covers in a full circle along their borders. The patterns were splendid and the work was done by skilled hands.

Stalking Wolf wondered if the *tivas'* faces were painted beneath them or if the ceremonial masks were their only adornment. He also wondered why never showing their faces was so important to them and their people. He could not surmise why *tivas* did not take mates or have children; they appeared to live only to feed, clothe, and protect their families and tribe. He could not help but ponder why they remained chaste and alone. What strange law made it wrong for a *tiva* to sate his desires within a female, to have a mate, and to grow his seeds in her body? Was it a chosen or a coerced demand of their mysterious cult and Great Spirit? Perhaps, he reasoned, it was a personal, difficult, and painful sacrifice like his people's Sun Dance ritual. Perhaps those denials of physical and emotional pleasures were a *tiva*'s way of offering something—a vital part of himself and his life—something only he possessed and controlled, which was also the motivation behind the Sun Dance.

Subtly, the Cheyenne studied Kionee. A circle of white swan feathers bordered Kionee's black mask. The upper half displayed a thick over-layer of raven feathers. A narrow fan of short snow owl plumes was positioned over the forehead area and came to a point between the brows; over it were red-tailed hawk feathers and in its middle was an inverted tipi-shaped crow one. From the ear locations, five long strips of leather dangled to the chest and were adorned with white and black beads, tiny hairpipes, and hackle feathers. The eyes were encased by green circles with stripes running from the inner corners along the edge of the nose, curling under its base, and halting at the nostrils. Another slash traveled from the outer corner of each eye hole downward near the jawbone and stopped close to the chin, upon which was painted a large sunny dot. White slashes accentuated the brows and journeyed along the jawline to the earlobes. The remaining section above them was yellow. Wiggly blue lines like rivers were painted from the inner eye corners, across the cheeks, and spilled into an oblong design like a lake in their hollows. Red stripes left the centers of the eye holes, then formed symbols like mountains on the cheekbones. Red lips contrasted against the black background to complete a dramatic pattern. He did not know if the pattern had a certain meaning or was only meant for decoration. It was odd to him that Kionee's mask seemed to depict femininelike features, if his memory were accurate.

In fact, Stalking Wolf reasoned, most of the *tivas* were thinner and shorter than the average man, had delicate-looking hands, smaller feet, and moved like females when they danced and walked. Yet, from the hunt earlier and from seeing their tipis, the *tivas* were among the best providers and skilled protectors of the Hanueva. Perhaps those unmanly characteristics were why they felt it necessary to use masks, to make them appear fearsome to enemies. Still, he mused, that did not explain why they shielded their looks at all times. They were a mysterious group who kept to themselves, but were friendly when approached. No one could be more likable and skilled than Kionee, and the bond between them felt good and strong and blessed.

He knew the meaning behind the grizzly claw necklace around Kionee's neck; it had been earned by saving Red Bull's wife and baby from certain death. He assumed the dewclaw rattle in Kionee's grip was a sacred item for rituals, as the *tivas* shook them at certain points. The sash that crossed the hunter's chest revealed many deeds of courage, daring, and strength, and Stalking Wolf was impressed. Kionee's shield was a near match for his own. Surely, he mused, *Maheoo* and destiny had crossed their paths for a sacred reason, one he would know soon.

Before the feast started, Taysinga approached the families of Sumba and Tall Eagle to present them with gifts and to ask mercy for being partly responsible for the two hunters' deaths. Taysinga confessed her shame.

"I was afraid of the Crow warriors," the hunter said. "They were many and we were few. They are skilled fighters; we are hunters. They carried shields, lances, bows, knives, and clubs; in our hands were bows and in our sheaths were knives. They care not if they die while seeking coups; we must live to take care of our families. It was the first time I faced such danger and evil. I could not thaw the ice in my body. I suffer for the loss of my brothers." She told the fathers, "I will hunt for your families when you lie sick or hurt upon your mats and when *Atah* calls you to live with Him. I will give you a share of my hides after the buffalo hunt. I will make twenty arrows for each during the next cold season. I will not refuse my duty to fight again. I will give my life to save others. After the feast, my *tiva* brothers will remove my fear, shame, and weakness."

The families granted forgiveness, as was the Hanueva way. Taysinga thanked them and returned to her place among the masked group.

Stalking Wolf noted that Taysinga had not been banished from the *tiva* society. It was the Cheyenne way—when one was to blame by fault or accident for another's death, he was no longer a member of his society and no other society could accept him. The event pointed out one of many differences between his and Kionee's people; some he understood and others he did not.

Kionee was eager for the ceremony to end so she could put distance between her and the man who disturbed her thoughts and created turmoil in her emotions. No matter how hard she tried to ignore his presence, she failed. Her gaze kept drifting to his stalwart body and handsome face. She found herself wanting to know everything about him. She caught herself wondering how it would feel to have his lips pressed to hers, his arms around her, to hear him speak words of love in her ears, inhale his manly scent, and to have their bodies join in mating. She tried to imagine how a child of theirs would look, if it would be a boy or a girl, what name it would carry, and what its destiny would be. She tried to think of ways to free herself from her *tiva* vow without causing her dishonor and suffering by her family and people. There was nothing she could say or do, for he was Cheyenne, an outsider, forbidden. She could be his friend and companion, but nothing more. *Help me keep my promise, Atah. Destiny mine, whatever and wherever you be, hold me true to it.*

As soon as the *tivas* ate, they gathered in their private lodge for the ritual Taysinga had requested. She sat on a mat and held out her trembling hands. One by one the *tivas* pricked her fingers with porcupine quills to drain the bad traits from her body. Blood dripped into a clay bowl before the girl washed her sticky hands and smeared on salve from the arnica and purple coneflower which was mixed with spider webs and bear grease. Taysinga stood, removed her shirt and breast band, and lowered her head.

A group of five of the oldest Guardians flung water from bunches of sage over her torso as they chanted the prayer for purification. Afterward, sweetgrass and herbs were rubbed over her skin as they evoked *Atah* to restore Taysinga's courage, strength, and honor.

Regim, the *Tiva-Chu*, dried the girl with a rabbit fur and helped her replace her deerskin breast band and shirt. The group's leader lit a tuft of buffalo grass and wafted it beneath Taysinga's nose as the girl took deep breaths to drive any lingering evil from her body. The young female coughed and her eyes ran tears as the sacred smoke did its task. Regim drew her knife and cut a slash on the back of Taysinga's left hand, a mark against her. "Do not forget, our brother: if another joins it, you will not be allowed to meet, sit, dance, sing, and hunt with other *tivas*. You will be set apart."

"I hear and obey, Regim, our *Tiva-Chu*. I have learned much from this dark deed and I will not ride that path again. I swear to you and *Atah*."

Regim placed the bowl with Taysinga's blood on hot coals in the fire. She added water, dirt, dried and finely crushed plants and leaves, and two small feathers to represent the domains of the hunter's prey: river, plains, mountains, forest, and sky. She added buffalo hairs from the "provider of life," a white arrowhead for the means of obtaining it, and a clay ball—*bihe*—to absorb measures of all those elements. As the liquid mixture disappeared into rising vapors, Regim said, "Gone is the bad, and new power has come. Do not lose it or shame it, Taysinga."

"I will live and be as *Atah* commands."

Regim told the others, "When the *bihe* no longer burns like fire, I will place it in Taysinga's *kim* and toss the ashes around it into the wind. While the heat leaves it, paint your faces and return to your families."

Kionee knew it would harden her heart to refuse to forgive Taysinga; such emotions cut into one's spirit until it bled from foolish wounds. As they worked with their paints, she said to the girl sitting beside her, "I will no longer blame you for Sumba's death. It was wrong to do so and I ask your forgiveness. In my suffering, I did not think with a clear head and kind heart. You are a good hunter and you will be a good fighter if that sun rises."

"Sumba was your friend and brother; I understand your anger and actions." Taysinga replied. "I will not be weak again; I will do what I must. I have learned who and what I am and I will follow that path."

"That is good, Taysinga, for *tivas* must not war with each other," Kionee said, and the girl gave a nonchalant nod. Yet, something about the girl's tone worried Kionee. She had a feeling Taysinga could not be trusted and should be watched.

Regim approached and said, "Stay and speak with me, Kionee."

She nodded to her leader and continued her task, wondering why Regim desired privacy. Surely, Kionee fretted, she had not exposed her feelings for Stalking Wolf to others. If so, she was in trouble.

AFTER THE OTHER *tivas* left the meeting lodge, Regim said to Kionee in a low voice and a worried tone, "As I put the *bihe* in Taysinga's *kim*, I found your vessel broken, hidden behind others and out of its place. That is a bad sign, Kionee, for your female spirit could escape to wander about in confusion and be thrust into danger. Do you know how it happened?"

"No, for I have not looked at it in many moons. There was no need."

The *Tiva-Chu* believed Kionee was innocent of wrongdoing and was convinced her surprise was genuine. For a time, Regim had feared that a love-blinded Kionee might have broken the vessel to free her spirit to pursue the Cheyenne. The older woman admitted to herself that the superior warrior was an enormous temptation to females, even to one as strong-willed and dedicated as her precious Kionee. Witnessing Kionee's reaction, Regim knew her suspicions could not be true; she was relieved, and scolded herself for doubting the girl for even a moment. Yet the breaking of her *kim* was a bad omen, one she feared. She did not want to imagine that evil spirits were trying to ensnare the girl she loved as her own child. Or that *Atah* wished to expose and punish Kionee for having forbidden thoughts and feelings. "I will find fresh clay and put it together again," she assured Kionee. "I will try to do so before others see it."

Regim did not have to speak her concerns aloud for Kionee to guess them and agree: others would wonder how and why the damage occurred; and they might watch her closely for answers. "Will Spotted Owl need to summon my female spirit back to it?"

"Perhaps it does not roam. Perhaps it waits nearby to return to its rightful place. Perhaps that is why your woman's feelings trouble you."

Again, Kionee grasped the *Tiva-Chu*'s meaning. Yet, she did not confess or deny the validity of Regim's fears about Stalking Wolf. "Did someone break it to cause me trouble? Is that what frightens you?"

"Who would do such evil?"

With ease and conviction, the name "Taysinga" left Kionee's lips.

"You speak cold and cruel words against your brother."

"I fear my brother hates me and wishes me harm and shame."

"Has Taysinga told you such things?"

"Not in words, but he does so with looks and sounds. This moon, I warned myself to watch him with eagle eyes and to listen with hawk's ears. I cannot tell you why; it is a feeling deep within me. I tried to make peace over Sumba's loss but I do not believe my words reached his heart. Have your sharp wits not told you Taysinga hungers for freedom from the *tiva* vow and hungers for Night Walker as a woman does for a man and a mate?"

Regim gaped at Kionee in shock. "This cannot be. What evil sneaks among us this season to steal our *tivas* from their ranks? It is bad the Cheyenne returned. He tempts you to forget your laws and ways. That darkness spreads to others. As a sickness, it has entered Taysinga; he was not weak until after the Cheyenne walked near our camp."

"Do not blame Stalking Wolf for the weakness of Kionee and Taysinga. He is good and brave; he has come to help us. I believe *Atah* brought him. Taysinga's heart was changed before Stalking Wolf entered our land, for I saw desire in her long ago. Our brother has tried to live as a man, Regim, but she is not a man. Perhaps some cannot battle against what nature made us at our births. Why is it so wrong and evil for a woman to have a woman's thoughts and feelings? If *Atah* had wanted us to be men, our bodies would reveal it. I understand how Taysinga thinks and feels, but I cannot tell her so. I wish she could win Night Walker as her mate; that would be good for him and our people. Perhaps she and a family could turn his heart away from war."

"You must not speak or think such forbidden things, Kionee. Atah will punish you; He will punish the *tivas*, your family, and your people."

"I will give Him no reason to harm us. I will honor my vow, for my family needs me. Father cannot hunt for them and protect them. It is not so for Taysinga; her father's body is strong. When it becomes old, Night Walker possesses the skills to hunt for them and for his mate and children."

"Do you seek to help Taysinga break her vow and *kim?*"

"I will not, for it is not the *tiva* way. But if she chooses him and he chooses her, it will please me."

"How can he choose Taysinga when I believe he desires you?"

"I will not accept him. I do not love him. I will not join him."

"You will not, for your heart belongs to another, a forbidden one?"

Kionee let Regim see the anguish in her eyes. "I must not hunger for food I cannot catch and eat. I will remain a *tiva.*"

"I pray you will, my son, or dark moons rise ahead."

Intent on their emotional conversation, the *tivas* did not hear someone sneak away from outside the lodge to avoid being caught spying when they departed.

"Will you tell me who you loved long ago, Regim?"

"It matters not. I did not yield to temptation."

Despite her leader's claims, Kionee perceived a lingering sadness at her loss. "Remember the love and desire you felt for him and understand what a fierce battle I fight this season."

"I understand, Kionee, but you must win it as I did. If you do not choose Night Walker or another Hanueva, you can have no mate."

"If that is true, I will remain a *tiva* until *Atah* summons me."

For the next three days, the Cheyenne warrior and selected Hanuevas hunted and scouted in groups of two, chosen by Kionee in private. Without asking, he assigned his friend to ride with him, and was not refused.

As Stalking Wolf and Kionee rode for camp on that third day, he said, "Our hunt was good; we bring back a large deer, four rabbits, and a turkey. Our eyes have not seen our enemies."

"Perhaps they saw Stalking Wolf and flew away in fear of his prowess."

"If Bird warriors saw us, they would challenge us. They would earn many coups to defeat Stalking Wolf and Kionee. They will come soon."

"I pray that is not true, but I fear it is."

"Why did you send Taysinga with Night Walker, Regim with Little Weasel, and Runs Fast with Red Bull?"

Kionee was prepared to respond and wondered why it had taken so long for him to ask that question. "Night Walker and Little Weasel are first friends; they desire to war with the Crow. If they ride together, trouble would come as swiftly as the arrow flies. Regim and Taysinga will prevent their rash actions. Red

Bull is a great hunter and fighter; he will protect the love of my sister, Blue Bird. I fear Runs Fast's mind is clouded by his feelings for her. I wish him to live and to join with her."

Stalking Wolf respected Kionee's honesty, but he suspected the hunter had another motive for pairing Taysinga and Night Walker. He did not grasp the reason, but the chief's son had watched Kionee in a strange manner. "What is the meaning of your ceremonial mask?" he asked.

Kionee glanced at him, for that query was unexpected, and began her explanation. "It is a symbol of the Hunter-Guardian, a *tiva*. White feathers tell of day and game that forages in the light; it speaks of all things good and pure. Black tells of night and game that forages in the dark; it also speaks of things which are bad and things which come when I cannot see, things I must fight and defeat. Yellow on my forehead speaks of enlightenment by *Atah*; the chin dot reminds me of His warmth from the sun, *Atah*'s shining eye. Beads are symbols of the circle-of-life, white for good and black for bad. Hairpipe speaks of the breath of life and bones of the hunter and his prey. The fan is to entreat knowledge for hunting and fighting. Hackle feathers are pointed like arrowtips, the Hunter-Guardian's weapon. Feathers evoke swiftness and come from messengers to *Atah*. Marks leaving my eyes help me see clear and far; they point to my nose and ears to help me catch the smells and sounds of prey and enemy. White near my eyes and ears helps me to see and hear dangers and evil. My mouth is red for the earth and its food to help me to taste what is good and bad. Dangles summon powers to hear game and foe. All are skills needed by hunters and protectors. There are five dangles: one for each direction of the wind and one for the center of life. It is much the same as when warriors paint their faces before riding out to war or raid: they choose patterns and symbols with meanings special to them."

"Is that the same meaning of the one you wear each sun and moon?"

Kionee touched her cheek and felt the covering that shielded her secret. "Black tells us we are nothing without *Atah's* creation, guidance, and protection. The colors and symbols tell of the hunter's lands: red is for earth, green for forest and plains, blue for water, and yellow for the sky with its sun. All *tivas* must wear these colors. Our fathers choose the sizes, shapes, and places for our marks when we are but five summers and paint them on in a sacred ritual. So we do not forget our masks when we bathe, they are placed on our hands. When we are young, other *tivas* paint them on after bathing until we are skilled enough to do so ourselves. Our fathers make our ceremonial masks and give them to us at our last ritual when we are sixteen summers old. *Tivas* are chosen by *Atah* before our births. Our duty is to our family and people. We do not join to mates or have children; they would distract us from our sacred vows. We wear masks to remind ourselves and others we are *tivas*. That is all I can tell you."

Stalking Wolf realized Kionee had told him more than most people knew about the mysterious society. He let his friend know he honored that request by talking about other things. "You are a great hunter and fighter, Kionee. You trained your horse and companion well; he is skilled and smart."

"Your words warm my heart. White Cloud is a good horse; you trained him to ride as one with you."

"He lets no one ride him but Stalking Wolf. No enemy can take him. He likes Kionee, for it is not his way to touch others as he does you."

Kionee recalled how the white stallion allowed her to stroke him and how he nuzzled her hand when she finished. For some reason, a bond had been made between her and the majestic animal. "He knows I am a friend to White Cloud and Stalking Wolf. The same is true for Maja, Recu, and Tuka; they are friends to my first friends."

"We are good companions, Kionee; we also ride and hunt as one."

Companions, her troubled mind echoed, that is all they could be.

After they entered camp and tethered their horses, Moon Child approached with fresh water for them. Kionee noticed her sister's suppressed giggles, and furtive looks at the Cheyenne. The girl had lived sixteen seasons and would soon become a woman when the blood flow came to her. It was obvious Moon Child found their visitor appealing. Kionee decided it was best to whisper a warning to their mother so Martay could scold the girl to prevent trouble and suffering.

Part of the meat, feathers, furs, and the hide were given to older *tivas* who lived in a large tipi. Stalking Wolf was impressed by Kionee's generous and respectful nature, as it was also the Cheyenne way to share with others and to show honor to elders, especially those left alone without families to care for their needs. Kionee possessed a gentle and kind manner which touched his emotions and caused him to like and admire the hunter more each sun. As he watched Kionee with the old ones from a distance, their laughter, movements, and voices reminded him of elderly women. He assumed it was because the Hanueva were a tranquil people, content to live in peace and happiness amongst themselves. It was sad the Crow would come to try to destroy their harmonious existence. He knew that threat was real because his shaman had seen it in his visions, and Medicine Eyes was never wrong. He was proud to be the one chosen by the Great Spirit to save Kionee and the Hanueva, for in doing so, great honor and magic would come to him and to the Cheyenne Strong Hearts. The two tribes' destinies were entwined this season. How, he did not know. Why, he did not know. When his test of courage and prowess would come, he did not know. As for Kionee's part in it, he did not know. But soon . . .

After the evening meal, many hunters and *tivas* gathered in a clearing to talk and play games. Once more, Stalking Wolf noticed how the *tivas* kept to themselves, when his societies intermingled at such times.

Night Walker called the visitor over to where he stood with Little Weasel, Red Bull, and other men. "We toss hoops. Is your aim true?" he queried.

Stalking Wolf sensed it was a challenge by the chief's younger son. "I will join you," he accepted with a genial smile, and saw the man's sly grin.

Stalking Wolf looked at the six hoops of willow, each one smaller than the one before it. He studied the stakes, each one set farther away than the one before it. Standing behind a line drawn on the ground, he was to begin with the largest circle and closest stake, decreasing the hoop's size and increasing the distance thrown with each of the six throws. He realized everyone in the clearing had stopped what they were doing to observe him. He checked the wind to make certain it did not work against him, then extended his left foot and wiggled its moccasin in the dirt to give him balance and control. He fastened his tawny gaze to the first target and concentrated on victory. He took the largest hoop from his right hand, brought it to his stomach, and flung it with the precise speed and angle to ring the slender post. Repeating his action five times, he then recovered the circles from their confining stakes and returned them to his rival.

The Cheyenne's success annoyed Night Walker. His tension caused his hand to quiver in dread of missing. He almost sighed aloud in relief when he did not. With haste, he passed the rings to Red Bull and refused to glance at Kionee, the object of his desire.

The chief's son was right; Kionee was observing the game with keen interest, and with worry. She suspected Night Walker had wanted to best the Cheyenne, and any opposition to their visitor could be perilous.

"Night Walker and Stalking Wolf have great prowess," Taysinga whispered. "They will help protect us from the evil Crow. They are both handsome and of age; I wonder why they have no mates."

"The son of Bear's Head needs a strong and brave woman to become his mate," Kionee whispered in return. "If his brother falls to our enemies, Night Walker will become our chief. What woman among us matches him? Your skills are as great as his, my brother, but you are a *tiva.*"

Taysinga did not get to respond, as they were summoned to shoot arrows with the rest of their group. As usual, Kionee and Regim struck their targets more times than the others and at greater distances.

When Taysinga fretted over her few misses, Kionee suggested she ask Night Walker for help. "It will enlarge his pride to be asked to do so."

Night Walker was pleased to be approached for guidance, so he could avoid the hand-to-hand practice fights. He did not want to be selected to battle with Stalking Wolf, as the Cheyenne's size and strength were greater than his own and he must not lose before Kionee. He needed to prove he was worthy of Kionee and to win her heart and acceptance. He worried he could not do so with such a skilled warrior around. To show his prowess was equal to or better than Stalking Wolf's would only be achieved in glorious victory over the Crow. Somehow that had to come about . . .

As Kionee moved her weapons stand outside, she stole glances at Stalking Wolf. He faced the dawn sun and prayed to his Great Spirit to guide him through the coming day. His torso was bare and his hands were uplifted as he performed his daily ritual, his communion with *Maheoo.* She saw the firm muscles ripple in his back, his broad shoulders, and his strong arms. She eyed the claw marks of the grizzly he had defeated, at the same time noting how narrow and tight his waist was, how tall he was. She watched the wind lift strands of his golden brown hair, which hung free except for two thin braids beside his breath-stealing face. How wonderful, she mused, it must feel to have hair unbraided and playing in the breeze. Hers was never loose long enough to enjoy that sensation, but she knew how glorious it felt to have the sun kiss her face and to have rain splash over her unpainted skin when she bathed in secret before reapplying her mask. How she wished she could enjoy that feeling every day.

When Stalking Wolf finished his ritual, he joined Kionee near the entrance, which did not face the rising sun as was his people's way. He noticed the excellent condition of his friend's weapons and their fine craftsmanship. He knew from overhearing requests for his services that Kionee was viewed as one of the best bow and arrow makers of the Hanueva. He also knew he had placed the "tipi-of-power" outside to allow the weapons to absorb the sun's power. The poles of the conical stand drew other powers from the earth to renew a hunter's skills. The same was true of his people's custom. But one item was missing: a medicine pipe. From his observations, no *tiva* possessed or used one. When he was with Kionee longer, he would ask why that was so, but not this soon. It was not because the Hanueva did not believe in the sacred pipe, breath of the Great Spirit, as all other men had and displayed one. It was another mystery about the *tiva* society he felt he needed to solve.

"The sun is warm this day, Kionee," he observed. "Grass grows fast; soon buffalo will gather in large herds on the plains and we will hunt them together."

Together, her mind repeated. How wonderful and painful that experience would be. Could he not sense her strong feelings for him? Could he not sense her torment? Could his instincts and skills not tell him she was a female? It would be agony to be near him and never touch him. But it would be greater agony to never see him again. To think of him with another woman ripped into her heart like a knife. "We must hunt game to prepare for our long journey. We break camp in eleven moons."

Stalking Wolf perceived that something grave distressed Kionee. He reasoned it was not polite to ask. If his friend wanted to tell him those worries, he must do so willingly. "I will bring White Cloud and Tuka while you get water and food. Come, Maja, walk with me."

The wolf looked at Kionee as if asking permission to go. At her nod Maja followed Stalking Wolf to the edge of the forest where the horses were tethered.

Kionee sighed. It had been three days since she watched the Cheyenne toss the hoops. It had been two since a joint hunting party where Night Walker fired his arrows before others were ready. She guessed he had meant to show off his skills before her and to best Stalking Wolf. Though he had not spoken openly to her about his feelings, she surmised Night Walker was worried about her being drawn to the Cheyenne since they spent so much time together. Even so, she could not refuse to ride with Stalking Wolf without creating suspicions that might lead to trouble. All she could do was hope and pray the chief's son did not expose her sex to their visitor. If Stalking Wolf ever learned she was a woman and he revealed any desire for her, her battle to resist him could be lost. If so, the punishment would be harsh.

Regim had repaired her *kim*, but perhaps her female spirit was still roaming free. Perhaps that was the reason why she was so tormented by her sacrificial existence. No, it began long ago, before the *kim* was broken. Stalking Wolf only intensified the reason behind her misery and unfulfillment. As surely as she breathed, what she felt for him were love and passion. *Fight them, Kionee, fight them as your worst enemies as Regim warned.*

As the sun rose high overhead, Maja stopped loping beside the couple. His body stiffened. His tail lowered as the ruff on his neck stood up and his ears lay back. His nose wrinkled and he growled.

At almost the same time, Stalking Wolf seized Kionee's arm and warned of approaching peril: it was a large band of Crow from the noise he heard, too many for them to battle. *"Haesto notseoo. Hoeeve."*

Kionee's ears detected the sounds of "many enemies" and realized they must "hide," not in cowardice but in caution and wisdom.

Without giving away their presence, they slipped into a deep ravine edged by thick bushes to conceal themselves and their mounts. They commanded their loyal horses to silence, and were obeyed by the highly trained animals. No order was needed for Maja, who sat down on his haunches nearby, ready to defend the one he loved.

Stalking Wolf and Kionee crawled up the bank, taking care not to disturb dust or small rocks. They peered through the lower branches of the bushes where no leaves obstructed their view.

"Ooetane," he whispered.

But it was unnecessary to tell her the men were Crow. She guessed from the markings on their bodies, possessions, and horses. There were ten heavily armed and painted Bird Warriors. The men were riding away from the Hanueva camp. She was relieved they led no stolen horses and had no captives from her people. She reasoned they were a scouting party and had not attacked the Hanueva. It appeared they were heading home or to a location to make camp. Their reprieve must be over and their enemies were preparing to raid them. She did not know if she should be pleased or more alarmed when her friend echoed her conclusions.

As the riders came nearer, Kionee saw the Cheyenne narrow his gaze and stare at the leader. *"Nevaahe tsethoe?"*

"Hawate-Ishte," he revealed the man's name through clenched teeth.

Kionee gaped at One-Eye, a fierce and famous warrior, a man who felt and showed no mercy to those whom he hated. She had heard terrible stories about him and his deeds but had not seen him until this moment. A chill raced over her body. When the Crow party slowed their pace to a walk and came closer, her heart beat fast in trepidation. She wondered how and if she and her companion could defeat such a force if they were discovered. Now she understood the terror and immobility Taysinga had experienced during that last confrontation. Yet, Kionee knew without a doubt she would unfreeze and fight to the death if they were attacked. She glanced at Stalking Wolf whose expression and gaze exposed no fear. She read an eagerness in him, but something stayed his hand; perhaps a sense of duty to protect her. When she stole another—longer—glance at him, she was calmed a little by his confidence and prowess. If she had to die, she mused, what better place or time than with the man she loved? Their bodies were close, touching in several areas. A heat spread over her and she knew it was not because of the warm sun overhead. *Are you my true destiny?*

A shrill cry of excitement escaped one of the Crow's lips, jerking Kionee's strayed attention back to their perilous threat. The band was moving so slowly that she feared they were about to halt and dismount. She caught words of their talk and was horrified by them. The winds of destiny were gusting over her and she warned herself to prepare for the storm they were blowing in. *Help us to survive, Atah. Let him live to help my people and I will obey all commands from You.*

STALKING WOLF LOOKED AT Kionee from the corner of his eyes. His friend's full attention seemed focused on the Crow party. For a few moments, he had imagined Kionee was studying him in a strong and curious manner like a female examining a pleasing male. He scolded himself and discarded such a foolish idea. He had reflexively placed his hand on Kionee's head and pushed it downward when One-Eye looked in their direction. To prevent more movement, he left it there, his arm resting on the hunter's small shoulders. Again, he was reminded of how little his companion was compared to most men. Kionee's body and garments smelled clean. His braided hair was as dark and shiny as a raven's wing in sunlight. A hoofprint of a buffalo—provider of life—was beaded into the Hanueva's browband. Once more he noted Kionee's delicate profile and features. For an instant, a wild thought flashed through his mind as he envisioned Kionee as a woman beneath that guise, the female he had dreamed about not long ago. He dashed that image aside when he found it arousing.

Kionee was stimulated by Stalking Wolf's contact. She found

strength and comfort in his arms and from his touch. His scent was rich and heady. His prowess was unmistakable. She felt torn between her world and the one she craved with him. For a life with him, she must defy and deny all she was and had. That would be selfish and wrong because her family needed her. In this season of perils, her people also needed her. She must ignore all female desires, emotions, thoughts, and actions. She must not battle her destiny and fail, or those she loved would be endangered.

"It is safe," Stalking Wolf said after the Crow were gone. When Kionee looked at him, the hunter's gaze locked with his and exposed an anguish—and other emotions—he did not understand. The Hanueva's gaze was almost pleading. *"Henovae?"* he asked what was wrong.

Kionee came to her senses and took a deep breath. "The Crow plan to attack my people. One-Eye says their shaman and his vision are dead. He wants captives, horses, and possessions; he craves the magic and power he thinks *tivas* have. He says he will become chief over Swift Crane if he can gather many coups from raiding us and the Cheyenne. One-Eye's heart is evil; he listens to no voice except his own. He goes to camp not far away, to wait for the coming storm to pass before he attacks in three suns."

Stalking Wolf gaped at Kionee, whose gaze returned to the vanishing enemy band. "How do you know his words? How do you know mine?"

"The tongues and signs and ways of the Cheyenne and Crow are known to my people. After *tivas* are marked at five winters in a sacred ceremony, we go to live and train in the elders' tipi and *tiva* lodge until we are sixteen summers and return to our families as their Hunter-Guardians. The Old Ones teach us so no enemy or trader can fool us with unknown words."

"You speak three tongues?" he asked in amazement.

"That is true. A trick came to me as—"

Kionee's words were halted as Maja climbed the bank and

squirmed between them as they lay on their sides facing each other and talking. The couple shifted to make room for the persistent animal. The wolf lay down, placed a paw on Kionee's chest, and licked the hand she held out to him.

Kionee smiled as she ruffled Maja's neck fur, impressed as always by the animal's intelligence, and grateful for his help and protection. *"E'fa,* Maja," she told him he had done good to create space between her and temptation. "We must go, Stalking Wolf. I will share my plan as we ride for home." As she scrambled down the bank with Maja close behind, she said, "It is good we have no fresh meat with us to call birds of prey to our hiding place; if Crow saw them circling, they would come to see what lured them here. Or they would have caught the scent of a fresh kill when they passed. *Atah* guides and protects us this sun." *He does not punish me for my weakness; He must have a great task awaiting us. I do not understand why He sent you into my life and heart—perhaps to test my strength and loyalty. When He takes you from them, it will be a cold, sad, and bitter moon, for I cannot help how I feel about you.*

Stalking Wolf sat up but did not follow right away. He could not forget the way Kionee's eyes had softened and glowed, the way his fingers had looked while stroking Maja, and the tone of his voice as the hunter spoke Hanuevan words to the animal. As for Maja, the silver male wolf almost seemed jealous of Kionee's friendship with him. It was as if the wolf saw him as a rival. What strange thoughts and images, he mused, were these which filled his head! How could the "son of Strong Rock" give him such strong physical and emotional stirrings? Was an evil spirit playing tricks on him and trying to defeat the sacred visions? Stalking Wolf knew he must clear his thoughts of foolish ramblings, as something mysterious was afoot.

"*E-hootseehe. E-neamookoho,*" he said as he joined the hunter.

Kionee glanced at the darkening sky, northward of their position. She saw the lightning he mentioned and agreed it was going to rain soon. Thunder rumbled. "We must hurry," he commanded. "The sky is angry; the storm comes fast."

The following day, Kionee and Stalking Wolf rode out as usual to hunt and scout, or so everyone thought. Their true purpose was to locate the perfect site and to make plans to carry out Kionee's daring and cunning idea to frighten off the Bird Warriors until the Hanueva could break camp and depart.

They reached the area where they had hidden from their enemies the day before and rode in the direction the band had taken. The storm had washed away all tracks and another siege of bad weather was approaching, so they hurried to find the Crow's temporary camp. Dark clouds concealed the sun. A brisk wind swayed trees and plants as it gusted through them. Muggy and oppressive air caused the riders to sweat. Perspiration glistened on their faces and wet their bodies beneath their buckskin garments. Soon a cooling and refreshing rain would come, and they must finish their task with haste as it was dangerous to travel when bolts of lightning shot like sharp and fiery arrows to the earth.

Kionee pointed ahead. "Smoke. A cook fire. We will hide the horses and sneak to their camp to see if more Crow join them. We must learn how many warriors we will battle soon and what weapons they carry."

They guided their animals into a dense timberline and dismounted.

"I will go alone, Kionee; it is safer for one to get close than for two. Be ready to ride if they see me and I return in a run."

Kionee decided it was best not to argue with Stalking Wolf, as his prowess and experience in such matters were greater than her own. The only thing that was important was success. She nodded agreement.

Kionee watched the Cheyenne head toward his target, using

the landscape to conceal his advance. Her breathing was shallow and swift and her heart beat heavy in dread of his peril. A nervous sweat dampened her garments and body, but it would not damage her mask if she refrained from wiping the moisture from her face. Her legs seemed weak and shaky; they begged her to sit, but she did not, as she needed to keep watch. She struggled to calm her fears and not lose sight of him. Yet, soon he vanished over a hill. She examined the span between her and the verdant rise which hid the enemy camp from her line of vision. No one slipped from behind a bush or tree to trail Stalking Wolf, and she sighed in relief. She strained to catch any sound of exposure. She reasoned that if she could not detect his presence, neither could the Crow.

Time passed and he did not reappear. The sky darkened. Thunder boomed in the distance, its peals louder and nearer with each series. The wind's force increased; it whipped limbs, bushes, grass, and wildflowers about as if determined to tear them from their trunks and roots. Displays of brilliant and multibranched lightning came at closer intervals and lingered for longer periods. As she waited in alert and tension, she feared the worst and prepared herself to come to his aid if necessary. When she heard excited yells coming from the Crow, she put her plan into action.

"You must help me save Stalking Wolf," she told his snowy stallion. "You must let me ride you and obey my commands."

As if the horse understood, he allowed her to touch him.

In a rush, she removed all Cheyenne items and covered all symbols with white paint to make the animal look ghostly. She put aside the feathers and tokens taken from his mane, tail, and forelock. She suspended a large sunburst medallion around the horse's neck, then added another lengthy thong which held the dewclaws of deer and jackrabbits' feet. After yanking on white garments, she tossed a coyote's skin over White Cloud's back and tied another around her body. She put on a special mask and leapt upon the stallion's back with her ceremonial shield clutched in her hand.

"Come, Maja, we ride as spirit warriors. Help us with this deed, *Atah*. Strike fear into their black hearts. Force them back to their land."

White Cloud let Kionee walk him toward the camp, his hooves almost soundless on the thick spring blanket covering the ground. He seemed to sense his beloved master was in danger and the person on his back could save him. Stalking Wolf had taught him stealth and caution, and he used the lessons well.

It was the same with Maja; the silver creature's paws treaded as silently as a mist drifting across a meadow. His taut, muscular body was ready and eager for action. His golden gaze and erect ears were alert in his great desire to protect Kionee.

Kionee halted and posed them on a grassy knoll that overlooked the campsite. She saw the Crow mounting their horses with weapons ready for use. Stalking Wolf was bound to a tree, but seemed unharmed. The Crow were probably planning to scout for Stalking Wolf's horse and for any companions concealed nearby.

Kionee lifted her shield and shook it as she shouted in an angry tone in their language, *"Apsaalooke, dee!"* Grabbing their attention and ordering the Crow to leave the area, she told the startled men that *Isaahkawuattee*—Old Man Coyote—wanted the *Isaauushpuushe daache*, the Cheyenne captive. She warned if they did not leave she would called down the *baleilaaxxawiia*—evil spirits—to *dappee*—kill—them.

Kionee heard panicked shrieks of *"Tset-scu-tsi-cikyata"* and *"chia cheete, baaaxualeete akbilikkuxshe. Apasaxxiahche, biilapaache!"* Her mind translated their words: "The Wolf Mask Wearer," "silver wolf, his spirit helper," and "Gallop to safety, friends!"

One-Eye stared at the ghostly sight which had appeared as if by magic before an awesome backdrop of nature's beauty. The

Crow leader studied the rider who wore white garments and a coyote skin, carried a wolf shield, and sat astride a cloud-colored stallion which displayed sacred symbols of his god's helpers: coyote, deer, wolf, and jackrabbit. His gaze moved to the silver beast and noticed its flinty-eyed glare and threatening posture. He knew of no warrior who had tamed a wild creature and rode with one as a companion. "Why does Old Man Coyote want the weakling Cheyenne?" he asked.

"He lives under the sign of the wolf," Kionee replied, "Isaah-kawuattee must take back that magic before he is slain."

"I will slay him for Old Man Coyote," One-Eye offered.

"No, if you slay him, the magic will flow into your body. Ha-wate-Ishte does not need it; he is a great warrior by his own skills. Iichihkbaahile stayed your hand; that is why the Cheyenne still lives until He could send me to claim him. Do you refuse Him this gift? If you do so, the Creator will turn His face from you on the battle and hunting grounds. If you do not obey, He will not guide you and protect you. Without the prowess of Ha-wate-Ishte to help them, your people will suffer. He will order the Sun to send down fiery rays to burn up the medicine tobacco plants. He will call the storm to send thunderbirds to attack. He will order the wolf spirit to take summer from your land; grass will not grow and buffalo will not come. This is not the time to raid and kill enemies. Return to your people and prepare for the great buffalo hunt and for battling many Lakotas. If you do so, the Creator will reward you with many coups. Go fast before the storm."

"Why do you not take the Cheyenne with you and leave us here?"

"The sacred ritual must be done where he was captured; it is not for the eyes of men to witness. If you do so, it will steal your sight. Leave this place where the spirits gather to take his power and magic."

One-Eye stared at the potent image. Strong winds danced through the horse's snowy mane and tail; it swayed fringes on the eerie rider's shirt and leggings. Constant lightning streaked behind the warrior like vipers snaking and hissing across the sky; it roared like a grizzly and flamed like a magical fire when bolts struck the earth. Thunder pealed around them. A downpour was imminent. Yet, if Stalking Wolf truly possessed such coveted "power and magic," One-Eye craved them for himself. His terrified companions urged him to leave:

"They are spirits, Hawate-Ishte. He has big medicine with him. He will slay us or call the thunderbirds to attack if we challenge him."

"The Sun hides his face from us. See, the white wolf—helper of the Sun—rides with him for protection. The Sun will punish us as he did the fool-dog who dishonored the Sun's mate and caused her death. We must go."

"They bear the marks of Old Man Coyote. The Creator's four helpers will take summer back to the Old Woman if we disobey. Without summer grass and the buffalo hunt, all *Apsaalooke* will die. He speaks our tongue."

One-Eye did not know if the ghost rider posed a true threat but decided not to challenge this day. "We ride," he said. "Let *Tset-acu-tsi-cikyata* have the captive. We will take others from the Hanueva in two suns."

The intimidated band gathered its possessions in a hurry.

As he mounted, One-Eye told the bound man, "If *Tset-acu-tsi-cikyata* does not take your life, Stalking Wolf, I will do so on another sun for you are weak." To make certain his enemy understood, One-Eye repeated his message in signs all Plains bands used for intertribal communication.

The taunt stung the Cheyenne's pride, and he glared at the man with one eye covered by a buckskin circle held in place by tied thongs. Embarrassed and angered by his capture, he yanked against his bindings. Unable to reply in sign language or in Crow, he scoffed in his tongue, "I am willing and ready to battle you."

One-Eye chuckled as if he grasped foolish words. He stared at the awesome sight on the knoll for a moment, then departed.

As the Crow party galloped away, Stalking Wolf stared at Kionee, White Cloud, and Maja who remained poised dramatically against a dark gray sky on a vivid green hillock. The majestic sight they created awed him. If he did not know the identity of the rider, he also would be deceived. He could hardly believe the hunter's daring challenge against such odds and wondered why Kionee had taken such a great risk to rescue him. He was also amazed that White Cloud had allowed anyone to touch and ride him. He did not know why Kionee had brought along such a disguise and why the hunter had not told him. Perhaps a vision had warned the Hanueva to do so. The mysterious *tiva* had greater medicine and magic than he had guessed. It was clear why the Crow feared the *tivas* and wanted to defeat them to steal their powers.

After the Crow were gone and Kionee joined him and cut his bonds, the Cheyenne said, "You saved the life of Stalking Wolf. Your trick was good and brave. What words did you say to frighten them?"

Kionee removed the wolf mask so she could speak and breathe easier in the heat. "When Bird Warriors came to our land, long before the seasons of my grandfather's father, their shaman told my people their ways and beliefs. Hanueva were given their language and traded with them, for they saw us as no threat or coup. My tribe taught them many things about our land and its game and showed them many mysterious and sacred places. Though we did not live and believe as they did, they thought the Creator honored us by placing so many wonders near us and He protected us. When the old *Apsaalooke* leaders joined their Great Spirit and other Crow bands came, friendship left our circle. The new chiefs and warriors saw us as weak and foolish—for my people loved peace and we did not raid, kill, and take captives. Hanueva were forced to defend our lives and camp when bold ones chose to raid us. If not for their past shaman's vision, they would have tried to slay or capture all Hanueva long ago."

Kionee checked the storm's steady approach, then continued. "Crow have many names for the Creator: Old Man, Old Man Coyote, and the Sun. They pray, dance, and offer gifts to the Sun, as do other tribes. It is said the Sun claimed a Crow mate, but a daring Bird Warrior forced her to his mat to steal her magic. In dishonor, she took her life. The Sun was angry and made all Crow suffer. It was the Sun's companion, the white wolf, who evoked mercy and forgiveness for them. They also believe that long ago a powerful Old Woman possessed summer. They say the Creator sent a male wolf, deer, coyote, and jackrabbit to trick Old Woman and steal summer for them. As long as they have summer to grow grass for buffalo and other game and to grow sacred tobacco seeds, they will have power, life, and victory. They feared to challenge, harm, or disobey me, for I carried and bore symbols of their Creator and spirits. They also pray to Thunderbeings and honor the Spirit Of Rain, so my coming near a storm frightened them. I was taught such things by the elders and our *Tiva-Chu* and used them to fool our enemies. It will be the same with our next trap."

Kionee related the talk between her and One-Eye. "They fear what they do not understand; they seek to escape evil spirits. They fear to offend Old Man Coyote or his helpers. If One-Eye had been alone, he would have challenged me; his hunger for coups and big medicine are large. He is hardest to trick. They will return to attack in two suns. We must be ready to defeat them again with fears of their own beliefs and spirits."

After hearing that explanation, Stalking Wolf was convinced the hunter's other plan would work. "You placed your life and Maja's in danger for me. I will not forget your generosity. I will repay it. I was reckless and was captured. A Crow guard hid in a tree and jumped on me as I sneaked close."

"*Atah*, the one you call *Maheoo*, dulled your wits to allow it; we needed to test our coming trick. We learned they can be fooled; we learned their strengths and weaknesses. Do not feel shame for being *Atah's* scout. We would not know their secrets and plans if you had not fallen into their hands. If it was not *Atah's* purpose, you would be dead. Hawate-Ishte would have killed Stalking Wolf when he was brought to camp."

The warrior did not know if that conclusion was true, but he was grateful to Kionee for helping him to save face over his capture. He smiled and thanked the hunter for such kindness. He stroked and praised White Cloud and Maja for their parts in the cunning victory. White Cloud nuzzled his master's hand, but Maja edged closer to Kionee.

They knew there was no need to conceal their escape tracks, as the impending deluge would do that task for them. Riding doubleback, they headed to where Tuka and their possessions awaited them.

The short journey suited Kionee, as her body was in constant contact with Stalking Wolf's. She wished it would be a longer trip but knew she should be relieved it was not. The insides of her legging-clad legs pressed against the outer edges of his. Her hands rested on his hipbones, as she dared not encircle his narrow and firm waist and put her chest against his broad back. His wind-whipped golden-brown hair tickled over her painted face and neck. She inhaled his manly odor. She gazed at his powerful shoulders and muscular arms in blissful torment. If only she could have him, she would be the happiest person alive. Yet, she knew it was reckless to wish for what could never be.

When Stalking Wolf halted the stallion, Kionee slid off its back. To avoid making eye contact, she busied herself with departure preparations.

Stalking Wolf was amused when Kionee slipped behind thick bushes to change garments. He grinned, then packed their things and loaded them.

"Why did you bring those Crow medicine signs with you?" he asked after the hunter returned.

"A dream warned me to be ready for danger."

"It was a good and powerful vision, Kionee. Why did you not tell me?"

She glanced at him and admitted, "I did not want you to think me foolish if nothing happened."

"I would never do so. We are friends, companions. I trust you."

"As I trust you, Stalking Wolf. If I had told you, my need for surprise might have been lost if your face revealed signs of knowing to them."

He smiled and nodded agreement with the clever precaution. "You are wise and cunning, Kionee. Your prowess is great."

"That is why we work well together; we match in many ways."

"That is true. We must hurry; the storm moves swiftly toward us."

They rode away side by side to complete the remainder of their task before racing the bad weather to camp, arriving only minutes before the downpour and nature's fury unleashed itself over the land.

>>>> <<<<

Near the bank of the river from the mountain of the Big Horn animals, Kionee waited in anticipation to spring their trap. She prayed they had selected the crossing which the Crow would take while en route to raid her camp. She and Stalking Wolf had agreed that this site appeared to be the best for safe and easy fording. They were fortunate that there were many trees, bushes, and rocks to hide behind. Lookouts were positioned for a long distance to watch for the Bird Warriors' approach; each would fire an arrow to the next in line until the message reached them.

Just yesterday the Hanueva chief and council had agreed to this daring and dangerous trick, and most of Kionee's people had helped prepare for it. She and Stalking Wolf had revealed the previous day's episode to the astounded council. She had lied to her people for the first time: she had told them Stalking Wolf allowed himself to be captured so they could test their ability to fool the enemy. The council had believed her, and had praised their courage and prowess. She had noticed envy in the gazes of Night Walker and Little Weasel at being denied participation in such a glorious and exciting event. When she explained her idea for this day's ruse, they had quickly agreed with her clever plan.

The signal came, halting Kionee's musings. She took a deep breath to calm her tension; it was win or die, be brave or be trampled as cowards. She cautioned everyone to be alert, still, and silent; and no one took offense at her words. She knew her camp was prepared for battle in case they failed in their mission. Spotted Owl had offered prayers to *Atah* for success and guidance, but she added hers to the wise and gentle shaman's. She glanced toward Stalking Wolf, but he was hidden from view. She wished she could have one more glimpse of him before the Crow arrived. She wondered if one or both of them would die today without him knowing of her love and true identity.

9

As the colorfully decorated party came close to the river, Regim made flashes with a shiny metal pan to distract them. The object was a gift from their chief to the *Tiva-Chu*. Bear's Head had received it in a trader's camp from strange travelers with white skin who passed through this land many seasons past and called themselves Lewis and Clark.

The flickers caught the enemies' attention long enough for Stalking Wolf to throw a war lance from his hiding place in a tree without being seen by the band. Its sharp point stabbed into the ground with a noisy impact, and its tall shaft wiggled for a time. That action startled the Crow's horses and caused several to rear, paw the air, and whinny, while others danced about in tension. The lance's hand-grip was a coyote skin with coyote tails dangling from its edges. The wood was painted bloodred; eagle feathers were secured along its entire length. Its wild movements halted as the riders brought their mounts under control and glanced about for signs of danger.

Kionee moved into the open. She was attired in the same manner as their last meeting, and was accompanied by silver-pelted Maja. She sat astride the decorated White Cloud, whose hide bore more of the enemies' sacred and magical symbols this time. Ravens' feathers were secured to his snowy mane, tail, and forelock; the black made a sharp contrast to his whiteness. "Halt! Why do you not ride for camp as commanded? *Tset-acu-tsi-cikyata* gave the Creator's words to Hawate-Ishte and his companions two suns past. Why do *Apsaalooke* disobey sacred messages?" When a large cloud drifted overhead and shaded her—and them—as she spoke, she motioned toward the sky. "See how Sun hides His face from such evil."

Hawate-Ishte shifted his head to compensate for the loss of vision in his left eye. He glared at the intruder. "How do we know the Creator sent you to us on both suns?"

"That is how I know where and when to find you." Kionee noticed that rapid and sly response made sense to One Eye's band. Yet the scowling and fierce leader did not look convinced. "I will prove my power and words." Kionee beat a small drum as she pretended to call forth the evil river spirit, *"Aashe Balei-laaxxawiia."*

Night Walker, who was hiding underwater with a reed in his mouth to obtain fresh air and clutching the alleged "monster," heard the drum signal. He used all his strength to shove the enormous and water-soaked doll into sight; only the head at first, then the massive torso.

Kionee was relieved at the success of the chief's son. She had feared the doll would become too heavy to lift or that Night Walker could not retain his position or his grip on it in the currents. They had made the creature from stuffed animal hides, the women stitching them together in a hurry. They had given it a hideous face and body: fox heads with jaws agape for hands, antlers protruding from its temples, two snake heads for eyes, sharp badger claws as ears, and eagle talons growing from its cheeks and chest. She prayed their belief in evil river spirits would terrify them into leaving.

In a hurry, One-Eye grabbed food from a pouch and tossed it

into the water to appease and distract the demon, as was the Crow custom. He realized their vivid colors did not frighten the beast, as usual. He watched his offering sink—or float away—untouched, as did his nervous followers.

"He does not accept your gift," one of them murmured in panic.

"We mean you no harm," One-Eye shouted to it. "Let us cross."

Night Walker, his face just above the swirling surface but concealed behind the large object, moved forward in the water and roared a warning for them not to enter his domain or he would eat them as punishment.

Kionee watched the warrior retrieve his bow and fire several arrows at the mythical creature in a bold attempt to slay it. Of course his weapons had no effect on the frightful "beast," who moved a few steps closer and roared in fury.

"You dare to challenge him?" Kionee shouted. "You are a fool-dog!" She beat her drum again as she pretended to call forth the mythical Little People—*Daaskookaate Bilaxpaake*—from Medicine Rock to give warnings against defiance. "Do you wish their arrows of death to pierce your bodies? Do you wish them to steal the aim of your arrows on the hunt and in battle?"

Hanuevas, concealed in bushes and trees and painted with disguises to resemble leaves, pushed small dolls with terrifying faces into sight and shook them with sticks attached to the backs of the dolls' waists. They clicked their tongues in anger and scolding and chattered, *"Dee! Dee! Dee!"*, to tell the Bird Warriors to leave fast. The noise was loud and eerie, and all except Hawate-Ishte looked persuaded and petrified.

Kionee held up a large hoop of buffalo hide with a huge all-seeing eye painted on its surface. As she did so, having timed the incident with perfection, the sun—viewed a great Crow deity—came from behind its clouds as she shouted, "See their defiance, Creator! Little People and River Spirit, prepare to attack if the *Apsaalooke* do not return to their camp."

As One-Eye gaped and listened and hesitated, Kionee shouted again, *"Xalusshe asshile!"*

"We go, Hawate-Ishte; we must not offend the Creator and His spirits."

"Itchia baawaalushkua," another warned of the "powerful magic."

One-Eye gave the order, whirled his horse about, and charged from the infuriating scene with his panicked party galloping behind him.

As prewarned, everyone remained concealed, quiet and motionless, until the signal was given the threat was gone.

The victorious and exhilarated group laughed and talked in merriment. Runs Fast and Red Bull extolled Kionee for her courage and cunning. Regim embraced her, smiled, and sent her silent messages of praise. Others banded together to discuss the deed with great zest. Even White Cloud and Maja were cheered, and the two animals pranced about as if they understood their important parts in the deception.

When Stalking Wolf came forward, smiled, and commended the hunter, Kionee thanked him. It was difficult, but she managed to conceal her feelings for him from the warrior himself and the others. In truth, she wished she could fling herself into his arms, kiss him, and celebrate with him.

Gray Fox, Little Weasel, and Taysinga helped Night Walker pull himself and the drenched "monster" from the river. The ecstatic man did not seem to notice he was soaked and chilled.

Taysinga handed her love a skin with which to dry off, then another to wrap around his body to warm himself. She savored his smile of gratitude. She watched as his brother and best friend congratulated him for his courage and success. More than ever, she decided he would make the perfect mate and father for her children; he was skilled enough to hunt for their tipi and for her family's. Somehow she must find a way to win him, to pull his eyes from Kionee to her. At least she now knew that Kionee did not desire Night Walker, but there was still a chance that the chief's son would find a way to compel Kionee to join with him. That must not be allowed to happen, she fretted.

If only, Taysinga mused, Stalking Wolf would seize Kionee and make her his, that fierce competition would be removed. She wished her rival would yield to desire for the Strong Heart warrior and would escape with him to his tribe. Yet, Taysinga doubted that Kionee would ever commit such a forbidden and perilous act; and it was wrong of her to hope and pray in that direction. She witnessed the scene, as did the Cheyenne, when Night Walker approached Kionee to embrace and compliment her on her successful plan.

"You also did well, my friend," Kionee told him. "We would not know victory if you and those with the Little People had not frightened them, for Hawate-Ishte would have challenged me this time before yielding to my words alone. It is good we worked together to defeat them. We must return to camp and tell the others we are safe. Until our journey begins or we reach the grasslands, the Crow will not trouble us again."

The elated Hanuevas returned to camp to be honored and exalted for their clever and brave deed. The chief and shaman acknowledged Kionee and Stalking Wolf as the two responsible for bringing this time of joy and feasting. He hailed his youngest son and the others for their involvement.

Kionee's parents and sisters, her paternal grandparents, Long Elk and Yellowtail, her maternal grandmother, Fire Woman, Regim, Little Weasel's parents, Four Deer and Swift Fingers, and the rest of her kin gathered close to praise and honor her for saving them. There were so many people around her that Stalking Wolf had to sit with Runs Fast and his family. She wished the Cheyenne were part of her family, but that could never be.

With the rising of the dark new moon two days later came Kionee's menses. She headed to the *Haukau* to endure her confinement in private, as was the Hanueva custom. She had told Stalking Wolf she was going to carry out a sacred *tiva* ritual to pray and purify herself for the tasks ahead before their departure on the sixth sun. She was pleased when he said he would hunt for her family and would protect them during her absence. He also had promised to tend her horses and to guard Maja. Her heart was touched by his generosity.

As she entered the willow hut, Kionee admitted to herself she needed some time away from the tempting man who was becoming more desirable to her each day. She was delighted to have her blood flow come while they were in camp. It would remove her from Night Walker's sight, and she hoped Taysinga would take advantage of that.

During the few days while Kionee was absent, Martay was compelled to scold her youngest daughter again about making romantic overtures to their visitor. She was glad the Cheyenne either did not notice the girl's infatuation or was politely ignoring it. She tried to keep her energetic daughters—Moon Child in particular—busy gathering spring berries, greens, and various roots, bulbs, tubers, and corms. It did not escape her notice that Runs Fast always went along to guard them when he was not hunting. The love between him and Blue Bird was strong; their joining—she decided—would be a good one. Perhaps she would have little ones to help tend by the next buffalo hunt after this one. Thoughts of the continuation of their family circle excited her. She wondered if Kionee ever resented the fact a *tiva* could have no mate and children, or was bitter because her mother had not born a son to be head of their family. They had never spoken of such things and feelings since Kionee returned home after her training. It was sad that a female would be denied such joys. Perhaps, Martay reasoned, it was not impossible. Kionee could be the first *tiva* in countless seasons to leave her role if she had not misread the way Night Walker looked at her son. Night Walker had the skills needed to fulfill their laws, and it would be an honor for Kionee to join to such a man, a man with great prowess and rank, one from the bloodline of a chief. For a wild minute, Martay was overjoyed at the idea of having Kionee back as a daughter. But, she cautioned herself, the decision belonged to Kionee alone.

The *tivas* and men hunted for extra meat to be prepared by the women in their family circles to be used during their imminent and long journey. The females gathered extra berries, roots, and so forth. They also made additional parfleches for carrying food and replaced any worn water bags. They stretched hides and pelts on racks or staked them to the ground to dry for tanning later. They repaired torn garments and moccasins and made any new ones needed. The best poles from winter tipis were chosen and marked to be used in the construction of travois for transporting their possessions. They believed it was wrong to cut more wood when using the tipi poles would prevent a waste of *Atah*'s creations, trees that might be needed at other times.

Men sharpened, repaired, or made new weapons for protection and hunting. They braided leather bridles and harnesses for their horses and travois. The camp was a busy and noisy place with many tasks to be done to get ready for the seasonal move to the grasslands.

Stalking Wolf supplied more than enough game and many hides for Kionee's family, so they shared the abundance with the older *tivas*. That generosity endeared the warrior to Strong Rock and Martay and to the elderly *tivas* who could no longer perform their duties.

In small parties, the hunters scouted and continued to place guards around the camp in case the Crow returned. But time passed and no trouble threatened. And as the days went by, the tribe grew restless and eager to get under way with the yearly hunt that would provide them with hides and food and other needs to sustain life during the long and harsh winter.

On one occasion to relax between chores, men played a game where bones—carved into squares with designs marked on their sides—were tossed from a wooden bowl onto the ground, certain symbols designating the winner. As the group enjoyed themselves, questions were asked about the plans for their trip to Thunder Basin to camp near the Cheyenne.

Stalking Wolf told them the plan again. "The tribe will travel down the canyon of the winds and round the mountains to journey along the river near the Medicine Bow forest. Four men will ride toward the place where it is Ten Sleeps to the yellow rock lands where water shoots into the air and bubbles in earth kettles. Leaning Tree and Yar will go with me and Kionee, for they are not the sole providers for their families; their fathers are strong, good hunters and fighters. The scouts will part there and take different trails to watch for Crow to see where they head to camp and hunt on the grasslands. They take the same trail each season; they first visit Medicine Wheel, then follow the river from the mountains of the Big Horn creatures, pass Ten Sleeps, and ride along one of the rivers with three forks. After they reach the grasslands, they choose a location to camp where many buffalo graze and there is water. The scouts must also prevent eager Bird Warriors from leaving their tribes to sneak raids on Hanueva. If we watch them and their tracks, we can learn their location and we can give the needed warning."

"Why do you take Kionee with you?" Night Walker asked.

"If Crow sneak near your people, they will see Stalking Wolf, Kionee, White Cloud, and Maja; they will know they were tricked at the river and in their raiding camp. Their anger and shame will provoke an attack. It is best for all if we are not found with the Hanueva. We can conceal ourselves along the way and work against them while your tribe's safety is guarded."

"You endanger Kionee's life too many times when he rides with you, great enemy of the Crow," Night Walker said. "His father is injured and his family needs him. You must choose another to ride with you."

Before the Cheyenne could respond, Spotted Owl said, "No, it is *Atah's* will for his companion-helper to be Kionee; that is why they met. Do you forget how many victories they gather when they ride as one? Kionee's skills and courage are great; he will come to no harm with Stalking Wolf. The Cheyenne's words are true and wise; it is dangerous if they are seen."

Stalking Wolf was intrigued by Night Walker's obvious concern over Kionee, and assumed they were longtime friends. He also suspected the Hanueva was envious of the coups he and Kionee were obtaining. To prevent problems, he said, "When camp is broken and the journey is under way, Night Walker will have one of the most important ranks and duties to carry out for his people." He noticed those words seized the man's attention. "While our scouting parties work their way over the passes and through the canyons, you must ride behind your tribe and protect their flank. If and when Crow strike, that will be their first target. You must choose and lead the band which will challenge and defeat those Bird Warriors. It will be a dangerous task, but Night Walker possesses the courage and prowess to do it. Little Weasel should be your companion-helper; he has great skills, and best friends work well together."

"How can there be danger when scouts will ride between us and Crow and will stop them before they reach us?" Little Weasel asked.

"One-Eye and others like him will be tempted to continue to ride along the river to your old camp and follow your tribe from the canyon to raid," Stalking Wolf reasoned. "We will be in the mountains and will not see them pass to halt them or to warn you. It will be your duty to stop them."

The chief's youngest son asked, "If Kionee travels with you, who will hunt for his family when fresh meat is needed?"

"Night Walker can do that generous deed when camp is made before the sun goes to sleep. You have no mate and children. Your brother, Gray Fox, hunts for your father when Bear's Head is unable to do so. Gray Fox will travel close to the chief to protect him from harm. If danger comes at their faces, a signal will be given for you and your warriors to come to help them. You must choose which warning sign is best to cover such a distance. You must also be ready to accept the rank of chief if injury befalls your father and brother. All know Night Walker is the best trained warrior of his tribe."

"Stalking Wolf speaks wise and true," Spotted Owl concurred. "We must follow his words for our people to survive."

The Cheyenne was relieved when others agreed with the revered shaman, leaving the two overeager men no way to argue or refuse.

Night Walker smiled and said, "I will hunt for Kionee's family and protect them from harm during our journey, as my love and respect for them is large. No hunger or danger will come to them while they live in my shadow. The same is true for my people in the rank you give to me."

"Your heart is big and good like your father's," Strong Rock said. "You will be as our son while Kionee is gone. We thank you and honor you."

From the corners of his keen eyes, Stalking Wolf saw Night Walker and Little Weasel exchange cunning grins and he perceived a suspicious undercurrent pass between them. Talk changed to other things as he took his turn in the game, but his observations were stored for later study.

During Kionee's absence, Stalking Wolf missed his friend's company. From furtive studies since his arrival, he noticed many things about the Hanueva customs and the mysterious *tivas*. They believed *Atah* was the creator of all things and He was the maker of the sacred Medicine Wheel and Great Arrow. They had been in this land since long before anyone could remember; they said their ancient ones were called Nahane, but he had never heard of such a tribe. They believed in and practiced peace, and fought only in self-defense. They buried their dead in the ground, in the "arms of Mother Earth," not upon scaffolds. They did not observe a period of mourning, as they believed a person went to join *Atah* and those left behind should not be sad. They did not raid or take captives. They did not join outside their tribe or with those close to their family's bloodline. They did not count coup, but they did have a special name for brave deeds called *Btu-i-geeshi,* and those who did them were praised and honored.

They did not decorate their horses or tipis with pictures and symbols of hunts and battles; only the father's name was painted upon the entry flap. They did not harm animals or the land; they took only what they needed for survival. When left to themselves, they were happy and serene.

The *tivas* intrigued and mystified him. They did not possess or smoke pipes, even during ceremonies. They did not share sweat rituals for purification or bathe with the other hunters, or have mates and children. Surely, he reasoned, they had more purpose in life than only being their families' Hunters-Guardians. What it was, he had not discovered.

On occasion, he had seen one or more *tivas* vanish for days into a special willow hut in the edge of the forest reserved just for that society to perform an unknown ritual. He had discovered the cult, the only one among them, had three tipis: a large one which seemed to be for society meetings and storing regalia; another large one where older *tivas* without families and youths-in-training lived; and the willow hut where solitary or small group rituals were held. It was evident no other tribe member—not even the chief, shaman, or parents—could enter any of those locations. A tall, solidly built man of great esteem and affection and dignity was their sole leader: the *Tiva-Chu*. The one called Regim was respected and loved in particular by Kionee. He already knew that Regim was the brother of Martay, so that close relationship was understandable. He had met others in Kionee's extended family circle: Martay and Regim's mother, Strong Rock's parents and brother, Little Weasel, and their families. He liked all of them except the son of Four Deer, whom he could not trust or admire.

His scattered thoughts returned to the *tivas*. The society members were never without their faces painted or ceremonial masks. He reasoned that only that group knew what the others looked like without their guises since they had been taken into the society at age five. Even so, he and others knew which names and identities belonged to each of them, having learned their facial patterns and differences. Those in training lived in a special tipi with the elders and were trained by them and other *tivas* until the age of sixteen. He had seen two youths—about twelve and fourteen—being instructed. The *tivas* seemed to have the same powers as the other men; they met and voted with the council, which included all males over sixteen; they danced and sang with the others, but sat in a group during rituals and meetings. No one had told him and he must not ask why the *tivas* had such unusual laws to follow which the other men did not.

Since Kionee was a *tiva*, he wanted to know all about them. He could not understand why his friend appeared so doelike at times and so wolfish at others. Kionee could be calm, gentle, and open; then be excited, strong, fearless, and cunning. It was as if two people and spirits that were opposites lived inside the hunter's body, as if Kionee possessed two faces—one real and hidden, and one spiritual and exposed.

Taysinga whispered to Stalking Wolf as she slowly passed him, "Follow me from camp. We must talk in secret. Let no one see you."

Intrigued by the hunter's serious tone and fearful expression, the Cheyenne obeyed. He left camp by another path, sneaked to Taysinga's tracks, and followed them to a meeting place. While en route, he made certain no one saw him or was nearby.

"You must swear on your life and honor, Stalking Wolf, not to speak of what I will reveal."

He witnessed how nervous the *tiva* was and how the man kept gazing around. "What troubles you, Taysinga?"

"Swear it or I will hold silent and go."

Stalking Wolf's tawny gaze studied the *tiva* whose facial pattern was so unlike Kionee's except for the black background. If he was going to solve this mystery, he *had* to promise his silence. "I swear on my life and honor never to betray you." *Unless you are evil.*

"If you do so, I will die. Kionee will be shamed and punished. The vision which sent you here will be broken. Many will suffer. Friendship between our peoples will end. You will die or know defeat and dishonor. Without you and the Cheyenne, Bird Warriors will destroy us."

Those claims took Stalking Wolf by surprise. "Your words will not leave my lips and head," he vowed. "What secret is so large and powerful?"

10

TAYSINGA GLANCED IN ALL directions and listened to confirm they were alone before she spoke. *"Tivas* are chosen by *Atah* at five winters to be trained and to live their lives as Hunter-Guardians for their families. Few in all seasons past have left this sacred rank to have mates and children. To do so, a Chosen One must pass twenty-one summers and join only to a Hanueva who fulfills the four deeds of our law. To do otherwise is forbidden. You must not lure Kionee off the *tiva* path or many will suffer and die."

Stalking Wolf stared at the hunter in bewilderment. This was not what he expected to hear and could not imagine how it applied to him. "I do not try to get Kionee to take a mate or follow me to my tribe or into battle. Kionee is needed by his family and people. I seek only to save Hanueva lives. He is my helper, for his skills and needs match mine. Uncloud your words."

"You make Kionee think and feel strange things, forbidden things; that is wrong and perilous for Kionee and our people."

"I do not force Kionee to ride with me. I do not pull him from his ways and laws and beliefs to follow mine. We are friends and companions on a sacred task. I do nothing to harm him or to lure him into evil."

"It is not by your choice or plan. Strong forces are at work— good and evil ones. You must obey the good and defeat the bad. Come. Speak no more. Walk as silent as the coyote. Be as unseen as the air."

Stalking Wolf was confused and curious, so he obeyed without question.

Taysinga led him to a place where water cascaded down a slick cliff and formed a basin before it escaped over little falls in stony crevices and traveled through the verdant forest to the river. Dense trees and vegetation concealed the location from view until one was upon it. Melting snow from the mountains fed the gushing stream; the noise of rushing water masked any sounds of their approach. Many large boulders and rocks encircled the hollow and guarded it against intrusion. Men and women washed in the river. Only *tivas* were allowed to use this site, and Taysinga had done so many times. She touched a finger to her lips to command silence, then signaled for stealth. She leaned toward Stalking Wolf and whispered into his ear, "Look, and you will understand the peril you can cause if you do not hold strong and true."

The curious Cheyenne was careful as he used his fingers to part the branches enough to peer beyond them. His keen gaze took in the lovely setting. A beautiful woman stood in nature's bowl with clear water to her knees as she bathed. Her body was slender and firm; her hips were rounded; her buttocks and thighs were taut; and her belly was flat. Her breasts were full and high, telling him she had borne and nursed no babies from them. Her flesh looked soft and sleek, even with the presence of tiny rising of chills from the cold water. Though she shuddered on occasion, discomfort did not encourage her to rush. Her black hair was soaked and shiny after many scrubbings, as was the dark fuzzy area between her thighs. Her eyes were closed and her lips were parted as she tossed handcupped water over her lovely face, and her neck and chest. Sun sparkled off the drops which missed and those which touched her skin. She squatted to rinse yucca soap from her arms, stomach, and hips. After she stood, she halted a moment to let the warm sun kiss her face and body. It was as if she savored the feel of the rays and water against her naked flesh, as if they were rare and cherished pleasures. "Is she real or a spirit?" he whispered.

"She is real. She is of my tribe. She is loved and respected among us."

He wondered for a brief moment if the Hanueva was planning to offer him this arousing maiden in gratitude for his help. Surely not, as that went against their law about mating outside their tribe. He had never come across her since his arrival seventeen suns ago, yet, there was something oddly familiar about her. The winter camp was large and spread along the river for a lengthy distance, but he had wandered through it many times and had witnessed rituals and meetings. Where, he mused, had she been hiding? What did this beauty have to do with *tivas*, Kionee, and such odd warnings? Was this the female whom Kionee desired as a mate? If so, why was he to blame for arousing natural hungers, when she would entice any man who looked upon her to crave her for himself? "Why did you bring me here to spy on this woman? Who is she?" he asked.

"It is Kionee," Taysinga whispered. "She has been in the *Haukau* during the blood flow season. She cleanses and purifies herself now to return home."

Stalking Wolf rushed his widened gaze back to the alluring sight. His heart pounded. His jaw slackened and his mouth went agape. He seemed unable to move, to speak, or to pull his eyes from the incredible discovery. Kionee was a *hee*, a female . . . Her mask and garments concealed this exquisite creature. The person who had become his close friend and constant companion, who had battled three Crow with him on the sun they met, who had saved his life at great risk to her own, who had defeated five Crow alone, who had battled and slain a grizzly, who hunted with great skill, who was solely responsible for her family's needs and protection . . . was a woman, was this heart-stealing woman?

The astonished warrior turned to ask more questions, but Taysinga was gone. He locked his gaze on Kionee as she walked to a flat-top rock and climbed upon it to dry herself. He recognized the possessions lying nearby: the beaded shirt and moccasins, the decorated medicine pouch, the browband with a buffalo hoofprint, the elk-handled knife, and the markings on her bow and quiver. He watched as she lay down on her back to flatten her breasts before she secured a wide strip of buckskin around herself to obscure those splendid mounds. She stood to don a breechclout, leggings, shirt, and moccasins. Now he understood why she slipped into the bushes to change clothes that day after rescuing him! He spied as she used a trade mirror to see herself as she replaced the concealing mask of nature's paints; soon her beautiful female face was shielded. He realized she had done this task so many times that it was unnecessary to use her handmark as a pattern guide. He looked at it as she braided her shiny raven-black hair and realized she would have that entrapping symbol and perilous rank for life: Mask Of The Hunter-Guardian. As she gathered her things, he sneaked from the enlightening location. He could not risk being caught there, and he needed to find Taysinga for answers.

Many thoughts and observations flooded his mind as he made his way back to camp. *Tivas* were women; that was why they wore disguises and avoided people outside their tribe. That explained why he felt drawn to Kionee in strange and potent ways!

His racing mind sorted through the gathered facts in a hurry. No *tiva* he knew had a brother, so the "Chosen Ones" were reared—and lived—as needed sons. No doubt the oldest was selected for that so-called honor and forced to believe it was her duty. He could not imagine what it was like to take a five-year-old girl and "change" her into a boy, or how hard it was for that child to obey. If they became mates and mothers, enemies would guess their secret, as the hand markings would expose them. That explained why unions were discouraged . . . forbidden. By the time a girl took her sacred vows at sixteen, no doubt her mind was so washed clean of her birth role and was too filled and controlled by years of sacrificial teachings that she obeyed her assigned duty without question.

In his flurry of thought, it did not escape him that such women of skill and prowess would be craved as worthy captives, even as mates of men who found it a stimulating challenge to tame their wild spirits. There was also the danger of enemies attacking them without mercy, believing a female was a weaker fighter and would be an easy conquest. It was fortunate no *tiva* had been captured or slain body been taken. That could be why Kionee had fought the Crow with such daring and desperation when Sumba was killed. To give up that rank, he realized, would leave those affected families sonless, leave aging parents without providers and protectors; that was true in particular in Kionee's life with a disabled father. She was trapped.

Stalking Wolf could not envision himself being made into a woman, by force or choice. Yet he knew the Crow had men among them who dressed and lived as females; the *batee* were respected and accepted, and their true sex was not kept secret. But the Hanueva were a smaller tribe and exposure could endanger them. He recalled he had never seen a *tiva* at a trade camp and realized they avoided other hunters on the grasslands; now he knew why they were so distant and mysterious.

A conclusion shot across his mind like a lightning bolt: Night Walker knew Kionee was a female! That was why the chief's son was concerned about her riding alone with Stalking Wolf. Or was there more to the man's feelings, he speculated, than envy and friendship? Had Night Walker ever witnessed the same revealing view of her as he had today? Did the chief's son crave Kionee for himself and feared him as a rival for that goal?

When Stalking Wolf reached the edge of camp, he saw Taysinga mounting . . . *her* horse to go hunting or riding alone. He took a path to intercept the *tiva* a good distance from camp. "Why did you tell me such an important secret?" he questioned her immediately. "Did you fear if I learned it, I would be angry I ride with a female, and leave your people in danger?"

"Why does it matter if your helper is a woman? Kionee has proven her prowess matches yours. A man of honor and confidence would not care."

"Do you wish me to be snared by her beauty and steal her?" he asked. He saw Taysinga's gaze and expression fill with anxiety, then immeasurable fear. Had she suddenly realized she had made a terrible mistake with the revelation and envisioned tragic repercussions from it?

"No, you must not!" she implored. "It would cause much trouble and endanger us. My people would turn against you and the Cheyenne; they would send fighters to battle for her return. We need the help of Stalking Wolf and his tribe against the Crow. You said in council a sacred vision sent you here to save us. You must do nothing to dishonor or prevent it. Your Great Spirit, chief, and people will be angry if you fail in your sacred task. You will do so if you steal Kionee or if you lure her away from us."

"What is your true reason for breaking your law and your silence?" He watched Taysinga search her mind for a good response. When no sly answer seemed to come, she appeared to him to speak the truth.

"Kionee does not think it is right or kind for *tivas* not to mate and have children when there are so few Hanuevas. She does not believe we should be forced to dress and live as men. Being women does not take away our skills. We can be female hunters and fighters. Other tribes have them. We are forced to be what we are not. Yet, we are not allowed to do all things men can. We must not show our faces and let others learn we are women. I wish freedom from such strong and painful bindings. I wish to break my *kim* and become a woman again."

"What is a *kim?* Tell me all about *tivas.* It will remain between us."

After Taysinga complied, he asked, "You say there is a path to freedom. What is it?"

Again Taysinga complied.

"You know of my shame and weakness," the *tiva* continued. "I was afraid of the Crow when they attacked us. I am a good hunter, but I am not a fighter. I do not wish to ride into war. I am smaller and weaker than our foes. I will be slain. I do not want to ride in fear and danger each time I leave camp to hunt. I want peace, love, children, a tipi, woman's chores, a mate, Night Walker."

The Cheyenne realized the last reason left her lips without meaning to do so. He watched her gaze lower in distress. "Why do you not leave the rank and join to him?" he asked. "He meets all of your laws." Taysinga's eyes showed anguish and her voice carried tones of it when she answered.

"How can I pursue and win Night Walker when he views me as a man, like a brother? How can a man lure another man to him? I try to do so in cunning ways, but I have failed to snare his eye and heart. If Kionee puts aside her vow, serious troubles will come. Two *tivas* leaving in the same season will be viewed as a bad sign, as evil medicine. They will blame you and Kionee for bringing darkness and evil into our camp."

"Why would Kionee leave her rank when she is needed? She has not revealed herself to me. Even if she does not believe your *tiva* laws are fair, she lives as one in all ways before me and her tribe."

"You are a great warrior and a man who pleases women's eyes and hearts. You have come to rescue us from great peril. She has not known a man such as you; she has not shared adventures such as those with you. To be your companion stirs her blood and heart in strange ways. I fear it will cause her to weaken, to hunger to become a woman. She is our greatest hunter and bravest guardian; she is a *tiva* of great honor, respect, and rank; all others try to be like her. If she puts aside her mask and rank for any man or reason, her defiance will bring much suffering."

Stalking Wolf's heart drummed in an odd manner and his loins warmed. He barely heard the words following her first few statements. "Do you fear she desires me as a man?"

"Even if such is true, it is forbidden. Perhaps Kionee would break her *tiva* vow and join with a Hanueva, but she would never break her tribe's laws. She would not shame herself and her family. She cannot leave; her father cannot hunt for them or protect them. Do not tempt her to do so."

Stalking Wolf recalled that Kionee would reach twenty-one seasons soon. "Is there a man among you she desires for a mate?"

"I do not know. We shared the *tiva* tipi and training for many seasons, but we are not close friends. We do not speak to each other of things hidden deep in our hearts. Sumba was Kionee's good friend."

Stalking Wolf suspected the only way Taysinga could know those secrets was by spying on Kionee and overhearing them. The only person he could imagine Kionee trusting that much was Regim, which would be the reason he had noticed the *Tiva-Chu* watching him on the sly. He warned himself to be careful in words, deeds, and looks around the society leader. "I have heard the name of Sumba."

"Sumba was killed by the Crow when I was afraid to battle them. Kionee offered me words of forgiveness, but she does not forget I am to blame for Sumba's death and for endangering the others by refusing to fight."

"There is no loss of face when fear is wise and brings caution. Do not feel shame for not wanting to ride against strong and skilled enemies. It is best to know your strengths and weaknesses and to yield to them, just as it is foolish to challenge greater forces." He saw her smile and her eyes mist in gratitude. "I will not betray your words to me and I will tell no one the *tiva* secret. If Crow or other enemies learn *tivas* are females, they will be hunted for captives and coups. I understand now why *tivas* conceal their sex to prevent men from desiring them, but it is sad they must make such sacrifices for their families and people. I will pray to the Great Spirit to turn Night Walker's eyes and heart toward you." *Just as I will pray for Him to turn Kionee's toward me. Somehow He will help me find a way to free her and win her, for surely she is part of my destiny.*

"You are good and kind," Taysinga responded in gratitude. "Now we must part before others see us together. Do not forget my warnings, but forget Kionee is a female."

Stalking Wolf watched Taysinga vanish into the trees. He suspected she had not exposed all of her motives for revealing the shocking truth to him. He surmised Taysinga wanted Night Walker, but the chief's son had his aim set on Kionee. The Cheyenne became agitated as he imagined the breathtaking beauty with such an aggressive man, one whom he believed was not trustworthy in all ways. He had been honest when he said he would pray for Taysinga to win Night Walker. He knew it would be hard, impossible, to allow Kionee to become that man's mate.

To rid himself of tension, Stalking Wolf took a long ride on White Cloud. He remembered his own and his shaman's visions: his true destiny was to be given to him during this hot season. That destiny included discovering and punishing his parents' slayer, guiding the Hanueva to his people for safety and survival for an unknown but important task, and finding a mate.

A mate . . . His eyes and heart had settled on no female among his tribe. He wanted and needed a special woman, one who would be friend and companion as well as lover, one who would provide all that was missing from his life. It was not against his laws or beliefs to join outside his tribe; his own mother—the chief's daughter—had done so. His father was as unlike the Cheyenne as Kionee was, yet their union had been strong, filled with love and passion, until they were slain without mercy. Like his father, Stalking Wolf did not want a timid and submissive wife. His mate must have strength and courage to be able to protect their tipi and family when he was gone on raids or battles. He wanted someone with whom he could share and tell all things. He craved a female whose desires and passions and dreams matched his own.

Kionee was that kind of woman. He did not feel threatened by her skills or worried she would try to outshine him. He no longer felt ashamed for being captured; her reasoning for it made sense, and no man or woman could control destiny or the Great Spirit's plans. He was certain she respected, liked, and trusted him. He was sure she enjoyed his companionship. They worked as one with ease and success. When necessary, she yielded to his words and experience, but she never did so in a cowering manner. She reminded him of light and warmth. They had a strong bond. If he was not mistaken or being wishful, Kionee had looked upon him with desire. He wanted her; he needed her in his life-circle forever. Yet, there were enormous obstacles between them.

He pondered the three paths to freedom and their complications: her parents' deaths, which would not come for a long time unless enemies slayed them; a son born to Martay and Strong Rock—which appeared impossible after three daughters and sixteen years since Moon Child's birth—plus the years required for him to train and replace Kionee; or meeting four hard deeds as a man worthy of her after she reached twenty-one circles of the seasons. In the last requirement, he was confident he could beat her in hand-to-hand fighting and arrow shooting, and become the Hunter-Guardian of her family in her place. Cognizant of his male prowess and appealing looks, he reasoned he could entice her to accept him by choice. But still, he was not Hanueva and there was no way he could become Hanueva in blood.

Stalking Wolf concluded that no matter what he did for this

tribe, they would never gift him with Kionee because she was a *tiva* and they could not permit that important secret to be divulged to others. If only she were just a woman, perhaps he could persuade them to let her join with him. But her handmark could not be removed. Besides, he could not even hint at wanting her without revealing he knew the truth; he had given Taysinga his word of honor to never do so. To make it appear Kionee had exposed herself would be dishonest and cruel. He must not become so desperate and eager to have her that he deceived and hurt her. Yet, he suspected from the visions and recent events that, in some mysterious and powerful way, the destinies of himself, Kionee, the Cheyenne, Hanueva, Crow, and his parents' killer would be entwined this season.

Kionee—"Wind of Destiny"—had connections to all except the last one. What, he wondered, could she know or have to do with the brutal incident that had taken his mother and father's lives so long ago? Less than three winters old at that time, he could not say who had slain them. If his mother had not hidden him before the attack, to be found later by her brother, he would either be dead or a Crow captive this sun.

Stalking Wolf pushed such tormenting thoughts from his mind and headed back to the Hanueva camp. He knew Kionee would be home, and it would be hard to "forget" she was a woman, one he desired above all others.

The following morning just before midday, Kionee and Stalking Wolf finished the arrows they were making for their journey and the buffalo hunt. They had sharped their knives and restrung their bows. They had talked as they worked on mats side by side, with him relating tales of past hunts and battles and enlightening her about other aspects of his life.

To her, his life sounded exciting, stimulating, and fulfilling. "There are many places and people I have not seen. You travel much and have many adventures. Do you become restless in camp in winter?"

"On some suns. But there is much to do when snow blankets the land. Hunting is a bigger challenge. Weapons must be made and repaired. Deeds must be painted on family record hides. Skills must be honed in practice. Bodies must be kept strong and agile. Camp must be guarded. Rituals must be done. It is also a time to rest and visit." *To make love and make babies.*

To Kionee, he seemed a little different this day: more relaxed, and talkative. This side of him made him even more appealing to her. "You miss your family and people?"

"Yes," *when I can think of anyone except you. I want to hold you and kiss you, take you to my mat, make you my own family.* Knowing what was beneath those paints and male garments, his heart longed to win her, his spirit yearned to fuse with hers, his body ached to have hers. He pushed aside those arousing thoughts. "Five Stars and Stalking Wolf are brothers and best friends. We ride as one when I am home, as we do here. When we reach the summer camp, you will become friends with my brother. My people will honor you for the victorious deeds we carried out together."

Kionee was dismayed to realize those things could not happen, but it made her heart leap with joy for him to consider her that worthy. *Tivas* were not allowed to mingle with others, and she did not know how she would explain that to him and his tribe without offending them. What acceptable reason, she mused, could she give for refusing and for avoiding them? She must think of something believable before that sun rose.

Stalking Wolf sensed her line of thought and perceived distress. He let the matter pass unquestioned for now. "Big Hump has lived many seasons; soon Five Stars will become a chief."

"He is older than Stalking Wolf?"

"No, a circle of seasons younger. I have lived twenty-three."

"Why will you not become a chief after your grandfather?"

"Five Stars has Cheyenne blood; mine is not all Cheyenne.

We can join with those outside our tribe, as my mother did. My half blood does not matter to our people, but it prevents me from becoming a high leader."

"Does that anger and sadden you?"

"No. Five Stars will make the best chief; Father trains him well for that rank. Holding the survival of your people in your grasp is a big task. In most Cheyenne bands, the society leaders have the power and control to tell their councils and chiefs what to do. With the Strong Hearts, we give our chief and council that power and control to lead us. What man among us could be more worthy than he who holds the four Sacred Arrows? It is the same with our shaman. Medicine Eyes sees and knows many things: we follow the visions *Maheoo* sends to us through him. It is my destiny to be a warrior and hunter and follower of *Maheoo*. That pleases me."

"I have heard the story of Sweet Medicine's prophecy, who gave your people their rituals, regalia, and sacred symbols for survival. Two arrows are for the people and two for the animals. This is the sign for your tribe," she said, and made it by drawing her right forefinger across her left one several times to indicate "Striped Arrows."

"You know much for one who lives apart from others," he observed. "It is wise to learn the ways of friends and enemies. This is a good day to work; the sun is warm; the land is green; the buffalo gather; we are good companions."

"All you say is true. We will gather our things and hunt." As they did so, Kionee watched the man she loved from the corner of her eye. He possessed such self-confidence, prowess, and sensuality. He was a mixture of rough and smooth, tough and tender, wild and tamed, giving and taking, pride and humility. He was irresistible. "You smile and laugh much this sun; you did not speak much on the past one."

"My head was busy with plans for our task. We ride soon."

"In two suns. You are eager to race the wind and seek challenges?"

"I am eager to begin our big task," *to be alone with you.* "We—"

A rider suddenly entered camp in a hurry and shouted bad news: a group of women gathering berries and plants had been captured by Crow raiders, along with their horses. A male guard had been killed and a scalplock taken, but Goes Ahead had witnessed the scene from the bushes where he was relieving himself. "I could not fight them; they were six," he announced. "I came for help. Their garments and symbols were Crow. The man with one eye was not among them; the others did not match those we tricked at the river."

"We will save them," Stalking Wolf vowed. "Goes Ahead, you warn the others that Crow were nearby and may return. Tell them to protect the camp and horses. Join us with Red Bull and Leaning Tree. We ride fast: follow our tracks. Bring food and water, for we will not return without them."

As they reached their horses, Kionee told him, "You must not ride White Cloud; he will be seen. Ride Recu instead; he is a good buffalo horse; he is swift and smart and surefooted. I ride Tuka. Maja, stay; no Crow must see you with us," she commanded the silver wolf who appeared to understand her caution.

"Goes Ahead said it was not Hawate-Ishte and his band."

"If this one escapes while we chase them, they could tell our looks. He could be waiting to join them in their camp. It is risky to expose ourselves."

"You are right, Kionee. I will follow your words and ride Recu. We must hurry. They are beyond us but must travel slower with captives."

"My sister Blue Bird is with them, Stalking Wolf."

He looked at her worried face and offered a smile of encouragement. "Do not fear, Kionee, we will not let the Crow harm her. It is good Runs Fast is hunting; in his fear, his thoughts would be clouded and his daring too large." *The same is true for Night Walker and Little Weasel; their eagerness for coups could pro-*

voke recklessness and dangerous actions. I must be careful not to allow your presence in peril to distract me. You are skilled and there is no reason I can give to prevent you from coming with me. Mounted and ready, he cautioned, "Take no risks, Kionee."

"I will obey you," she replied, bewildered and warmed by his tender gaze and tone. "With you at my side, we will defeat them. We go," she said, and off they galloped to face another dangerous challenge.

KIONEE AND STALKING WOLF found the women's discarded pouches and the enemies' tracks where Goes Ahead had told them to look. They trailed their targets across a stream, along the riverbank, past a forest, and over a span of grassy terrain. They traveled hard and fast to catch up with the raiders before the daring men reached their tribe or other friends along the way. They had paused in a group of trees to study the open area before them; they knew they could not be seen and the damp earth had prevented any revealing dust clouds. There, atop one hill, they saw the band and bound captives.

"There is a shorter way to them, Stalking Wolf," Kionee announced. "A hidden opening between the mountains they ride around. Come, I will guide you."

He nodded and followed her through a canyon which had appeared impassable to him until they weaved their way beyond a dense thicket and toppled boulders that obscured its entrance. The space between the ridges was winding and narrow, but wide enough for their horses to traverse in single file.

They reached their destination before the Crow came into view, and set a trap.

As Kionee had hoped, the band halted at the seep nearby to rest and water their horses and themselves. The bound females were pushed to the ground near several large boulders and ordered to be quiet and still. The frightened, weary, and thirsty women obeyed. The warriors drank first, removing and laying aside their weapons as they did so. The men seemed to feel it was safe halt and relax. Kionee pulled her gaze from her sister's pale face to ready herself for action.

The moment the men gathered to one side to talk and joke while their mounts refreshed themselves, Kionee and Stalking Wolf loosened a rain of arrows on them in rapid and accurate sequence. Taken off guard, the startled warriors could not defend themselves in time to save their lives. Two were struck in their hearts with the first series of arrows. Two more were slain as their heads jerked in the direction of their companions' cries. As grim reality dawned on the last two foes, they darted toward their weapons, but did not reach them before being taken down by arrows.

The women screamed and huddled together in panic. Kionee rushed to them and shouted above their noise, "It is Kionee and Stalking Wolf; you are safe; they are dead." She knelt before her trembling sister and coaxed, "Do not be afraid, Blue Bird, your brother is here. We will take you home. We must hurry before more enemies come and our people worry."

Stalking Wolf cut the other women's bonds as Kionee freed her sister. "Drink, do your private tasks, and mount your horses," he told them.

As the nervous women obeyed, Stalking Wolf removed their arrows from the enemies' bodies to avoid leaving clues. He also collected things he wanted as coups. Though the excised plugs of hair would be small and damage would be minor to the dead men's heads, he did not take scalplocks in front of the frightened females, as it was not the Hanueva way and might offend them.

After the women were calmed and mounted, Kionee guided them into the twisting pass. Stalking Wolf was to follow with the Crow horses and conceal their trail for a while. Kionee moved as fast as possible in the restrictive canyon. She wanted to reach the far end and get into the open before the Hanueva party passed that location. After they emerged, she sighted five men beyond them. She yelled to the rescue party and caught their attention.

Goes Ahead and Gray Fox rode the fastest to join them, as their mates were among those taken by force.

Summer Lake, sister of Night Walker and Gray Fox, urged her horse forward to meet her beloved, overjoyed and relieved to see him alive and coming after her. As they leaned forward to embrace, she said in a choked voice, "I feared they had slain you."

"I saw them from the trees but there were too many for me to battle," Goes Ahead told her. "I rode to camp for help. Did they harm you?"

"They did not have time. They are dead. Kionee and Stalking Wolf saved us. We hurried away before others came to attack."

The chief's eldest son grasped his love's hand and smiled. "I feared we would come too late to rescue you, my flower," Gray Fox said. "I thank you, Kionee, Stalking Wolf, for this great and brave deed. You saved the lives and honors of my mate, my sister, and the others. My father will be happy to have his daughters returned unharmed."

Kionee smiled and nodded, as did the Cheyenne. She saw her sister gaze about for her love and look disappointed to find Runs Fast was not among the group. Kionee whispered to her that the man was hunting and did not know of her capture. If he had learned it by now, he would be coming soon.

"I would die if he was lost to me," Blue Bird murmured. "He is like the air I breathe, the sun which warms me, the food which feeds me. I could not become a captive mate to our enemy. Thank you, my brother."

Loving and desiring Stalking Wolf as she did, Kionee understood her sister's feelings toward Runs Fast. She smiled at Blue Bird.

Red Bull, Leaning Tree, and Yar—a *tiva*—praised the rescuers and asked questions about the victory. Stalking Wolf related the stirring story of Kionee's ingenuity.

"*Atah* was kind and wise to give us a fighter as skilled as Kionee. *Atah* was kind and wise to send Stalking Wolf to help us. You ride well, brave, and cunningly as companions; you are well matched."

"Your words warm my heart, Red Bull," the Cheyenne warrior replied. "I thank you for them. Now, if we ride fast, we can reach camp before the light is gone. We will halt for food and water when we are away from this place."

"We brought them with us; we did not know how long the chase would be. The camp prepared for attack before we rode from it."

"That is good. We do not know if more bands will raid. I say One-Eye did not tell others about the warnings we gave him or they would not come and risk angering their spirits. We will leave soon to join my people for safety; our tribe is large and strong."

"We begin our journey in two suns," the future chief said. "All is being prepared. We will take down our tipis and load our possessions soon. We hunt on the next sun for the last time before we go."

"That is wise, Gray Fox, for Bird Warriors grow daring this season. I recovered the scalplock stolen from Little Beaver. We will return it to his head before he is placed in the arms of Mother Earth."

"His family will thank you and honor you," Red Bull replied.

The still angered Goes Ahead vowed, "We will be ready to fight and defeat them. You give us courage and tell us how to battle them to victory."

Stalking Wolf smiled. "Hanueva are brave and wise. It is best for them to seek peace first, and battle only when it is threatened." The warrior believed that since the Hanueva tribe was small and the Crow large, truce—if possible with honor—was the safest and smartest trail to ride, unless the Hanueva could be persuaded to settle near the Cheyenne for protection. That move would place Kionee near him all winter . . .

"Many times our plans come from Kionee; he is to be honored for them, and for his prowess."

"We do so, for his deeds are many and large," Red Bull replied. "My mate and child live by his hand and courage."

"Come, we must go," Kionee said after smiling her gratitude. Maja would wonder where she was when the wolf returned home after hunting and found her absent.

Before they reached their destination, they were joined by Night Walker, Little Weasel, and Runs Fast.

Blue Bird's brown eyes glowed with love and happiness when she saw the man she would join after the buffalo hunt. As the two talked and touched hands, the scary and victorious tale was repeated.

"We came fast after we heard about the Crow," Night Walker said. "We hoped to battle them at your sides. Your chase was swift and good."

"You must be on alert when the journey begins," Stalking Wolf told him. "With their shaman dead and his vision lost, I believe more Crow parties will attempt raids for horses and captives. It will be your rank and duty to guard your people well," he reminded to appease the other man.

"No Hanueva will die or be taken captive while we defend them. Night Walker and Little Weasel will slay any Crow who threatens us."

"Do not allow boasting to make you careless," Runs Fast cautioned.

"Do you doubt my skills and honor, Runs Fast?" Night Walker asked.

"Not when your head is clear of seeking coups. You have an eagerness in you which is dangerous to our people if you let it run wild. You spoke many times of battling them only for praise when gathering coups is not our way."

"If they are beaten many times and learn fear, they will leave us be. There are times when we must do more than defend ourselves."

Kionee halted the quarrel. "We must not fight with our brothers and friends. We have much work to do. Let us ride and do our tasks in peace. Our people wait to see if we live."

"Kionee is right," Gray Fox told the men. "We will waste no time on bad words and feelings."

Out of respect for their future chief, they departed in silence.

The following morning, Gray Fox, Runs Fast, and Goes Ahead came to the tipi of Strong rock and Martay to bring gifts of gratitude to Kionee and Stalking Wolf for rescuing their cherished women.

The chief's son spoke for them, "You are our friend and brother, Stalking Wolf of the Cheyenne; your name and deeds will not be forgotten; they will be recorded on our tribal hide, and on those of the families you have saved. The same is true for Kionee, son of Strong Rock and Martay, whose past markings are many upon it. You bring honor to your father and your people. As long as you are with us, we will learn and gain much from your courage and skills. You trained your son well, Strong rock; *Atah* chose him well. In this season, no Hunter-Guardian matches him."

Kionee was glad her father thanked the men. She had done nothing more than perform her duty out of love for her family and tribe. She was happy the Creator-High Guardian had guided and protected her and her companion. She was pleased and touched by the admiration and respect her people felt for Stalking Wolf. She hated to think of the day, after the buffalo hunting season, when he would be gone, forever. Her life would seem so cold and empty without him. Thoughts of being alone with him soon both excited and intimidated her. Yet she knew how things would change between them after they joined his people and the great hunt began.

Stalking Wolf was elated by the Hanuevas' respect, friendship, and praise. He realized he had to do everything within his power to increase his standing with them in order for them to even consider allowing Kionee to join with him later. As he walked toward that goal, he must be careful not to reveal his knowledge of the *tiva* secret.

"Come," Goes Ahead invited, "hunt with us this sun."

Kionee and Stalking Wolf gathered their weapons and departed.

Strong Rock rested on his sitting mat, lost in thought and worry.

Martay returned to the tipi with wood and water. She noticed her love's strange mood and asked, "What troubles you, my mate?"

"Kionee is a great hunter and fighter, but I fear for our son's survival when we part. The Crow are eager for his scalp and medicine, and those of Stalking Wolf. They are too close as friends and companions. They will be alone and far from us for many suns and moons. Another should go, one who is not a mask-wearer. I fear the Cheyenne might learn the *tiva* secret."

"Kionee will not forget or dishonor the *tiva* rank and duty. You are no longer able to guide and protect our son. He was safe in your large shadow, but it is gone now. The Cheyenne is brave and skilled; he can guard our child from danger. Kionee will be careful to hide the truth from him."

"Perhaps evil spirits attack Kionee's life and heart this season. Our son has much feeling and respect for his new friend. Kionee takes much happiness and pride from working with him; our son has known no man such as he is. I do not want Kionee to be misled by the excitement and joy he finds while they ride together, for those moons will end. Then Kionee must return to a quiet life and must not hunger to share more challenging moons as Stalking Wolf's companion." Strong Rock took a deep breath. "They both have the symbol of the wolf. What if that is a bad sign, Martay, one of warning?"

"If our son's destiny is to change, only *Atah* can do so. *Atah* has chosen them to work together; that is why He sent Stalking Wolf and why Kionee was the one in the forest to meet him. We must not intrude."

"Stalking Wolf is unlike Hanueva men," Strong Rock stressed. "He does not know our ways. What if he stirs her female spirit to life?"

Martay suspected her child's attraction to the visitor, but she told herself she must trust Kionee to hold true to their laws, so she kept those doubts to herself. "Kionee will not dishonor his father, himself, our people, and our laws."

"I will pray for *Atah* to give her strength and courage to do so."

Martay noticed that he used the word "her" for the first time since Kionee was age five, but she did not correct his slip. It was natural for Kionee to admire and be impressed by a man with Stalking Wolf's good traits. She believed her loyal and obedient child would and could resist such a temptation. "I will do the same, my mate," she responded. "Do not fear, Strong Rock, for Kionee is strong and true."

The Hanueva women packed family possessions, took down tipis, and loaded travois as men readied weapons and horses. Plans were discussed for a last time, children were given instructions, babies were placed in cradleboards, and the elderly were assisted with tasks too heavy or difficult for them.

The setting was noisy and everyone was busy with their tasks. Water bags were full. Food was ready for consumption on the trail. Anticipation and suspense filled the people, who hoped they would get away without trouble.

Gray Fox, Bear's Head, Spotted Owl, and their families took the lead. Others followed according to the position they were assigned. Night Walker, Little Weasel, and his chosen band rode at the end of the long line. The defenders were alert and prepared for any threat; two of them were eager for it.

After final waves were exchanged, Kionee, Stalking Wolf, Leaning Tree, and Yar headed in the opposite direction from the departing tribe. Maja loped beside Kionee and Tuka, ever watchful for danger.

The journey was under way.

Three days later, the scouting party halted to camp at the base of the mountains of the big horn animals where it was ten suns' travel to the yellow stone land, wintering ground for the Crow. Red cliffs and white sandstone hills presented an awesome sight. Their journey had been quite easy in the canyon of wind nestled between two ranges and across the rocky terrain of black slate outcroppings they had just traversed. Scrubs and grass were abundant, as were colorful and fragrant wildflowers. The scent of countless pines wafted on clear and pleasant air. Water was plentiful, most of it a vivid blue like the sky above it. Snow was visible on the highest peaks and in deep crevices northeast of them. Game roamed the vast forest beyond and frequented the benchland nearby, but there was no need to hunt this day. Many species of birds and insects were busy hunting food, mating, and building nests. Red, blue, and green dragon-flies whose iridescent wings were patterned like spider webs glided, hovered, and performed loops on air currents. It was a wildly beautiful and verdant spot to spend the night.

The signs were apparent to all four that a large Crow party had camped there many days ago. There were no messages left on trees, in rock piles, or by grass knots, so they assumed there were no stragglers left behind as scouts or raiders. From the direction they had taken, they knew the Crow had chosen the easiest canyons and passes to use to reach their final destination.

Kionee, Stalking Wolf, Yar, and Leaning Tree ate *honovohko* and *ame* and drank water from the river. The dried meat and pemmican were necessary trail food as they dared not make a fire. If the night turned cool as was probable this time of year so close to the white-capped mountains, they had buffalo hides upon which to sleep and robes with which to cover themselves. Besides, no worthy hunter or warrior ever complained of being tired, hungry, thirsty, or afraid; to do so made him appear weak in body and prowess.

Stalking Wolf gave clear instructions to Leaning Tree and Yar; "When the sun rises, you will travel along the red fork of the river of Powder. Cross to the south fork and go to meet your people near the badlands of flaming rocks. Look for tracks which say others do the same. If you see Bird Warriors sneaking to find and attack your people, do not challenge them if they are many. Circle their party, ride fast, and give warning. If Hanue-vas have passed that area, check for Crow tracks following them. Hawate-Ishte and others are sly and eager; I believe they will shadow your tribe and nip at their heels for horses and coups and captives. Warn Night Walker to be alert and ready to battle them. Tell your chief and council we follow the big Crow party along the north fork to the grasslands. After we see where they camp for the first hunt and count their number, we will join you."

"It is a good plan, Stalking Wolf, and we will obey."

"Thank you, Leaning Tree; your tribe's survival is in our hands on these early suns. With Our People as allies, Crow will not slay or raid them."

They talked a while longer before they settled down to beneath a waxing half-moon. Yar and Leaning Tree went to sleep within minutes. Stalking Wolf pretended to do the same, but his thoughts were too consumed by Kionee, and the reality of being alone with her the following day.

Kionee kept her breathing slow and even to conceal her restless state. For the past three days, the short distance kept between riders to be ready to react speedily to danger and enforced attention to their surroundings had saved her from concentrating on their leader. But now that they were so close . . .

Maja lay beside her, providing warmth and protection and comfort. As Kionee's fingers nestled into the animal's ruff she felt the beaded collar she had placed around his neck to make certain the Cheyenne people knew he was a pet when they reached the joint encampment. She thought about the collection of *kims* that were hidden in a small cave near their winter living grounds, left behind to prevent breakage and the extra work of transporting and guarding them on the plains. She recalled the repaired cracks in hers and wondered if she should hope and pray they held fast. If the Spirit Vessel crumbled, her female essence would soar in freedom. But for now, she was with Stalking Wolf and should enjoy his companionship; she did not want to think about how soon their time together would end, forever.

12

DURING THE NEXT TWO DAYS, Stalking Wolf and Kionee journeyed at a.tranquil pace as they rode northeast while her friends headed southeast. They did not want to catch up with the Crow; they only needed to learn where the enemy would camp on the plains and how large their band was. On a separate path from Leaning Tree and Yar, the quiet and watchful couple traveled into the lofty range which was forested with aspen, pine, juniper, fir, and other trees. They made their way over grassy knolls, sharp ridges, through canyons, over passes, around piles of boulders, and across short flower-filled meadows where deer and antelope grazed. Sandstone bluffs were covered in dense stands of tall pines and spruce. Red rimrocks and gray cliffs made a startling contrast against the expanse of green below and azure above.

Waterholes and seeps bubbled and pooled at the foot of the cliffs and fish were plentiful in the many streams and rivers. Small animals bathed and drank in shallows along verdant banks. A vivid blue sky was clear of ominous dark clouds. The wind was brisk and air was cool. In the distance to the north, snowcapped pinnacles dazzled in brilliant sunlight at midday and softened in the sunset's fading glow.

While the trip was physically undemanding for Kionee, the company of the handsome and virile warrior was extremely exciting. Soon they would make camp for their second night alone, and she did not know how or for how much longer she was going to be able to continue her deception. Kionee's wayward heart begged her to tell him the truth, but she dared not relent to the yearning to expose herself, or yield to her desire for him. Every moment spent with him was a mixture of bliss and anguish.

Kionee watched him furtively. He sat tall and straight on his horse. His unadorned buckskin vest did not conceal the strength and beauty of his torso. His back and shoulders were broad and hard, and covered with dark and smooth flesh; his arms were muscular and strong. His flowing golden-brown mane was clean and shiny. She smiled in pleasure as mischievous winds lifted and played with strands of it. His waist was narrow and firm; his legs, long. She caught glimpses of skin and hipbones where his leggings were attached to his breechclout belt. Those two garments and his moccasins also were unadorned with beadwork. He had told her the plain clothing was worn to prevent revealing his tribal identity and rank if they were sighted by enemies. He was so cunning and wise, so skilled and strong, so fearless and generous. Just the sight of him made her heart beat rapidly. Imagine how she would feel if he took her in his embrace . . .

Kionee glanced at the encompassing terrain to calm herself, as she was becoming aroused just looking at him and thinking such forbidden thoughts. They had not talked much since their journey began; both realized how reckless it was to let their attention stray when flanking Crow scouts could be lurking ahead. She let him be the leader, the one who checked the tracks and watched for messages left behind. Rarely had he paused to look back at her or even glance over his shoulder. He appeared in tight control of himself and the situation.

Kionee's stomach told her it was nearing meal time. Roots, berries, and edible plants were abundant in this territory, and she had collected some during rest stops to eat at a later time. She knew from observation while guarding Hanueva women which ones were safe to consume and could be eaten raw, as a cook fire remained a hazard they could not risk. Yet, what she longed to taste were his lips, and to feast herself full in his arms.

Kionee saw Stalking Wolf halt, so she reined in her pinto. He twisted on his horse, propped a hand on the animal's haunch, and told Kionee it was time to camp. She followed him off the well-worn trail and into the forest to a stream where she dismounted and unloaded her belongings while he did the same. Tuka was well trained and loyal, so she left him untethered to graze and drink, to be free to escape if danger came. She ruffled the fur on Maja's neck and allowed the silver wolf to go hunting and roaming; she knew he would return to her side before departure.

After eating their sparse meal, Kionee and Stalking Wolf reclined on their mats.

"What tribe did your blood father belong to?" Kionee asked. "You said he was not Cheyenne. How did he join to a chief's daughter?"

Stalking Wolf was glad she wanted to know more about him, but hoped his mixed bloods would not matter to her. "My father's name was Adam Stone. He was a man with white skin who came to our land from far away to trap beaver and other animals for their pelts. A band of Crow stole his possessions and he tracked them. He found them attacking a small hunting party of Our People and helped defeat the Bird raiders. They took him to our camp and he stayed with them for many moons. He honored and accepted the Indian ways and became a friend. The Strong Hearts made him a blood brother and he lived and trapped near our tribe. He won my mother's heart and eye, and

Big Hump allowed them to join. Her name was Morning Flower. Others have told me she was craved by many warriors for her beauty and rank and gentleness."

Stalking Wolf watched water flow in the nearby creek as he revealed his history to her. "I do not remember my parents; they were slain by Crow when I was two winters' old. We lived in a wooden tipi, what his people call a cabin, on the river near the Medicine Bow mountains and forest. Mother was gathering plants and berries when the Crow attacked. She hid me in my cradleboard in a tree and went to help Father, for she was skilled with a bow and knife and her love for him was as large as the sky. Flying Eagle, her brother, found me two suns' later and took me to Grandfather's camp and tipi. I was raised by him and the Strong Hearts as Big Hump's adopted son, as a hunter and warrior. When I was found, I was wrapped in a wolf skin, so Grandfather named me Little Wolf and I was no longer called Joshua Stone, my white name. In my visionquest, I was told to take the name of Stalking Wolf, to take the wolf as my spirit sign and helper. Many seasons later, Flying Eagle and his mate were killed by Bird Warriors while camped on the grasslands. Their son, Five Stars, was adopted by Grandfather and we became brothers. Flying Eagle's death was avenged by his friends, but we still do not know who killed my parents. When I find the man who wears a hairlock like the blazing sun, I will know who slayed them."

Kionee realized that his hair was lighter than an Indian's because of his father's legacy. And the color of Adam Stone's eyes must have made Stalking Wolf's a tawny shade instead of brown like his mother's. She thought about his quest. If the attacker had taken possessions as coups or to place in his medicine pouch, the killer could be exposed when those belongings were found, if the man still lived. It was possible the man had since died or been killed during a battle.

"It is sad to lose parents at such a young age," she said wistfully. She knew that terrible feeling from experience: when she was five, she was taken from her home and parents' arms and forced to live and train with *tiva* elders until she reached sixteen. It had taken her a while not to feel abandoned and afraid, to put aside girlish things to become as a boy, to learn to mask her true feelings as she was compelled to mask her appearance. Kionee discarded those bad memories for now.

She looked at Stalking Wolf and said, "It is good your grandfather took you as his own son and you have a brother like Five Stars. The moon will come when you will have your revenge; *Atah* will guide you to the Bird Warrior who took their lives, for such evil must be punished."

The warrior locked his gaze on Kionee. He longed to view her lovely face without the colorful guise. He craved to caress her soft skin and stroke her unbound hair. He yearned to hold her and kiss her, to make her his in all ways. Surely she was the woman in his vision and dreams who would become his mate. How he would win her, he did not know, but he was going to do everything within his power to capture her heart. "That is what the visions of Medicine Eyes and Stalking Wolf told us this season. Our shaman is never wrong; his words and dreams always come true."

Kionee was touched by the tender expression in the man's eyes and on his face. He could be so gentle for someone so strong. It would be joyous to press her mouth to his, to be held in his embrace, to lie with him on the joining mat. She had overheard whispers between men and women about the pleasures of uniting bodies, and she longed to experience them with Stalking Wolf. She realized from his curious look that she must be staring at him oddly so she lowered her gaze and asked, "Those are the same visions which told you a Hanueva will do a great deed for your people? That is why you were sent to protect us and why we were asked to camp with the Strong Hearts on the grasslands?"

As Stalking Wolf nodded, he barely controlled a potent urge to seize her and kiss her; the way she watched him stirred his already kindled passions to blazing life. He was convinced now that she desired him, and that conclusion caused his heart to soar with happiness, but he must not reach out to her too soon. He did not wish to offend her or frighten her away. They had many similarities, yet many differences, and there was a great obstacle between them to be conquered. She took her *tiva* vow and duty seriously, and he must not treat them lightly. When he trusted his voice not to betray his emotions, he said, "The visions did not tell us who would do the deed or what it will be."

"*Atah* knows all things; He will guide the chosen one's path."

Maja returned and lay beside Kionee's mat, placing himself between the two people as if determined to keep them apart. He rested his muzzle across Kionee's outstretched arm and relaxed when she used her other hand to stroke his head and neck. He wriggled closer to her and closed his eyes, as if to dream of running in the forest with a she-wolf.

"We must sleep," Kionee murmured.

"Rest well, my friend and companion."

They traveled along the North Fork of the Powder River, so named because the dirt became like dust when handled. Winters were always milder along riverbanks which were guarded against harsh nature by rimrocks, cliffs, and sloping ranges. In the cold season and early spring, winds howled through the canyons and through passes like a pack of starving wolves on the chase and blizzards often buried everything in sight. In late summer, sudden and violent thunderstorms sent water sweeping over their banks and carrying away anything in its path. There were sections where bogs, quicksand, and flash floods could devour man and beast. Aware of those perils, Kionee and Stalking Wolf traveled with caution.

Game thrived in this area where water, grass, plants, berries,

> 168 <

and trees were abundant. Deer, antelope, and other creatures grazed in juniper-scented draws. Moose and elk feasted in wetlands and peaceful meadows. Wildflowers were everywhere. Sage and rabbitbrush dotted the landscape.

Ancient rock cairns marked the trails, but the couple did not need them for direction. They continued to follow the tracks of the enemy band; from the marks in the dirt, the doused campfires, and condition of broken grasses, they estimated the Crow to be two days ahead of them.

Suddenly Stalking Wolf halted, turned, and gazed behind them. "Two riders follow us. Come, we will trap them." He was pleased when Kionee obeyed without hesitation or doubt. He guided them to a side river and told her, "Ride into the edge, turn fast, and leave the water there." He pointed to an area where dense brush was near the bank with a thick cover of trees behind it. "The Crow will think we crossed here. They will be fooled and will follow and be snared by the eating sand. We must hurry. Be careful. Go no farther out than an arm's length."

Kionee guided Tuka into the river and stayed close to the bank as she walked the pinto downstream. She kept Maja close and opposite of harm's way. She urged the horse up the bank, and Maja followed with an agile leap. She watched Stalking Wolf do the same and join her.

They dismounted and hid the animals, then concealed their tracks. They ducked out of sight as two Crow warriors came into view, both leaning over to study the ground for signs. One pointed to the river and said their targets must have seen them coming and had crossed to elude them. The two men were excited to have them on the run and heading into an apparent box canyon ahead. Both galloped into the water as if each was trying to be first to reach their goals to earn the coups and possessions.

Kionee watched as the horses staggered, whinnied, and became wide-eyed in panic as they grasped their peril. Both riders were unseated and the animals struggled backward, somehow escaping the threat their owners could not. Kionee hated to watch their futile attempts to survive, but the enemies would have slain them if caught and would still do so if she and Stalking Wolf helped them escape.

Soon it was over, and Kionee lifted her gaze once more. She watched her companion unload, unbridle, and free the two horses. She joined him.

"We cannot take them with us. They could endanger us by not obeying our commands when we near the Crow camp in secret. They are strong and smart; they will survive in this good land."

"You are wise and cunning, Stalking Wolf," she said in agreement.

"Come. We cross to the Red Fork. We will ride its waters to hide our trail and plan if others come behind us to reach their people. Perhaps some warriors remained longer at Medicine Mountain to seek visions at the Great Wheel or were off hunting or raiding when their tribe left. Fresh tracks atop old ones of their band will be seen and followed. We take no risks."

Since other stragglers might be trying to catch up or could be riding as flanking scouts Kionee agreed it was best to leave the tribe's trail for a while and pick it up in a few days downriver where the Red limb joined the Middle branch which joined the North Fork. This way, they could conceal their presence and intention, and they could relax their constant guard temporarily. After six suns of being on full alert, that plan suited her fine.

The following night, Maja brought a rabbit into camp and dropped it at Kionee's feet. She smiled and knelt to stroke the beloved animal. "You are good and cunning, my friend, but we cannot make a fire to cook it. I will skin it for you and keep the pelt, for it is unharmed, my fine hunter."

Stalking Wolf watched Kionee remove the fur with skill. She gave the meat to her pet and scraped the fat from the pelt before rolling it and putting it with her possessions, to be cured later by her mother. He could not seem to take his gaze from her. Soon he was lost in stimulating memories of what he had viewed at the waterfall near the winter camp. His heart drummed as he remembered how she had looked without the painted mask and male garments.

Kionee looked up to find him watching her with a strange gleam in his eyes. Enticed, she asked, "Why do you stare at me this way?"

"You are beautiful and special, Kionee," he murmured rashly.

She gaped at him and trembled. "Your words confuse me."

Stalking Wolf drew a deep breath as he caught his mistake. Perhaps, he reasoned, this was the time and place to expose his feelings, to begin his quest for her. "I know you are a woman, Kionee." He watched her brown gaze widen in alarm and he heard her gasp in surprise.

13

"**D**O NOT BE AFRAID, Kionee; trust me to tell no one your secret. The words in my heart spoke swifter than my wits could halt them. You walk into my thoughts when I sleep and race into them when I do not." He came and knelt before her and captured her gaze with his. "There is no other like you. We are matched. Destiny drew us together to find each other. You are the woman for me. I want you as my mate." He lifted his hand and stroked her colorfully painted cheek. As she stared at him in panic and disbelief, he pulled her head toward his to kiss her.

Maja leapt upon the warrior and knocked him backward. The wolf took a menacing stance between them and growled in warning. His ears were erect and the ruff on his throat bristled; his tail was motionless. His golden eyes were clear and threatening. He was ready to attack on her command.

"I mean her no harm, Maja, for she has captured my heart." Stalking Wolf met Kionee's troubled gaze. "I hunger to taste your lips, to hold you, to make you mine, to share a life and tipi with you. Do you feel the same for me?"

Kionee leapt to her feet and urged, "You must not speak such words! You must forget I am a female in body. To mate with you is forbidden."

Stalking Wolf decided he must urge his chosen one to face the truth about her feelings, if she had not done so already. As long as she denied or resisted them or remained unaware of his love and desire, he could not win her. Worse, he could have a rival for Kionee in Night Walker, who was an acceptable choice by her tribe and under her laws. "Do you say you do not desire me as a man and mate? Do I misread your signs?" His last words seemed to stun her, so he appeased, "Only I sense them, for you hide them with skill and cunning. Do you not want me as I want you, Kionee?"

"It is forbidden," she repeated in rising distress. "Why do you speak such cruel words?"

"*Ne-mehotatse*," he murmured in a tender tone.

Kionee's heart fluttered and she trembled. "How can you love me? You do not know me."

"We have spent many suns and moons together, and you live in my dreams and visions. I know you, Kionee, as you know me."

She did not know how to respond and turned her back to give her time to think.

"If it were not against your laws, would you come to me in love?"

Anguish flooded Kionee as she yearned to tell the truth. If she did so, that would make the futile situation worse. "I must not speak such words; I must not think them. I am a *tiva*. I can be no less or more."

"You are much more, *Na-htsesta*; you are the woman I love and desire. You are a vital part of my destiny."

Kionee turned, and Stalking Wolf attempted to rise from the ground. When Maja growled, she commanded in a gentle voice for the animal to sit. The creature obeyed but remained alert. He had called her "my heart" and warmed her soul. "How did you learn the truth?"

"It was revealed to me. My vision and those of Medicine Eyes said I would find my mate this season," he answered in honesty without betraying Taysinga as promised.

"I am not the woman in your vision, Stalking Wolf. I must remain true to my vows and laws. I am the Hunter-Guardian for my family, for my mother bore no son to take that rank. They cannot live without me. To break my vows would bring shame and anguish to my family and people." *It would also lead to my punishment, and almost certain death.*

"What do you want for yourself, Kionee?"

"I can ask for nothing more than *Atah* gives to me."

"How do you know He did not send me to you to become your mate?"

"*Tivas* do not join and have children."

"Never?" he asked, needing her to tell those things he should not know so they could discuss and resolve these obstacles they presented.

"Only if a son is born and she is released by our law."

"There is no other path to freedom?"

"Yes, but it has been traveled few times and long ago."

"Why can you not travel it this season?"

"You are not Hanueva; it is forbidden to join outside our people."

"No female of your tribe has joined to one from another?"

"Never; it is our law. It cannot be broken or changed. To go against it would reveal the *tiva* secret. That would endanger our survival."

"Not if no one learned you had been a *tiva*."

Kionee lifted her hand. "I am marked for life."

"What of the others who left the *tiva* rank? What of their marks?"

Kionee stared at him. "I do not know," she admitted. "No *tiva* has left the rank since I joined it. I have not seen marks removed. I have not been told how it is done." *But it must be possible!*

"The few who left the rank to join mates, how did they do so?"

Kionee told him the requirements and the reasons why mating and bearing children were perilous to a *tiva's* family and to the tribe.

"I am of high rank. I can be the Hunter-Protector for your family until they join your Great Spirit. When that moon comes to pass, we can go to live with my people. The mark can be removed and we will tell no one your tribe's secret. I can win a challenge against you. I have done many good deeds for your people and they can reward me with you."

"You do not carry Hanueva blood."

"I can become a blood brother as my father did with the Cheyenne."

"That is not the same, and it is against our law. My people will never break it or change it, or reward you for any reason with a *tiva.*"

One point remained to be settled for now. "If the Great Spirit shows us a path around the blood law, will you accept me? Do not sting my pride and knife my heart with words you do not mean."

"My feelings do not matter; they change nothing."

"They are important to me. Speak them, my love, if only one time."

Kionee did not want to hurt him. "If my laws did not stand between us, I would accept you. I have known no man such as you. No man has made me feel this way. But it is forbidden, Stalking Wolf, so I cannot break my vows. You must forget I am a woman beneath this mask and these male garments. You must forget your desire for me. You must choose another as your mate."

The Cheyenne saw her anguish and ached to comfort her. "How can I do so, Kionee, when I love and desire only you?

When my sacred vision said you will be mine? You are part of my destiny, as I am of yours."

"You misread the vision, Stalking Wolf; it cannot be true. I am captive to my rank and, even with your great skills and prowess, you cannot free me. Even with mine, I cannot free myself. Ours together are not strong enough to release me. It is hopeless. To try to escape my laws and vow will bring pain and trouble to many. Do not attempt such a futile task," she pleaded.

He grasped her small hand. "If the Great Spirit wills it and He clears the path between us, will you join to me?"

Tears mistied her brown eyes and her heart ached in denial. "Do not ask me to hope and dream for what will never come to pass."

"Your words are clever, but they give me the answer I need. I will be patient while *Maheoo* clears a path for us. Will you touch lips with me?"

Kionee warmed from head to feet. "That is perilous."

"All we do in life is filled with dangers and challenges. Say yes, and I will ask nothing more from you this sun and speak no more on this matter."

Kionee nodded in suspense and pushed aside nibblings of guilt. She yearned to experience that thrill once in her life, and this was her only chance. She allowed him to pull her into his arms and kiss her for what must be the last time. She quivered in the flames that surrounded her as their mouths meshed and their bodies made contact. She followed his lead and let their tongues dance with joy and defiance. The kiss was long and deep and filled with powerful emotion. His embrace was possessive, but gentle. His taste was wonderful. She closed her eyes and permitted blissful sensations to wash over her.

Stalking Wolf's control was strained, but he knew he must not break his promise and seduce her. She was too special to him to be tricked, and to do so would harm their new relationship and make him an dishonorable man. He had needed proof her feelings were as strong as his own, and he had obtained it. She was his match in all ways. She fit into his arms and life to perfection. Somehow and some way, he would win her. He hugged her and ended the kiss with reluctance. He stared into her gaze of wonder and passion. "I love you, Kionee, and I will wait for the moon when we can join, for it will come."

With daring boldness, she smiled and said, "I love you, Stalking Wolf of the Cheyenne. I pray your words are true, but I fear you are wrong. We must not reveal our feelings to others or trouble will part us too soon."

Safe in the sheltered canyon, they slept peacefully that night, with Maja resting between them.

They reached the Red Fork River and traveled its banks without encountering trouble. When it flowed into the Middle Fork, they located another sheltered canyon to make a safe and hidden camp for the night. It had been three days since they had kissed and embraced. They had laughed, talked, and enjoyed each other's company more than ever in their new closeness and with their shared secrets. They had exchanged tender gazes and light touches. They had refused to speak of the obstacles between them; more accurately, against them. But desires were building within them, enormous hungers craving to be fed.

The moon was full and romantic, and it cast a soft glow over them as they lay on their mats beneath it. Maja was off hunting and roaming, so nothing separated them. They were vulnerable to surrender, and both were aware of that temptation.

Stalking Wolf turned his head to look at Kionee, to find her watching him. Their gazes locked and searched and spoke forbidden messages. He extended his hand and she grasped it.

"In a few suns, we will be on the Crow trail and on alert again," he said.

Kionee knew their brief time alone would soon end. Did she dare yield to love, to passion, to him? Was it a risk worth taking this one time? If she did not, she would never experience the full joy of being a woman, of being in love, of having Stalking Wolf. Yet, could she endure the shame and punishment if discovered? How would her family survive without her?

Kionee told herself she had lived an existence of sacrifice to others for over twenty cycles of the seasons and would do so for the rest of her life after this one moment of weakness and defiance. For tonight, it was her turn to grasp happiness. "I will return soon," she said as she left her mat and took a parfleche and blanket with her to the river.

Kionee removed her garments and bathed. She scrubbed the mask from her face. She dried herself with the blanket, then loosened her braids to brush her hair. She would go to the man she loved as a female, not as a *tiva*. She would seize this wondrous event before the chance was lost forever.

Do not punish my family and people for this deed, Atah, for I must have him. I must know love this one time. If it is Your will, I will return to my duty when I reach my camp. If he is my destiny, guide us and protect us as we seek Your path to each other.

As Kionee turned, Stalking Wolf approached. He had feared she left camp to sleep elsewhere to avoid temptation. He had come to tell her he would not press her to surrender to him if she returned to her mat near him. The sight of moonglow splashing over her naked body, unbound hair, and lovely face was breath-stealing. He halted, stared, and the words caught in his throat.

"I will be yours for this moon, Stalking Wolf, but that is all I have to offer you. Unless *Atah* changes my destiny once more. Until He does, I must remain a *tiva*. Do you accept those terms and honor my vow?"

Stalking Wolf hurried to her and said, "It will be as you say, my love, but I will convince the Great Spirit and your people to let us join."

"You must say nothing to my people about joining with me, for I live as a man and you must not reveal you know the truth. Swear it."

"I swear it, but the Great Spirit will help us."

"If it is not the destiny He wants for us. He will not. You must understand and accept that bitter truth. To battle it will bring great trouble and perils to us and my tribe." *To me, certain death.* "This has been our way since the beginning when *Atah* created us; it will not change because we desire it to. When you face a band too large and strong to fight, you do not, for it would be rash and fatal. It is the same with my laws; do not challenge them with the misguided hope you can win me with skills and cunning. It would be as if I asked you to throw away the Sacred Arrows and to forget Sweet Medicine's prophecy. These are our beliefs and customs; they are as binding and important to me as yours are to you. To betray them by leaving my rank is unforgivable and dangerous. My love for you is great, but I cannot accept it by destroying others."

"I will retreat when and if the time comes to do so," Stalking Wolf promised.

"It will come, my love, have no doubt. I live in a trap which I cannot escape without harming others; that would be wrong and cruel, selfish."

"Then I will share your captivity as long as possible."

Stalking Wolf removed his shirt and tossed it to the ground. As he continued to undress, Kionee admired his virile body. She saw Sun Dance scars and the Strong Heart symbol on his chest; marks of the grizzly on one arm. His waist was narrow; his stomach, flat and taut. She noticed that his long legs—which had been covered during the winter—were lighter than the brown of his torso and face. As he stripped off his loincloth, she realized the area it concealed was even lighter, almost shaded white when compared to Indian flesh. Dark, curly hair surrounded his manroot, which was already thickened in eagerness to enter her body and seek pleasure there.

That sight did not frighten or discourage her. Her gaze lifted to fuse with Stalking Wolf's, who stood still for her appreciative study. She smiled.

The warrior's gaze took in her features. "You are beautiful, Kionee, more so than any woman I have seen." he w hispered as he caressed her cheek. "It brings joy and pleasure ' ɔ gaze upon you without your mask and garments. My spirit soars when I touch you. My body burns to possess yours. I have loved no woman but you." He cupped her chin and kissed her as his arms banded her body and removed all space between them. Her breasts were warm and titillating against him. His fingers trailed up and down her spine as his mouth feasted on hers.

Kionee's arms encircled his waist and her palms flattened against his back. She felt her nipples grow erect and was aware of a strange tensing in her woman's region. She knew she had made the right choice.

Stalking Wolf lowered them to the thick grass and lay half atop her. His left hand brushed over her breast peaks and caused her to quiver. His mouth journeyed her face, pressing kisses everywhere. His fingers stroked her sides before claiming her breast once more. He drifted his mouth down her throat and fastened it to one bud. He heard Kionee gasp, and felt her arch her back a moment at the sensation. His tongue swirled around the nipple as his hand fondled the firm mound.

Kionee's fingers entwined in his thick hair. She seemed warm and tingly from head to feet. She relished his bare skin next to hers. Her hands danced over his shoulders as she let herself explore his torso. When his hand slipped lower and lower with its caresses, she tensed in anticipation of giving herself to him. She moaned in bliss and parted her thighs to allow him access to all her secrets.

Stalking Wolf kissed her as he aroused her with his fingers and skills. He savored the way she sighed and wiggled and stroked his back. His tongue played with hers and he nibbled at her lips. He labored with love and tenderness until he knew she was ready for more. With his mouth capturing hers with heady kisses, he eased atop her and entered. Knowing she was pure in body, he was gentle and unrushed. From her reaction, he had not pained her; even so, he hesitated a moment to relax her.

Kionee had been active all of her life, so the union did not create much discomfort, and that passed quickly in the heat of desire. She was too aroused to feel anything other than love and rapture. She was eager for each thrust and caress and kiss, and responded to all of them.

Stalking Wolf knew he was giving as much pleasure as he was receiving. He was glad he knew how to enflame her and how to sate her. He wanted her to remember this moment always. He wanted it to be as special and satisfying for her as it was for him. He strove to tantalize her beyond thought or control, and accomplished his goal. He realized when she was at the pinnacle of release as she writhed beneath him and her kisses deepened and quickened. He drove with speed and purpose to carry her over that last boundary.

As the passion uncurled within her, Kionee clung to Stalking Wolf. Her womanhood seemed to quiver with delight as ecstasy consumed her. She had believed the experience would be enjoyable, but it was magnificent. She was fulfilled at last. She had won the man of her heart; she belonged to him in all but one way. She now knew what she had been missing and what she would miss later. But she had this joyous memory and would not regret it. She would love and desire Stalking Wolf until she left Mother Earth for the stars. If *Atah* was kind and generous, He would make her dreams come true.

Stalking Wolf moaned and tensed as his climactic moment arrived. He cherished every sensation to the fullest, and the woman who provided them. His heart brimmed with love and happiness. Kionee was his, at least for tonight and until they reached the joint encampment. But she would remain his forever if he could find any way to free her from her rank.

"You are my love, Kionee. My heart swells like a flooding river. I have never known such joy, pleasure, and peace."

She gazed into his eyes and knew he spoke the truth. Her

fingers placed his long hair behind his ears so she could see his face better in the light of the brilliant full moon. "You are my love, Stalking Wolf. My heart overflows with happiness. The pleasure was large, and your skills on the mat are many. My heart sings just to look upon you, to hear your voice, to feel your touch. We are as one this moon."

The Cheyenne lowered his head and kissed her in gratitude. He thanked the Great Spirit for bringing them together long ago and tonight. He cherished her as he held her in his embrace. "Yes, my love, we are as one this moon."

A short distance away, Maja rose and returned to camp. He sensed a strong bond had been made between his companion and the warrior. Kionee had someone now who was closer to her than he was. He lifted his head and howled at a loss he could not understand.

Kionee heard the odd-sounding wail which seemed filled with sadness and longing. "Maja has no mate, as is the way of the lone wolf when his pack has died or been slain. Others will not accept him. He lives as I do, apart from others and without fulfillment," she observed sadly. "Now we must bathe and return."

"Will you leave off your mask until the sun rises so I can look upon you longer?" the warrior entreated.

Kionee smiled and nodded, elated that he found her appearance pleasing. She took his hand and was helped to her feet. After rinsing in the cool river and drying off with the damp trade blanket, she gathered her things and followed him to their camp. She saw Maja lift his head, look at her, then lower it to his front paws again. She sat down and stroked the jealous creature. "Do not fear, Maja; you will always be my friend and companion. I also love you." She hugged the animal, and he nestled close after she lay down on her mat.

"If I could be that near you all the time, I would ask *Maheoo* to change me into a wolf," Stalking Wolf jested.

Kionee laughed. "Do not, for I like you as you are."

His gaze roamed her face as he smiled. "Sleep well."

"It will be the best sleep I have known."

"The same is true for me."

The happy couple journeyed for many days along the river-bank in a tranquil canyon to reach the Powder River basin. There, after checking tracks and signs, they headed eastward to spy on their target, both ever alert and ready to defend each other with their lives if necessary. They were forced to resist their desires to mate again as it was perilous to be that distracted where Crow had passed recently and others could come along at any time.

At night in sites well selected for concealment and defense, the couple snuggled and kissed and whispered, with Maja lying on Kionee's other side and noticeably resigned to the new situation.

As they lay close together, they told each other about their pasts and their tribes. By the time they reached the edge of the plains and the landscape altered its face, they seemed to know almost everything about each other and the two tribes; and their bond was tighter and closer than ever.

A seemingly endless expanse of gentle knolls and flat terrain stretched out before Kionee and Stalking Wolf. They took care to conceal themselves well as they rode amid the hills and streams. Wildflowers were plentiful, but a variety of short and tall grasses now outnumbered them. Hawks, falcons, and eagles soared overhead as they hunted prey with their keen eyes. Ground squirrels, voles, rabbits, mice, and sometimes a weasel darted about; and many of them used deserted or stolen prairie dog burrows for homes, as did rattlesnakes.

They saw coyotes, pronghorns, and deer. Small herds of buffalo roamed the area, their large and dark bodies easily sighted; but the largest herds were farther ahead.

The sky was clear and blue, but storms were frequent and violent and short this time of year. In the vast openness, one could be seen coming for a long way as it built to ominous level. Huge rainbows often followed them. With nothing to block the view, lightning put on dramatic displays.

Days appeared longer on the plains because there was nothing of great height by which to shade the extensive landscape. Distance was deceptive and had to be judged using markers, pace, and past knowledge.

During a rest stop, Kionee said, "*Atah* created Mother Earth and the animals for people's use, and they cannot be owned. But the Bird Warriors try to claim them and keep others from those hunting grounds. Each season their number grows and they want to control more land. The canyon of wind where we live in the cold season is a good place to camp. I believe they have cast their greedy eyes upon it. If we do not frighten them away after the buffalo hunt, they will come to claim it and take my tribe captive. My people do not want war and deaths, but they push them upon us. Soon Hanueva will become warriors as often as we are hunters. That is bad. We must increase and hone our fighting skills and stay ready to battle them."

"Perhaps it is time to leave the canyon of wind and to live near strong allies. Our People will welcome yours and will help protect them."

"I do not know if my people will agree. Do you seek a path to keep me near you?" she teased.

"It is a clever trick, but that was not my thought. I do not want the Crow to capture any Hanueva; I would track and slay anyone who took you as a slave. Perhaps I will camp with your tribe this winter for defense."

"You must not. To do so will summon suspicion about us. *Atah* controls our destinies; He chooses when we live and die. It matters not where we are or who is guarding us when our dark moon rises."

"Between hunts, Crow will try to raid our camps to count coup. The first ones of the new season are important to their ranks, and they have need of more horses to carry home their meat and hides. If we show them we are too strong and cunning to be defeated, they will seek others to raid."

Days later at dusk, Kionee and Stalking Wolf left their horses behind a hill and sneaked toward the Crow encampment. They halted their approach and lay on their stomachs on a grassy knoll. In the distance, they counted many colorfully painted tipis. Horses were picketed beside them; weapons' stands were near the entrances. Women cooked over buffalo chip fires as children raced about playing games. Some men stood in groups talking and planning. Others sat on rush mats and tossed marked bones from a wooden bowl. It was obvious the camp was set up and ready to begin its summer tasks.

"This was a good place," Stalking Wolf whispered. "Water is in three directions. Trees grow on their banks for wood, and chips are plentiful in the grass. Many buffalo graze in all directions. Other game is nearby. No enemy band can reach them without being sighted in time for defense."

"How far away is your people's camp?" Kionee asked.

"Three suns' ride toward the Medicine Bow forest," he answered.

"We travel to it after this moon?"

"Yes."

Their sad gazes locked in understanding; they had only three days of privacy left. Loud hoops and thundering hooves seized their strayed attention. They crouched low for a minute, then— with caution—peered over the knoll toward the enemy camp to assess their peril.

14

K IONEE AND STALKING WOLF saw warriors racing about the village and whooping in exhilaration as they challenged each other to see whose horse was the fastest and which rider was the most skilled.

"We must go, Kionee," Stalking Wolf commanded. "They could ride this way. They are too many to battle and defeat. If we are captured, we will be slain. I know a safe place to camp."

Kionee followed him with vigilance to their horses and Maja, who had guarded the animals and their flank against a sneak attack. Both thanked the intelligent and fearless wolf and stroked its head before they mounted. They backtracked a safe distance to where hills would protect them from view, then headed southeast, making certain to conceal their tracks for a lengthy time. They traveled in the great basin of Thunder until near darkness blanketed the grasslands beneath a waning half-moon. They halted for the night in a cluster of trees on a stream-bank.

Tuka and White Cloud grazed and drank behind bushes

which kept them out of sight, though it was unlikely anyone would be traveling this late.

"Guard and protect, Maja," Kionee instructed the animal, who loped away to make rounds of the secluded location. "He will warn us if an enemy approaches."

After they ate and unrolled their sleeping mats, he asked, "Will you lie with me this moon? It will be our last chance to be together."

"I hunger for you, Stalking Wolf, as you hunger for me."

Kionee took off her shirt, leggings, moccasins, and breech-clout while he did the same. "I cannot remove my mask, for we may have to put on our garments and ride fast if enemies come, or scouts from your people. No one must view my face as a woman. Besides, the moon offers little light and it will be gone soon, so you will not be able to see me as I am beneath it."

As Stalking Wolf unfastened the band around her chest and dropped it on the pile of her clothes, he said in a husky tone, "My heart sees you as you are in truth. Your beauty lives in my memory. One day, with the Great Spirit's help, nothing will hide you from me or stand between us."

She lifted her hand to run her fingertips over his parted lips. "I long for that sun to rise. What if it does not?"

Stalking Wolf embraced her and comforted, "Do not doubt the sacred visions; they will come true. They tell me you will be mine."

Kionee wished she had his same confidence in those mystical dreams, but stark reality prevented it. She knew that no matter how urgently she prayed for release to become his mate, it might never come to pass. How—her aching heart questioned— would she live without him after winning him? She did not know, and that dread tormented her. For now, she must put aside her worries and fears and take advantage of this precious opportunity. She clutched his head and pressed it closer as he kissed her neck, teased her jawline and cheek, and wandered to her lips. She sealed her mouth to his and shared his breath between numerous and sensuous kisses. Her eager hands stroked his back and moved along his spine. She felt the coolness of his buttocks against her warm palms and trailed her fingers over the slight protrusions of his hipbones.

Stalking Wolf's mouth trailed kisses down her throat as she leaned back her head to give him plenty of room to tantalize her. His lips nibbled at her collarbone and danced lightly over her shoulders. His hands slipped down her arms and grasped her slender waist. She was strong and agile, gentle and giving. He guided his hands upward at a leisurely pace, stroking and memorizing every inch they passed. He cupped her firm breasts and kneaded their nipples to taut buds. His thumbs moved back and forth across those peaks to stimulate them further. Then he lifted her, placed her on his sleeping mat, and lay beside her there.

Kionee slid her fingers into the hair near his ears and led his willing mouth to hers. She gave and took quick and short kisses, teethed his lips, and titillated him with her mischievous tongue. She laughed when he gave her chin a playful bite and made noises at the bad taste of her paints. She sighed in pleasure as he fastened his mouth and attention on her breasts. She squirmed and moaned as his hand stroked her to throbbing need. "My heart, you steal all thoughts except those of you and your skills," she murmured in near-breathless delight.

"We need no wits this moon, my love, for Maja guards us from harm and will give us warning." His lips and deft fingers returned to arousing her to a greater height of desire. He sucked in a rush of air when she grasped his manhood and moaned in pleasure at the sensations she created.

Suddenly Kionee could wait no longer to feel him within her as before near the river. She released her grasp on his maleness and used her hands to shift him into place between her thighs.

Stalking Wolf caught her message and obeyed. He entered her with a bold thrust and grinned with satisfaction at her gasp of pleasure. She held him tightly and possessively within the circle of her legs, matching him stroke for stroke. When she reached her pinnacle, his shaft quivered, and blood pounded through his body as his heart soared with joy. After she relaxed beneath him, he dashed aside his control to savor the same kind of splendor she had found.

Afterward, Stalking Wolf held her in his arms, kissing and caressing her until their soaring spirits settled and their bodies calmed. "I love you, Kionee; you are my wind of destiny. Forever my heart and body are yours."

"I will love you and belong only to you until my last breath is taken."

"It will be as my mate."

Kionee did not want to spoil the special moment so she did not argue with him. "We must bathe and put on our garments. We must sleep and be rested for what lies ahead."

After doing so, they nestled together on the same sleeping mat for the first and only time they would allow themselves to have that pleasure. Maja returned and took his place near them, yet remained alert.

Daylight was almost gone when Kionee and Stalking Wolf reached their destination. Hundreds of conical abodes were outlined against the horizon. The Cheyenne camp was enormous and colorful. The Hanueva camp was smaller and plain. Horses were tethered beside every tipi and dogs were tied to stakes near many of them. The outside fires were nearly all extinguished, as the evening meal had passed. Few people were in sight, and those who saw them waved a greeting to their returning warrior and stared a moment at her.

Kionee knew it was her mask which caught their interest. She did not know what would happen between them now, but they could not seek out each other without a strong reason. There seemed no hope for a private union. Yet, she prayed he was not lost to her forever. Her heart beat heavily and a sadness flooded her body. She told him they must hurry to locate their families' tipis before the invisible new moon made their search harder and longer. There was also the risk of tripping over things and being injured, or of alarming the camp with fears of a sneak attack.

"I will help you find yours." Stalking Wolf answered. "Mine will be easy, for our chief camps in the center of our circles. Your tribe spreads out and uses no bands."

"We have our places, so I know where to look. You go to your people and I will go to mine as you promised. We must not expose our secret to anyone. You must tell your chief and people that *tivas* stay to themselves and mean no insult by it. I love you and will miss you."

"I love you and will hunger to see you every sun and moon. I will be careful to guard us from danger. We must both pray and watch for a path to freedom for you. I will not be happy again until you are mine."

"If we are careless and exposed, there will be no chance for us. We must part before others wonder why we linger."

Kionee rode to the right and Stalking Wolf headed to the left, both suffering over their separation and angered by the obstacles between them.

She located her family's tipi when she saw Recu tethered beside it. She picketed Tuka with him and unloaded her possessions. She ducked and entered her family's dwelling, to find them preparing their sleeping mats. She had hoped they would already be asleep, for she was in no mood to talk. "We have returned safe." Kionee said quietly. "It is good to see you unharmed."

Strong Rock, Martay, Blue Bird, and Moon Child greeted her with joy and relief. All voiced questions at almost the same time.

"Our journey was a success, but I will share the news on the next sun. The ride was long; I am tired and must rest. Maja will sleep near me until others see he is not wild and is no threat. I placed the band you beaded for him around his neck, Mother, but it does not show in the dark. After we awaken, Father, you must tell me of your journey and about the Cheyenne."

"It will be so, my son. Sleep, you have done well. Our hearts are filled with joy to have you returned alive and uninjured."

"Thank you, Father."

"After we rest, my brother, we have many things to tell you."

"When the sun rises, I will be eager to hear them, Blue Bird."

I am not a "son." I am not a "brother." I am not a man. I am a woman. Why can you not see and accept that truth and let me live as I am? Remorse filled Kionee as she realized her family was not to blame for her dark fate; her tribal laws were. *Forgive me, Atah, for my anger, for my heart is filled with pain and sadness. Help me, help us, I beg you.*

>>>> <<<<

The following morning, Kionee did not have time to speak with anyone before she went to visit the *Haukau* for two and a half days. One had been erected by the *tivas* for their use soon after the tribe's arrival. For once, she was glad to make this trip; after her two nights of passion with Stalking Wolf it was a relief to know she was not with child.

Another *tiva* who joined her on the third day told her the first buffalo hunt of the season was to begin the following day. A great ceremony was planned by the Strong Hearts, and Hanueva were invited to observe it.

Kionee wondered if she and others like her would be allowed to attend. If so, she would get to see her lover and observe him with his family and people. She also would learn if any female of his tribe was pursuing him. She prayed for *Atah* to permit her a glimpse of Stalking Wolf. But would He be kind and generous after what she had done in the mountains and on the plains?

From a distance near the Hanueva camp, Kionee sat on Recu's back to witness the Strong Heart ritual before their departure. The eight-year-old chestnut was well trained, and skilled for the task ahead of them. Tuka was a good riding and hunting mount, but it took a special animal to race with the buffalo, one used only for that purpose and honored for its prowess and courage. Kionee was bathed, wearing clean garments, and ready to begin. Her mask was vivid, painted to perfection, her braids were neat and tight. Her disguise was unquestionable. She knew her poise and expression did not expose the turmoil that bubbled within her. She knew Maja was safe, as he was with her mother, so she did not have to worry about him. He would stay close to Martay as ordered. When the women followed them later to butcher the game, to help haul it to camp, then prepare it, her beloved companion would remain with her father.

The other *tivas* waited alongside her, as did most of the male hunters. They would leave as a party and separate as needed to pursue their prey. Her gaze sought Stalking Wolf but could not find him among the crowd. She had not seen him since their arrival. She wondered if their passion would be evident to others if he came to Strong Rock's tipi under the guise of visiting friends. Her family and tribe could do nothing more than suspect them of breaking the *tiva* laws unless they gathered proof she was guilty of betrayal. If she and her beloved were careful, she reasoned, they should be safe. But what would she answer if asked outright about her feelings and conduct? She did not know if she would be honest, for the punishment and repercussions were too painful to imagine. She loved and respected her family, and they would suffer greatly from her misdeeds. She knew what her punishment would be and doubted she could survive it, so she had never discussed it with Stalking Wolf. He probably assumed she would be banished and would come to him, but he was wrong about her punishment, very wrong . . .

Kionee forced herself not to dwell on such grim thoughts. Instead, she tried to think of ways to dissuade Night Walker from his ongoing pursuit of her heart. After she reported on her journey to the Hanueva council last night, the persistent hunter had followed her outside to ask more questions about her absence. She did not know if he was suspicious, or only jealous of the time she spent alone with another man. She had tried to appear calm and genial but Night Walker strained her control and their past friendship. As Taysinga neared them, Kionee had hailed the other *tiva* and drawn her into a talk about the impending hunt. When an opening arrived, she excused herself and left Taysinga and Night Walker together. She noticed Taysinga's smile and nod, as if the woman caught her trick and appreciated it. Night Walker was in the midst of a story that Taysinga found exciting; she was heaping praise on him, and he had no choice but to linger and finish his tale.

Kionee's strayed attention returned to the Cheyenne camp. The Cheyenne warriors sat in a group astride their best buffalo horses, and were clad only in breechclouts and moccasins. Their hair was braided to prevent winds and movements from blowing it into their eyes and creating hazards. Knives were in sheaths on their belts. Quivers filled with arrows—marked by signs of ownership—rested on their backs. Bows were in their hands. They wore no adornments, and neither did their horses. Before the riders stood the Strong Heart chief and shaman, and all gazes were fixed upon the two men.

Big Hump lifted the bundle of Sacred Arrows and held them over his graying head. He wore a flowing bonnet of eagle feathers with a half-moon circle of snowy plumes from ear to ear. Buffalo horns were attached, with hackle feathers dangling from their points. A beaded browband held everything in place, including the wolf's tails suspended near his temples. His chest was covered by a hairbone breastplate, and a matching choker

was around his neck. The front flap of his breechclout was decorated with beadwork; his leggings, with tiny scalplocks. His face
was lined by age and sixty summers of exposure to the sun. His
expression and bearing revealed reverence, dignity, and power.
It was clear to Kionee that he had been a great warrior and was a
beloved leader. She noticed his body was no longer firm and
straight and strong. She knew he would remain in camp with
the elders, as the event was too dangerous for him.

The Keeper of the Arrows began the ritual, and she strained
to catch his words, spoken as loudly and clearly as possible so
everyone could hear him.

"Great Spirit, our Creator and Provider, we call to you to
give us victory this season. Our People have need of many buffalo hides and much meat for the coming winter. Protect our
hunters and return them to camp and their families unharmed.
Guide us to the provider of life You placed on Mother Earth for
us to use. Give our arrows true flights. Grant us our needs. We
will honor You in dance and song and with many offerings
when this season passes. Hear us, Great Spirit, we send this
prayer to You."

Kionee watched him slide the bundle of Sacred Arrows into
a leather and beaded quiver and kneel to wrap the holder in a
buffalo skin with decorative paintings. She was glad she was in
the front row and no one leaned forward to block her view. She
observed as Medicine Eyes held skyward a weather-bleached
buffalo skull whose white surface was painted with a variety of
colorful marks, but she was too far away to see what the pictures
were. She saw sage, sweet grass, and herbs protruding from its
eye sockets and mouth cavity; and knew those were symbols of
the plains, feeder of the buffalo. She listened as the shaman
prayed.

"Great Spirit—Creator, Provider, and Protector of the Strong
Hearts—we come to honor You for all things You give to us.
Guard our hunters and give them success in their deeds. Give
them eyes like the eagle's, strength like the bear's, cunning like

the wolf's, swiftness of the deer. Make them fearless as the badger, sure of foot like the horned ones who travel the rocks of the mountains. Let their horses ride as one with them with those same skills. Great Spirit, we send this prayer to You."

Medicine Eyes placed the ceremonial skull on a piece of buffalo hide, handling it as the sacred object it was to him and his tribe. He lifted a ritual arrow which was a longer and thicker shaft than normal. Hoofprints of buffalo and bighorn sheep were painted on its smooth surface. A length of deerskin was secured around its middle. Eagle feathers, grizzly and badger claws, and wolf tails dangled from the skin's edges where a thong was tied for hanging it in the shaman's lodge. As several men beat a large drum with sticks, he danced and chanted as he raised and lowered the arrow many times. When he and the drumming halted, he pointed it toward the north and said, "It will guide you to many buffalo. Go, Strong Hearts, and return with many hides and much meat."

At that signal, the large band whooped and yelled and galloped off across the grasslands.

Bear's Head gave the sign for the Hanuevas to do the same. The moment the words left his mouth, Night Walker and Little Weasel dashed off toward the departing Cheyenne as if they intended to overtake and beat those braves to the herd which was chosen for their attack.

They approached the last hill between them and their goal. At the assigned leader's signal, everyone drew in their mounts to prevent startling the herd before everyone was ready. They stretched out in two rows—long with the number of men and *tivas* present—with Cheyenne to the right and Hanueva to the left. Sharp arrows were nocked on strong bows. Horses pranced in eagerness and excitement, knowing what was about to occur from many seasons of training and participation. The two parties were filled with suspense and exhilaration. The signal was given, and the great event commenced as they raced over the last hill and charged the peaceful herd.

Hunters selected their first prey and focused on them, never singling out another until the previous one was defeated. The closest beasts stopped grazing and looked toward the riders. A rain of arrows was released. Slain animals thudded to the ground. Wounded ones bellowed in rage. Merciful hunters quickly sought to end the creatures' suffering, as they were creations of and gifts from their Great Spirit. The Indians would not slay more than needed for food and clothing and other necessities, as waste and sport were against their beliefs. Only males and motherless females were selected, as the herd must be able to reproduce in—and for—future seasons.

The hunters of both tribes were skilled horsemen and marksmen. They knew where the vital sites were located and aimed for them. The early hunts were important because the animals had not shed their winter coats; the thick mantles around their enormous shoulders would provide warm robes and long hairs for other needs. As they plunged into the herd, the beasts began to scatter and attempt escape. Riders took extra caution to avoid sharp horns and head battings which could injure horse and man.

Buffalo lying in wallows got to their feet with amazing swiftness and agility for such large and sluggish-looking creatures. Their massive dark heads swung in the direction of the noise. Bulls, young and old, seemed to surround cows and calves, unaware the females and young were not in jeopardy. The more aggressive males appeared to take stances of attack and intimidation. Many were brought down fast by the hunters' prowess.

Clouds of dust were kicked up as the herd dispersed in three directions, and determined riders pursued them. Bulls snorted in anger and tossed their heads in warning. Mothers guarded their calves as they urged their offspring forward. The beasts moved with surprising speed. They seemed to know the intruders presented danger and death. Their pounding hooves sounded like ceaseless roaring thunder; the loud noise seemed to reverberate in the warm air and in the ground.

Kionee was pleased by the number of buffalo, as the herd dotted the grassland for as far as she could see to both sides and beyond her. The beasts' hides were in splendid condition this season; they would make fine robes, tipis, shields, quivers, drums, parfleches, and other possessions. The thick hair of winter mantles was sturdy and long for braiding ropes and soft for padding cradleboards. Shiny horns would become good drinking holders or be made into scoops for eating and cooking. Strong bones would be carved into knives and tools; their marrow, would be used in cooking. Sinews would hold tipis, garments, moccasins, and other things together. Galls would be collected for making yellow dyes. Part of their meat would be eaten now and the rest would be made into winter supplies. She already knew which greens and herbs her mother used for flavoring certain cuts and for tenderizing tough ones.

Kionee clutched Recu's belly with her knees and feet for balance and security and drew back the bowstring for her first strike. She watched the arrow enter the selected point. She fired another, and the beast stumbled and fell. She glanced up to mentally mark its location before taking off after a second target. A large bull was nearby, and she focused her skills and attention on him, bringing down the powerful creature. Again, she made a mental note where it had fallen. Though the symbols on her shafts proclaimed the beast to be hers, she wanted to be able to guide her mother and sisters to the sites.

Groups of antelope and solitary coyotes fled in panic. Prairie dogs barked warnings and disappeared into their burrows. Other small critters scampered into their holes. Birds were flushed from their nests in tall grasses. Butterflies took flight to avoid being trampled.

Frantic buffalo stampeded over a prairie dog village where many broke legs and were trapped. Alert riders used caution in picking their paths into the hazardous area. With skilled shots, they made certain the creatures suffered no more.

Kionee withdrew an arrow with Taysinga's markings. She

had decided to help the other *tiva* who had promised to hunt for Sumba's and Tall Eagle's families. She also reasoned a successful hunt would make Taysinga look good in Night Walker's— and in others's—eyes, make her appear more worthy of the chief's second son. Kionee brought down five buffalo with the arrows she had painted with Taysinga's symbols.

The huntress halted in the shade of several trees on a creek bank to rest, drink, and eat from the pemmican pouch suspended from her belt. Recu drank and grazed, at the same time. Kionee was grateful the summer sun did not blaze down on the plains without mercy this early in the season, but their exertions caused both woman and horse to perspire. Kionee's disguise— the face paints, breast band, buckskin shirt, and leggings—increased her discomfort. It was also a dirty chore, as dust, animal hair, broken grass, and other debris clung to her and Recu. She was glad creeks snaked across the plains to provide water for man and beast, and that a few trees and bushes to grew along their edges for shade. She knew, as the hot season progressed, many of those water sources would either slow to tiny trickles or dry up until rains nourished them back to life. Then it would be necessary to bring along water bags to wet and soothe their dry and scratchy throats. Also, hunts would be done early or late in the day to avoid laboring in scorching and dangerous heat.

When their break ended, Kionee returned to hunting for her family. Many hides were needed to make Blue Bird's tipi for the time when she would join to Runs Fast; any excess meat would be given to elder *tivas* and to others. The thought of herself being unable to mate to her secret lover saddened her, so she pushed it aside to prevent distraction. She returned to the noisy action and shot several animals from a small group that came her way as countless other hunters darted in and out amongst the large herd.

A wounded bull made a charge toward her, which Recu avoided with nimble footing. A Cheyenne warrior chased it, took it down, then returned to Kionee to make certain she was all right. "He did not injure us. Recu is quick and alert," she said as she stroked the chestnut's neck in gratitude.

"Another ran against my target, so my arrow was not true. I am Five Stars, adopted son of Big Hump, our chief, and my grandfather long ago," he identified himself. "Strong Hearts welcome Hanuevas to camp and hunt with us."

She studied the handsome man. She was pleased by his kindness and concern. "I am Kionee, son of Strong Rock and Martay." She saw his brows lift in recognition of her name and watched his intrigued gaze roam her colorful mask and small frame. When he smiled, it was a genial gesture; and his expression was one of respect and surprise.

"You are the friend and companion of my brother, Stalking Wolf. He says your skills and prowess are great. He spoke of your coups in our council meeting. It is an honor to look upon you. It is good you rode with him to find our enemies, the Crow. It is good your people join mine for safety."

Kionee hoped her astonishment in hearing that news and the sheer delight in the name of her secret lover did not show. "We thank the Strong Hearts for their protection. The name and deeds of Five Stars are known to the Hanueva. You are a great warrior, as are your brother and father. Our protectors and guardians can learn many things about battling Bird Warriors from your people. We desire peace with all tribes but the Crow will not allow it. They hunger to take us captive, to steal our lands and possessions."

"The Strong Hearts will not let them do so. The Great Spirit sent us a sacred vision and commanded us to protect the Hanueva. My brother told us of the cunning tricks you played on Crow raiders. My father, our shaman, and our people want to chant your many coups. You must come to our tipi where we can speak more after the hunt," he said, nodded, and rode away.

Kionee watched him race beside a bull and fire several arrows as he made another successful kill. She saw him glance back at her, smile, wave his bow, and gallop off in search of his next goal. She longed to see Stalking Wolf but doubted he would seek her out amidst the commotion, and both knew he should not do so. Most of the Cheyenne were hunting to the right, far away. The only reason Five Stars had neared her position on the left was to pursue of the buffalo he had wounded and end its suffering.

She was glad she had met Stalking Wolf's brother. She had taken an instant liking to the man who would become chief of the Strong Hearts after Big Hump's death. From stories told about his prowess and many coups, she reasoned that Five Stars was more than worthy of his destiny. Now she knew she was on her lover's mind, as he was on hers. He was praising her to his people and family; that made her happy. But how could she refuse his brother's invitation without offending Five Stars, Big Hump, and their tribe? They wanted the chance to thank her, to honor her. She must speak with her parents, chief, and council to receive an acceptable and harmless reason; for they were the ones who made the *tiva* law and should deal with the repercussions.

With the herd racing away from the south where the joint camp was situated, it was safe for the women to arrive with the travois to begin their tasks. When Kionee sighted them, she ceased hunting to find her mother and sisters to guide them to her first kill. They first gave thanks to *Atah* for His gifts and Kionee's success. She stood guard against a sudden turn of the enormous herd as the women collected any undamaged arrows and handed them to her to be sharpened and used again. Broken shafts, mangled feathers, and ruined points were discarded; but good tips were knifed out and saved. She watched for perils and stole brief observations of tasks she hoped to do one day as they skinned the beast, carved out the meat, removed the horns, and cut out the sinews and other parts for which they had uses. Everything collected was loaded onto the travois and wrapped in the hide, which was spread out on the wooden frame.

That process was repeated many times as they moved from

carcass to carcass. When the three travois were full, Kionee removed the arrows from her remaining kills to let others know they could claim them. Hunters who had been less fortunate than she was today, or those who had larger families to feed and clothe, thanked her and placed their marks upon the beasts.

Kionee knew she would hunt several more times this season, but the amount they were hauling back to camp on this trip was as much as could be preserved, eaten, and cured before spoilage would occur. After this supply was handled, the task would be repeated until enough hides and food for winter were gathered. Martay, Blue Bird, and Moon Child mounted the horses, and the travois were dragged to their tipi, with Kionee guarding them. The weary group arrived with just enough daylight left to remove their loads, tend the horses, wash off the blood and sweat, and cook.

Strong Rock greeted them upon their return. "It is a good day, my son; success was yours. My pride and joy are large. We thank you."

Kionee noticed the look in his eyes and heard the wistfulness in his voice which revealed how much he missed the stimulating hunt and the thrill of victory. She knew he tried to accept his fate without becoming bitter, but it was hard for a man to be almost helpless in a normal male role without feeling that way at times. She was glad and proud he did the best he could; she loved and respected him for doing so. She embraced him and said, "I thank you, Father, for good training. The *tivas* taught me many things, but I learned more from you when we hunted together."

Kionee watched Strong Rock smile and his gaze mist with deep emotion, so touched by her words and hug he could not respond. His was a condition which could never be altered, but was it the same for her? Could she be denied her dreams and desires and not become resentful and distant? In all honesty, she did not know, and that admission troubled her.

Martay smiled and said, "No family has a more skilled

hunter and brave guardian than Strong Rock's. Our love, respect, and joy are as big as a mountain on this day, our son."

"Thank you, Mother" was all she could reply at that tormenting moment to the woman who had everything she herself craved and could not have.

"I thank you, Brother," Blue Bird said, "for the hides you helped gather. Now I can make a tipi for me and Runs Fast. Your heart is good and kind."

Kionee forced out a merry laugh. "We must both work hard and long, for a tipi takes many buffalo skins."

"I will tan all you can bring to me, even if I must work at night and my fingers become raw and bleed."

Kionee wished she could recover the words that escaped her lips and heart before she could halt them. "Love should not hurt and punish, my sister; you must enjoy your task, for it is a special one."

"That is true, my brother; you are as wise as you are skilled."

"We must eat and sleep," Kionee said, "for much work awaits us."

Martay and the girls hurried to prepare the meal while Kionee tended their horses and visited with Maja.

But as she cooked, Martay worried over the unfamiliar and suspicious tone of her son's voice and the expression in his eyes when responding to Blue Bird's jest. Could it be, she fretted, that female emotions and urges were chewing upon Kionee this season? If that were true, who was the man who sparked them to life? Was it Night Walker, a good and acceptable choice? Or was it another man, a forbidden and bad choice? Surely, the anxious mother reasoned, that could never happen.

>> 15 <<

IONEE JOINED HER MOTHER and sisters outside to construct
meat-drying racks for them, ones tall enough that disobedient camp dogs could not reach them and strong enough to
resist being toppled by winds. She dug four holes in the shape of
a square, put a forked-topped stake in each, and secured sticks
across their tops with pieces of thong. She repeated the task
many times in front of their tipi in the area assigned to them.

While she worked, Martay pegged the buffalo hides to the
ground with the fur side down. Kionee knew her mother and
siblings would scrape off all flesh and fat, rub the hides with
brains and grease to soften and condition them, then tan them
with sumac berries and other things from nature. After the skins
dried, they would be twisted, pulled, and rubbed until they
were pliant.

Kionee glanced at Blue Bird and Moon Child as they sliced
meat into strips to hang on the racks to dry in the sun and wind.
Some pieces were cut smaller and thinner for eating as jerky,
while others were left thicker and longer for use in pemmican.
The larger pieces would be pounded into grainy powder, mixed

with fat and dried berries and nuts, rolled tight in cured deer-skins, and stored in parfleches for winter food.

Strong Rock sat on a rush mat with a willow back as he braided hair into rope, sharpened Kionee's arrowheads, and fed wood to the fire that was roasting their meal. Hanueva men helped their women with some chores during this particular season, as they did not have captives or multiple mates to handle so much work. Strong Rock smiled at Martay as she approached the fire to sprinkle crushed sage, thistle, and other herbs on the skewered meat. As his tender gaze roamed her face and body, he was glad his accident had not rendered him useless on the mating mat. He never tired of this woman or of uniting his body with hers. He knew she felt the same about him, so his heart soared with joy at remaining a man for her.

Kionee watched her mother's actions without being noticed. She had learned which berries, greens, roots, tubers, corms, bulbs, stems, fruits, flowers, nuts, and herbs to gather; and how to smoke them or boil, bake, or roast them in or over coals. She knew how to make soups and how to prepare many foods and cuts of game. She was very familiar with gathering things for preparing paints, dyes, and medicines, which was not considered all woman's work by her people. She liked collecting earth pigments and plants for those uses, some which were mixed with water and others with grease, and others simply dried. After meeting Stalking Wolf and yearning to become his mate one day, she made it a point to discover all she could about the new rank she craved.

The following morning, as Martay and her two daughters tanned hides and dried meat, Kionee and her father sat nearby to work on her weapons. Maja rested beside her and on occasion lifted his silver head to check out movements or noises. Moon Child was in an elated mood on this her seventeenth birthday, as she was now considered a woman who was available for joining.

A hunter of their tribe had caught Moon Child's eye during the recent journey. Kionee was relieved her youngest sibling was no longer attracted to Stalking Wolf and asked no questions about him. She reasoned that her second sister would be mated by the cold season which would follow the impending one. Also, another season of buffalo hunting would be needed for gathering the hides for Moon Child's tipi. Kionee did not mind helping her sisters obtain new homes, but she experienced natural resentment at not being allowed to have one herself. After both girls were gone, that would leave only her parents to protect, feed, and clothe. Yet, she would still be a *tiva*; she would still be forbidden to join with her love.

As if thoughts about Stalking Wolf summoned him to her, two Cheyenne warriors came to visit, before the sun was high overhead. Kionee saw them approaching and had time to compose herself before she and her family greeted Stalking Wolf and Five Stars.

"We came to offer help if it is needed, and to hear of your hunt. My brother said his wounded buffalo tried to charge you."

"Five Stars has many skills, as does Recu," Kionee replied, "They did not allow me to be harmed. My hunt was good. Speak of yours."

"*Maheoo* gifted us with many buffalo for hides and meat. Big Hump's mates tend them; he has four, but Morning Light is his first and best. She is the mother of my mother and the mother of Five Stars' father. He took other mates when it was past his season to give seeds for more children, but we are as his sons. We know it is the Hanueva custom to have one mate, so her work is much; that is why we come to offer help to our friends Martay and Strong Rock."

Kionee was pleased he had not given anything away. "Your heart is good and kind, Stalking Wolf, but Hanueva men help with chores during this busy season. We do not hunt again until this work is done. We thank you."

"My son speaks words of truth, Stalking Wolf. I thank you."

As her mother responded to their generosity, Kionee noted the differences between Stalking Wolf and Five Stars. The younger male was shorter and leaner, but well-muscled and solid. His skin was darker than Stalking Wolf's. He carried himself with the same self-confidence his adopted brother possessed. His looks would please most women, but he was not as handsome as Stalking Wolf. His black hair hung loose and spread around broad shoulders. The only marks she saw on him were scars of the Sun Dance and a red handprint on his chest.

"Sit, speak more about your hunts," Strong Rock invited. "I can no longer do the chase; it gives me joy to hear of others' rides and victories."

Kionee had an odd sensation that her mother was slyly observing her with Stalking Wolf. She thought it best to take her leave for a while. "While you speak, Father, I will take the horses to drink and graze at the water," she said.

"Keep alert for cunning Crow, my son," Strong Rock cautioned.

"I will do so, Father. I will return after my task, Mother."

Stalking Wolf also felt Martay's eyes upon him, so he said and did nothing to provoke suspicion. He and Five Stars took seats on the sitting mats Blue Bird brought to them. He made certain he did not even glance at Kionee's departing form as he plunged with seeming enthusiasm into the tale of his successful quest.

As she led the horses away, with Maja trailing beside her, Kionee noticed that Moon Child paid little attention to either Cheyenne male. Yet, the girl kept stealing glances at a hunter nearby: Shining Star of their tribe.

While Kionee was tending her family's horses and her own, Taysinga arrived to thank her for the unexpected help during the hunt.

"Your heart and ways are kind, Kionee. You slayed many buffalo with my markings, for I know the skill of your arrows when I see them. Others do not know my hunt was not good that sun, for my arrows were on many of the fallen. I shared the abundance with Sumba's family and that of Tall Eagle, as was my vow in the winter camp. Tall Eagle's mate has joined to another, so the buffalo I gave to her is enough to repay her loss. I will hunt again for Sumba's family to fulfill my promise to them. I thank you and honor you."

"I did not help because I believe you are weaker and slower; I helped because it was much work for one hunter to do, and you are my friend, my *tiva* brother. It is good and wise for us to help each other. You would do the same for me. Did you tell Night Walker of your great success?"

"Yes, and it pleased him. Is it wrong to trick him and others?"

"Not when holding silent helps many. You desire him as a woman desires a man?" She was surprised she had asked that bold question, and was more astonished when the older woman replied in honesty.

"It is true, but I must tell no one I hunger to mate with him. Why are we punished by our laws because we were born to families without sons? We are women; why can we not have the joys of being mates and mothers?"

"I do not know. If there were no *tivas*, only female hunters and guardians, there would be no dangerous secret for our tribe to conceal. If those without brothers whose fathers become too weak to do their duties helped each other by tending others' children and chores, we could still hunt for our families as needed. If an attack came, a few of us could guard all *tiva* children while the others battled enemies, so our tribe would not lose its protectors. If one or more guardians were slain in a fight, their men could take new mates. The risk of us being slain as sons is no greater than the same risk if we lived as daughters."

Kionee noticed Taysinga's intense concentration on her

words. "Other tribes have female warriors; it could be true for Hanuevas. I do not believe it is fair for us to be the only ones to make such sacrifices. But the *tiva* laws are old and strong; I fear they cannot be broken or changed. If you wish to leave the rank and join to Night Walker, it must be done by our customs. I see no uncrossable mountain between you and your love. He is worthy of you and you are worthy of him. But I warn you, hold silent while you play the hunter. With cunning and patience, you can capture him. I hope your chase will find victory; you would be good mates; you are well matched. In your heart and head, you are a woman; that is how you should live, not alone, unhappy, and in peril. I will tell no one your secret."

"My heart overflows with happiness to hear your words and to earn your friendship. I will do as you say and be careful."

"I will pray for your victory on love's battleground."

Taysinga checked their privacy before saying, "There is a secret I must tell you. I am unworthy of your help, friendship, and respect."

Kionee studied the female's hesitation and was intrigued by her words. "That is untrue, Taysinga, but free your mind of its guilt and shame."

"I am the one who broke your *kim*. I was ashamed and afraid after the Crow attack; I was angry and did not want to blame myself. I was jealous of your deeds. I lifted your spirit vessel to drop it but knew that was wrong. It slipped from my grasp before I could return it to its place. I feared to tell you or our *Tiva-Chu*, so I hid it behind others. I am sorry."

"Regim repaired it, so do not worry. I was also angry after Sumba's loss and spoke in cruel haste. You must forgive me."

"We will be friends from this sun until we join *Atah* in the stars. I will help you in any way you ask of me."

"You are good and kind, Taysinga, and I thank you."

Days later as the seasonal chores continued, Kionee offered to watch her cousin's two children while the anxious and weary mother tended her chores. "They wish to run and play, White Flower, and you have much to do. I will be their shadows until it is time for them to rest upon their mats. Little Weasel and Night Walker visit the Cheyenne to hear their stories and to learn tricks to battle the Crow with when we part from them."

"Thank you, Kionee, for they are restless and distract me this sun. I must work harder to teach them obedience and patience, for theirs are small." She wanted to say she feared her husband had forgotten his help was needed and he was too eager to learn of war and coups, but she dared not.

Yet, Kionee saw her frustrated expression and grasped the unspoken message. Since she had approached the woman, it was unnecessary for White Flower to use a talking-feather to ask permission to speak with her. As the mother gathered the active children and a few playthings, the *tiva* thoughts wandered. She felt pity for the young mother who had mated to Little Weasel at eighteen and must have discovered too late she had made a wrong choice. It was their law that only death or an evil deed broke a union, and the guilty were banished for life. Unlike most Hanueva men, her cousin was selfish and too proud to do any "woman's work" in any season. Kionee had observed him using skinny reasons not to do so, even when White Flower was ill or too busy. She guided the five-year-old boy and his three-year-old sister to the grass on the edge of their camp. She sat down to observe them while they raced about chasing a deerskin ball stuffed with buffalo hair. She wished she was watching her children, hers and Stalking Wolf's, but that joy was impossible. In misery and longing, she stroked Maja's neck for comfort. The silver wolf licked Kionee's hand and rubbed his ears in her palm as if he sensed her anguish and need for solace.

The children came to sit before Kionee and rest from their exertions. She smiled at the sweaty and dirty youngsters. "Your throats must be dry. Do you want water?" Both nodded in eagerness. She gave them drinks from the bag she had brought along, as the air was warm today.

"Are you a great hunter and fighter like my father?" Weasel Boy asked.

Kionee assumed her cousin had boasted of his prowess to them. "I am a good hunter and guardian, but a man must know when to battle and when to return home without challenging an enemy. It is wrong to war if truce can be made. Peace saves the lives of those we love, so we must seek it first and fight only to defend our lives and camp. A man is not weak and unworthy if he retreats from foes who are larger and stronger. With hunting, a man must not take more animals than his family needs and he must not slay any creature he does not use for food and garments and tipis. No woman," Kionee said to Weasel Girl with a smile, "should pick more berries or plants than her family can eat. *Atah* and our laws tell us it is bad to waste His creations, and there are others to be fed and clothed. If we gather all of one animal or plant, there will be no seeds to grow more in seasons to come, and Hanuevas will not survive."

"Father says we can take what we need from the Crow. They are bad and must be punished. We must not be afraid and run when they raid us. Will he fight them when he rides from camp? Will he kill many Crow?"

Kionee was stunned and alarmed by the things Little Weasel was telling his susceptible and trusting son. She guessed the child's defiance came from his mother telling him to walk a path of peace and self-sufficiency when his father was telling him it was braver and easier to ride a trail of theft and coups. She wondered if her cousin's parents and her grandparents knew about this. Surely Four Deer, Swift Fingers, Long Elk, and Yellowtail would not allow such things to continue if they were aware of the problem. Since their grandparents lived with his parents, they might not know. Perhaps she should whisper into her father's ears so he could enlighten his brother and father. She must be cunning as she did not want more trouble between her and Little Weasel.

"*Atah* and our laws say it is wrong to take from others, even enemies," Kionee said. "The Creator gave us skills and wits to do our own work, not force others to do it for us; that is lazy and unworthy of an Hanueva. There are good bands of Crow; we cannot punish and harm all of them to hurt those few who are bad. They are strong and many, Weasel Boy, to challenge them to war before we try to make peace or try to trick them out of our path is dangerous and foolish; many Hanueva would die or be captured. There are many good things about the Crow, but they are unlike us. It is best to remain separated and alive. Men who wish to raid and fight like the bad Crow seek out those bands who like to do the same, not those who have no hunger for killing and stealing."

Several older boys and girls came to the area and enticed the children to join them in a hoop-and-stick game. Kionee watched them until Weasel Boy, who was losing and getting annoyed, suggested a mock battle, with some of them playing Bird Warriors. Since it was time to eat and nap, she gathered Little Weasel's children and took them to their mother. The boy did not want to stop playing or to go to sleep. Kionee was relieved when Four Deer and Swift Fingers arrived in time to give White Flower needed assistance with discipline. She accepted the mother's gratitude and left.

The Cheyenne braves gathered early one morning and left on a second hunt, while the Hanuevas stayed behind to complete their tasks from the first one. From messages sent to camp, the large herd which their scouts had sighted was farther away after the last chase, so the men expected to be gone for several days, unless the buffalo changed directions. The last report said the animals had halted and were grazing contentedly, as if they awaited what was to come. The Cheyenne women and captives who were to butcher and transport the meat home were told to follow them later; they also planned to spend a night or two on the grasslands. Their children would be tended by aging parents, grandparents, older siblings, or trusted captives during the mothers' absences. Some would be cared for by female friends who could not go along because they were too heavy with child or were nursing babies.

As Kionee observed the scenes, she gathered information about her lover's people. She was happy to see how they helped each other in times of need. She was also pleased to learn that their captives were treated with kindness and that most accepted their altered fates. She could not imagine such an existence, but it seemed a way of life with other tribes.

She had not even glimpsed Stalking Wolf since his visit six suns past. It was frustrating to know he was nearby, but out of reach and view.

She knelt by the circle of rocks to make a fire for her mother. She grasped two sticks and placed sand on one. Amidst a small bed of dried grass, she rolled the second stick between her palms with fast movements until it created sparks and made a tiny flame. She fanned it until the dried buffalo chip caught fire. When that one was burning, she added others.

Just as she completed her task, a shadow fell over her. She looked up and saw a smiling Night Walker. She wished her mother and sisters were nearby, but they were gathering more chips in parfleches and fetching water in bags.

"You work hard and long and good, Kionee. No other . . . matches your skills on the hunt, in the battle, or in camp."

She nearly flinched as she saw his ravenous gaze devouring her and heard the husky tone of his voice. She guessed he had almost called her a woman, but she pretended not to notice. "Thank you, my friend and brother."

The chief's youngest son lowered himself to one knee. He propped an elbow on his thigh and watched her. "It is good you know much about women's chores and help your mother and sisters with them."

"It is our way to lighten the burdens of others."

"You would not need much training to become a mate and mother."

She focused a strange and reproving gaze on him. "I do not need such training; I am a *tiva*."

"One season that could change."

"Only if *Atah* wills it, and He does not do so."

"What if the Creator speaks to you but you refuse to listen?"

She looked at him as if he had lost his wits or insulted her. "He has not done so, and He will not. I am needed in my rank."

"Another could do it for you, one who is skilled and desires you."

"I hope there is no man among our tribe who hungers for me, for I cannot feed him the food he craves. It is not in my heart or head. I pray if such a man lives among us, he will not speak of such unwanted things to me. I do not wish to injure his feelings or pride with a refusal."

"Are you certain there is no pursuer you would not think to turn away?"

"Yes. I am a *tiva* and I will remain a *tiva* until I breathe no more." She knew she had made her voice and expression harsh and firm to silence him. She watched him shrug, grin, and drop the matter.

"I go to ride with Little Weasel. We scout for enemies and shoot pronghorn not far away where they graze. Will you come with us?"

"I have work to keep me here, but I thank you. Ask Taysinga to go. He sees you as the greatest hunter and protector among our people. He also thinks there is no Cheyenne or Crow with prowess to match yours. He seeks to learn much from you about hunting and fighting. You can speak while you ride. It would be a good deed for you to help him."

"If it pleases you, I will ride and talk with your *tiva* brother."

"It would please me and Taysinga. Thank you."

Night Walker stood, stared down at her a moment, then left. Kionee sighed in relief of his departure.

Later, as Strong Rock's family worked during the afternoon, Martay edged close to Kionee. She said in a low voice no one could overhear, "Night Walker is a skilled hunter and fighter of high rank. I see a glow in his eyes this season when he looks at my son. I think he will seek you in joining after we leave the grasslands." When Kionee gaped at her, Martay smiled and coaxed, "Do not fear, my child; that is good. To join with our chief's son is a great honor. It will please Night Walker, Bear's Head, and our people for two of such high ranks to join. It will bring happiness to your father and mother, for a union will remove you from the path of peril on the hunt and in the battle. You can become a female again; you can have love, children, a tipi, and a mate. Our people need more children to make us larger and stronger, for our enemies grow bolder. One sun, Night Walker could be our chief. Others will not understand why you dishonor such a great man who is worthy of you and who meets our laws to leave the *tiva* rank. He rode as our son on the journey to the plains. We love, respect, and trust him. We will live in your tipi while he provides for us and protects us. I will have my lost daughter returned. We will work together again as we did before you took your vows and left me. That moon was hard for me, Kionee, for my selfish heart loved you above your sisters. They will be gone soon, joined to mates and with their own tipis and families. You need not speak of your thoughts and feelings this day, but think on my words and this good deed." Martay rose and left before her firstborn could argue the matter.

Kionee stared after her mother in astonishment and distress. She wondered if Martay spoke the entire truth or if her parent feared she would take off with Stalking Wolf if she refused Night Walker. Dread and fear washed over her as she felt the trap tighten around her. She could not accept Night Walker for a mate, and she did not know how Stalking Wolf would react to such an event if she were compelled somehow to consent.

It was midnight when Maja slipped inside the tipi and nudged Kionee awake. The entry flap had been left tied back for air to enter and then leave through the top opening. The silver wolf placed his mouth around her wrist in a gentle grip and tugged on it. Kionee suspected something was wrong. Without disturbing the others, she took a bow and quiver and a knife from her tipi-of-power and followed him.

Soon she discovered what Maja had sighted or smelled as he roamed the area for a last time: two Crow warriors were sneaking into the partially deserted Cheyenne camp. It was as if they had spied and knew most of the braves and many women were away on the hunt, and the others were slumbering on their mats. She wondered why they did not steal horses and possessions near the edge of the many circles, then surmised the daring enemies' target from the direction they took. With caution, she and Maja hurried forward. The two Crow seemed to travel alone.

Kionee and the wolf reached Big Hump's tipi just after the last Crow ducked and vanished inside. After discarding her bow and quiver and drawing her knife, she entered without making any noise. In the remaining firelight, she saw one with his blade lifted, ready to slay the chief as he slept, while the other was searching through the leader's possessions with his back also to her. She feared there was not enough time to reach the defenseless man before a fatal blow was struck; and the moment she revealed her presence, both would attack her. Yet, she knew she must try to save Stalking Wolf's grandfather, his adopted father, even if it cost her her life.

"No!" she shouted in their language, causing both of the armed and experienced warriors to whirl and notice her. *Two against one,* her keen mind warned as they charged her with weapons brandished.

16

AJA BOUNDED THROUGH the opening and leapt upon one attacker, seizing an armed wrist with powerful jaws and disabling it before Kionee could be hurt. The growling animal clamped down tighter, despite the rain of blows to his body and head. Finally letting go, Maja snapped at the man's flailing arms, bare belly, and legs; as he did so, his strong mandibles inflicted many gashes which spewed blood. He began to nip at the man's chin and chest in an attempt to reach his throat.

The silver wolf's sudden appearance and the Crow's yelps of pain and terror caused the second man to be distracted long enough for Kionee to prepare for his impending assault. He came at her in a crouched position, holding the blade point toward her. She made certain her weapon's grip was secure and held herself loose for quick and easy movement. She knew it would require skill, cunning, and careful timing to best him. The man grinned to intimidate her and slashed at her, but she dodged his strike.

The Crow hurled himself at his smaller opponent, sidestepped, and slashed out again. He noticed the trick did not cause the *tiva* to stumble off balance or react with reckless abandon. His eyes brightened with respect for the masked challenger, whose prowess he had misjudged. He knew he did not have time to outwit or wear down the other fighter. He went closer and raised his arm, hoping his rival's gaze would follow the weapon while he slammed a fist into a vulnerable belly. His ploy failed and he received a stunning wound as the Hanueva ducked, surged forward with speed and agility, and sliced his side in passing.

Kionee watched the enemy whirl and glare at her. She heard the growls and scuffles and yells of Maja's fierce battle, but did not dare a look to ensure her beloved creature was unhurt. She knew Big Hump had awakened and was calling out for help amidst the noise. She could hardly believe it when the Crow stormed at her and knocked her backward, for it cost him another injury on his arm. He snatched up the bundle of Four Sacred Arrows his friend had dropped and jumped through the entry hole. She raced after him, pausing only long enough to recover her bow and quiver outside. She yanked out an arrow and continued the chase. Without missing a step, she nocked it and fired. As the shaft left the bow, a drumbeat warned of peril and rousted the sleepers. She heard her target yell out in pain and watched him hit the ground.

Kionee rushed to where he had fallen and knew a blow from her knife was not necessary; he was dead. Big Hump and Maja joined her as people left their tipis to check on the commotion. She looked up at the elderly man who was staring at them in amazement. She reached for the bundle, then withdrew her hand. "Do you wish me to not touch them?" she asked. "They are sacred to you."

"He who saves them is worthy to touch them" was the reply.

Kionee picked up the bundle and returned it to their Keeper, who clutched it against his bare chest with reverence and joy. She stroked Maja's head with her fingertips. Without his help, she would not be alive; nor would the man before her; something the chief also understood.

Big Hump shouted to the onlookers, "The danger is past. I am safe. Morning Light lives. Our enemies did not escape with our Sacred Arrows."

The drumming ceased, and more Cheyenne observers arrived. People from her band hurried to the location, awakened and drawn by the noise. Night Walker, Little Weasel, and Red Bull were among them.

"You are Kionee and Maja of the Hanueva, friends and companions of my adopted son. Stalking Wolf told me of the skilled masked warrior and his cunning animal helper. I am honored you camp with us. Your coups are many and your courage is great."

The ever-enlarging crowd parted for Medicine Eyes to approach. Her family, Bear's Head, Spotted Owl, Regim, Goes Ahead, Taysinga, Runs Fast, and other Hanuevas merged with the group during the chief's words.

With a look and in a tone of gratitude and esteem, Big Hump revealed, "This *tiva* and his wolf saved the life of your chief and saved our Sacred Arrows. Two Crow are dead, one in my tipi, both by their hands and skills."

The shaman lifted his hands skyward and said, "The sacred vision is fulfilled: this Hanueva has done a glorious, brave, and generous deed for us. This is why *Maheoo* told us to protect them. After our hunters and women return, we must have a feast and sing the coups of Kionee and Maja."

"It is so," many Cheyenne agreed aloud.

"Tell us how you did this deed," Medicine Eyes said.

After Kionee complied in their language, Big Hump ordered his braves who were present to place more guards around both camps. "Other Crow may raid or attack while our number is small," he explained. These were cunning, for they sneaked past those watching us."

"It will be done, my chief," responded the man in charge,

who felt shame and weakness at allowing such a dangerous incident to occur.

Medicine Eyes sensed the man's torment and said in a gentle tone, "You are not dishonored, Sharp Lance; lift your eyes in pride. This deed was in the hands of *Maheoo*. When the Crow do not return in victory, their tribe will know we are strong and alert and should not be challenged foolishly. It will make others slow to come. The Great Spirit chose Kionee and Maja for this honor and His will must not be questioned."

"We must go to our mats and sleep," Big Hump said in dismissal. "We will feast and honor our two friends after our people return."

The chief thanked Kionee again and stroked Maja's head after she told the animal his touch was a friendly one. He carried the precious bundle back to his tipi. The Cheyenne returned to their tipis, and the Hanueva walked to their camp.

After receiving praise from many of her people, Kionee accompanied her family toward their dwelling, with Night Walker close by. She had to repeat the tale for them, and they commended her courage and skills.

"You risk your life too many times, Kionee," Night Walker rebuked. "We do not want to lose you to death."

Without even glancing at him, she said, "I can follow no path except the one *Atah* makes for me. If He did not want me to save the Cheyenne chief, He would not have shown the enemies to Maja or sent Maja to guide me to that peril."

"You should not walk into danger alone and outnumbered."

Kionee was fatigued, and annoyed. If he had been the victor tonight, she fumed, he would feel differently. "There was no time to summon others, and Maja was at my side," she snapped. "We are skilled fighters, and we have proven ourselves in past battles with greater numbers of enemies. It is the duty of a guardian to protect others, with his life if *Atah* so wills it. If *you* had sighted the Crow, you would have gone alone."

"My son is tired," Martay told Night Walker. "He must rest.

Speak to him again on the new sun when his head is clear and he is calm."

For the first time in her life, Kionee almost had to bite her tongue to keep from scolding her mother for daring to make an excuse for her behavior. When Martay looked at her as if to say, You should not do that to him, Kionee narrowed her gaze in warning and stared at the woman for a moment without smiling, then quickened her pace to reach home. She put away her weapons and stretched out on her mat. When her family arrived, she rolled to her side away from them and closed her eyes to let them know not to disturb her. She called forth images of Stalking Wolf to comfort her until she could become a captive of slumber and lovely dreams.

When Kionee's pattern of breathing told Strong Rock she was asleep, he whispered a reprimand to Martay, "Do not ever speak to our son before others in such an angry way. It is shameful and wrong."

"*Kionee* should not speak with sharp tongue to the son of our chief. Have you not guessed he desires our child as a woman? After the last hunt, he will come to ask for her in joining. Our law says it can be done. She will be freed of her rank and will face no more dangers which can take her from us."

Strong Rock noticed Martay used "she" many times and that . troubled him. "That does not change what you did this moon. Kionee is no longer a child to be punished with words or deeds. He is our hunter and guardian. Since I can no longer do my duty, our son took my place as the leader of our family. No woman speaks to a family leader as you did. And, you spoke to Night Walker without asking permission."

"I am sorry, Strong Rock, but I forgot my talking-feather in our rush to leave. I acted without thinking out of shame for Kionee's actions."

"You also forget Kionee was tired and tense from a death battle. You must ask our son's forgiveness when light returns and you must not do these bad things again. Now, tell me of Night Walker's desire for Kionee."

Martay related her speculations and observations about the young man's feelings and intentions, and confessed that she had spoken of all this to their child.

"You must not mention anything to Kionee again about leaving his rank, even to join to a chief's son or to protect his life. Do not fill his head with confusion. Do not blind him to *Atah's* will with your desires to regain a daughter or to pull him from a perilous trail. That is for the Creator to choose and for Kionee to agree. Do you wish her to join to Night Walker if she does not feel love and passion for him as we do for each other?"

Martay dared not mention her suspicions about Kionee and Stalking Wolf, for she had no proof she was right. Even if she was, that did not mean the warrior could lure their child away from them. She prayed she was wrong, as breaking their law would endanger Kionee's life. Whether or not Kionee was guilty of wrongdoing, Martay knew she could not bring about Kionee's exposure and punishment, for she loved her daughter. Too, they needed the Cheyenne people's protection for survival during the hunt; to accuse the adopted son of the Strong Heart chief of trying to ensnare their child would be an insult that could break their bond. Perhaps, Martay excused her behavior, those fears were why she was pushing Kionee toward the safety of Night Walker's arms.

After a patient Strong Rock asked his question again, Martay said, "No. I only wish for our child to be safe in the perilous suns ahead. As Night Walker's mate, that would be true. He would be a good son to us."

"Kionee's happiness is more important, Martay. Our son has given up much to take care of us. He has earned many deeds of courage and generosity for his sash. If Night Walker does not catch his eye and heart, he cannot become a woman again to join to him to please you. That is fair and that is our law."

Martay realized her mate had forgotten or had discarded his

> 222 <

previous concerns about Kionee and Stalking Wolf, and she should do the same. She should rely on her trust in and love for Kionee to convince her not to worry. "You are right, Strong Rock. I will speak no more about it."

"That is good. We must sleep now, for there is work on the new sun."

Kionee, who had been listening silently, smiled to herself in joy and relief at her father's words. She had feared her mother would convince him to help persuade her to join with Night Walker. Now, she told herself, she could relax and sleep in peace. But a new worry came to her: Had Martay hesitated to answer Strong Rock's last question because she suspected something had happened between Kionee and Stalking Wolf? Kionee cautioned herself to do and say nothing to increase her mother's concerns. Exhausted, she slept at last.

Two days later, the Cheyenne hunting party returned and was told the astonishing news about the Crow raid.

Stalking Wolf yearned to rush to Kionee's side to make certain she was safe and unharmed. But he could not. With one rash move, he reasoned, he could destroy the truce between them, an alliance needed for his love's and her people's survival. He told himself he would see her soon at the feast. *If tivas are allowed to come,* his mind shouted in anger. *How,* his heart argued, *can they refuse when she is to be honored? Help unite us as one, Great Spirit, for she is my destiny and I love her.*

The moment Stalking Wolf craved arrived when the Hanuevas reached the edge of their camp and the *tivas* were with them, wearing their ceremonial masks and best garments. He struggled against the almost overpowering urge to go speak with

Kionee, but warned himself he must not approach the group which sat down together near a large campfire as directed by his shaman. He watched the rest of her tribe take places to the *tivas'* left. As everyone was getting settled, he calmed a little when he sensed Kionee's sly gaze on him. Without looking at the source of his desire, he smiled and nodded his awareness.

On the other side of the large fire sat the Cheyenne chief, council of forty-four, and the society leaders. Behind them were the warriors and braves, followed by women and children.

As the last rays of daylight touched the grasslands, Medicine Eyes stood in the center of the enormous circle of people and began the event. He lifted the ceremonial buffalo skull and asked for the Great Spirit's guidance and protection and thanked their creator for life, successes on the first two hunts, and divine intervention during the Crow attack.

Kionee watched with interest as the shaman prayed and chanted; sometimes his words were clear and other times they were like mere sounds. His expression and tone were solemn; his mood, reverent and respectful. His face and hands were lined by weather and aged and his flowing mane was more gray than black. His brown eyes beneath thick brows wore small white clouds. There was a slight bend to his back and rounding of his shoulders. The fringes on his shirtsleeves swayed from his movements. It was evident he was loved, esteemed, and trusted by his people.

Kionee allowed her gaze to roam the Strong Heart band with its seasoned warriors. She saw Stalking Wolf with the Dog-Men, the largest and most powerful and respected society. As were those near him, he was clad in their chosen regalia: red-striped leggings, eagle-bone whistle around his neck, and a striking headdress, which was made of four tailfeathers from a golden eagle. Those from hawk and crow filled its sides; and all feathers stood erect and were attached to a beaded band. The Dog-Men held ceremonial rattles and their faces and torsos were painted red. Most of them were bare-chested; a few had donned buckskin shirts with hairlocks, evincing the fact they had performed heroic deeds for their tribe. Some wore beaded bands around their upper arms or on their wrists. So many warriors clad in their finest garments or different regalias was an awesome sight. It made her glad they were allies.

Big Hump stood after Medicine Eyes took a seat on a willow mat. He called Kionee forward to join him. He handed his rescuer an eagle feather with two red dots painted on one side. "It is a coup feather; it says you killed two enemies in hand battle at great risk to your life. Wear it with pride on your headband when you remove your ceremonial mask. For saving my life and our Sacred Arrows, I give you a captive to help with your work. I will call them forward and you will choose the one you want."

Kionee picked her words with care so she would not insult him and his tribe. "I thank you, Big Hump, but it is not the Hanueva way to have captives. *Atah* commanded us to be a people of peace and to fight only in defense. Please keep her as my gift to you for your protection of my people."

Stalking Wolf had explained the customs and ways of the Hanueva to him, so Big Hump did not take offense at the refusal. "It will be so. I also give you ten buffalo hides, tanned by my mates. I give you this necklace which says you are a friend to Big Hump and the Strong Hearts. Our tribes will be bonded forever in friendship. Your people are invited to live close to mine near the forest of the Medicine Bow wood, out of the Bird Warriors' reach and under our shadow of protection."

"You are kind and good and generous, Big Hump, but my people must return to the land where the Creator-High Guardian placed us. That is where He told us to live in the cold seasons. We honor your friendship."

"If danger comes, summon the Strong Hearts to help you."

"We will do so, and we thank you."

Kionee and Big Hump returned to their places. Five Stars and three other men entered the circle to reenact the Crow attack and to chant Kionee's coup. The next chief played Kionee's part, two played the Crow raiders, and one donned a wolf pelt to perform Maja's role. Everyone watched with interest and pleasure as the "enemies" were defeated again.

Kionee was filled with elation and surprise to be so honored. She looked at her parents and smiled, for they were gazing at her with deep emotions tugging at their hearts. From the corners of her eyes, she saw Night Walker's gaze on her, too, but she refused to return it. She wished she could enjoy this special event sitting beside Stalking Wolf. She feared to even glance at him and allow a softened expression to betray her true feelings. They were so close in distance and so far apart in many ways.

When the men finished, Kionee nodded her appreciation to them. The feast ensued, and she concentrated on eating and talking with friends. She tensed when she noticed the chief's grandsons heading toward her. She struggled for poise when they stopped before her. Five Stars presented her with a beaded wristlet and a hairpipe choker. Stalking Wolf gave her a sienna shirt with beaded designs, in her size.

"These are gifts to thank you for saving the life of our father and chief and for saving our Sacred Arrows," the youngest man said.

"I thank you, my friends and allies," she responded.

"Enjoy the feast and tell us if you have need of anything."

"Thank you, Stalking Wolf, but I have more than I can eat and drink. My heart is so filled with happiness, speaking is hard."

The two Cheyenne nodded in understanding and left.

It was a strain for Kionee to keep her gaze and thoughts off her secret lover. He appeared so wild and sensual tonight in his society regalia. The red paint on his face did not hide his good looks; nor did the covering of it on his torso mask his virile physique. He moved and held himself with an undeniable air of self-confidence, pride, and control. There was no doubt he was a man of abundant skills and courage. To think of never kissing, touching, holding, viewing, and surrendering to him again was torment.

Kionee was relieved when Red Bull, Leaning Tree, and Runs Fast came to visit with her, distracting her from anguish and yearnings. The remainder of the evening passed in swiftness and in resignation to her fate. When the time came, she gathered the gifts and returned to Strong Rock's tipi and a lonely sleeping mat.

The next three days were consumed by many chores; including preparations for Blue Bird's tipi. Kionee had given the ten hides from Big Hump to her sister to add to the number required, nearly complete now. Cooking, fetching water, tending horses, and gathering fuel were daily tasks.

During those busy days, Kionee noticed how often Shining Star visited them and guarded the women during chores away from camp. He could not seem to keep his gaze off Moon Child, who had blossomed like a flower since winter departed and she became seventeen. The same was true for her youngest sister: the girl appeared to be in love with the hunter who would reach twenty circles of the seasons soon. It was clear to Kionee that the man would be playing the flute for her sister before they left the plains or shortly afterward.

It made Kionee miserable to see both of her sisters nearing a joining sun when she was older than them and could not do so. They both seemed so happy and playful, and with good cause. Kionee tried not to resent their joy and or to become bitter over her lack of it, but it was difficult not to do so at times. On occasion, she found herself wishing one of them was the oldest daughter and had her rank. Then she would realize even that would not change her problem: Stalking Wolf was simply not of her tribe.

The following day, Kionee was given a chance for diversion. She and others were asked to fetch wood from the Medicine Bow forest: a two-day ride there, a day's work, and two days' travel to return. The wood was needed before the next hunt to make more stakes for drying racks, pegs for tanning hides, shafts for arrows, and replacement poles for their travois. While there, they would collect various herbs and arnica for food and medicine.

Kionee mounted Tuka and left camp with Maja and another horse which was dragging a travois for her load. Red Bull, Goes Ahead, Leaning Tree, Gray Fox, and Yar went with her. They also brought their travois, food, water, sleeping mats, and weapons. They headed across the expanse of flats and knolls as wind raced through the grass and billowy white clouds.

They used a tall peak in the forest of the medicine bows as a landmark, as it could be sighted in clear weather for many days' ride from most directions. A dense timberline of pine, fir, spruce, and aspens covered the ridges and foothills. Mountain mahogany was located there, a fine wood for making bows and for use in healing rituals; it was the source of the site's name. At the range's feet grew many other kinds of trees and bushes. Grassland with abundant wildflowers, sage, and rabbitbrush walked to its base. Amidst the verdant forest were glacier-carved ravines, sparkling lakes, and rushing waters. The area was filled with birds and animals. Beaver and other water creatures were plentiful in rivers and streams for obtaining meat and pelts.

The mountains almost appeared to be a dark bluish color as the party approached its destination. On occasion, the riders sighted small gatherings of buffalo which were grazing near or dust-wallowing in prairie-dog villages. The large beasts seemed unconcerned about their distant presence, but the furry dogs fled down their holes after some barked warnings. Burrowing owls did the same after clacking their beaks and hissing like rattlesnakes. Buntings, longspurs, and meadowlarks took flight. Hawks soared overhead and sent out shrill cries as they threatened invaders to leave their territories.

The Hanuevas found a narrow and shallow spot to cross the river, then entered the foothills. Soon they halted to set up camp. Afterward, they ate and slept, as their task would begin early the following morning.

Kionee looked up from her work and could not believe that her gaze encountered her lover standing nearby and motioning for her to sneak away and meet with him! She furtively glanced at her friends to make certain they had not sighted Stalking Wolf. Dare she slip away, she mused, and join him for a few blissful moments? To go was taking a big risk, one larger than the unenlightened warrior could imagine. She looked at the place where she had glimpsed him; he was gone, hiding. The choice was: Be safe and denied, or risk danger and be happy.

17

KIONEE REASONED SHE COULD steal a few precious moments with him without getting caught. She told the others she was going to take care of private needs and left the work party. Maja walked beside her as she hurried deeper into the dense forest until Stalking Wolf stepped into view and grinned. "Guard, Maja," she commanded in a soft voice and rushed from the wolf into the warrior's beckoning arms.

"I had to touch you, feel your lips on mine, hold you," he whispered.

Her gaze devoured his face and smile. "The same is true for me."

"I love you, Kionee, and keeping distance from you is hard."

"It is torment, for I love you and need you close."

The elated couple hid behind a section of trees and thick bushes, in the unlikely event someone came looking for Kionee. They kissed deeply as their hands roamed in reckless abandon.

Kionee did not mind the rough bark which pressed into her back as she leaned against a pine to steady her shaky knees. It was not discomforting enough to distract her from this dream come true. It had been so long—too long—since they had touched and kissed, had privacy to show their feelings. With Maja on guard, she yielded to him and this blissful moment, ignoring the lethal threat of exposure which loomed over her head.

Stalking Wolf's arms slipped with gentle purpose around Kionee. He nestled his cheek against her hair and felt her braid press into it. He held her close as he thanked the Great Spirit for bringing her to him. He could not imagine his existence without her.

They kissed, embraced, and caressed in heady pleasure. That was all they had intended to do until fiery passion burned away any resistance. They gazed into each other's glowing eyes and admitted they craved and needed more. They nodded messages of eager surrender. They wanted to move slowly, but a shortage of time did not permit leisure today. They could not even remove their garments.

Kionee eased her breechclout over its front loop and let it fall between her legs; Stalking Wolf did the same with his. They kissed and embraced again with the bare flesh below their waists in stimulating contact. His aroused manhood brushed against her softness and they delighted in that glorious sensation. He fondled her breasts and stroked their points through the snug band around them as his mouth explored hers.

Kionee experienced a flood of desire. The only thing which would feel better was if his lips and fingers were touching her naked skin. In leaps of joy and delight, her hunger for what was to come mounted with haste and urgency. She trembled when he nibbled her lobe and hot air entered her ear. She leaned her head back to give him more room to roam her neck from side to side, and moved one foot to allow his eager hands to move ever lower.

Stalking Wolf's mouth sought hers again and plundered it in a feverish pace. He found it exciting to kindle her beyond will or thoughts of grim reality. Her hands teased over his chest and back beneath his shirt, and he savored her touch. Her lips replied to every signal he sent to her. He gazed into her glowing eyes, so full of love and desire for him that it caused his breath to catch in his throat and his pulse to quicken. His fingers below became bolder as they prepared her for his entry. He dared not speak more tender words which might be carried too far in the quiet forest where only birds sang and squirrels chattered.

Kionee smiled and pressed kisses to his nose, cheeks, and chin. His strong hands grasped her hips and he lifted her so he could join their bodies. She gazed into his hungry tawny eyes before he rested his golden brown head on her chest as he held her in place and thrust within her. She clung to him and savored his masterful thrusts in exhilarating bliss. The rough bark could not bite into her buttocks, as the trailing breechclout protected them. The same was true for the shirt on her back. Even if she had been naked and the tree was clawing her raw, she would not care. Perhaps, she thought for an instant, fear of discovery and their cunning boldness made their lovemaking more intense and sensual, more gratifying.

Stalking Wolf could barely maintain his control. The fire within him blazed higher and hotter. His muscles rippled as he drove onward and upward in his quest to sate them. When the mutual moment arrived he raised his head and kissed her to prevent cries of rapturous fulfillment which would lead to exposure. After she calmed, he held her tightly.

They kissed and hugged as a rush of tenderness washed over and between them. They gazed into each other's eyes and smiled, their moods and expressions speaking words their lips could not.

Stalking Wolf lowered her feet to the ground. He recovered his water bag and a soft pelt from nearby, as White Cloud awaited him at a safe and hidden distance. He let her wash away any signs and scents of their forbidden union, then he did the same. He adjusted his breechclout while she replaced hers. He kissed Kionee again, caressed her painted cheek, and let his fervent gaze speak of his love for her. His happy smile faded as he signaled he must leave.

Kionee smiled, stroked his jawline, and nodded agreement. She watched him vanish into the trees before she went to join Maja and then the others in her party. She was aglow with love, happiness, and contentment. She warned herself to conceal those suspicious emotions. She stroked the silver wolf's head and mouthed a thank-you for his guard and understanding. She did not know how long she been away, but when she joined her friends, no one seemed suspicious. The huntress returned to her chores, fantasizing about Stalking Wolf as she worked.

On the fourth day following the wood party's return to camp, the third buffalo hunt for the Cheyenne and second for the Hanuevas took place. Once more, Kionee helped Taysinga with kills to complete honoring the promise to Sumba's family. Again, any abundance would be shared with others.

Kionee spotted a white buffalo almost hidden in trees on a creek bank. She knew the rare creature was considered good fortune, "big medicine." She shot it with arrows which were marked with Taysinga's symbols, making certain no observers were nearby: it was meant to be a secret gift to bring Taysinga honor and attention as the alleged slayer. She located the woman among the busy hunters and racing herd to reveal her deed. "It will bring you good luck with Night Walker and honor from our people," she told the astonished *tiva*, "Tell no one I took its life, for it carries your arrows."

Tears of gratitude dampened Taysinga's lashes and caused her eyes to sparkle. She swallowed hard to clear her throat and struggled not to weep in happiness.

Kionee smiled and said, "Words are not needed between friends. You must accept this gift to catch your love's eye and heart, and to show our people your honor and prowess have been returned by *Atah*." She related why she believed the white buffalo was meant for the other *tiva*.

"Your heart is good, Kionee. I pray *Atah* will grant any desire in you. Even if this does not bring Night Walker to me, I will never forget your kindness and generosity. Somehow, I will repay them."

"You owe me nothing but friendship, Taysinga."

"You have it and more, my respect and love and loyalty."

Upon return to camp, the Hanuevas crowded around Taysinga and praised her skills and good fortune. The *tivas* and shaman congratulated her and said it was a good sign, as was the fulfilling of her promises to Tall Eagle's wife and to Sumba's family. Almost everyone touched the white hide in admiration and respect, and many prayed for its departing spirit.

Night Walker examined it with envy, and extolled Taysinga for her success. He was stunned and pleased when she presented the hide to him as a gift for all he had taught her. At that moment the man suspected the *tiva* of having female feelings toward him. But he was a chief's son, could become the next leader if his and Gray Fox's fates changed. In such a rank, he should have the best woman in camp for his mate, and that was Kionee. He thanked Taysinga, accepted the gift, and took it to his tipi.

Kionee and Taysinga exchanged smiles and went to join their families.

The remaining number of hides Blue Bird needed for the impending couple's tipi had been obtained. Their tanning would begin the following morning. The girl could hardly contain her excitement and pleasure. She thanked her brother many times for his skills and gifts. In appreciation and affection, Blue Bird gave Kionee a browband she had beaded, one with wolf symbols.

The *tiva* accepted it with matching feeling, for it was not her sister's fault that Blue Bird could join when she could not.

Two days later, Kionee went to spend time in the *Haukau*, again relieved her blood flow had commenced.

While she was there, Martay, Blue Bird, Moon Child, and the two grandmothers—Fire Woman and Yellowtail—punched holes in the cured skins and sewed them together with strong sinew. Skilled in tanning, the mother and daughters had cured the more than twenty hides until they were soft, white, and waterproof. The tipi would be a strong and warm one. When the task was finished, it was rolled and stored until needed. Before the conical dwelling was pitched and the two young people could join and go to live in it, many pine poles would be cut, debarked, and rubbed smooth after their return home.

On the second day after she left the *Haukau*, Kionee and other Hanuevas were surprised by a nocturnal Crow raid on the edge of the Cheyenne camp. Guards were slain and many horses were led from the area in quiet stealth. Again, it was Maja who caught their scent upon the earth and found a slain man, then alerted Kionee. She trailed her pet to alarming clues, and saw the daring enemies before they were out of sight. She went to Big Hump's large tipi and awakened Stalking Wolf and Five Stars to report her findings.

Five Stars was placed in charge of security in case the raid was a trick to lure warriors away from camp. He promised Kionee if an attack occurred, the Hanueva people would be defended by members of their societies during her absence.

Several braves were chosen to form a rescue party while Kionee fetched her weapons. She awakened her father and told him the bad news so her family would not worry when they found her missing in the morning.

"Why must you go with them into danger?" Martay reasoned in fear.

"There is little light from the moon," Kionee began her explanation. "Maja is needed to follow their smell in near darkness, and he will obey only me. If we do not leave now, the Crow will reach their camp before we can overtake and defeat them."

"Kionee is right," Strong Rock said. "He must go. Do not be afraid, Martay, for he is a skilled fighter and he will have others with him for protection."

"Be careful, Kionee, and return alive and unharmed."

"I will do so, Mother, if that is *Atah*'s will."

"We will pray it is so," the frantic mother murmured.

"Do you summon other Hanuevas to ride with you?"

"No, Father, for we must hurry. The Cheyenne are skilled fighters who have battled Bird Warriors many times, so we need not risk the lives of our hunters and friends. Our tribe is small and needs no losses. Is that not true?"

"That is true and wise, my son."

"It is good and kind, my son," Martay added.

"Thank you, Father, Mother. You will see me again soon."

Kionee left and joined her lover and his party. With Maja leading the way, they followed the silver wolf across the grassy flats and hills beneath a sliver of moon. She was glad Night Walker and Little Weasel had left for several days to hunt and scout, as they could cause trouble on the trail. She knew the two men would resent missing the action and a chance to gain coups. She fastened her gaze to Maja's loping body as she wondered what challenges and perils lay ahead for them.

The next afternoon, the raiders and stolen horses were sighted not far ahead, galloping along at a steady pace. Neither party had halted to sleep, only to rest themselves and their mounts for short periods and to drink water from creeks they passed. Yet, progress had been slowed by the near darkness, a large sleeping buffalo herd in their path, a few snaking ravines, and several perilous prairie-dog villages. Though they were unaware of being pursued, the Crow had continued to move; so had the Cheyenne and Kionee. Maja's acute nose had sniffed out their tracks and the silver wolf had used his sharp vision to watch for dangers.

During the chase, the Cheyenne praised the creature many times for alerting them to unseen hazards and for guiding them around unfamiliar locations. They were amazed that a wild animal had accepted and lived with a person. They noticed his loyalty and obedience to Kionee, who had found him injured and tended him back to health. It was clear the creature loved Kionee, and the hunter loved him. They knew, too, from word passed through their camp that he could not be touched by others unless Kionee commanded it. Since Maja had helped save their chief and Sacred Arrows, no one bothered him, not even the children. Most just watched him in awe, respect, and gratitude.

"They see us and run!" Sharp Lance shouted to his friends.

"Look, they part," Fire Dancer added. "Five go straight and one turns toward the sacred hills where the sun rises."

"It is Hawate-Ishte!" Stalking Wolf exclaimed as he saw the man's patch and the enormous eye on the enemy's shield. "Go after the horses, my friends; we will capture or slay their leader."

"Perhaps he leads you into a trap," Three Arrows worried aloud.

"He is the one who will be snared," Stalking Wolf replied. "They did not know we would see them taking coups from our camp in the shadow of darkness and follow. They have no war party waiting to attack us. Do not allow any to escape and boast of their deed, or tell of spying on our camp. If others learn of

Maja and White Cloud from One-Eye, they will know we tricked them in the canyon of winds near the old Hanueva camp."

"We will slay his party and recover our horses."

"That is a good plan, Brave Badger. We will meet you in our camp. Come, Kionee and Maja; we go to make challenge and trick his people."

Rides The Wind led the other four warriors northward in swift pursuit of their targets while Stalking Wolf, Kionee, and the silver wolf traveled northeastward after the enemy.

Hawate-Ishte rode toward Lodgepole Creek. He did not halt for darkness, as there was a certain place he wanted to set his trap for those following him, those who had tricked him twice. He knew Stalking Wolf, the masked warrior, and silver wolf were trailing him. First, he plotted, he had to place an arrow of death in the ferocious animal so it could not attack him or help them. With haste, he would wound the *tiva*. Then he would take the life and possessions of the Cheyenne who had escaped his knife. Afterward, he would cut out the *tiva*'s heart while it still beat and remove the colorful skin from his face and hand. He would eat the heart to take its big magic and sew the dried skins to his shield to give him great power and medicine in battle. He would add hairlocks from both heads to his shield and shirt, and he would wear the wolf pelt as a robe this coming winter. When his tribe saw his skills and power, he would take his chief's rank.

At dawn, Stalking Wolf warned wearily, "We must be careful, Kionee, for One-Eye is cunning and daring. He will seek a place where he has the advantage before he halts to challenge us."

"He knows who we are and what we have done. He is eager

to slay us. Why do we not trick him?" Kionee suggested, and related her plan.

"It is a good and clever one, my love," Stalking Wolf praised when she had finished.

Kionee apologized to Tuka for riding him so fast and hard. She thanked him for obeying her and praised his skills and strength. She gave him water in a cupped hand, then left him to graze in silence while she and Maja sat on a knoll and watched for their enemy. She, like Tuka, was fatigued from two nights and almost two days of exertions. She had to struggle to stay awake and alert, and did so with Maja's help.

At last, she saw One-Eye coming toward them. Concealed by bushes, she knew he could not see her or glimpse the pinto behind the hill. She hoped he would not suspect them of separating and galloping around him in a wide circle to lay in wait for him. When she saw him pause and gaze over his shoulder, her hope came true. She was relieved they had guessed his eventual location with accuracy, for he had continued to ride in the same direction. With luck and *Atah*'s help, Stalking Wolf should be hidden behind the hill ten tall tree lengths from her position.

Suddenly her lover topped the other hill and shouted to their enemy, "Hawate-Ishte, Stalking Wolf challenges you to a death battle! Do you fear to fight me? Is that why you run from me?"

The Crow warrior reined in his horse and gaped at the unexpected sight. His mount's forelegs reared slightly and his back legs dug into the earth when his master yanked on his bridle. The warrior grabbed an arrow and nocked it, then glanced around for his challenger's masked companion and the ghostly wolf.

Kionee and Maja remained in their positions, so the warrior would not panic and flee in fear of being outnumbered. She noticed he was dressed in plain garments and wore no adornments on his body or in his hair; nor had he decorated his buckskin-colored horse. Those precautions were no doubt taken for his raid on the Cheyenne camp.

Stalking Wolf laughed and taunted, "You fear to fight me face-to-face? You fear my skills and courage are larger than yours? You are weak and worthless."

"You seek to trick me again. Where are your companions?"

"They were tired in mind and body and returned to camp. Stalking Wolf will not halt his chase until One-Eye fights him."

Kionee kept her armed bow ready to fire if Hawate-Ishte attempted to do so. Maja was poised to race toward the enemy and distract him. Both were determined that Stalking Wolf would not be harmed.

"Where is the wolf who rides with you?" One-Eye demanded.

"He is the companion of the *tiva* and travels only with him."

"They tricked me two times! They are cunning but foolish. When you are dead, I will find them and slay them."

"After our fight, Crow dog, you will be dead and seek no one to slay."

"If the battle will be fair, between us, I will fight you."

"You have the word of Stalking Wolf and I will honor it. Drop your bow to the ground and ride toward me. I will do the same."

The warriors met halfway, and dismounted. Both held sharp knives in their hands. They glared at each other as each checked his opponent for strengths and weaknesses. Their gazes sent forth insults and dares. Both were fatigued, not at their best. They moved in a circle, careful not to trip one foot over the other.

Stalking Wolf halted, crouched, and bored his tawny gaze into Hawate-Ishte's dark-brown one. He glanced at the patch and grinned, for he assumed that disability gave him an advantage. He began to move again, stepping to his right, as Hawate-

Ishte's lost eye was on the man's left. Stalking Wolf leapt toward the enemy with the agility of a puma.

Hawate-Ishte reacted in haste, but not fast enough to avoid a slice to his left arm in passing. He whirled to face his cunning foe. He stormed forward, waving his knife in rapidly slashing motions and causing the Cheyenne to hurry backward and almost stumble. He sent forth cold, harsh, and confident laughter to unnerve the man. When that ploy failed, he tried another one to unsettle the Cheyenne. "Do you run from me like a scared rabbit from the eagle's talons?" He used his wiggling fingers to summon his cautious opponent closer. "Come, fight me, weakling, if you have the prowess to do so."

Stalking Wolf charged the man, deflected a blow, and slammed his lowered shoulder into Hawate-Ishte's chest. One-Eye was thrown to the grass, but he did a quick and nimble roll-over and bounded to his feet. As he did so, Stalking Wolf pursued and kicked at the hand holding a weapon, but One-Eye held on tight to it. The Cheyenne flung himself upon the unsteady man, and both hit the ground. They tumbled, scuffled, kicked, and pounded with hard fists. Sweat poured from their bodies. Dirt and grass clung to their hair and wet flesh and stained their garments.

Kionee stood to see better. Her heart pounded in trepidation. Her mouth and lips went dry. Her gaze was fixed to the fierce confrontation. She could not allow her lover to be slain, so she lifted her bow in readiness. Yet, she held to her difficult position, having promised Stalking Wolf she would not intrude on his challenge. To do so would make it appear as if she doubted his ability to win.

Maja's muscles were taut with the strain of controlling the urge to race to the scene to help his friend. He would attack the instant Kionee's signal was given, or before it if one seemed too slow in coming to save his friend.

Hawate-Ishte straddled Stalking Wolf and raised his knife to plunge it into the man's heart. The Cheyenne imprisoned his enemy's right wrist between his hands. The Crow used his left hand to give his right one more strength to lower the deadly blade. The sharp point came closer and closer to Stalking Wolf's chest, almost provoking Kionee and Maja to rescue him. The Cheyenne arched his back and thrust upward with force, sending the Crow toppling over his head. Stalking Wolf scrambled to his hands and knees, then stood.

Hawate-Ishte had done the same. In bent positions, they hurled themselves at each other. Their muscles bulged, their armed hands cramped from gripping knives so long and tight. Stalking Wolf nicked the man's shoulder, and avoided a slash to his side in the process. As they bumped and struggled, Stalking Wolf's deft fingers ripped off the patch covering Hawute-Ishte's eye and he gazed into an empty socket. Reflexively, the Crow's left hand darted upward to cover the gaping hole and his right one lowered a little; that action slowed Hawate-Ishte long enough for Stalking Wolf to defeat him and take his life.

"Hawate-Ishte took the lives of Big Hump's daughter and her white-skinned mate," the Crow taunted with his last breaths. "They were my first coups. He is the one who stole my eye. If they had not hidden you, Stalking Wolf would be dead . . . or he would be my adopted son." He extended a bloody arm skyward. "Hear me, *Isaahkawuattee*, I come to join you. Punish the mixed-blood who slayed Your creation."

Stalking Wolf gaped at the dead man in silent shock at his words. He cut off the medicine pouch around Hawate-Ishte's neck and dumped its contents on the man's stomach. Among them was a lock of blond hair secured by a narrow thong. He saw a gold circle with a strange tie on it. Without a doubt, Hawate-Ishte was the one who had slain his parents.

"Are you harmed?" Kionee asked in worry as she knelt beside him, for he had not risen and his expression was odd.

Stalking Wolf shook his head. He related what the Crow had told him and what he had found. He lifted the hairlock and watched sun brighten its yellow shade. He clutched it in his hand, closed his eyes, and said, "Adam Stone and Morning Flower are avenged. The visions of Stalking Wolf and Medicine Eyes have come to pass. There is only one part of the vision which remains: I am to take a mate this season. I have found the woman I love and desire. Our joining will come to pass before winter covers our land."

Kionee placed a trembling hand on his arm and tried to clear his head of false hopes, though it pained her deeply to do so. "That is your destiny, Stalking Wolf, but it is not mine. I was chosen to help you fulfill it but not become a part of your life. I do not see how we can join; I wish it was not true with all my heart, but too much stands between us."

"The trail will be cleared for us by *Maheoo*, He you call *Atah*. He crossed our paths. He gave us the same spirit sign. He gave us love and desire for each other. We have fulfilled His sacred messages to me and to our shaman; He will reward us."

"I am not Cheyenne, not one of *Maheoo's* people. I cannot leave my rank and duty until *Atah* changes my destiny. He has not done so."

"He will," Stalking Wolf murmured with confidence.

"Do not allow your belief in the visions and your desire for me to cause you to say or do anything to expose us," Kionee warned. "If you hope discovery will change matters for us, it will not and many will suffer. Swear to me you will not trample a law you do not understand and accept, as I would not trample you. To do so is selfish and wrong; it will bring great harm to me, my family, and my people."

"I will guard our secret," he vowed.

"Do so and you will not injure my trust and love." *Or imperil me.*

"We must go trick the Crow and return to our camp," he said to alter their line of thought and to end their tormenting words. He gathered the items he wanted before loading Hawate-Ishte's body onto the man's horse.

"I have all we need to trick them," Kionee assured him. "But first, we must eat and sleep."

"I know where we will camp until the sun rises. Come, my love. We will lie together before we challenge Swift Crane's band."

Kionee was eager to join with him, as they would look into the face of death again soon.

18

A S MAJA GUARDED THEIR privacy and their enemy's body from nocturnal scavengers, Kionee and Stalking Wolf surrendered to their soaring passions, rejoicing in the absolute wonder of their love.

Kionee felt the sleek strands of his golden-brown hair as she twirled them around her fingers. She wished she could look into his tawny gaze, but the moon did not yield enough light. Yet, her mind's eye could envision his features, and her fingers and lips could roam them with ardor. She relished his slow kisses and seductive caresses. Of their own volition, her arms looped around his neck and drew his mouth closer and tighter to hers. There was not a spot on her that did not burn or quiver with longing and pleasure. She cherished this man with all of her heart and soul. She could think of no thrill greater than being his lover. She responded to the signal from his nudging hand to part her thighs so he could tease and tantalize her very core. She moaned in rapture as his finger slipped within her, delving, thrusting, moistening her. This time, he continued until rhythmic spasms of ecstasy assailed her. She moaned and thrashed and drew every drop of splendor from that new experience.

Stalking Wolf brushed his fingers over her rib cage and traveled the curves and planes of her pliant body. She was caressing his shoulders, arms, and back with feather-light but highly arousing gestures. He ached to bury himself inside her, but he did not want to rush as he had been forced to do so the last time. His fingers dove into the shiny and thick waves of her black hair, and reveled in the freedom from their braided bonds. Her lips brushed kisses over his neck, throat, and face while he did the same with hers. He loved feeling her naked flesh next to his, and it made him wild to have nothing between them. His mouth captured her breast and claimed its nipple. He kissed, teethed, and brought it to full attention.

Kionee savored the magic of his deft tongue and hands. Another blast of searing heat stormed her body, one so potent and demanding and swift that it astonished her. She felt the hardness and erotic heat of his desire against her hip. "Come to me, my love," she coaxed.

Stalking Wolf moved atop her, the force of his weight controlled. She wrapped her arms around his back and pulled him close. His mouth melded as he slid the tip of his manhood into her, paused a moment to draw a deep and needed breath for renewed restraint, then thrust further and deeper until he was totally concealed by her soft, wet heat.

Kionee trailed her fingers over his back. She felt the muscles in his firm buttocks contracting and relaxing with each thrust. It was as if she were staked naked beneath a blazing sun and it was burning her to willing ashes. She matched his pace and pattern, clinging to him, almost ravishing his mouth, refusing to allow him to withdraw for any distance or any length of time.

Stalking Wolf's ravenous appetite for her heightened as she welcomed him deeper and deeper into her honeyed core. Nothing could have seized his attention at that moment, so enrapt was he by her and their wild joining.

A landslide of pleasure tumbled over them and carried the couple away as they found their release. Their greedy mouths and hands continued to send sweet messages of satisfaction, happiness, and serenity to each other. They remained cuddled for a long time; both knew that precious moments like these were few and far between. Finally, exhausted and sated, they slept.

Kionee took a position atop a high hill. She was clad in the regalia of a spirit warrior and sitting astride White Cloud, who was adorned with sacred symbols and items. Maja stood beside them on stiff alert. On her other side was the horse of Hawate-Ishte, his body lying across its back. There was just enough daylight left for her to be seen. She shouted, *"Apsalooke!"* several times to seize the Crows' attention.

It did not take long for the Crow band to gather at the base of the hill, where she halted them with commands and signs in their language. Some had snatched up burning torches to help them see in the darkness which was trying to blanket the land. She heard the murmurs of *"Tset-acu-tsi-cikyata"* and *"Chia cheete"*: "The-Wolf-Mask-Wearer" and "Silver wolf." She prayed they would be too frightened or awed to doubt and attack her. If so, she and Maja would discard the trick and flee.

"I bring you the body of Hawate-Ishte." She watched their expressions and movements closely for any hint of a challenge. "Hawate-Ishte *daase xawiia.*" She explained how One-Eye's "heart" was "bad" and how he had disobeyed Old Man Coyote's warnings. "Do not attack Hanueva; *Iichihkbaahile* and His spirits protect them. I was sent to Hawate-Ishte two times to give him the Creator's messages. He broke his word and raided the Hanueva again. He is dead and punished; those who followed him are dead and punished. All who defy *Iichihkbaahile* will be punished, too. Other Crow bands accept the words of the

Creator; the band of Swift Crane defies them. That is wrong and dangerous; it will destroy you."

She pointed northward and said, *"Dee asshiia Bahkashua Aashkaate,"* telling them to leave this place and to go camp on Cottonwood Creek. "Do not ride away from the cold wind direction to raid and kill Hanuevas. If you do so, the Creator will hide the buffalo from your eyes and skills; He will destroy the sacred tobacco plants; He will turn his face from you. Hawate-Ishte is gone; let his evil die with him; let no other follow his bad trail and ways." She smacked the enemy's horse on the rump and sent it trotting down the incline and into the crowd. She watched braves capture its bridle and stare at the lifeless body.

Kionee motioned to the camp and said, "Hawate-Ishte *ash-taale alaxiia."* She had glimpsed the smoke and knew One-Eye's tipi was burning. As prearranged, Stalking Wolf had set it ablaze as an intimidation. When everyone turned to look in that direction, she and Maja slipped over the hill and out of sight, leaving no tracks because of the furry pelts that were tied to the horse's hooves and wolf's feet.

As they hurried into the shadows which had closed in, her ears caught shouts of *"Bilee!"*: "Fire!" She had assumed with accuracy the tribe would race to save its camp, unaware only one man's tipi was being destroyed. Her love's clever distraction gave her and Maja time to escape. They headed for the location where Stalking Wolf was to join them.

Kionee was relieved they did not have to wait long to learn he had gotten away without being seen. She listened as he revealed how he had removed sleeping children without awakening them before torching the tipi. She was happy he did not feel a need to punish the man's family.

"A storm comes soon," Stalking Wolf observed. "We must hurry to be out of its path. It will cover any tracks we make. The Crow will believe the storm is a bad sign, a warning meant to push them from this place. After we move our tipis, our camps will be far apart. They should not raid us again during the hunt."

"That brings happiness to my heart, Stalking Wolf."

"You bring happiness to my heart, my love."

"As you do to mine," she responded before they kissed and embraced.

They loaded their belongings and rode as fast as the light permitted with Maja scouting for them. They did not halt to sleep until they were a safe distance from the storm-drenched enemy camp. They cuddled together on one mat, sharing kisses and caresses. They yearned to yield to their searing passions but felt it was not the time or place. A violent storm often spooked buffalo or antelope and caused them to stampede, so they had to remain clothed and ready to react to such a peril.

Kionee, Stalking Wolf, and Maja reached camp at dusk on the eighth night after their hasty departure. He related the news of One-Eye's defeat, the man's guilt for slaying his parents, and how they had tricked Swift Crane's band into moving farther northward. He held up Hawate-Ishte's eye patch and shield for his family and friends to view. An enemy warrior of great prowess and high rank, the taking of such possessions and the man's defeat were great coups. The rest of the Cheyenne party had returned days ago with the stolen horses, the Crows' mounts, and the enemies' weapons. A celebration was planned for that night to honor the seven victors and Maja and to chant their recent coups.

Big Hump told Stalking Wolf the necklace he had found in One-Eye's medicine pouch had belonged to Adam Stone's mother and had been given to Morning Flower when they joined. He showed the young man how to open it to view the paintings of his white grandparents and his father.

Stalking Wolf held the locket with reverence as he studied

the image of the man he could not remember, a father taken from him when he was two. He perceived the mixture of strength and gentleness in Adam's face. He wished there was a painting of his mother, too, but she had been described to him many times by her mother. Morning Flower was said to resemble her. He gazed at the image of his white grandparents and was glad to learn of their appearances at last. He clutched the necklace and hairlock in his hands and knew he would always treasure these keepsakes of his lost family, and would cherish the woman who had helped him recover them.

During the feast while the party's coups were being chanted and their tales related once more, Kionee furtively observed Night Walker and Little Weasel. She sensed their anger and jealousy at being excluded from such glorious adventures and at being denied a chance to gather coups. Kionee could imagine how such behavior affected her persistent pursuer and envious cousin.

The following morning, as prearranged between the two chiefs, the mates of Big Hump and Bear's Head struck their tipis. That was the signal it was time to move their camps to another location, one fifty miles westward where the buffalo were heading to new grazing grounds. The leaders' tipi poles were removed and their hide coverings snaked to the ground. The rest of the women dismantled their conical dwellings and packed them on travois. They loaded the remainder of their belongings and mounted their horses.

With the Hanueva, elders and pregnant women were always given horses to ride if the travois were too full to hold them, even if a male or *tiva* had to loan one a mount. The only animals never ridden or used for hauling possessions were the buffalo horses, for they were too vital to survival to risk injuries. Babies traveled in cradleboards on their mothers' backs. Small children rode with a parent or sitting upon the travois, but older children walked. Everyone had an assigned position and kept it.

In a short time, the second journey was under way as the noisy and steady procession spread out on the vast plains.

As the group camped for the second night, Kionee visited with Fire Woman. She realized her maternal grandmother would join *Atah* soon, as Fire Woman grew frailer with the passing of each season. She told herself she should not grieve over that natural event, as the woman's spirit would become one of the sparkling stars which brightened and filled the night sky. Yet, she was saddened by the reality of how much she could have shared with and learned from her grandmother if she had lived as a female and they had worked together as her mother and sisters often did. As she glanced at the darkening sky, she recalled that one of the stars to appear soon belonged to her third sister, who had died while she was in *tiva* training. She wondered why the Creator had taken a young girl to live with Him, but *Atah*'s will was not to be doubted or questioned. She gave her grandmother two soft rabbit skins with which to line her moccasins for the winter. The elderly woman stroked and admired them before thanking her.

Regim, "son" of Fire Woman and "brother" to Martay, joined them after fetching water. She asked the young *tiva* to go with her to get her horses where they grazed a short distance away. When they reached the animals, Regim patted one's neck as she said, "We have not talked alone since I repaired your *kim*. Does your female spirit roam free or did it return to its vessel as it should?"

Kionee stared at her aunt, astonished and worried by the unexpected query. "It would serve no purpose for it to escape, for there is no man among our tribe who summons it to him with my willingness."

"What of Stalking Wolf? You have spent many suns and moons with him. Does he still cause your body to flame and your wits to cloud?"

"Even if that were true, he is forbidden, out of my reach."

"It pleases me you see and accept that truth. I wish you did not have to suffer from this harsh test of your strength and loyalty to your vows. *Atah* will soon release you from their pain, for He does not give us burdens too heavy to bear. He crossed your paths so great deeds could come to pass and our people could survive. After all things are as He desires them to be, He will part them again and all will be as it was before you met the Cheyenne. Be strong and patient, and be true to your rank. *Atah* will bring you honor and contentment and He will reward you for your many sacrifices."

Reward me by stealing Stalking Wolf from my arms and returning me to a lonely and miserable existence? I will never be as I was before he entered my life, for he and his love have changed me forever. "Do not fear, for I will walk the path *Atah* marks for me." *I have no choice.*

"That is good and brave, Kionee. My love and respect for you are enormous."

It is not "good and brave," Regim; it is the hardest trail I have ridden and the most perilous and wounding battle I have fought. You do not know how it torments me to win it, but I know I must. "I go to visit Long Elk and Yellowtail before they sleep. Do you wish to go with me?"

Regim shook her head. "I have tasks to do. Come to me if you have need to speak of things others should not hear or learn. My ears and heart remain open to you always."

"I will do so, my leader and friend. Thank you for your kindness and worry." Kionee left to spend time with her paternal grandparents, for they also were advanced in age and would soon live among the shiny stars.

After five days on the move, the second camp was set up near several water sources and a safe distance from a large herd of buffalo. Chores and rest consumed that day and the following one.

The eighth morning of the journey, the fourth hunt for the Cheyenne and third for the Hanueva occurred. They took much meat and hides, but lost the oldest son of Chief Bear's Head. The body of Gray Fox was hauled to camp across his horse, after an enraged bull had unseated him from behind and trampled the man to death.

The Hanueva gathered to mourn their loss and to bury Gray Fox beside trees near a creek bank, for the use of scaffolds was not their custom. Big Hump sent words of sorrow through a short visit by Five Stars, but his people stayed away to give the other tribe privacy to grieve.

Kionee did not like the gleam she witnessed in Night Walker's eyes as he gazed at his older brother's dirt mound or the look he focused on her afterward. The man who was now in line to become their next chief soon approached her.

"Come with me to walk and speak," he whispered.

She did not glance at him as she said, "I have many tasks to do."

"Come, or I will say words aloud others should not hear."

Kionee was stunned by his near demand, though he smiled and his tone was gentle as he spoke it. She had no choice except to go with him to a place where they could not be overheard but where they would remain within sight of others to prevent shame.

As he gazed across seemingly boundless grasslands, he murmured, "My brother is with *Atah* in the stars and I will become our next chief."

Kionee knew the obvious fact he stated, and dreaded the motive behind it. There would be no vote for who would take Bear's Head's place, for it was their custom for the oldest son to do so. Only if a chief did not have a son or have one old enough to take his position after death or an injury was a vote taken to select another man and to pass the honor to another family.

She responded to Night Walker when he did not continue. "That is true. To survive to lead and protect our people, you must be careful on the hunt," she cautioned. "You also must avoid battles with the Crow which could bring your death or a disabling injury like my father's."

Night Walker turned to face her and smiled. "Your words are wise, and the same ones entered my head as we covered my brother with Mother Earth's blanket. I will take no risk with the Bird Warriors. My prowess is known to all, so I do not need Crow coups to prove it to them or to others. For my children and people to live, we must be a tribe of peace."

Kionee suspected he was not being honest. How, she mused, could a man change his thoughts and feelings so quickly? Did he only seek to deceive her with words? She pretended to believe him. "That is true and wise, Night Walker. I am pleased your wits have unclouded and you now accept the value of peace."

"A leader cannot think of himself first; his people's needs must rise above his own desires. I must prepare to become our chief, for Father could join *Atah* as swiftly as my brother did. I must choose a woman, join with her, and give her seeds to grow the chief who will walk after me. The highest ranking woman of our tribe is the best choice for a leader's mate. Only the *Tiva-Chu'* skills match yours, but Regim is too old to bear children and cannot be considered. Kionee and Night Walker will make great leaders."

She looked at him, like the last time, as if he had lost his wits. "I am a *tiva;* a Hunter-Guardian, son of Strong Rock and Martay. You must not approach me in such a manner."

"If your *kim* is broken, you can become a woman again, as

you were meant to be. I can fulfill our laws to free you from your rank."

"With Gray Fox gone, you must become the Hunter-Protector for your parents. You have many skills and much courage, Night Walker, but you cannot be the provider and defender for three families. You must choose a female who will not bring her parents to your tipi to add to your duties." She silently apologized to Taysinga for making that desperate excuse, for it might also exclude the other *tiva* from consideration.

"I will be the Hunter-Protector for our family and for your parents, and I will do so for my parents when needed. Have you forgotten: our people show their gratitude, love, and respect for past chiefs by providing their needs and protecting them?"

Yes, that reality had eluded her panicked mind. She sought another path to discourage him. "To be Hunter-Protector for even two families is a hefty task for a man who also bears the rank and duties of a chief."

"By the time I step from the shadow of Bear's Head to stand before him, I will have sons to help me hunt, and to fight if necessary."

Her heart pounded as she reasoned, "Even if your mate bore a son before the next buffalo hunt, he would be too young to help hunt and fight when your father gives up his rank and you take his place. What if you have only daughters as my mother and those of other *tivas* did?"

"My seeds are strong enough to make sons."

Kionee looked insulted. "Do you say *tivas* come from weaker seeds?"

"No, but *Atah* will bless me with sons, for I have been true to Him."

She sent him an expression of annoyance, one which did not have to be faked following his arrogant words. "Do you say those who have no sons were not blessed because they were weak or false?"

"That is not my meaning, Kionee. I saw my sons in a dream."

"Our people do not follow dreams unless they are sent to our shaman from *Atah,* so your dream means nothing but what you desire. Do not ask me to join with you, for I cannot. I look upon you as a friend and brother, not as one to be desired as a man."

"If I but hold you in my arms and put my lips to yours only once, I can change your thoughts and feelings for me."

Kionee observed the sparkle of desire in his eyes. "No, Night Walker, you cannot, for we are like brothers. I have no woman's feelings for you, and you do not possess the power or magic to create them within me. I am a *tiva,* and I will remain a *tiva.* I do not seek to wound your pride and heart, but I must speak the truth. Ask another who will and can accept your offer. Taysinga is of high rank: she has taken many buffalo this season; she has fulfilled her vows to the families of Tall Eagle and Sumba; she has slain a white buffalo and given its hide to you. Perhaps those are signs from *Atah* she is a worthy mate for a chief, for you."

"Do you say Taysinga desires me as a man?"

Kionee witnessed his surprise at her bold suggestion. "I cannot speak for her, but I believe it is true. She is a good match for you. She would do all you ask of her to make you proud and happy. Her female spirit is strong and it craves freedom. Without her paints and male garments, I have seen no female in our tribe who has greater beauty of face and body," Kionee asserted, knowing that stretched the truth very little. "She would please you greatly in all ways."

"You say this to turn my eyes and heart from you. Kionee wastes time and words, for she is my choice. You have always been my choice; that is why I waited for you to approach freedom. After the last buffalo hunt, I will come to you for your answer. Until that sun, think much on the great honor I offer you. If you come to me, I will use my wits and rank as chief to end the *tiva* custom. With more women free to become mates and mothers, our tribe will grow larger and stronger. We can make new laws and customs to help parents without sons. Do this worthy deed for your people by becoming the mate of their chief and the mother of their next chief. I will speak no more of such things until after we chase the provider-of-life for a last time this season." Night Walker smiled, turned, and walked back to his father's tipi.

Kionee felt trapped in a whirlwind. She was being pulled between two men, two different roles in life. Stalking Wolf offered love, passion, respect, excitement, and protection—but he was out of her reach. Night Walker offered her the chance to have a mate, her own tipi, children, honor from her family and people, safety from perils on the hunt and in battle, and the rank of being a chief's wife. She admitted that Night Walker could be the hunter and protector of their family and her parents with one hand bound behind his back, so great were his skills; and he was within her reach if she agreed. But she suspected his feelings leaned more to lust and control and obtaining a woman of high rank as his seed-grower than they leaned toward love and passion and equality.

Yes, she reasoned, it would be an honor and joy to bear a child who would become their chief and leader. Perhaps even bear other children who would hold high positions, perhaps even a warrior who saved their tribe from total destruction. Her children also would bear other children to help her people survive. And there was a chance he would keep his promise to help strike down the *tiva* law so future daughters would not have to become "sons" and endure the anguish and denial she was experiencing. Could she make a final and binding sacrifice of herself in order to help other unfortunate women? Though Night Walker was handsome and virile, could she ever surrender to him in fiery passion and total abandonment as she had done with Stalking Wolf? Was it possible to learn to love and desire someone? She did not think so.

Kionee's heart felt crushed in a tight grip. She had to stop hoping, even praying, for release. She had two choices: remain a *tiva* for life and be unfulfilled as a woman, or join to Night Walker.

The only way she could have Stalking Wolf was to defy all she was to share his destiny. If she escaped into his arms, they would be forced to leave this territory to save her life, and probably his—if any man or group had the ability to capture and slay him. Would Stalking Wolf give up his whole existence to have her? Was she worth that much to him? She could not ask him that question without revealing her grim jeopardy, and she hated to let him learn how many times he had imperiled her. Also, her escape would endanger the needed alliance between their tribes.

Kionee wanted to weep uncontrollably for the first time in her life. Agony ripped through her body like the sharp claws of a grizzly. Arrows of anguish, dipped in bitterness, pierced her heart. A sensation of utter hopelessness captured her soul. Was her brief time with Stalking Wolf over forever? Could Night Walker be her true destiny, whether or not she loved him? Had *Atah* sent her a message, a command, in Gray Fox's death that she was refusing to hear? If she chose to join their next chief, she was convinced Stalking Wolf would not expose or harm her in any way; but he would be hurt deeply and painfully. A bitter betrayal of one side or the other was a certainty, she admitted in torment, but of which one?

19

MANY DAYS HAD PASSED since Kionee's intimidating talk with Night Walker. The warrior kept his distance but always seemed to be watching her. She prayed no one noticed his interest in her. As promised, Stalking Wolf kept away from her and the Hanueva camp. She longed to see him but knew it was perilous to seek him out. She hungered for his kiss and touch; her body ached to join with his.

She kept busy with chores, but her troubled mind was elsewhere. That disobedient part of her persisted in chasing dreams while she struggled to remind it of the futility and the agony those thoughts inspired. Yet, it was difficult not to think of love and passion when Runs Fast and Blue Bird could not conceal theirs. The same was true for her younger sister: Moon Child and Shining Star were spending much time together and sharing looks of love and desire. The joyous couples made her yearn for what they possessed.

Kionee told herself she had faced the harsh reality she could not have the man she loved. Either she could remain a *tiva* for life or she could join to Night Walker to help her people. She worried over what would happen to her parents if she were injured or slain; she knew Night Walker would be obligated to remain the Hunter-Protector for them. Could she give Strong Rock and Martay that security at such a great sacrifice? She had been taught and trained not to think of or to yield to her wants and needs, only to be a captive to those of others. But must that role be a lifelong burden? Was there no time and in no way her feelings could come first for a change?

There was another factor to consider: who would do the female chores after her sisters were gone if her mother fell sick or when she became old and frail? If she chose to remain a "man" and either of those events occurred, Kionee could not do both the female's and male's roles for her family. Was it selfish and wrong, she pondered, to want only Stalking Wolf or no man, when joining to Night Walker would bring joy and help to her parents and others? Also, if she became his mate, she could help keep peace by discouraging him from seeking war and obtaining coups. If she rejected him, Kionee feared he might be influenced to act in a destructive manner.

There also was the possibility Night Walker could expose his desire for her and make his quest for her known to their tribe. That would make her refusal harder for others to understand and could cast suspicions on her and Stalking Wolf as the reason she rejected Night Walker. Whatever decision she made, it could not come while her head was clouded by confusion and her heart was suffering in anguish over her true love's loss.

Kionee made a visit to the *Haukau*. Again, the blood flow and her sensitive breasts pointed out she was a female, one who wanted children, one who could have them only with Night Walker or with another Hanueva male. Yet, no other appealed to her; nor did her pursuer, only the Cheyenne beyond her reach.

For several days after her return, a series of violent thunder-storms with downpours of blinding rain and streaks of brilliant lightning assailed the plains and forced everyone to take refuge inside their tipis. Outside chores were delayed. The hunt was put off until they ceased.

When the weather cleared, scouts reported bad news: the storms had frightened and stampeded the large herd to a loca-tion three days' travel northeast. That distance was too far for easy hunting and travois trips to haul meat and hides back to camp, so another move was necessary. Other scouts were sent to check on the new location for Swift Crane's Crow band to make certain the Cheyenne and Hanueva would not halt too close to it.

While that party was gone, Bear's Head and Big Hump gave the signal to dismantle their tipis again, as they must follow the buffalo herd.

Their third camp was set up within distant view of tall and majestic buttes. Despite the late-summer heat, wildflowers and grass were plentiful after nourishing rains. The herd had settled down to graze in contentment a half-day's ride beyond them and near another prairie-dog village, the type of site which they favored. They ate and drank, dust-wallowed, tended their off-spring, and romped in ignorance of the impending fates of many of the huge beasts: to become meals, garments, shelters, and more for the nomadic Indians.

Near the camp, water for drinking, bathing, and other needs was abundant in creeks and catch-basins. Countless buffalo chips provided ample fuel for cook fires and for drying some cuts of meat. Roots, bulbs, tubers, corms, leaves, flowers, and stems offered themselves as other sources of food. The sky was clear and blue, and a gentle breeze wafted through the verdant ground covering. Everyone liked the favorable site, which would be their last for this season. Everyone, except for Kionee and Stalking Wolf, who dreaded the end of summer and the necessary parting which would come with it. Both still prayed the Creator would find a way to let them join; but both feared nothing would change for them. If only they could see each other on occasion, their pains of denial would be lessened during those arduous days and nights when they were so close in proximity and yet so far apart.

The Cheyenne left on their fifth and final hunt. There was no need for Hanuevas to go, as they had sufficient meat and hides for winter. Yet, the small tribe stayed near the larger one for safety—among other reasons while completing its tasks. There were things they needed to gather in this area before they left the plains to return to their winter campground.

As Kionee did her chores or stood guard for women doing theirs, she wondered if it was only wishful imagination or if Night Walker was watching Taysinga closely during this busy time. Few things would please or calm her more than for the two hunters to fall in love and join. She whispered words of encouragement into the older female's ears, who was thrilled to hear them.

"How can I pull him toward me when I live and look as a man?" Taysinga wondered.

"He knows you and all *tivas* are females. Tell no one, not even Night Walker, I heard him say he believes the *tiva* custom should be cast aside, for we are needed as mates and mothers to make our tribe larger and stronger. There is no better match for him among us than you are, my friend. He has taken no mate, for he will accept only the best female among us; this season, you have proven your rank is high and your skills are great."

"I have done so only with your help and good heart, Kionee."

"But no one knows that secret, so the honor is yours. We must never reveal it to others. If only there was a sly way he could view your face and body, he would desire you. He would play the flute for you and ride you behind him many times during our coming journey."

Taysinga glanced around to make certain no one was approaching. "How can I show him the woman beneath my mask and garments without getting caught and punished?" she asked.

"I do not know yet, but I will think of a clever way to do so without you taking risks. You must do the same, for my wits may fail me. Do you have the strength and courage to do anything to win him?"

"Yes. But what if he does not like and desire what he views?"

"He will, Taysinga," Kionee said, confident of Night Walker's lust, and her own desperation to elude it.

Kionee's tension mounted every day as the moment for separation from her beloved grew closer. She decided to scout the buttes from which foes could spy on them or gather in for an attack. Swift Crane's band had not been a threat since the trick she and Stalking Wolf had played on them. But, she worried, what about defiant raiders from other bands? She left camp with Maja, and no one seemed to take notice of her departure.

She galloped toward the cluster of three mountains with flat summits and protruding bodies which were shaded like burnt ochre. Their odd shapes and sizes made them markers for travelers, as they could be seen for a long way as they rose above the mixture of flat and rolling terrain. She approached them with caution and looked for fresh tracks, but sighted none on this side. Maja sniffed the ground and discovered nothing suspicious. She dismounted to allow Tuka to rest before they checked the remainder of the area and headed back to camp.

"*Maheoo* shines with favor on us this sun, my love, for He guided you to me," a mellow voice said.

Kionee whirled and stared into the tender and glowing gaze of the man who consumed her thoughts and ruled her emotions. "Stalking Wolf! Why are you here? Why are you not hunting with the others?" How had he found her? What if somebody came and saw them together? Without being told, the astute Maja left them alone and went to guard their privacy.

"I made many kills and was returning to camp. I came to scout this place for enemies, but I saw you coming toward me. I hid so I would not frighten you away before you saw it was me. I watched behind you and no one trails you. If another comes, Maja will warn us."

Kionee smiled and raced into his open arms. She laughed with joy as he lifted her and swung her around in playful delight, her body held snugly against his. "*Ne-mehotatse*," she murmured her love for him after he lowered her feet to the grass.

"*Ne-xohose-neheseha*," he entreated her to say it again, his smile broad, his eyes sparkling, and his manhood aroused.

"I love you," she complied with honesty and desire. Her expression and tone shouted her sadness as she said, "We leave soon." She saw his sunny smile fade and his gaze dull. She felt his fingers on her forearms tighten for a moment.

"*Tonese?*"

"In fourteen to sixteen suns." She drew a deep and ragged breath before she reminded, "We can say and do nothing to help us be together until the Creator-High Guardian clears the path for us to join."

Stalking Wolf felt as if his heart skipped a beat. "What if He does not?"

Kionee lowered her misty gaze and murmured, "That is the only way we can be together."

The troubled warrior cupped her jawline and lifted her head to lock their gazes. "You are mine, my love; I cannot lose you."

"I belong first to *Atah*, then, to my family, my tribe, my laws, and my rank. I cannot betray them for selfish reasons, though I crave to do so. I could not live with that shame and anguish or burden you with them. How could we be happy if we destroyed many and much to grasp our love? How can we risk endangering the alliance between our tribes? We cannot, my love." She watched him conceal his anguish and dismay.

"It is true, but it knifes my heart. I cannot ask you to go against your beliefs and laws for me; if I did so and you obeyed, you would not be the special woman I love. You would not ask or expect such treachery and weakness from me, and I must not do so of you. For us to live in the light of Good, it must be with *Maheoo'* blessing and by His freeing you of your rank and duty, without imperiling our tribes' bond."

Kionee's eyes teared with gratitude and love for his understanding. She perceived how hard it was for him to say such things as it was different for women in his tribe. Cheyenne females and captives obeyed men and yielded to their wishes. She was glad and relieved he respected their differences.

Their lips fused in an intense, soul-stirring kiss. Each knew they had only a short time for one final and blazing bout of passion before they were parted. They knew it could be next summer before they saw and touched each other again, so this union might have to last them a long time.

With haste and eagerness, they joined in an almost desperation to seize every pleasure possible in such a short span. They reached ecstasy's pinnacle, wavered there a brief spell, and plunged over its glorious edge with willing eagerness. Splendor captured and enthralled them until bleak reality returned.

Stalking Wolf stared into her eyes and said, "I love you, Kionee; you are my destiny, the air I breathe, the sun which warms me, the food which feeds my spirit, the water which sates my thirst. Use the power and magic of your name to blow back into my life and arms soon."

"You are those things to me, my heart. I will do all I can to come to you. Now, I must wash and go before I am missed," she said with reluctance.

He waited while she bathed, then resecured her garments. He held her and kissed her one last time before watching her ride away with Maja loping beside her. He murmured to himself, "Guard her for me, my friend and spirit sign, for she will become my mate, the mother of my son. Bring her to me before winter, *Maheoo*, or I will be forced to disobey and capture her."

In the days which ensued, Kionee protected her mother and sisters and other females as they gathered chokecherries, prickly pears, mariposa bulbs, goldenrod, bullberries, beeplant leaves, berries, other edible plants, and many herbs for flavorings. She shot six turkeys for meat and plucked certain feathers for arrow fletchings. She brought home four slain pronghorns and three deer for hides and food, and removed their teeth for use in adornments. As always, she shared any abundance with others and, in particular, with the elderly *tivas*.

Some afternoons after the sun lowered and the air cooled, she sat on a rush mat with a willow backrest while she sharpened existing weapons or made new ones to use for defense during the impending journey. Not a day or night passed that she did not realize it was one sun and moon closer to a parting force beyond her control to halt and beyond her skills to battle.

How, she fretted, could she turn and ride away from the man she loved, perhaps forever? Yet, how could she escape into his life without—*Do not think of such a painful event, for you cannot stop it from coming.*

The scouts returned to report that Swift Crane's band was camped far to the northeast. They told of how the enemy was being raided and challenged by the Crow's fierce rivals, the Oglala, known to Cheyenne as *Hotohkeso*, friends and powerful allies of the Strong Hearts.

It calmed the Hanuevas' lingering fears to learn all their aggressors' stamina must be used to battle the mighty Lakotas. Hanuevas delighted in the fact the Bird Warriors would have none left to focus on them.

The scouts also said that no other *Apsaalooke* bands were within sight of their travels, so both camps relaxed and concentrated on their tasks.

Days later, Stalking Wolf rode to where Taysinga was tending her horses away from the Hanueva camp. He stayed mounted as he cautioned, "I will point to where a herd of deer graze. You look that way and nod. Tell others that is what I came to tell you. We must speak swift as the arrow flies." He got to the matter occupying his every thought. "If I seek Kionee's heart, is there a way to remove the hand mark to protect the *tiva* secret for others?"

Taysinga was—and yet was not—stunned by the question. She allowed her gaze to follow the direction in which he pointed. "Those who left the rank after sons were born had them burned away with hot coals. After the place healed and old skin fell off, a scar hid it." She turned back to look into his imploring gaze. "Do you love and desire her?"

"That is true, but I will do nothing to bring her trouble and shame, and I will never betray your words to me. I will await until after the Great Spirit clears the path between us before I speak and act. Help me, Taysinga, for she has won my heart and eye."

The *tiva* wished there was something she could do or say to help him obtain his goal. There was nothing, and Taysinga told him so. "If you expose her as a female, she will face great peril, certain death," she warned. "The punishment for breaking her silence and vow is exile into the highest mountains during the coldest season. She must remain there alone, without weapons or other needs, for the span of three full moons. If she survives, she can return to camp to be forgiven and purified and her rank returned. If betrayal comes during the other seasons, no one can speak to her, she cannot meet with our council or with *tivas*, she cannot visit or hunt with friends, she must exist as unseen as the air, until deepest winter comes and her punishment and purification are done. Even Maja would be halted from helping her."

Stalking Wolf hoped his dismay did not show. He made it appear as if he was waiting for his horse to finish drinking from the creek before he left the location. "I cannot allow her to endure such danger and suffering."

"If Kionee commits treachery, Stalking Wolf, there is no choice for her to make, unless she escapes from our people in secret," Taysinga continued revealing the shocking details. "Her family would be left in dishonor, left in need and anguish. Kionee would not do that to them, for her heart is good. For you or anyone to intrude on a sacred rite is forbidden and perilous. If you did so, it would destroy the truce between the Hanueva and Cheyenne, and you would be viewed as an enemy. You and Kionee would be forced to flee to far away to elude my tribe's search. To stain the sacred visions of Stalking Wolf and Medicine Eyes which united us will anger and displease your father, shaman, people, and Great Spirit. To protect her and our bond, you must keep her secret and keep your distance from her. I am sorry I exposed her to you and fueled such futile love. I know these words cut into your heart, for I also live the pain of chasing one I cannot seem to catch while hiding my secret."

The warrior forced out a wide smile for anyone who might be observing them. "Our union will come to pass, Taysinga, for it also was in the visions of Stalking Wolf and Medicine Eyes. I do not know how or when, but Kionee will be released to become my mate. Do not fear punishment, for your words and deed are safe with me forever." He nodded to her and rode toward his camp. He wondered why Kionee had not revealed to him such dangers to herself. In ignorance, he had subjected her to many risks of exposure so they could steal moments together. From this sun onward, he must not do so again.

He thought the punishment practices were cruel, but that was the Hanueva way. He realized that some of his rites and customs no doubt seemed just as heinous to her tribe. The only escape was to steal Kionee and flee to another tribe and territory, but that, he reasoned, was not an acceptable or honorable solution to their problem. All he could do was wait for the Great Spirit to solve the matter for them. Now, he fully grasped why Kionee had said and felt their union was so hopeless.

Eight days later, Kionee left the tipi of Big Hump to prepare for her people's imminent departure. The Chief had sent Five Stars to summon her to thank her a last time for all she had done for him and his tribe. While concealed from the Hanuevas' view in the midst of Cheyenne tipis, Stalking Wolf halted her to speak for a moment, which was all the time they had left together. "I love you," she whispered in a rush. "My heart will yearn to see you on each sun and moon we are apart. I promise I will come to you as soon as *Atah* releases me from my rank and duty. If it is not while snow blankets the land, I will see you on the hunt during the next hot season."

"I love you, Kionee," he responded huskily, "and I will wait and pray for that sun to rise. Do and say nothing to endanger yourself. Our love is strong; it will be patient until we can be together; it will last forever, even beyond death."

"That is true. Now, I must go before someone comes to seek me; we ride soon. Tipis are being taken down and packed. Travois are being loaded. Horses are tended and ready. Until our eyes touch again, I love you."

Stalking Wolf watched her walk away from him and his heart thudded with heaviness. *Return her to my arms and life soon, Maheoo, and guard her from all harm while she is not within my reach and protection.*

Kionee felt his potent gaze upon her back. She missed him already. She was too aware of the possibility of never seeing him again, too aware of the enormous obstacles between them, too aware of what faced her in the days to come with Night Walker in hungry pursuit. She prayed that *Atah* would send his eyes to Taysinga and let love enter his heart for her.

Kionee glanced at the *Haukau*, which was being dismantled. It was a little beyond the time for another visit, one which her troubled body was delaying. As soon as it returned to normal, she would begin her flow, she reasoned.

Kionee joined her busy family, sent them feigned smiles to imply everything was fine, and did her tasks. Within a short period, she mounted Tuka, moved into her assigned position, and left her lover far behind.

20

THE HANUEVA TRIBE had traveled south for five days when they reached the large river where it bent southwest. They halted to camp on its bank near the forest of medicine bows. They would remain there long enough to rest from the plains' heat and their exertions and to gather needed things which grew in this area. Afterward, they would head northwestward to skirt the base of the mountains of the bighorn animals until they arrived at the mouth of the canyon of the river wind. There, they would journey through a large pass between two ranges to their destination near the hot springs.

At dusk when others were busy and distracted, Taysinga and Kionee put a daring plan into motion after the older *tiva* made a wild suggestion to which the younger agreed. Taysinga approached and asked Night Walker if he would guard the path toward a secluded spot where the two women were going to bathe and to repair their sweat-smudged masks.

"Kionee waits for me to join him at the river," Taysinga said, "but we need a strong and brave man to protect us from animals and enemies."

"Where is Maja?"

"Kionee said he hunts in the forest and will not return soon."

"I will watch the trail and guard you from any danger," Night Walker agreed.

"Thank you, Night Walker. There is no better hunter and defender among us."

"Your words are kind and they please me, Taysinga."

"I will go and tend my tasks, unafraid with you nearby."

Taysinga hurried to the place where Kionee sat on the bank with her bare feet in the cooling water. She stripped off her garments, waded into the river, and scrubbed her face clean of paints. She unbraided her hair, washed it, and allowed the air to dry the dark strands that cascaded down her back. Standing in knee-high water, she faced Kionee. "Why do you not join me?" she asked.

Kionee nodded the signal that Night Walker was spying on them, for she had listened and watched in furtiveness. "You took long to come. I have finished. I stayed so you would not be alone if danger approaches."

"We are not in peril, for Night Walker guards the path for us. No threat is larger than his prowess and courage."

Kionee smiled and teased, "You glow and your voice softens when you speak his name. Is there something about him which touches and warms the woman hidden within you? I will tell no one what you say to me."

Taysinga laughed, and did everything she could to reveal and enhance her feminine side. "His face is easy to look upon. His body is sleek and hard and swift; it has no weaknesses or scars. When I gaze upon him, I have a strange craving here," she murmured and placed a hand over her loins. "It is like a hunger which must be fed or I will starve. When I hear his voice or see his smile, I feel strange. When I am near him or touch him, I quiver. Why do I do this, Kionee?"

"You love and desire him as a woman for a man. You live as

a male, my friend, but you are female; that is what your feelings tell you."

"I fear what you say is true, as a great battle rages within me."

"Why does what is natural trouble you? We cannot control instincts."

"Just as we cannot control our destinies. We are *tivas*, Kionee. We are trapped by our ranks and duties. If I lived as a woman, I would be a good mate and mother."

"A *tiva* can be freed to join if our laws are met."

"How can I tell Night Walker my feelings when he views me as a man? If I approached him, he would be insulted. If he would accept me as his mate, I would do anything he asks to please him."

Just keep standing there naked and lovely to enflame his loins, and keep voicing bold thoughts to stimulate him. "I cannot speak of Night Walker's feelings and hungers; only he can do so. If *Atah* chooses you for his mate, our chief's son will ask you to break your *kim* to join him."

Taysinga continued to pose seductively to ensnare her concealed love. "What if a man of our tribe asks you to become a woman again for him?"

"He would waste words," Kionee answered quickly, "for there is none among us who steals my eye, stirs my heart, and heats my body as Night Walker does for you. You shiver," she suddenly observed.

"Darkness and cool air come soon; I must finish my tasks. We will speak of this again on another moon when we are alone."

Kionee saw Taysinga step from the water and dry herself, then braid her raven hair, all the while using graceful and provocative moves and facing toward the woods. Kionee waited as the *tiva* concealed her shapely body beneath male garments and lovely face beneath colorful paints on a black background.

"I am ready to return to camp, Kionee. Pray I do not expose my feelings for Night Walker if nothing can come of them."

"Pray for what is best and right and that is what will come to pass," she replied, and hoped that was true for both of them.

Carrying their possessions, the two *tivas* walked to where the chief's son leaned against a tree with a knife in his hand, prepared for trouble if it struck. Taysinga smiled and thanked Night Walker for his protection. The man gazed at her a moment, nodded, and glanced toward camp.

Kionee spoke her gratitude without smiling or using extra words. She wanted to stress that although she was disinterested, Taysinga was just the opposite. She noticed beads of moisture on Night Stalker's upper lip and forehead, a slight flush to his cheeks, and a gleam in his dark eyes. She surmised they came from an attack of lust after the stunning sight he witnessed. Since Kionee had told him he could not have her for a mate, surely the splendid sight of Taysinga's face and body would prove to him the older female should be his next and best choice.

Kionee walked a little ahead of the two hunters as she listened to Taysinga praising Night Walker for his prowess, kindness, and past deeds. Since the *tiva* truly felt and thought that way, her honesty was obvious. Kionee reasoned it must be heady and arousing to such a vain man to learn he was so adored and desired and respected. If she was not mistaken, the huskiness she heard in his voice proved her conclusions were right.

Kionee excused herself to join her family to complete daily tasks before the evening meal. Maja returned and lay down nearby, resting his muzzle on his forelegs. He glanced up at her when she stroked his ears, then looked at the ground, which was unlike him. Kionee reasoned that he also missed Stalking Wolf's companionship.

Since striking camp, Maja's normally shiny and alert gaze appeared dulled; his tail hung low as he walked beside her and Tuka; his pace and vigor seemed slowed. Kionee worried over the animal's lack of attention, and sluggish manner. It was as if the vital creature had grown old and listless overnight.

Kionee leaned over and hugged the silver wolf. She whispered in his ear, "I love you and need you, Maja, my best friend. I cannot lose you as I lost Stalking Wolf. Call your lost spirit back to you, for we will live as companions for life if *Atah* does not hear our prayers and answer them."

Maja moved his head to lay it on Kionee's thigh, seeming to sense her need for comfort. He had a need for the same things for which she yearned: a companion, a mate, someone lying beside him. But each time he felt the urges to return to the wild and to mate, he quelled them. Kionee had saved his life and she loved him, needed him. If he left her side, both would be alone and miserable; and she would be in peril if she did not have him to protect her.

In that forest and in the one on the bighorn range which they reached many days later, Kionee, Taysinga, and others guarded the women as they gathered nuts, berries, roots, and plants. Afterward, the *tivas* and men collected woods for bows, tool and weapon handles, and arrow shafts. During the long and harsh winter when much time was spent inside their tipis, the hunters would work on those tasks. Certain types of rocks were picked up to be used for arrowheads; they would be shaped and sharpened for lethal tips to bring down prey and to thwart foes. Turkeys and other large birds were hunted for fletchings; their feathers were packed with care to avoid damaging them. Sturdy sinews and thin strips of rawhide were ready for use as ties and were stored in parfleches. All they required for survival was in their possession.

It was on the south fork of the river of powder banks that Kionee noticed how often Maja left her side to roam in the forest and foothills. The wolf vanished many times during the day and was gone for most of each night. She dreaded to imagine he was being pulled back to his old life. She could not envision her existence without her constant companion; yet, if a return to the wild made him happy, she should not stop him from going. Maja had not lived in captivity so he had not lost any of his survival and hunting skills and would not be in peril. She noticed how his vitality and the shine to his eyes had returned, and that made her happy. When he was with her, he seemed to pace in eagerness to take off into the woods again. Sometimes, she sensed powerful eyes on them, but she knew they did not belong to Stalking Wolf, was something only known to the silver beast that enticed him to frequent lengthy disappearances. Yet, he never failed to rejoin her at least once or twice a day, usually at dawn and at dusk. He seemed to do so to make certain she was safe and to ensure she was not forgotten and deserted. Even so, Kionee suspected and feared she was losing him to an unseen and potent force.

On a moonless night near the creek of bad water, Kionee spoke with the chief's son again. "My heart and answer have not changed, and they will not change," she told him after he said this was the last time he would approach her about becoming his mate. "I want to remain your friend and brother, but I cannot become more to you. I am honored you view me as a worthy choice and I do not wish to injure your pride and feelings. Seek another to ask, one who loves and desires you, one matched to you in all ways. That is not me, Night Walker."

Night Walker nodded and said, "It will be as you say. Tell no one I came first to you, as knowing could hurt the heart of my second choice."

"Such words will never leave my lips." She was surprised and relieved when he appeared to accept her response. That arduous task was over. Now, if she never won Stalking Wolf, she was fated for a life alone and childless.

Five suns later, Kionee saw Night Walker with Taysinga. She hoped and prayed he was seeking the other *tiva* as his mate. She could not tell, for afterward the handsome male did not start playing the flute for the *tiva* or take her for rides on his horse. Others were present every time Taysinga was around her, and they could not speak in private so she could learn if their trick succeeded. Nor did Taysinga's mood and expressions reveal anything to Kionee. Perhaps, Kionee reasoned, the couple had agreed to join but felt they must wait to reveal their plans until after they reached camp.

The following day, the tribe halted early to bury Fire Woman who had died in peace and without suffering as she lay asleep on Regim's travois.

Kionee sat beside the earth mound for a long while after everyone left that lovely location; she wanted to visit with her maternal grandmother for a last time before her spirit reached the stars. She told herself she should not grieve over the woman's departure from Mother Earth, as Fire Woman had enjoyed a happy and safe life with Regim as her Hunter-Guardian, and with Martay to give her grandchildren.

That blessing was not true for some *tiva* families who had no other daughters to continue their bloodlines; those circles closed forever when unmated and childless *tivas* died or were slain by enemies. Sumba's parents were fortunate to have other girls to continue theirs after the *tiva* was killed during the Crow attack. Kionee still missed Sumba and often thought of her lost friend.

A tiny smile appeared on Kionee's face when she wondered what Sumba would say if she knew Taysinga had become such a good friend. She had worked hard to effect the truce with Taysinga. At first, Kionee admitted, her overtures were only for purposes of making peace; later, real friendship had been born. Even so, she thought it best to conceal her love and desire for Stalking Wolf from the older *tiva*.

Kionee went into the woods to empty her stomach of tainted food she must have eaten. Afterward, she chewed on herbs from her medicine pouch to settle her churning belly and to refresh her mouth. As she did so, she learned the reason for Maja's joy and disappearances when she saw the silver creature playing with a gray wolf. She watched the male lick and stroke the female's muzzle with his own. She watched him rub himself against the female's furry pelt, moving along one side and then the other as if caressing a lover. They let their tongues dance together before they raced deeper into the forest to savor their discovery of each other.

Kionee smiled and warmed as she realized Maja had found a lone she-wolf to become his mate. A mate . . . That was a joyous victory for her companion. Yet, she would miss him when he left her side for theirs, which he would and must. If only she could obtain a joyous victory of her own.

Not a day or night had passed without thoughts and dreams of Stalking Wolf and the life they could share if her destiny changed. She had assumed it would be easier to adjust to his loss with distance between them; she was wrong. She yearned for him. Her body craved a union with his. Her lips hungered to taste his. How could she ever forget him and what they had shared? How could she ever be happy again without him? How could she clear her wits when anguish over his absence dulled and clouded them?

Kionee knew it was dangerous to be so distracted and dispirited. It was difficult to pretend nothing was wrong when her heart had been knifed from her body. No captivity could be stronger than Stalking Wolf's hold over her. No torture could be more painful than the denial of him in her life, at least in her arms.

Help me, Atah, her wounded heart and soul cried out, *for I am alone and injured and in great need. Can You not find a way to join us?*

Kionee dried her tears, took a deep breath, and headed for camp.

On her way there, she encountered Regim. Both women halted and looked at each other. Regim shook her head in sad awareness, for Kionee had not been given enough time to conceal her troubled emotions.

"The light is gone from your eyes, and tears have replaced it," she observed. "The smile has left your face, and pain makes lines in it which your mask does not hide. Joy has escaped your body. Weariness steals your spirit, and you move as one who is old. Your heart bleeds over the Cheyenne warrior's loss as mine does over Fire Woman's."

Kionee lowered her gaze. "Yes, my *Tiva-Chu* and friend, for I love him and need him. If I cannot have him, why did *Atah* put such powerful desire in my heart and body?"

"I do not know. You are strong, brave, and good, Kionee. *Atah* has blessed and gifted you with many skills and strengths. If it was possible for anyone to battle and defeat such a force and challenge, you could do so. As I watch you and sense your sufferings, it brings back thoughts of the long past moon when I loved and desired a man and could not have him. Does he know you are a woman? Does he also love and desire you?"

"Yes, but I did not tell him or do anything to expose myself to him. His instincts and skills are great, so he guessed my secret. He promised to tell no one, and he will keep his word. He said it was in his vision and those of their shaman for him to find a mate this season; he believes I am the woman for him and that is why our paths were crossed and why the signs of our animal spirits match and adorn our shields." That thought elicited another one as her distressed mind wandered for a moment. "Maja has been given a mate; she follows us and they meet in the forest; soon he will leave me to return to his old life and I will be alone."

She sensed Kionee's despair and fear as she asked, "Did Stalking Wolf ask you to join to him?"

"Yes, many times, but I told him I could not leave my rank and family. He knows I cannot run away with him and endanger our alliance. He said he would wait until my destiny changed and *Atah* freed me."

"Perhaps I was wrong when I said this was a test, an evil, you must fight and conquer. Perhaps, for reasons we do not understand and know, *Atah* brought you together for more than the deeds you carried out as companions. Yet, until He changes your destiny and our laws, you cannot go to him, for the risks are too great and the dangers are too painful."

"There is no hope for us to be together, for I cannot betray what I am."

"With Fire Woman gone to live with the spirits in the stars, if *Atah* freed you, I could live with Strong Rock and Martay; I could be their Hunter-Guardian. But for me to take your place and for you to flee without *Atah* releasing you first, you and your family would face dishonor and endure great anguish. To choose Stalking Wolf—an outsider—over your parents, rank, people, and laws would stain you and your family. Stalking Wolf would become our enemy if he helped you. Our bond with the Cheyenne would be broken. Does his love and a life with him mean that much to you?"

"I cannot make that choice on this moon while my heart is in pain and my wits are dulled. I must wait and pray for *Atah* to send me a message to tell me what I must do before I act."

"That is good and wise, Kionee; your heart is not selfish. I love you and I am proud of you. I will be near when you need to speak again, and I will be near if you decide to act upon your desires for him."

Kionee hugged the older woman and thanked her for comfort and understanding. It had taken much for Regina to confess an unrequited love and to speak with such honesty and openness. It felt as if a heavy burden had been lifted from her shoulders now that she had the woman to help her carry it. She smiled. "I thank *Atah* you are my friend and my mother's . . . sister." Yet, Kionee realized, Regim had said such things because the *Tiva-Chu* did not know she had already broken their law by yielding to passion. Kionee decided this was not the right time to confess such shocking news to her.

Regim smiled in return, took Kionee's arm, and guided her away.

On the journey's final night, Taysinga managed to whisper to Kionee as they passed while tending chores, "He asked me and I accepted. Tell no one until he reveals it to others. Thank you for helping me, my friend."

Kionee was happy for the *tiva*, and relieved Night Walker's futile and intimidating chase of her had ended. Joy and victory, she mused. So many fortunate people were experiencing those glorious things. Why not her?

At last, the Hanuevas reached their old campsite near the northern mouth of the Wind River Canyon, close to where hot springs bubbled from the ground and sent steam drifting into

the sky. The air after sunset was getting cooler with every passing day; in another circle or two of full moons, winter with its
blanketing snows and powerful winds would arrive.

The people settled among the trees and rocks beneath evergreen foothills which drifted upward into tall mountains on
both sides of the river. Tipis were raised. Possessions were unloaded. Travois were taken apart, their wood frames to be used
in cook fires. Horses were tended and tethered. Hides and meat
from the seasonal hunt were stored until it was time to complete
their preparations. The evening meal was started.

Kionee stroked Maja's head before he vanished to join his
mate for the night. She glanced to where several *tivas* were hauling willow sapplings into the edge of the trees to put the *Haukua*
in its place. That sight reminded Kionee she had missed one visit
there shortly before their journey began. In a few suns it would
be time to walk through its entrance again.

The next day, a signal was given by Regim for the *tivas* to go
to the nearby cave where their *kims* were hidden. They would
recover the female spirit vessels and place the clay pots in their
meeting lodge. After the group reached that concealed location,
a shocking discovery was made.

21

HE STARTLED *tivas* eyed the destruction of their *kims*. Large
bear tracks were abundant around and in the cave and
amidst the alarming sight. Smashed spirit vessels were
tossed everywhere, their broken pieces and previous contents
scattered and mingled beyond repair.

Regim and Kionee exchanged glances as both wondered if
this was a sacred message from *Atah* to tell them it was time to
end the masking custom and sacrificial rank.

"Is this a bad sign, our leader?" a young *tiva* asked the *Tiva-
Chu*. "Have we displeased *Atah* and He punishes us with a
warning? Do we purify ourselves and make new *kims?*"

"Perhaps *Atah* wishes to change our destinies again and He
released our female spirits to return them to our bodies to make
us women once more," Regim speculated, "Perhaps He knows
our people need more mates and children to make our tribe
larger and stronger so the Bird Warriors will not attack and destroy us."

"If that is true," Taysinga ventured, "we must remove the

> 283 <

paints from our faces and the marks from our hands so males will seek us out."

"Bring Spotted Owl to us," Regim told one of the younger *tivas*. "We will ask our shaman to tell us the meaning of this sign."

The holy man arrived and examined the shocking damage. "In my last dream when an owl whispered in my ear, I did not see masked hunters walking among our people. This custom began in a time when the Ancient Ones had more females born to them than males. That has changed; each season more families have sons than those who do not. Yet, our tribe grows smaller, for males cannot join females close to their bloodlines and we join only one mate."

"Do you say it is time to halt the *tiva* custom and masking ritual?"

"That is what this sign and my dream tells me, great *Tiva-Chu*. We will wait until after another sign is given to tell others."

"When will that message come, Spotted Owl? What will it be?"

"I do not know, Regim, but we will know it when it appears."

After the mystified *tiva* group and the aging shaman returned to camp, Night Walker announced his choice of Taysinga to become his mate and her willing acceptance of him. Standing before his surprised father and the gathered tribe, he agreed to be her parents' Hunter-Protector. After he defeated her in a contest of skills, all requirements of their law for her release were met.

The smiling *tivas* guided a glowing Taysinga to the forest

cascade. Her face was scrubbed clean of paints. Her soot-black hair was unbraided, washed, brushed, and allowed to hang free for the first time since she was five years of age. Her skin was rubbed with dried herbs, fragrant grasses, fresh sage, and wild-flowers. The mark on her hand was burned away with hot coals, then the injury was tended with nature's medicines. After it healed and the scab dropped off, only a scar would be visible. With the use of oil from the coneflower, Taysinga had felt little pain during the symbol's destruction. She kept glancing at Kionee and smiling, as she knew without her friend's help, this event would not be happening. She silently prayed that some-how Kionee could find this same happiness with Stalking Wolf. Though Kionee had not confessed love for the Cheyenne, Tay-singa sensed it lived within the younger *tiva*'s heart and body; and she knew it lived within Stalking Wolf's. Yet, even with their *kims* broken and possible release ahead for all mask-wear-ers, he was not Hanuevan. How sad, she mused, for them to suf-fer such denials because of their law.

After the bathing ritual, Taysinga—dressed as a woman—began her next task. Excited women grouped to make the cou-ple's tipi from gifts of buffalo hides which were donated by delighted tribe members. Many people presented her with par-fleches of dried meat and pemmican, tools, sitting or sleeping mats, and an assortment of other things required to start a new tipi and union. The women laughed, talked, offered Taysinga advice, and sang merry songs as they worked in a genial circle.

From a short distance, Kionee furtively watched and listened in near-envy of that occasion which she probably would never enjoy. If she had accepted Night Walker's offer, she would be in Taysinga's place right now, preparing a home and awaiting a ceremony, but dreading the night ahead in his arms. It was the Cheyenne warrior's tipi, embrace, passion, and mat she wanted to share. It was their children she wanted to birth. It was his des-tiny she needed to mingle with hers.

As soon as the tipi was erected near the lodge of Bear's Head, just as sunset arrived, the chief's son and ex-*tiva* took positions in front of the shaman. They spoke words to reveal their intention to live as mates until death, and the tribe cheered them. Spotted Owl thanked *Atah*, blessed the couple, and handed Taysinga a talking-feather, which the woman gladly accepted and tucked inside her belt. The shaman wrapped a buffalo robe around them to signify they were now as one; then the smiling couple entered their cozy dwelling to seal their bond.

Members of the tribe told their current chief and Running Otter that they would provide the leader's needs and protection, now that their son had a mate and her family as his responsibilities.

Bear's Head smiled and thanked his generous people.

The crowd dispersed, leaving to eat, tend chores, and sleep.

Kionee sighed a deep breath of relief to have the threat of Night Walker removed. She headed for her family's tipi where she would spend the rest of her life in a mask-wearer's rank unless *Atah* changed His mind.

Blue Bird and Runs Fast were joined the following day at dusk, after their tipi was erected near Strong Rock's. As soon as the happy couple entered it, Shining Star asked Moon Child to become his mate. That did not surprise any member of Kionee's family, as the young man had spoken to the father and mother earlier that day.

"I accept you, Shining Star," a beaming Moon Child said, "but we can not join until after the next buffalo hunt, for we have no hides for a tipi."

Regim returned the smile to the girl's face and sparkle to her eyes with a reassuring suggestion. "I will give you the tipi I shared with Fire Woman. I will go to live with the *tiva* elders as is our way after parents are gone."

"That is kind and generous, my brother," Martay said.

"We thank you for your good heart and ways," Strong Rock added.

Regim nodded and smiled, as that left only her parents for Kionee's duty.

"Can we join on the next sun, Father?" the excited girl asked.

Strong Rock grinned and nodded permission. "Shining Star, go to speak with Spotted Owl and your parents so they can prepare for this event."

The young hunter caressed Moon Child with his tender gaze, then left to do those elating tasks. The girl hurried inside to check her garments, as she wanted to wear the best and prettiest one tomorrow.

Kionee took a walk with Regim, for her silver wolf companion was gone for the night. "You brought great joy to Moon Child's heart. By the time the sun sleeps again, my sisters will be with their mates. Taysinga is happy; she glows like a small sun; they are a good match. Soon the cold season will bring snow and they will all lie close to be warm and to share desires. Soon Maja will return to the wild, for he has taken a mate. Will the moon ever rise when I will know such freedom and happiness?"

"After the next sign is given to us, I will speak to the council to free you to join your love. I will offer to replace you in your tipi and rank."

"Even if they cast aside the *tiva* law and free all of us to become women, they will not agree for me to join to an outsider."

"Perhaps after there is no secret to guard, they will do so. After all he and his people have done for us, he is worthy of you, if the path is cleared."

"I fear to have hope for such a dream to come true."

"If it is *Atah*'s desire, Kionee, it will happen."

> 287 <

"Yes, *if* it is His desire," she murmured in despair and doubt.

"If it is not, Kionee, you must accept that denial and obey our law. Do not call down great harm upon you and others with defiance."

"Do not fear, Regim; I know where my first duty lies."

As soon as Moon Child and Shining Star were joined and cuddled in Regim's former tipi, Kionee walked in the forest with Maja. Now she was the Hunter-Guardian only for her parents, but that awesome rank and her tribe's restrictive joining law still loomed over her head and kept Stalking Wolf out of her reach. She knew Regime could take charge of her duty if she deserted it, but nothing could be done about the other perils, nothing she could imagine. "I am still trapped, Maja, unless I flee and bring shame and anguish to myself and others. If I dared to take that risk, would they come to understand my choice, forgive me for making it? Would it destroy the alliance between Hanueva and Cheyenne? Could my people survive if that black sun rises? Could I live with such dishonor, live with such damage and death to others?"

The silver wolf licked Kionee's hand and nestled close for comfort. He glanced toward the treeline where the female of his species awaited him. He seemed to feel torn between an urge to stay where he had lived so long and an urge to leave to roam as destiny intended. The call of the wild had never been stronger in him than it was today. He appeared to perceive Kionee's torment and loneliness, so his choice was hard. A teasing wind brought the scent of his mate to his nose; he felt her tug on his instincts. He looked in the direction where the she-wolf was concealed from Kionee's sight and knew his place was in the wilderness with the other female.

Kionee stroked his head and the soft ruff on his neck. She had glimpsed the gray wolf in the trees and noticed how many times Maja's gaze was pulled toward the creature. She sensed the battle within him. "We have been companions and friends for many seasons, Maja," she said tenderly as she stroked him. "A chance for happiness has been given to you. It brings pain to think of your loss, but you must return to the life you left for me. You must be free. You must live as your kind does. You must cling to your mate, not to me. Go, Maja, join your mate and run in freedom and with love."

The silver beast sensed the meaning of Kionee's words and the deep emotions behind them. He nuzzled her shoulder, licked her cheek, and loped off to be with his waiting mate. He halted beside the sleek gray creature, gazed at Kionee for a time, then raced into the forest as she commanded.

Kionee watched them running and leaping joyously side by side until trees and bushes blocked her view. She told herself she had done the right thing, for Maja would not have left her until she insisted. It was done; he was lost to her, just as Stalking Wolf appeared to be lost to her. Yet, she should be happy that at least one of them had love and freedom. She took a deep breath to calm her odd tension, fought back tears, and returned to camp.

On the morning of the second day after Maja's departure, Kionee sat near the place where her horses were tethered. Dread and panic filled her. She realized she had been sick too many times for it to be caused from eating tainted food. She often felt tired and sleepy and moody, and her breasts were tender. She also realized she had missed two visits to the *Haukau*. She had witnessed this same kind of illness in women, females who were carrying babies within their bodies.

She wondered if this was a sign from *Atah* to force her to make a choice she had delayed, the choice to join her lover. Or had it only happened to expose her passionate deeds and to punish her? She added up the time since her last blood flow and reasoned she had seven passings of the full moons before the child's birth. Yet, she had only one or two cycles of it before her blooming body would reveal her situation to others. Even so, Kionee knew she could not act in haste or with dulled wits.

Joining with Night Walker could no longer be a means to resolve her problem. She was glad that was true so she would not be tricked by fear into accepting him as a mate. There was no time to select another Hanueva male and ensnare him, even if she were tempted to do so, which she was not. Of a sudden, she comprehended in alarm, her exposure and punishment would now imperil her unborn baby as well as her tribe and herself. It complicated the predicament for her, forced a decision upon her.

Kionee needed to speak with Regim. She went to her family's tipi to ask the woman to walk with her. She found Martay writhing and weeping in great pain on her mat. Strong Rock and Regim were bending over the woman to tend her.

"What is wrong with Mother?" Kionee asked in dread.

"We do not know," Regim replied in worry. "I will summon Spotted Owl to pray for the evil spirits to halt their attack." She left in haste.

Martay gripped Kionee's hand. "Something bites into my body and tries to claw its way out. I have displeased *Atah* and He punishes me."

"That is not true, Mother," Kionee refuted. "You are a good woman; there is no reason for *Atah* to harm you. You will be well soon." Yet, troubled Kionee feared this suffering was her fault; she had brought torment upon the woman who gave her birth, a mother whom she had betrayed in secret. In rising alarm, she watched Martay squirm and struggle as she suppressed screams of pain.

Spotted Owl arrived. The others moved aside for the shaman and medicine man to examine Martay. He looked confused as his hands roamed her lower abdomen as it tightened and relaxed. He saw a rush of water soak the woman's dress, mat, and legs. His skilled hands checked her again. In surprise, he announced, "A child struggles to come forth."

"What do you say, Spotted Owl?" Strong Rock murmured.

"I feel the body of a child. It is near birth. I must send women to help her, for I am not the one needed here." He left to seek that special help.

Martay shrieked in pain as the child's head surged from her body. "There is no time. I must remove my breechclout. It is coming now."

"We are men," Strong Rock reminded his mate, feeling helpless.

Martay seized Kionee's and Regim's hands. "Do not leave me, my sister and my daughter, for I am afraid and I cannot do this alone," she pleaded. "The child will be injured if its escape is blocked or slowed. Remove my breechclout and let it seek freedom as it wills."

Kionee yanked a knife from her sheath, lifted her mother's wet dress, and cut off the garment since there was no time to untie and remove it. Her astonished gaze sighted the baby's head, dark with black hair. "It comes, Mother!" She watched Martay bear down and push with her stomach muscles, and the infant slid onto the soaked mat. Her gaze widened. "It is a boy, a son." She glanced at Regim, who nodded.

"Take a thong and cut it. Tie two pieces on the string which unite him to me, this far apart, here," Martay instructed as she pointed to those spots. "When they are tight, cut the string. You must hurry."

Kionee did as her mother said, with Regim's assistance. She lifted the slick infant and placed it in her mother's outstretched hands. She watched Martay clear its nose and mouth. She heard her brother cry out as he took his first breath of air. Her heart and spirit soared at that sound.

"How can this be?" Strong Rock murmured in awe and joy.

"I do not know. I have not grown fat in belly as one with

child. I have grown large over all my body, for I have been eating much and often. I feared I would not be good to look upon as I changed. My blood flow tried to halt many times during the last hot season; it left me while winter was upon us. I did not know I carried a child, for I am beyond those suns as a woman."

Strong Rock laughed and teased, "*Atah* says that is not true, my love. A son," he almost whispered in amazement and reverence. He looked at Kionee. "You have been a good son; now you can become a daughter and woman again when he is old enough to take your place."

Blue Bird and other women rushed inside the tipi. Kionee and Regim left to let them finish tending Martay. Strong Rock met with Spotted Owl outside to relate the good news. Word of the stunning event was passed around the camp.

Many came to view the unexpected child, this blessing to Strong Rock and Martay. Gifts were brought, and the tribe was in a cheerful mood. Some women teased Martay about waiting until her tipi had room for another person before she gave birth to the baby. Blue Bird and Moon Child were elated to have a little brother; so was Kionee.

Yet, the *tiva* could not decide if this was a sign from *Atah* that she had His permission to leave, now that her family had Regim and a son to care for them. The fact remained that Stalking Wolf was not Hanueva. Another reality flooded her mind: she had shared forbidden passion and committed betrayal with the Cheyenne and she was carrying a baby.

Away from camp and the tribe's ears, Regim was taking that choice out of Kionee's hands as the *Tiva-Chu* spoke with the shaman . . .

Spotted Owl called a council meeting the following night. It was held in a large clearing so the *tivas* and men could hear every word. The shaman revealed the destruction of the *kims*

and his belief for the reason. *"Tivas* wear dried ovaries of she-bears, and a bear was sent to destroy the spirit vessels. It is a sign from *Atah* to release our daughters from enforced ranks. Tay-singa has joined to Night Walker, our next chief. Kionee's mother has born a son to free her. I say, the Creator wants all mask-wearers freed to become mates and mothers so our tribe can grow larger and stronger to defeat our enemy. What do you think and say, my people?"

The stunned crowd glanced at one another in confusion as to what they thought and felt and should say.

At last, Bear's Head asked, "Is this a message to you from *Atah?"*

"He has revealed it to me in many ways, my chief and people. The *tiva* rank was made by the Ancient Ones long ago when females born outnumbered males, and families without sons went in want and lived in peril. The Ancient Ones, those who came before our Hanueva band, painted their daughters' faces and dressed them as men so others would view them as males when they hunted and battled. As seasons passed, more laws were made to bind *tivas* tighter to their ranks, laws used to guard that secret to prevent enemies from knowing they were females, fighters who could be easily defeated. Such laws made it hard for *tivas* to leave their ranks. By the moon the custom came to us, we no longer needed those laws as the Ancient Ones did, but we kept them in place, for no one spoke to end the custom. If we keep it alive, we deny our daughters their instincts to become mothers; we place them in danger on the hunt and in battle. They sacrifice much to honor their ranks, for they are taught and trained to do so when they are too young to think for themselves. It is time to reward them with freedom, to let them live as they were born, to make no new mask-wearers of our daughters."

"Who will hunt for us and protect us when we are old and cannot do so?" one sonless father asked.

Regim caught the shaman's signal for her to respond. "The

men who join to freed *tivas* will become your sons while you remain on Mother Earth. If those men also have a duty to their parents, *tivas* can help hunt for their parents, and fight for them if trouble comes. Sisters, mothers, and friends of *tivas* and their mates can help with a *tiva*'s children and chores if she is needed on the hunt and in battle. Those *tivas* who wish to remain as hunters and defenders can do so, but as females, as it is with other tribes. If there is no secret to guard, it cannot harm us. With the Crow frightened away, our *tivas* can give us needed sons to fight in days when their courage or daring returns, for it is certain to do so. They can give us daughters to bear more sons to increase our number and strength. Hanuevas are people with many wits, so we will find ways to care for our families and people. Few *tivas* have left their ranks to join, for men viewed them as brothers, as other men. Night Walker had the courage to do so when he claimed Taysinga as his mate, and she is worthy of him."

The chief's son spoke up. "My vote is with Regim and freedom. If we are to survive, Hanuevas, we must cast aside this law and custom."

Little Weasel agreed, knowing that change would remove Kionee as a hunter, as fierce competition in their bloodline. "Night Walker and Regim speak wise and true; my vote is for freedom of the *tivas*."

Many others spoke for release. Only a few spoke against it, those who feared change and how it might affect their lives.

"We vote," Spotted Owl announced when there was silence.

Kionee's heart was elated when that unfair law was discarded by a near-unanimous vote. Yet, that did not remove the remaining obstacle between her and Stalking Wolf. Nor did it change the fact she had broken the law while it existed. Would she still be punished, she wondered, in the old way?

"*Tivas*, when the new sun rises, you are women again," Spotted Owl said. "Remove the paints from your faces and seek mates among our men." He turned to Regim. "Speak now of what we talked about in the forest."

The *Tiva-Chu* stood and said, "It is the law for our women to join only to those men with Hanueva blood. There is one among us who must be freed of that law. Kionee must join to the Cheyenne warrior called Stalking Wolf; that will bind the alliance between our tribes tighter. *Atah* crossed their paths so they could do many great deeds; He also seeks to join them as mates. This I believe with all my heart, as does Kionee and Spotted Owl."

"I dreamed of two wolves mating, wolves who protect our people from harm," the shaman said. "I did not understand until Regim spoke of the love which has come to be between Stalking Wolf and Kionee, both who wear and carry the wolf's sign. We must free her of our law to join him."

Kionee stared at the two speakers in astonishment, as Regim had not warned her of this plan. She felt many gazes on her.

The shaman continued, "Strong Rock and Martay were given a son as a sign to release her from our law; I say, to go to him. *Atah* called Fire Woman to him so Regim could be the Hunter-Protector of them until the boy is grown and trained. Maja was given a mate and has left Kionee's side to be free with his kind. I say these are sacred signs, messages from *Atah.*"

The chief looked at Kionee and asked, "Do you love this Cheyenne friend who helped us, son of the man whose life and Sacred Arrows you saved? Does he know you are a female? Does he wish to join to you?"

"His skills and instincts are great," Regim responded for her. "He guessed she was a female. She did not betray the *tiva* secret to him. He loves Kionee and waits for her freedom to become his mate. She has proven her loyalty and love for us by sacrificing him for her rank and people. This union was in the sacred visions of Stalking Wolf and Medicine Eyes; though Hanuevas do not use visions to guide us, we know they have mystical powers. We know that all the warrior and shaman saw in their visions has come to pass. Even so, Stalking Wolf is a man of honor and a true friend to us; he respects our laws and customs and did not lure her away from them. Their love and union are destined by *Atah*. He they call *Maheoo*. We must release Kionee to join to him in honor and in reward for their great deeds together."

"Is this true?" the chief asked Kionee, who answered for herself this time.

"Upon my life and honor, Bear's Head, Regim speaks the truth. I do not know why *Atah* put such love in my heart, but it lives there for him. I could not put aside my rank and vow to stay with him as he asked. He is a man of honor, so he keeps my secret from all others. He does nothing to sway or to force me to come to him if I must hurt my family and people to do so."

"Who votes to allow Kionee to leave our tribe in honor to join with the mate chosen for her by *Atah*?" the shaman asked.

Red Bull, father of the girl named after her, said, "I vote yes, for she saved my mate and child from the grizzly and has done other good deeds."

Runs Fast, mate of Blue Bird, said, "I vote yes; she saved my love from the Crow, as she did with those of others."

Goes Ahead, one of those mentioned, agreed for the same reason.

The father of Sumba said, "I vote yes, for she saved my child's face and hand from adorning the shield of our enemy."

Older *tivas* agreed, for Kionee had helped them many times.

Others consented because she had helped save their people and had helped strengthen the Cheyenne alliance, which she refused to threaten even at a great sacrifice to herself.

Strong Rock smiled at his daughter and said, "This is why *Atah* gave me a son. I vote yes. Kionee has done her duty to us with skill. She has earned the right to seek love and happiness with *Atah*'s choice for her."

Kionee smiled at her father in love, respect, and gratitude.

Little Weasel concurred, eager to have Kionee gone.

"If she loves the Cheyenne, let her go to him," Night Walker said. "Let her find the happiness I have found with Taysinga.

She has done much for her people and we must reward her with freedom."

Kionee smiled at him in gratitude, for he sounded sincere. During these last few days, he had seemed like a different, better, man; she assumed that was because of Taysinga, who pleased him greatly.

Soon, all who wished to speak had done so and the vote was taken.

Kionee could hardly believe her good fortune. Her heart leapt with joy. Victory sent her spirit and wits soaring. She was moved by her people's love and esteem for her, by Spotted Owl's and Regim's words and actions. She thanked them, and she silently thanked *Atah* for this blessing. She was now free in all ways to go to her cherished lover. She could leave without exposing her condition.

She had to travel a long distance to find Stalking Wolf. She hoped and prayed the Strong Hearts had not decided to camp elsewhere for the winter. Even if the Cheyenne did not return to their usual site, surely she could track and locate them which would only lengthen her search for a while. Timing was vital in order to conceal the presence of the child. *I am coming, my love.*

22

KIONEE GAZED AT THE colorful mask on the back of her hand; Regim and Spotted Owl had told her it was unnecessary to burn it off since the *tiva* custom no longer existed as a secret to safeguard. She was told to wear it in honor of her past deeds and rank. She had been given a new name to go with her new life: Morning Dove—a bird of peace, beauty, lovely song, and messenger to *Atah*. Since she was going to join a Strong Heart warrior and live with his people, the Cheyenne language was used for the chosen name: Hemene. She loved the sound of it and the reason she had earned it.

A special ritual was held to bury the broken *kims* and she-bear ovaries, returning them to Mother Earth from whom they had come. Ceremonial masks were suspended from thongs on past-*tivas'* tipis-of-power where weapons were hung for safety and display. The group had removed their facial paints, discarded their male garments, and released their braids. In the two days since the council meeting, several men were pursuing eager ex-"brothers" for their mates. New tasks were being learned; old tasks were being assisted by many males. The tribe appeared to have grown closer as men and women worked together in unity, respect, and affection.

Martay watched Kionee as she held her baby brother, played with his tiny fingers, laughed, smiled, and made cooing noises. Martay was elated to have her oldest daughter returned to her birth role, and was thrilled by Kionee's success. With all her heart, the joyous mother believed that Kionee's joining with Stalking Rock was destined by *Atah*. She thanked their Creator for His many blessings, guidance, and protection. Her other daughters were happily mated to good and brave men; if they gave birth to only females, those girls would not be faced with enduring the *tiva* rank, for which Martay was grateful and relieved. She was glad to have Regim back as a sister, living with them and taking over Kionee's place until the son in her child's arms was old enough to do so. There was none better, she felt, to train him than Regim and Strong Rock. She was awed by the boy's coming, and amused that she had not guessed his presence within her body. At last, Martay thought with a smile, all was as it should be.

That afternoon, Kionee presented the coup feather from Big Hump to her father, who accepted it with pride and joy and misty eyes. She gave Recu to Regim, for he was a well-trained and skilled buffalo horse. The woman was surprised and pleased, as Regim's pinto was nearing the season when he would become only a riding mount. Kionee kept Tuka and one burden horse for her use, but left the others for her family's. She knew that Stalking Wolf had or could get enough animals for their needs.

Kionee gifted her mother with her ceremonial mask to hang

in their tipi, for she would never don it again. She handed Martay the browband with buffalo hoofprint to pass to her little
brother to wear during his first hunt for good luck. She wished
she had other special belongings to give to her two sisters, but
providing the skins for their tipis and garments and being their
Hunter-Guardian for so long was more than generous, they told
her. She hugged Blue Bird and Moon Child before the three
laughed and talked for the first time as sisters. Her siblings
whispered stimulating advice into Kionee's ears, unaware those
words were unneeded by one who already had experienced
wild passion with the man she loved and would soon join. She
smiled and pretended to take their words to heart.

As they talked, Kionee fingered the necklace which the
Cheyenne chief had given to her without realizing she would
become a member of his family and band one day. She had female garments to take with her, generous offerings from her sisters and friends. Her possessions were packed in parfleches and
her weapons were readied for self-defense, as she would leave
when the next sun arose. She would take with her the wristlet
and hairpipe choker from Five Stars, and the buckskin shirt with
beaded designs from Stalking Wolf: gifts for saving their grandfather's life and for preventing the theft of their Sacred Arrows.
She did not need to make a talking-feather, as that was not a
Cheyenne custom, one she hoped her people would discard one
day. It seemed foolish to her for a woman to be compelled to
shake a feather in front of men to ask permission to speak to
them. Now that Hanuevas had changed a law as significant as
the *tiva* one, Kionee mused, perhaps that ancient custom also
would be cast aside.

A mixture of joy and sadness, anticipation and tension, filled
her as the awesome moment for departure approached. Soon
her family and people would be left behind, but she would ride
into the arms and life of the man she loved.

Before dusk, Kionee visited and spoke with her closest friends for a last time before leaving. She knew she would see them again on the plains during the next hot season and joint buffalo hunt and was elated this was not the last time she would be with them.

She talked with Red Bull and Blowing Rain, and held the daughter named after her. She visited her paternal grandparents, Long Elk and Yellowtail. She spoke with Four Deer, Swift Fingers, White Flower, Weasel Boy, Weasel Girl, and Little Weasel. She guessed why her cousin was so exhilarated by her change of fate and why he was being so friendly today; yet, she refused to allow anything or anyone to darken her shiny joy.

Kionee responded to Taysinga's eager summons to her tipi. She dreaded confronting the chief's son after the startling turn in events, as he now grasped the reason she had rejected him and could not love him. She smiled and embraced the ex-*tiva*. For a few moments, their gazes studied each other's full appearances as women.

"I am happy for you, Hemene; this is the will of *Atah*."

"Thank you, Taysinga, for I also believe it is true. I did not seek love and joining, but they found me, as you and Night Walker found each other."

The chief's son grinned and said, "Joining Taysinga was the best choice for me. She is a good and skilled mate. Her female spirit was strong; it is good it was released to unite with mine. It is also good you have found a perfect match, one blessed by the Creator. Go, be happy and free, as we are."

Kionee caught his cleverly wrapped dual meanings. She was cheered by his change of heart and ways. Perhaps, in time and under his influence, he could inspire those same needed changes in her cousin. "You are kind, and your words bring joy to my heart. You will always be my friend and as a brother to me, as Taysinga will be a friend and as a sister."

"We have a gift for you, Hemene," the bubbly Taysinga revealed. "It is a dress for your joining ceremony with Stalking Wolf; it was made from the white buffalo hide for good luck and to reward you for all you have done for our people. Night Walker gave it to me and asked me to make it with the help of others. We worked fast to do so."

Kionee held the soft and lovely garment with fringes and adornments. She lifted a misty gaze to the couple. "There is much love and respect in my heart for you, my friends. Never have I seen a finer or prettier dress."

"That is not all," Night Walker hinted before handing her matching moccasins. "My mother made them for you. Martay gave her your old ones to mark the prints of your feet."

Kionee accepted the second gift and fingered the beadwork on the moccasins' tongues. "Such joy fills me that I can hardly speak," she murmured.

"There is no need, for your glowing eyes thank us," Taysinga said.

"Ride in safety and alert, Hemene, and be happy," he added. "I will never forget the great sacrifice you were willing to make for our people's survival, and other good and brave deeds you did for us and your family."

"Thank you, Night Walker. You and Taysinga be safe and happy. When that sun rises, you will be a great chief. It is good our people will have one such as you to lead and protect them. It is good Taysinga is at your side."

Kionee left them to halt by Bear's Head's tipi to thank Running Otter for the moccasins before she returned to her family to eat the evening meal. She needed to take to her mat early to get restful sleep before her journey.

The entire tribe turned out to watch the ex-*tiva*'s departure. After words of parting and good wishes from many of them, she embraced her parents, sisters, Regim, and grandparents. She kissed her little brother's forehead and glanced gratefully at Regim and Spotted Owl. She mounted Tuka, took the braided reins of her burden horse from Regim, and walked the animals away from the group. Just before she left their sight, she paused, turned, and took in the view one last time. She smiled as she remembered Stalking Wolf doing the same thing at their first parting. She signaled a farewell, which was returned by family and friends, and took a deep breath.

Kionee kneed the pinto's sides and off they went toward an exciting challenge. Kionee was no more; Morning Dove had taken her place. Golden rays of dawn touched the land and licked at morning dew. Dark days, like moonless nights, were gone; a fate, like a bright sun, was rising before her. Soon she would unite with Stalking Wolf; the birth of a new and splendid destiny was at hand.

Kionee rode close to the riverbank in the canyon of wind between two ranges of mountains. Behind her, some high peaks displayed white tops from last winter's snows, as if defiantly refusing to melt completely. Nearby, trees, bushes, grasses, and late-blooming wildflowers were plentiful, and would remain verdant for a while longer. Days were still warm, but nights had cooled since their return to the valley. Within a few more suns, she knew, the cold season would blanket the land.

That reality told Kionee she must hurry to find Stalking Wolf before the Cheyennes' trail from the plains was concealed by snow. First, she would ride to the location her lover had given to her on the grasslands; she hoped the Strong Hearts were camped there again. It would be perilous to wander about in snow and harsh winds while she searched for him. She told herself that *Atah* would guide and protect her. Even so, nibblings of worry kept returning to trouble her.

Be waiting and looking for me, Stalking Wolf, Kionee prayed.

Why should he when he will not expect you to come so soon? her defiant mind asked. *Be alert to enemies making their last raids for coups and captives,* it warned. *Halt your doubts and fears, Hemene,* her heart advised, *or you will lessen the glow of your happiness and victory.*

Traveling a well-worn trail and over relatively easy terrain, Kionee covered a long distance that day. She used every ray of sunlight available before halting to make her first camp. She needed to reach her destination as fast as possible to outrun winter's steady approach and a body that would soon enlarge. She tended the horses, leaving the loyal and well-trained Tuka free to drink and graze at will, but hobbling the other near the pinto. She ate the food her mother had given to her, then reclined on a sleeping mat with weapons lying within reach if needed to use against wild beasts or foes.

Kionee heard a wolf howl not far away; then another answered that soulful call. It reminded her of Maja, and she hoped he and his mate were safe. She listened for other howls that would indicate a pack was near, but only peaceful sounds of night entered her keen ears: frogs, crickets, birds. She fingered the bow, arrows, and knife close by and relaxed a little. Still, she must not slumber too deeply and be unable to catch noises of threats and to react to them in time to save her life and her baby's. *My baby,* her dreamy mind echoed as she caressed her belly. *Are you a son or a daughter? Will your face be like mine or will it be like your father's? What joy it will bring when I hold you in my arms. I—*

Kionee's happy thoughts fled as she heard a branch snap nearby. She sat up with haste, grabbed her bow, and nocked an arrow. She struggled to peer into the shadows of dense trees. The waning full moon failed to help her locate the cause. She waited in tension for it to reveal itself. She knew from the crunch and her hunter's training that it was not a small creature or nocturnal bird. Tuka whinnied and moved about near the river, telling Kionee he also sensed something unfamiliar approaching. Her heart drummed fast and hard in her chest. Her body was taut. Never had she felt such fear and dread, for the life of her unborn child was at stake.

"Maja!" she shrieked in elation as she saw the silver-pelted animal leave the darkness, enter the moonlight, and run toward her. She laughed as he licked her unpainted face and nuzzled his head against her shoulder. "Did you not know me as a woman?" she teased. "It is good you remembered my scent and Tuka's and did not attack us. Did you return to protect me from harm, my friend? Where is your mate?"

Kionee smiled as she noticed the skittish gray animal in the edge of the woods, the unfamiliar smell of the she-wolf no doubt the cause of Tuka's anxiety. But with Maja there, the pinto calmed and returned to grazing. She knew from experience that the other horse was too dull-nosed and too dull-eared to be depended upon as a guard; that was why he was only a burden-bearing creature. She watched the she-wolf sit to await Maja's return; it was obvious the female sensed there was no threat from the human whom her mate was visiting. She reached for a parfleche, removed strips of dried meat, and tossed them to the gray animal. Kionee observed as the she-wolf sniffed the air, crept forward, sniffed again, and snatched up the offerings.

Maja went to his mate, rubbed her sides with his, and licked her face. He returned to Kionee and sat down. She assumed he was telling the creature it was safe to join them, but the wary and untamed beast did not.

Kionee did not know how much Maja could understand from her words, but she told him everything that had happened since he left. Even if he did not grasp her meanings, he perceived her happiness and licked her hand once more. As she spoke, she fed him strips of meat, knowing her mother had packed more than enough to last during her journey. But if she ran out, she was a skilled hunter, and game was still abundant. "I wish you could travel with me to Stalking Wolf's camp," she addressed Maja wistfully, "but it could be dangerous for your mate, for she is unknown to them and remains wild in spirit."

The silver beast's ears stood up and he gazed at her as he heard that familiar name. "That is right, Maja, I go to join Stalking Wolf. Now, we will both have mates. We are free. I must rest. Will you guard me?"

Kionee knew Maja recognized the command of "guard," and he lay down beside her to obey. She saw the other wolf stretch out on the ground at a distance. Safe and happy, Kionee was slumbering soon.

After her breathing told the she-wolf the human was asleep, the gray creature sneaked to Maja's other side and lay down. Both females were protected all night by the powerful and alert animal.

At dawn, singing birds awakened Kionee. She yawned and opened her eyes. She smiled at Maja and stroked his massive head. "Thank you, my friend; I had great need of sleep." She saw the she-wolf at the wood's edge, where she had loped at first sign of Kionee's coming awake, watching them. "She waits for you to join her. Go to her. Return again when the moon comes if you are still near."

Maja licked her hand and raced off into the beckoning forest, with the agile gray female running beside him.

Kionee ate, washed in the river, packed her possessions, and departed the tranquil location.

At the mouth of the canyon, Kionee saw outcrops of rocks where they were scattered across grassy hills. Sage and rabbitbrush dotted the landscape. Mountains were a mixture of black and gray and sand, with occasional red rocks. A mesa loomed in the distance, as did other mountains and ridges.

Kionee knew the forests and mountains of the medicine bows was seven to ten suns' travel southeastward, according to weather, which could change in a short time during this season. In their sheltering canyons was her destination, the place where Stalking Wolf lived and waited.

She halted to make a second camp where the Muddy Creek would flow into the river if it was not dry from a lack of recent rain. She used a copse of trees to conceal herself and the horses from any passersby's view. She refreshed herself in the cool blue water. She ate while sitting on a rock, then squatted to unroll her sleeping mat.

"I knew you would come to me this season," a husky male voice murmured. "The visions said so, and they are never wrong."

She leapt to her feet and whirled so fast she almost stumbled, but a grinning Stalking Wolf caught her arms and steadied her balance. She stared at him in astonishment. "How?" was the only word she could speak.

The man chuckled as he caressed her cheek. "Maja came to where I camped and guided me to you. Another travels with him, a gray female."

Still dazed, she told him the recent events in Maja's life. "Where are you camped?"

"Not far away. I did not mean to frighten you but I did not know where he was leading me. I hoped he was traveling with you, but I did not know if you were in peril. When my eyes touched upon you and joy filled my heart, I spoke without thinking to alert you I was near. I did not see or hear your approach, for I was hunting in the hills for fresh meat. Maja found my camp, knew my scent, and tracked me. I have waited here for the passings of ten moons," he said as his gaze roamed her adoringly.

Her trembling fingers roamed his parted lips. "What if I had not come?"

"I did not doubt the visions; it is our destiny to unite as one." He lifted her right hand and stared at the colored mask still in place, then kissed it with tenderness. His tawny gaze fused with her brown one. His fingers slipped into silky black strands that flowed around her shoulders and relished the sensuous feel of them against his flesh. His gaze roamed her flawless skin and delicate features, visible and enticing with the painted mask gone. "To look upon you as a woman steals my breath, for no other's beauty compares with yours. My heart races faster than the deer flees danger, and it beats with love for you. My body quivers with desire to have you near, to touch you, to hear your voice, to see your smile. My love for you is strong; it grows with each sun. I will make you happy, Kionee. Do not be sad for leaving your people to join to me; you face no dishonor. I will make sure no trouble comes between the Hanueva and Cheyenne for your action. Now, we must rest before we leave. We will ride far so you will be safe from any hunter who might come after you, and I will not be forced to take his life to protect you. One day they will forgive us and we can return to this land, for we only obey *Maheoo*'s will and vision."

She smiled, aware he misunderstood the reason why her hand mark had not been removed. "There will be no trouble or danger, my love. My people freed all *tivas*, and they voted to release me from our law to join to you." As he stared at her in astonishment this time, she related the events that had taken place since their separation on the plains. "I am called Hemene now, for I will join a Cheyenne and live with the Strong Hearts."

"Morning Dove," he murmured, then smiled. "That is good for you. The visions said the wind-of-destiny would blow over me this season, and it has done so in a female once called by that name; that is how I knew you were the woman for me and that *Maheoo* would find a way to bring us together. When I became a man and warrior, I sought my naming vision and spirit sign. We are both guided and protected by the wolf. That is how it is with you, a new name for a new life and rank, with me, as my mate."

Kionee stroked his jawline and gazed into his tawny eyes. "You have removed my mask of the Hunter-Guardian and replaced it with a mask of love and joy which I will wear forever. The Great Spirit has smiled upon us and freed me so we can live as one in the stars even beyond death."

Stalking Wolf cupped her face in his hands and said in a husky voice, *"Ne-mehotatse, na-htsesta."*

"I love you, my heart," she echoed his stirring words.

"Ne-haeana-he?"

"I am hungry only for you," she answered as passion's flames ignited.

Their mouths met in a kiss filled with yearning and joy. At last, they did not have to fear exposure of their love. They were free to join in all ways, to surrender to the yearnings within them. With Maja nearby to guard them, they did so.

With leisure and delight, Stalking Wolf unlaced the ties on her dress and removed it. His hands fondled her naked breasts and tantalized their tips to eager hardness. He trailed his fingers over her rib cage, across her abdomen, and downward. His seeking finger found her sweet heat and teased her lovingly. His mouth wandered down the sensuous column of her throat, brushed over her collarbone, and climbed one firm breast to nuzzle the nipple until she writhed with desire.

Kionee was consumed by love and desire for him. She slipped her hand under his breechclout; his maleness felt hot, hard, and eager against her palm. She massaged the shaft as best she could with the leather obstacle restricting her movements, rejoicing in his groan of pleasure. Soon, all their garments were discarded so they could enjoy every inch of each other, and savor the sensation of skin against skin. As if a signal was given, they united their bodies as one.

Kionee's legs encircled his muscled thighs and locked him in place. Together they undulated like ripples on a river's surface.

He entered and half-withdrew countless times with her coaxing him onward to greater swiftness, depth, and strength.

With tight control, Stalking Wolf managed to time his release to come simultaneously with hers. They clung together, their bodies quivering and their hearts pounding, as they found splendid victory together.

At last, sated and contented, they snuggled on Kionee's sleeping mat. Both thanked Maja for protecting them; then the two wolves went off to hunt, roam, and cuddle in the forest for the night.

As his breathing slowed to normal and his body cooled, Stalking Wolf's gentle fingers traced the outlines of her facial features, which were so calm and lovely and peaceful. "I love you, Hemene, and you are mine forever, as I am yours," he said.

She tingled with joy and sighed. "I can hardly believe we are together like this, free and in honor and soon to share a tipi and new life as mates. I fear it is only a sunny dream and I will awaken soon to a dark reality."

Stalking Wolf kissed her parted lips and smiled. "We will always be together, for nothing and no one will ever take you from my side and life. I will use all of my skills to protect you and to make you happy. The sun our paths crossed when I rode to the sacred Medicine Wheel, you stirred something powerful deep within me. I did not understand what it was until I learned you were a female." To avoid having to explain how he made that shocking discovery and betraying Taysinga's trust, he asked, "Did your people visit the Medicine Wheel before making camp?"

"We did not do so this season. Bear's Head told us we needed to elude the returning Crow, for they also stop there after the buffalo hunt, and we remained on the grasslands with your people too long to risk it. My people will go when Mother Earth's face is green again after the cold season." Kionee grinned and added, "The next time we climb Medicine Mountain, we must take gifts for *Atah* to thank Him for all He has given to us."

"The Creator cleared the path between us so we can join; that is much to be thankful for," the warrior concurred in reverence and gratitude.

"There is another blessing for which to thank *Atah;* I carry our child."

Stalking Wolf stared at her in amazement. He watched her stroke the area of her womb in delight. "Our baby grows within you?"

Her glowing gaze fused with his proud and astonished one as she caressed his cheek. "That is true, my love, my daring Cheyenne."

Ever so lightly, he touched the place where her hand had visited. "How did this happen?"

Kionee laughed, and her brown eyes sparkled with amusement. "You planted your seeds within me many times; one came to life."

"When will I look upon his face? Or her face," he added with a laugh.

If she was right, it would be in *"Matse-ome-ese-he,"* she told him.

"During the Spring Moon when Mother Earth puts new leaves upon the trees, flowers bloom to give her beauty, and the grass becomes green and plentiful to feed the buffalo and other creatures. That is good, Hemene. You will be strong and well before the summer hunt."

"We must hurry to your camp and join before others learn our secret. Where did you tell your family and people you were going?"

"To seek the answer to my vision alone. Medicine Eyes understood what I must do; our shaman is wise and sees much in his visions. He will not be surprised to see a mate return with me."

"Big Hump, Morning Light, Five Stars, and others will be."

The warrior chuckled. "That is true, but our joining will make them happy and proud. When they learn Hemene was once called and lived as Kionee, they will be happy to have one with such large and abundant coups in our tribe and family. You will be accepted with great honor and joy."

Since *tivas* were no longer a secret, the Strong Hearts could be told who she was she realized. "We must rest, for our journey is long."

"Sleep, my love, for I will guard you and our child. White Cloud will be safe not far away, and I will tend my camp after the sun rises. I love you, Hemene of the Cheyenne, Kionee of the Hanuevas."

"I love you, Stalking Wolf of the Strong Hearts."

They nestled together and went to sleep.

Maja and his mate visited the couple the next morning as they were packing to leave. As usual, the she-wolf remained at a safe and wary distance. The silver beast licked Kionee's and Stalking Wolf's hands as his way of saying good-bye for a final time, as their paths would probably never cross again.

The warrior stroked Maja's thick ruff and thanked him for all the years the loyal animal had loved and protected Kionee and been her companion, a rank he now held. He was amazed that the creature seemed to understand.

Kionee hugged Maja and whispered in his ear, "Be free, safe, and happy, my old friend. Go with your mate and run in the wild. I love you."

Maja licked her cheek, nuzzled her shoulder, and joined the gray she-wolf. His golden gaze watched the embracing humans for a moment, then, the wolves raced into the engulfing forest to live and hunt as a pair for life.

Kionee stood with Stalking Wolf's arms wrapped around her as they witnessed the heart-stirring sight. Soon those fortunate creatures would mate and give birth to offspring who would roam the wilderness as they should. For a while, her path had crossed and mingled with Maja's; now, she rode a loving trail with a Cheyenne warrior who had stalked and stolen her heart. She was no longer a Hunter-Guardian, no longer Kionee, for she had hunted and captured her last prey and would never release him. She turned and kissed the virile and handsome man, who responded in ardor. *Destiny mine, I have found you.*

EPILOGUE

KIONEE STOOD ON THE barren top of Medicine Mountain and gazed out over the majestic mountains, tranquil valley, and evergreen forest that stretched beyond the sacred site. After the seasonal ritual to give thanks to *Maheoo* and to seek His guidance and protection, everyone had left the pinnacle and returned to a temporary camp at its base. Stalking Wolf waited nearby, but she wanted a short time alone to reflect and pray.

She thought about how her destiny had been changed atop this lofty mesa at five and at sixteen in *tiva* ceremonies. She reflected on her years as her family's Hunter-Guardian, and on the joy she had found with Stalking Wolf. She called to mind her past adventures and her once-forbidden love.

Kionee turned and looked at the giant wheel of limestone slabs and boulders, the stone cairns of gray rocks, and the center altar. The torches were gone, not even the smell or sight of their smoke lingered. The weather-bleached and painted buffalo skull, sweet grass, and sage had been taken away by the elderly shaman. Medicine Eyes still held that position and continued to amaze her with the accuracy of his mystical visions and prophesies. No trees or bushes grew on the lofty site, as if that was *Ma-heoo*'s way of preventing any distraction from the true reason for being there. No animals roamed this barren area, and nesting birds seemingly avoided it out of respect to the Great Spirit who had created them and all things.

Kionee noticed that the setting sun gave a fading blue sky kisses of vivid colors which warmed her soul. A full moon was making an early ride on the eastern horizon, still pale at this time of day. The wind was calm for a while. This section of Medicine Mountain was quiet, holy, isolated. No peril harmed or threatened any visitor, as all tribes honored the sanctity of this ancient spot. During the passings of many seasons, truces had been formed with other bands—even with most Crow—which allowed everyone to use this vital place in privacy and peace, as it was revered by all. So far, no man—friend, foe, or ally—had broken that agreement, for which Kionee was grateful.

It had been twelve cycles of seasons since she met Stalking Wolf and her destiny changed again. No, she refuted, not changed, only taken its rightful path. It had been eleven springs since the birth of their son, Little Stone. It had been eight since the birth of their first daughter, Morning Dew, five since the birth of a boy named Blazing Sun, and two since the birth of a girl called Golden Dawn. Their two sons and two daughters were happy and obedient children. The oldest boy was in training as a hunter; one day, to be a warrior. Her daughters and youngest son were delights, and she cherished each of them, as did great-grandparents Big Hump and Morning Light, whose tipi was near theirs.

The colorfully painted tipi of Stalking Wolf and Kionee was large and comfortable and neat. Between her mate's prowess and her own learned skills, they wanted for nothing. Strong and able, she had refused friends' offers of captives to help with her chores. She was relieved Stalking Wolf had no hunger for more than one mate—a custom of his people, not hers—as she knew she could not share him with another woman. She remembered him telling her, even before he knew she was a female, that he would love only one woman and take one mate for life, as did the wolf, his spirit sign. He not only had kept his word, but revealed no desire to ever change it.

Long ago, she had been welcomed into the Cheyenne band, and honored once more for her past coups. No member had forgotten she—as Kionee—had saved their esteemed chief's life and their Sacred Arrows. Four winters past, Five Stars had become chief of the Strong Hearts and Keeper of the Sacred Arrows. Everyone, including his three mates and seven children, considered Five Stars a brave and wise leader, as did she.

Kionee was overjoyed that her family and tribe were safe and well. Her parents and little brother had wonderful lives, thanks to Regim. The past *Tiva-Chu* had not taken a mate but was happy and fulfilled being the Hunter-Protector and the trainer of Comes-Late for Strong Rock's tipi. Her grandparents still lived tranquil and healthy lives, as did Four Deer and his family. Even Little Weasel had given up his ugly thoughts and ways, under the influence of his best friend and now chief, Night Walker, who had changed dramatically because of Taysinga's love. Bear's Head and Spotted Owl still walked on Mother Earth and served the Hanuevas on their council and as shaman. The girl named for her, Ae-Culta-Kionee, was now twelve, and had two brothers. She saw her family and friends almost every summer on the grasslands, and sometimes at the annual intertribal trading camp. One past love she had not seen since leaving the canyon of the river wind was Maja; yet, she somehow sensed the silver wolf and his mate were alive and running free somewhere, members of a strong pack they had created.

Other changes had come to this vast territory. The large Cheyenne Nation had divided into two groups: the Northern and the Southern. The Strong Hearts stayed with the Northern branch and in this territory, for which Kionee was relieved and grateful since it kept her close to her people and on familiar terrain.

Large and strong men with white skin and furry faces had come five winters past to trap—with permission—in the streams and rivers; most had become friends with Cheyenne, Crow, and Hanueva. The pale-skinned men who sought pelts looked nothing like Adam Stone or his father. To her, they had strange ways and appearances, but they were genial and respectful of the Indians and of Mother Nature. A few had taken Cheyenne or Crow mates—wives, they called them—but no Hanueva female had joined one and gone to live and work in the same type of "cabin" where her love was born after his father—also a trapper—joined Big Hump's daughter.

Kionee fingered the gold locket on a gold chain around her neck which carried pictures of her love's family: his father and his grandparents. Stalking Wolf had given it to her on their joining day when she was adorned in the beautiful white buffalo-hide dress and moccasins. She kept those precious garments packed away and wore them on special occasions, as they still fit her slim and firm figure. She was happy being a female in all ways, and did her role with skill. She had no doubts this was meant to be her true rank in life. Sometimes, she admitted, she missed being a huntress who roamed the woods and plains at will; during those times, her kind love would take her into the forest with him to track and hunt while his generous grandparents lovingly watched over the four children. On a few occasions, she had missed the exciting and stimulating buffalo chase; but she agreed with Stalking Wolf that it was too risky a diversion to indulge in. Two things she had never missed were wearing a *tiva* mask and a binding breast band. She touched her clean face in delight of feeling flesh instead of layers of paint.

Stalking Wolf came to stand beside her. He hated to disturb her memories, so spoke softly. "Darkness comes soon, my love."

She faced him and smiled. "I am ready to leave."

His gaze swept over her flowing hair, tresses as black and

shiny as the bunting's feathers beneath the sun. Her skin was still soft and flawless, and invited his touch. Her body, small and taut, aroused his desires. "You steal my breath when I look upon you. My love is strong and endless. If we did not have children waiting for us, I would carry you to our mat and—"

Kionee's fingers touched his full lips and halted the remainder of his wishful and stirring words. "They are fine with your grandparents for a short time. There is a place over there," she said, pointing to one in the distance, "where we can steal a visit alone if we hurry, as we did long ago when our love was forbidden. *Maheoo* will not mind, for He has smiled upon us and we do not use the sacred site."

The Cheyenne warrior chuckled and caressed her soft cheek. "It is true, my love, my heart, my Morning Dove."

Hemene, the mate and mother—no longer Kionee, The Huntress and Guardian—took a grinning Stalking Wolf's hand and guided him toward the beckoning arms of rapturous and never-ending love and passion.

AUTHOR'S NOTE

For those of you who enjoy learning more about the Native Americans I feature in many of my novels, you should know that the Hanueva tribe and words used in this story are fictional. I based my imaginary Indian band on the historical Nahane tribe, on their legend and custom of boyless families making "sons" of their oldest daughters at age five. These girls were reared and trained to be hunters and protectors, to live and dress and behave as men. They wore the ovaries of a she-bear in a pouch on their belts. If you want more information on the Nahane, contact your local public library and/or bookstore.

The Cheyenne and Crow nations and languages used herein are factual. More information about them is available from the library; bookstores; Indian colleges; certain reservations and missions; the National Museum of the American Indian in Arlington, VA; and the Bureau of Indian Affairs, United States Department of The Interior in Washington, DC.

The sacred and mystical Medicine Wheel—builders, origin, purpose, and date unknown—is located in the Big Horn Mountains on highway 14-A, thirty-four miles east of Lovell in the state of Wyoming. The giant wheel, stone cairns, and worn travois trails are still visible and are accessible by road. The Great

Arrow, fifty-eight feet long and five-and-a-half feet wide, which points toward the mysterious Wheel, is located on a hogback east of Meeteetse. Pumpkin Buttes, a landmark for past travelers, is northwest of Pine Tree Junction. Mile-high Laramie Peak is visible for a hundred miles from the north, east, and south. It was a landmark to past travelers, and on the Oregon Trail, and is located in Medicine Bow Forest, twenty-five miles northwest of Wheatland. Two other areas of enormous beauty and historical meaning are the Powder River Country and Wind River Canyon, also in glorious Wyoming.

American artist, R. W. Adamson, is widely known for his authentic and magnificent replicas of ancient Medicine Masks. From years of research and with great skill, he has reproduced the masks in his collection with accuracy and beauty. A talented poet, he writes an emotion-stirring poem to accompany each piece of fine art. In a desire to enlighten owners of his works, he includes fact sheets about each mask and how to take care of it.

I am delighted to announce that R. W. Adamson has used the description of my heroine's mask to create a new collection for Shamanic Arts, with her ceremonial mask being the first piece, and my story's hero used as inspiration for the second. "Kionee, The Huntress" and "Stalking Wolf, The Companion" will be released by Shamanic Arts of Salt Lake City, Utah, simultaneous with this novel's publication by Kensington Books in February of 1995. "Kionee, The Huntress" is handcrafted of black pigskin over a clay form, handpainted with her colors and symbols, and adorned with feathers and tassels. It comes with a certificate of authenticity and a copy of the "Kionee's Destiny" poem. The masks are numbered, dated, and signed by the artist. Later, they will be withdrawn to increase value.

As a thank-you to my readers and booksellers, I am sponsoring a contest where the Grand Prize will be one of Kionee's ceremonial masks, lovingly created and generously donated and hand-signed by R. W. Adamson.

Second and third prizes—also artworks symbolic of this story—will be given away during the same drawing. To enter the contest, all you have to do is send a postcard *(postcards only* **will be accepted for this drawing/***no letters)* with your name, return address, and phone number to:

Kionee's Ceremonial Mask Contest
P. O. Box 211646
Martinez, GA 30917-1646

The entry deadline is May 31, 1995; the drawing will take place June 10, 1995. The prizes will be mailed promptly to the winners whose names are selected from a sealed box. Your postcards must be addressed to the contest exactly as listed above to make certain they reach the right source to get placed in the contest box; you must print your name and address clearly on the reverse side. If I can't read your name and address, I can't send you your prize! As required by law, no purchase of any kind is necessary to enter the contest or to make you eligible to win.

I own four of R. W. Adamson's splendid pieces, so I know you will be thrilled to win such an exquisite and valuable prize. Good Luck, and I hope you enjoyed Kionee's and Stalking Wolf's story, and Maja's!

If you would like to receive a free Janelle Taylor Newsletter, book list, and bookmark, send a Self-Addressed Stamped Envelope (long size best) to:

Janelle Taylor Newsletter
P.O. Box 211646
Martinez, Georgia 30917-1646

Reading is fun and educational, so do it often!